TELL NO LIES

A FAITH MCCLELLAN NOVEL

LYNDEE WALKER

SEVERN RIVER PUBLISHING

Severn River Publishing
www.SevernRiverBooks.com

This is a work of fiction. Names, characters, businesses, places, events and incidents are either the products of the author's imagination or used in a fictitious manner. Any resemblance to actual persons, living or dead, or actual events is purely coincidental.

ISBN: 978-1-64875-468-5 (Paperback)

ALSO BY LYNDEE WALKER

The Faith McClellan Series

Fear No Truth

Leave No Stone

No Sin Unpunished

Nowhere to Hide

No Love Lost

Tell No Lies

No Secrets Remain

The Nichelle Clarke Series

Front Page Fatality

Buried Leads

Small Town Spin

Devil in the Deadline

Cover Shot

Lethal Lifestyles

Deadly Politics

Hidden Victims

To find out more about LynDee Walker and her books, visit

severnriverbooks.com/authors/lyndee-walker

The getting of treasures by a lying tongue is a vanity tossed to and fro of them that seek death.
—Proverbs 21:6, King James Version

1

It takes more force than most people think to remove a human head.

A man of average size and strength who is inexperienced with the beheading process would likely take five or more swings even with a sharp axe, especially if the victim was upright rather than prone.

The secret is in the propulsion, and in the blade itself.

A run-of-the-mill hardware store axe, with its convex curve, is a poor choice of weapon—anyone who's ever wrenched a shoulder on a knot trying to split logs knows hitting a dense structure causes the chopping blade to recoil, impeding the task and even injuring the executioner.

A blade that's too thick can't be sharpened enough to get the job done, but enough width is required to allow a wide, slow taper to a razor-thin edge. Live targets pose strategic challenges, because their movements must be anticipated and accounted for in the approach.

He knew all of this. He'd done his homework. He'd built his weapon.

He ran a cloth carefully up one side of the double-ended scythe, both blades angled at a perfect forty-eight degrees. The steel gleamed in the light.

His muscles were well conditioned, his mind clear. He had a message to send, and the weapon balanced perfectly in his hands would carry it.

Eighty-two pounds of force—that was the magic number. The weight on a guillotine blade, falling at twenty-one feet per second.

Cliché as it sounded, it really was all in the wrist. He had to spin for velocity on the approach, but it was straightening his arm at the precise right instant and flicking his wrist just enough to send the angled blade cleanly through the spinal cord and vertebrae that elevated death to art.

He opened the door. The stench of urine burned his nostrils, the wide eyes inches above the thick layer of silver tape staring at him with equal parts terror and pleading.

The condemned scooted backward, his legs flailing, his shoulders still pushing against two walls when there was nowhere left to go.

"It's time."

The executioner grabbed the collar of a shirt so filthy he couldn't tell what color it was, the detail not important enough to stay with him over the past few days.

Hauled to his feet and thrown toward the door, the man stumbled headfirst outside with a sickening *crack*.

Running to the door, the executioner looked down, shaking his head at the angle of the condemned's neck, the dead man's glassy eyes staring up at nothing.

Years of work and study had gone into a weapon of attack, and it would be reduced to the boring, sloppy level of surgery on a cadaver. Nothing more than a practice round. He clicked his tongue as he jumped down, landing neatly beside the body.

No matter.

The blades would still cut.

The executioner would have his trophy.

He slid the toe of one boot under a limp shoulder, rolling his victim over. The skin of the neck stretched almost comically before the head snapped over, open eyes staring into the sand.

The wood of the handle was warm in the executioner's hands as he raised his weapon to strike.

2

"Has a medical examiner been here yet?" I squatted in shallow water two yards from a corpse, a bead of sweat running from my ponytail down the back of my neck before it seeped into the starched collar of my white button-down.

"The local JP is in Hawaii this week on his third honeymoon, and the closest ME is in San Antonio." Drew Ratcliff tipped his wide-brimmed Stetson back and shrugged from his perch atop a palomino gelding. The horse had wide, knowing eyes and the kind of fearless streak necessary for police work, easily balancing in the slippery mud of the partially exposed river bottom while ignoring the rotting human parts sticking out of the water. "I put in a call for assistance Thursday but haven't heard back."

"They're buried in a turf war among three street gangs." I pulled out my phone and zoomed in with the camera, studying the image on the screen. One arm was missing entirely, the hunks of flesh hanging on around the remaining wrist and ankles gouged away in deep trenches, bone gleaming grayish-white in the voids. The skull was nearly devoid of tissue, as was the chest wall peeking through the tattered shirt. The whole mess was stuck between mud and wood in a narrow low spot under a fallen tree limb, water lapping at the fabric of what probably used to be faded jeans, part of a Nike logo visible on the lone exposed sneaker. I could tell the body had been underwater awhile, but I needed an expert to determine the difference between a week and a month.

My Laredo boots sank into the muck of the riverbed, my stomach recoiling at the smell wafting off the remains in the nearly nonexistent breeze, even through the menthol gel slathered on my upper lip. "Bexar County won't call back. I'll get my guy from Travis to come down. This unfortunate soul has been out here awhile. Another day won't hurt."

I squinted, looking up at a silhouette of Ratcliff and his horse outlined against the kind of clear, wide sky that gets photographed for travel magazines and brings people to the Texas desert. "Was the medallion here?" I pointed to a yellow evidence marker slightly embedded in the mud about a foot closer to the remains than I was.

"It was. I didn't want to chance anything happening to it before you could get a look at it, so I marked the spot and took it back to the office."

"You have a perimeter secured?" I asked.

He waved one hand, and the horse took a step to the side. "As much as I can out here. In theory, my whole life is supposed to be about securing that perimeter there," he pointed to the opposite bank of the Rio Grande, "but in practice, I know folks who really want in will find a way in."

He pointed to the canyon a few football fields upstream along the Pecos, which met the Rio Grande in a Y shape just yards from where the corpse was stuck. "The state park starts there, so we called in Parks and Wildlife for assistance, but they have limited ability to help out in their busy season."

"Busy season?" I picked a wide circle through mud and puddles, my eyes scanning the ground for anything that might not belong. I noted and photographed two sets of boot prints that weren't mine, though at least one of them might've belonged to Ratcliff. I held a pen up in one side of a hoofprint and snapped a few closeups of it for depth reference. "Does anyone actually camp out here in the devil's armpit in August?"

The confluence of the two rivers and surrounding desert was beautiful country, but the relentless sun seemed hell-bent on destroying everything it grazed, the mercury soaring past a hundred degrees before eight in the morning.

"The kind of people who have RVs with air conditioning do." Ratcliff laughed, loosening his hold on the reins so the horse could dip his head to drink from a puddle.

"Not even then," I said. "Especially not in this drought. How many days is this for y'all?"

"Three hundred fifty-nine. We broke the record last week," he said, clucking softly to the horse and nodding in the direction of the Rangers command station double-wide parked a few hundred yards downstream amid the cactus, yucca, and grasses lining the riverbank on the Texas side. "Speaking of this heat, let's get out of it for a minute."

"And away from the smell," I added, moving carefully to walk alongside the horse where he could see me. "He's beautiful. What's his name?"

"Dodger," Ratcliff said. "He's bred from a line of Rangers service animals. They say his great-great-great-great-something-grandfather was Frank Hamer's mount a hundred years ago. So I guess working out here is in his blood."

I stepped out of the riverbed onto the sand of the bank, moving to one side to allow the horse an easier path. Ratcliff, a decorated ten-year veteran with the Rangers' border intelligence team, had emailed me late the day before with a photo of a prayer medallion he'd found sunken in river mud near a set of human remains, his message referencing an old case of mine he'd come across searching files.

"I read up on the case you worked with the medallion guy," Ratcliff said. "Seven victims, all women, all found with a medallion on their person somewhere."

"All found with only a medallion on their person," I corrected. "And Jerry Burkett was executed two years ago for those murders, so whatever happened here, I know he didn't have anything to do with it."

The truth was that bodies along the border, especially in the river, weren't uncommon—along some stretches out here, the rate ran as high as one a day when the river was high. Officers in this part of the state didn't usually call for help from homicide when one turned up, though the peculiar wear pattern on the flesh and the expensive sneakers had me thinking this wasn't your average drowned wannabe American, either. Whatever insight Ratcliff was hoping to get from my work on the Burkett case was bound to disappoint him, but I'd made the trip anyway—partly because I was curious about why he'd asked me to come, since Google could've told him in half a second that the State of Texas had put Burkett to death, and partly because I didn't have anything better to do with my weekend.

The heat choked off any desire for further conversation as we hiked through the hard-packed, clay-mixed sand just off the bank. I mentally catalogued the body parts I'd seen above water and wondered about my chances of actually getting Jim Prescott to drive all the way out here on a summer Sunday. We were friends, but there was a limit to what even friends could ask. I needed a strategy, though, because I needed Jim's sharp eyes and decades of experience if we were going to figure out who the dead guy was and how he ended up stuck under that log.

In front of the trailer that served as headquarters for his one-man unit, Ratcliff swung down out of the saddle and led the horse to a two-stall stable, hastily constructed going by the gaps between the siding boards and the shiny new tin roof. He plunked a large block of ice into Dodger's water bucket, checking to make sure the horse had hay before he turned on a fan, shut the door, and waved me into the trailer. The first blast of AC was so welcome I sighed.

"I forget that some folks don't have to work out in the heat all day," Ratcliff said, shutting the door and gesturing to a worn gray cloth-and-faux-wood chair that was probably older than me before he opened the fridge and tossed me a bottle of water. "After a while, you don't notice it as much." He opened another bottle and drank half in a single gulp, the red Ozarka label crackling under his fingers as the plastic shrank away from it. "Thank you for driving down."

"Always glad to help out where I can." I put my empty water bottle on the edge of his desk and crossed my legs at the knee. The office was small and sparse but tidy, his desk neat, from the four black pens in the Rangers coffee cup to the stack of fourteen perfectly aligned file folders on the corner nearest me. I sat back in the chair, fixing Ratcliff with a flat-faced gaze and waiting for him to tell me why I was there.

He played with the bottle, peeling the label off in long strips. "Have you really cleared every homicide case you've ever worked?"

"I'm more persistent than most people, that's all." I studied him for a second. "Why did you really ask me to come down here?"

He sighed. "My story about the medal didn't fool you?"

"Google knows Burkett is long dead," I said. "But you've got my attention, if that was your goal. And I'm pretty stubborn when it comes to finding murderers. What I don't understand is why that's what you think you've got here."

Ratcliff put the empty water bottle on the desk. "Ma'am, right now I'm praying to every god who might listen that you are the most stubborn person ever born. I can track a smuggler with the best of them, but everything I know about homicide came to me in two weeks of training under a guy who had never actually been at a murder scene, which means it ain't much. The feds want to pretend these bodies aren't stacking up, but that don't make it true. And letting murderers run unchecked out here seems like a bad idea."

"Bodies?" I leaned forward. "How many bodies?"

"By my count, he's an even half dozen since last September and the second one this summer."

"How can you be sure they were all murdered?" I asked.

"The first five were missing their heads when I found them."

"That would do it, sure."

"And then this guy..." He waved one arm in the general direction of the river, widening his eyes as he closed one hand around his opposite wrist.

"Was weighted down and thrown in the river, " I finished for him. The gouged flesh at the wrists and ankles wouldn't have given way just because he was tied up—it was ripped by something heavy. Something heavy that wasn't out there anymore, from what I'd seen. I tapped one finger on the desk. "You have an ID on any of the victims?"

He shook his head. "The feds really didn't seem interested. They sent a couple guys out, but they didn't do much but look around and mutter about illegals. To my knowledge, they were all officially counted as crossing casualties."

"With how much investigation?"

He raised both hands. "None that I know of."

"Why? That's solidly in a gray area for lying on a report."

"You're the murder whisperer, McClellan. You tell me."

The border was a special jurisdiction with its own dangers and challenges, but Ratcliff was more than a little bothered by these corpses, or he wouldn't have called me. There were a lot of things in my world I couldn't control at the moment, but I could solve these murders.

"I'll need all the information you have on every one of them." The words left my lips on a shiver of unease that had nothing to do with the AC. Falsifying a report was a serious offense, which meant these victims weren't random corpses.

"It's not a lot, but it's all here." He passed me a file folder that was way too emaciated to give me much of anything worthwhile about six dead bodies. I flipped it open anyway, studying a black-and-white still of a headless corpse in a Prada shirt, a gaudy pin hanging from torn fabric over his chest.

"Was this real gold? Do you remember?" I asked.

"Looked like it, but I doubt anyone took it to a jeweler."

"A random bandit interested in money would've stolen it, though." I flipped past the photo to a single-page report on the remains discovery, written by Ratcliff. Bare bones was a generous term for the information it held.

"You can figure this out, right?" Ratcliff said. "I'm not here to kill your perfect record."

"I don't give a damn about the record. I never have." I closed the file and tapped it on the desk as I stood and handed him a card. "I'm at the Cherry Lane Motel outside Duncan if you think of anything else, and I'll be back out tomorrow with a coroner. Just try to make sure nobody messes with the scene before we get here. Where were the other remains taken?"

"To the Bexar County ME's office, but if they have victims coming in from a gang war..."

"Then they're out of storage space, and it's been months. These people probably aren't still there. But I'll check anyway."

I nodded when he thanked me again as I stepped back outside, wondering what kind of situation it takes for five beheaded corpses to just slide under radar.

My truck cruising toward the nearest motel, which was forty-three miles back toward civilization, I dialed Jim Prescott to ask for his help.

Someone in a position of power didn't want anyone else nosing around this case, and Jim and I had experience walking this particular tightrope. I just wasn't sure he'd be willing to step onto it again, even for me.

3

"It's Sunday, McClellan. Aren't newlyweds supposed to be more interested in each other than they are in dead people?" Jim didn't bother with hello when he picked up the phone, his words wrapped in the kind of weary resignation that stung a little.

"How do you know I'm calling you about dead people?" I stared down the road stretching flat and straight as far as I could see, the heat throwing shimmers off it in dancing waves.

"When do you call me about anything else?" He didn't sound mad, but he didn't sound friendly, either. He hadn't in months, and while I couldn't blame him for being frustrated, I didn't know what to say to make him feel better, either. I'd nearly been killed in the line of duty a dozen times in as many years, but Jim didn't sign up for a job that carried that kind of hazard. He was still a little too far from retirement to be mad at his job, so I was catching the brunt of it. I could take that for a friend—for a while, anyway. And to be fair, I was calling to ask him a favor.

"Not today, I'm afraid," I said. "I have a water-bloated corpse revealed by the drought, I think. Looks like someone sunk him to the bottom of the Pecos just up from the juncture with the Rio Grande. On purpose."

"Dumped in the river at the border." Jim's tone changed as he considered that, the puzzle pulling his thoughts away from his frustration.

"Our guy down here says there are more victims—five of them beheaded." Interesting cases were Jim's reason for getting up in the morning.

"Organized crime?" he mused. "The cartels are pretty famous for beheading people."

"It's good theater when you're trying to keep criminals from stealing from you," I agreed. "But I'm not making any assumptions yet. The MO itself is common knowledge—it would be a hell of a way to throw suspicion if the killer wasn't cartel, too."

"Either way, not exactly a safe investigation," Jim said.

"I know," I said. "But we can have the remains delivered to your lab. The new security there makes Huntsville look easy to break into and out of."

The legislature had approved emergency security updates to every medical examiner's office in the state after Jim was attacked back in March, because if our MEs started quitting en masse, we'd be up to our eyeballs in dead bodies pretty quick, with no way to find the evidence needed to catch killers. Nobody wanted that. Least of all the governor in the summer of an election year.

"Can we do that quietly?" he asked.

"As quietly as we can in this line of work."

He sat for long enough that I looked down to see if the call was still connected. It was. I stayed quiet.

"Okay."

"Can you come check out the scene tomorrow? Just this one. Because they just found him, and I want to make sure I'm not missing anything. And their JP is in Hawaii."

"You can't call Bachman down in San Antonio? He's closer."

"Gang war. He's drowning in gunshot vics."

Jim sighed. "I'll come down. But just for the morning."

"Thank you." I put every bit of warmth I could muster into the words.

"I'm..." He sighed again. "I know none of this was your fault."

"I'm just glad you're okay, Jim. Take all the time you need. See you in the morning. I'll text you the address of the local luxury accommodations, just in case."

"I'm sure they're the very best 1971 had to offer."

"There's not even a hair dryer."

"I'll see you and your wet hair in the morning, Faith."

"Looking forward to it."

And for the first time in months, I was. I needed a problem I could solve and a villain I could catch. Ratcliff's dead people would do.

"You coming over to watch the game today?" Archie Baxter's low drawl sounded positively blissful, putting a smile on my face for the first time all day.

"It's preseason. It's not a real game," I said.

"It's football and it's on the TV, I'm not at work for the first Sunday in a month, and I've got a pot of vegetarian chili on the stove."

"Tempting as that does actually sound, I'm down in Terrell County with what appears to be a body dump and a border unit officer who says they've had a whole string of murders out here and the feds are turning a blind eye."

"I worked the border unit a thousand years ago," Archie said. "What's your gut say about the guy you talked to?"

"Like do I think he's shady?" I asked.

"Several were back in my day," he said. "A whole lot of valuable things cross that border every day. It takes a sort of blind allegiance to justice to be immune to the temptation down there."

"Common red flags?"

"Same ones as always, really. Secrecy is never good, neither is a whole-hearted embrace of the whole 'Lone Ranger' caricature—mistrust of fellow officers is often caused by a guy's own guilt," he said. "And piles of cash are always a reliable sign something is happening that shouldn't be."

"Every time, in my experience," I said, my thoughts going to Ratcliff's one-man show and his dismissive attitude about the local sheriff and whatever federal agency he'd been dealing with. Fan-goddamn-tastic.

But if Ratcliff was on the take, why would he have called me for help?

"Anything I can do from here with very limited time?" Archie asked. "Any other summer, I'd hop in the truck and come help you, but I'm buried up to my ears right now."

"I know. I really wish you could tell me why, but I'm glad you're home today." I paused. He didn't fill the silence with case details.

"I'm set," I said. "Jim is coming down in the morning to look at the scene, and I've ridden this horse before. But thank you."

"Of course." His turn for a pause. "Jim is coming out there?"

"Six suspicious corpses total, and our guy swears the feds are ignoring them. I think Jim's curiosity got the better of him."

"That would be a hard one to stay away from." His words sounded slightly strained. Did that mean my case sounded more interesting than his top-secret one?

"Enjoy your day off, Arch. Give Ruth my love."

"She's at the spa until just before kickoff," he said. "Like she's not beautiful enough. But I'll tell her. You take care of yourself. I don't want you getting too far into this without a partner."

"I'm not alone," I said. "The border unit guy is here."

"Just make sure you can trust him."

"I appreciate the heads-up."

I clicked the call off and turned onto another long, dust-laden stretch of highway, turning the radio up and singing along with Robert Earl Keen about a small-town dealer and a cocktail waitress who got in over their heads with big-time criminals.

Time to figure out just what kind of party Ratcliff had invited me into.

The Cherry Lane Motel sported a neon sign with a pair of cherries that resembled certain human anatomy so closely even I noticed, and Graham would've made a joke about it before he could stop himself.

I laughed as I killed the engine outside room 17, imagining what he'd have said. Running a finger over my wedding band, I sent up a silent prayer for his safety and hopped out of the truck, strolling slowly toward the office, sweat beading in new spots with every step.

The motel was the kind of run-down a place got with time, the wood decking, covered walkway, and wood-framed screen doors as typical of the late 1950s as the patterned carpet and black-and-white rabbit-ear-topped

TVs in the guest rooms. It was clean, and owned by the same family for two generations, according to the small talk I'd made with the teenager who'd checked me in four hours ago.

The last part was what interested me. A family who'd owned this business this close to the border for so many years would know who came and went from the area frequently—and which local bad guys might lop someone's head off for crossing them.

I spotted an older woman with gray hair so long and full it spilled out every side of the wide-brimmed sun hat she had tried to contain it with as she knelt weeding a flowerbed that skirted the far front edge of the building. I walked a little faster until I found a spot in the shade a few feet from her.

"Good morning." I let the words hang for a minute, waiting for her to reply before I said anything else. A simple response to a friendly greeting is a good way to get an early read on a person.

"When you get to be my age, they're all good as long as you wake up, sugar." She brushed her hands off and sat back on her folded legs, squinting up at me from under the brim of the hat. I saw her eyes widen the way most people's did when they lit on my badge. "What can I do for you, Ranger?"

"Call me Faith," I said, putting out a hand that she shook with a firmer grip than I would've expected from a woman of her age and size. I waited for her to offer her name.

"Doris Dushane," she said, fanning her face. "The damned summers get hotter every year, hand to God."

I nodded, tugging my button-down away from my damp skin, not that letting the oven-roasted air run over it really did me any good.

"Miss Doris, I wonder if I could trouble you for a glass of ice water and a little information?"

"I can do better than that." She stood in a motion more fluid than I could manage myself, removing her gardening gloves. "I've got a pitcher of fresh lemonade around to the house. Though I can't promise the kind of information you need, I'm happy to share whatever I know that might be useful to you."

"You've got yourself some company," I said.

She waved for me to walk with her, rounding the back of the motel to a sprawling ranch-style home of the same era, a metal TV antenna poking up off the roof and three cars in various states of disassembly scattered around the yard amid small beds of gladiolas, hibiscus, and roses that would make even Ruth McClellan gasp, especially in this climate.

"My husband." She waved a hand at the cars. "Keeps him happier than a mistress would, so I try to see them as decorative. I put Christmas lights on that one," she pointed to a Trans Am with a rusted front quarter panel and colorful lights wrapping the mirrors and vacant spaces where the T-tops should be, "last November, and he hasn't ever taken them off."

"He fixes them up to sell?" I couldn't help noticing the lack of license plates on the cars. While they didn't have to be registered if they were inoperable, selling cars with no plates to the wrong kind of people was probably a lucrative trade for the mechanically inclined around here—which might be good for me to poke into a little further, given the alarming number of headless dead people Ratcliff had seen in the past year.

"These days he piddles with them when he feels like being outside." She opened the front door, and I stepped in, the door closing quickly behind us. "Have to keep the bought air in here as we can. This place has enough leaks to strain spaghetti." She led me through a living room with plastic-covered sofas and chairs to a kitchen with a gorgeous triple-oven range in fire-engine red that I'd bet was original vintage, the black-and-white tile under my feet and flecked Formica countertops straight out of an episode of *Happy Days*. A blue bowl with a chipped edge, a spoon, and a simple blue coffee mug rested in the sink, not a dishwasher in sight.

Pulling a large glass pitcher from a Frigidaire with rounded corners and a single exterior door, she poured two glasses and set them on the table. "Have a seat and tell me what brings you out here, Faith."

"I'm wondering if you've had any regular customers at the motel the past year or so—maybe folks who haven't been in the area much before that?"

She guzzled half the lemonade and wiped her mouth with the back of her hand, letting out a belch that would win a fraternity contest. "I don't harbor criminals in our place, no matter how much cash they flash under my nose. My daddy would roll over in his dusty grave." She paused, eyeing me like she was sizing me up. "Never seen a lady Texas Ranger before."

"There aren't many of us," I said. "Even still."

"Guess that means you're pretty good at your job?"

I nodded, keeping quiet. People like Doris dislike silence and will fill it when it lingers.

"They camp," she said. "The folks you're looking for. Ain't another motel for fifty miles, and it's a hellhole. They sleep in their fancy SUVs and pickup beds, only for a few days at a time. Cross the border and come back the next day. They like to drink and pop their pistols off in the air. We lost a horse two months back to a stray bullet. Damned fools never learn that what goes up has to come down."

I kept my face neutral. For someone who said she didn't know if she had the sort of information I needed, she was pretty forthcoming with it—and didn't much like whoever she was trying to turn in, too. "They camp, you said. Did these people try to stay at the Cherry Lane?"

"They did, once. I told them never again. Trashed two of our rooms, dirt and blood all over the sheets and towels. One wanted to talk to us about the pickup out there in the yard, but I didn't like him on sight. Told him it wasn't for sale. They had the nerve to come back about a month later, and I had my son, Timmy, show them the door."

"Blood?" I asked, my eyes widening. "Did you call the police?"

She shook her head. "Do people call the law over some soiled linens where you're from? Four went in, four came out. And our sheriff don't like to do much in the way of detective work, anyhow."

Four that she saw went in. But I filed her assessment of the sheriff away for future consideration.

"Has anyone disappeared from around here this past year?" I asked. "Not moved away, but gone missing unexpectedly?"

Her eyes filled, a tear hanging from her lower lashes for a minute before it dripped off, zigzagging across her wrinkled skin. "Timmy. I saw him the evening of May ninth, he came for dinner, and by morning he was just gone. Didn't take his things, say bye to anyone, nothing. But the law around here didn't want to hear it. They said he's a grown man and I had no proof of foul play. Told me he took off with his whore. My son wouldn't up and leave without saying goodbye to me." She pinched her lips into a thin line.

Oh my. Doris Dushane wasn't just agile for her age, she was canny, too. I'd pegged her as a helpful old woman, but the hospitality came with an agenda: she saw my badge and thought I'd be able to track down her son.

Maybe I could. Maybe the local sheriff was right and he didn't want to be found. But I had time to listen to her story while I waited for Jim. Besides, she might still know something I could use to get a bead on Ratcliff's headless horseman.

I pulled a notebook and pen from my back pocket. "Do you mind if I take notes?"

"Sugar, if you're thinking you might help find my boy, you can take notes, video...I'll stand on my head and sing for you. Whatever you need." A sob muffled the last word.

She was milking the anxious mom thing for all it was worth, I'd give her that.

I flipped to a fresh page, hoping Ratcliff hadn't already found her son in the riverbed.

"Start at the beginning," I said. "Tell me everything you remember about the rowdy guests and everything I might need to know about your son and his girlfriend, even if it's embarrassing."

Doris wiped her eyes, finished her lemonade, and leaned back in her chair as she started to talk.

4

"I'd have to check the guest register, but I think it was February or March when that crew came through our place," Doris said. "Like a tornado. They seemed to drop right out of the sky, checked in late and slept most of the day, left around sunset, and came back about four o'clock for two nights in a row, Timmy said. He worked the night shift at the desk because he never could sleep when it was dark. Been like that since he was a baby."

She took a deep breath and continued, and I kept my hand moving across the page, not missing a word.

"Did they say anything about where they were from or why they were here? Or happen to pay with a credit card?" I asked.

"They used cash. I remember because I always think it's suspect when people pay for a room with cash money nowadays. Not that I dislike it, but for years now, the hikers we get through here who want a hot shower and a real bed, they all pay with plastic. Hell, we've had some lately who were flat befuddled that I didn't have a way for them to pay with their fancy cell phones. Nobody carries real money anymore. So when people show up with it, it sticks out. Makes me wonder why they got it."

She didn't miss a trick. I couldn't tell if she realized I usually don't, either.

"You said something about blood in the room they used?"

She nodded. "Our housekeeper, Jenny, she came running back out of room sixteen like something out of a cartoon. Blood all over the bathtub and the sink, a handful of towels soaked through, and some on the sheets."

"And you really didn't think the sheriff would want to know that?" I asked.

She shook her head. "The sheriff rarely wants to hear from the average taxpayer around here. I figure maybe one of 'em got hurt doing whatever they were doing. Folks do all kinds of dumb stuff so they can post videos on the internet nowadays."

She wasn't wrong about the internet, but with Ratcliff sitting on six bodies, five of them beheaded, I wondered how closely her son had watched who was going in and out of that room. My Granny McClellan was the sort of old-school country Texas broad who could handle anything on her own with either a broom, a rake, or a twelve-gauge, but even she probably would've called the sheriff if she'd ever walked into a bloody motel room. Nothing to be done for it now, but it added to my suspicion that something was off about this place.

"I told Timmy they weren't welcome back," she continued. "I had to scrub those rooms clean myself because Jenny wouldn't touch them, and I'm too old to be bending over a tub with a scrub sponge and a box of lye."

She seemed plenty spry enough to handle anything a given day could throw at her, but I kept that observation to myself.

"Besides," Doris said. "I don't need nobody coming through my place shooting it up looking for the likes of them. We run a decent establishment. No rooms by the hour. Most folks are quiet. Jenny and her little boy live in room twenty-seven. The occasional fraternity group looking for a hiking adventure in the parks gets rowdy drinking, but that's about all the trouble we ever see here. And I aim to keep it that way."

So she didn't think they were up to anything worth a phone call to the sheriff, but she didn't want anyone coming for them with guns? Those two things didn't add up.

I stopped my scrawl when she paused, looking up to find her biting her bottom lip, more tears hanging in her eyes.

"Did turning those boys away get my son hurt or killed?" she whispered.

It might've. But me telling her that without more information wouldn't do her any good.

"I don't have any way to know for sure, Mrs. Dushane, but what I can say is that neither did you. You did what you thought was right for your business and your guests at the time, and you shouldn't beat yourself up for lacking a crystal ball." The last words rolled out of my mouth effortlessly—as well they should. I'd been on the receiving end of them from one therapist or another several dozen times since I was fourteen. "I know that's a tough thing for some of us to do." I reached across the table and patted her hand. "But you really should try."

Doris's eyes narrowed when my fingers went to the charm bracelet on my right wrist as I spoke, my voice catching just the barest bit. "Who did you lose, sugar?"

"My sister. I was fourteen. Her murderer was never caught."

"Well, I guess that tells me all I need to know about why a pretty gal like you is a police officer. I'm so sorry."

"Thank you. I'm sorry you don't know where your son is. Can you tell me what happened when this same group came back?"

"It was later in the spring, after it started to get hot," she said. "April, because I was away in Laredo taking papers to the accountant for the taxes. Government's always gotta have their thumb in every pie, you know."

I jotted *early April* in my notes.

"Timmy called me and said them same boys were back here trying to check in to two rooms, near midnight when they got here, just like the first time," Doris said. "I told him to turn them away, and he put the phone down and tried, and they said he had no right." She barked a short laugh. "No right! This is a private business on private land, and I have the right to do as I damn please when people have left our rooms in a sorry state." She slapped one hand on the table. "I've never once turned a customer away on account of how they look or what they believe or who they're with—none of my business as long as they're decent folks and they pay their way. Still gets my back up that those young men told my Timmy I had no right to tell them to move along."

Her cheeks were flushed, her voice louder. I jotted that down, too, half wondering if she was spry enough to weight down a body and chuck it in the river if she had come across one of the guys she suspected of foul play in her son's disappearance.

"I don't blame you a bit for not letting them stay again," I said. And I didn't. But I did wonder what parts of this story she was leaving out.

"Damn straight. Timmy had to get out the shotgun, but they left. He saw them camping in the desert about fifteen miles toward the river the next day. He recognized their vehicles when he was driving out to meet Lucia. Said they were sleeping in the truck, mostly, but two of them was in sleeping bags on the ground in the middle of the day, under one of those canopy things people take to the football field to sit in the shade. Damn wonder they didn't get snakebit."

"Is Lucia your son's girlfriend?" I asked.

"I wasn't being hateful when I called the woman a whore, officer. She's a prostitute. Mexican, pretty—Timmy thinks he's in love," she scoffed, rolling her eyes. "Border guard he went to school with looks the other way when he brings her across as long as she don't stay more than a day. He was talking about marrying her." She shook her head. "She runs with some dangerous men who wouldn't like that none. I heard her on the phone one night after Timmy went to sleep. She slipped out of the room they used and was crying, bickering with a man she called Armando, who was yelling *'puta'* loud enough for me to hear it even without her speaker phone."

"But you don't think this Armando had anything to do with your son disappearing?" My eyebrows shot up.

"Damned fool up and proposed to her anyway. She told him no half a dozen times, and then she stopped coming around. It was right before Mother's Day I noticed we hadn't seen her in a minute. Them rednecks came back the following weekend, and Timmy disappeared."

I wrote down every word. She'd been talking for fifteen minutes, and I had multiple suspects already.

"You haven't heard anything from him since just after Mother's Day?" I asked.

"Not a peep. He was just gone that Tuesday morning—no boo, bye, kiss my ass, folks, nothing. He wouldn't do that." She set her mouth into the thin line again, her head shaking. "It isn't at all like him."

"Did he take things with him?" I asked. "Clothes, a computer, a phone?"

"No, ma'am, he did not. His clothes are all still in his room, and his laptop and phone are on his desk."

That didn't point to a voluntary disappearance. Unless he was running from something she either didn't know about or wouldn't admit.

"Do you have a photo of your son, Mrs. Dushane?" I asked.

She stood, holding up one finger, and disappeared around the corner.

I tapped the pen on the paper, raining dots all around my notes and turning that fact different ways in my head. When I don't know which trail is the right one, asking a lot of questions and looking at both often helps me figure out which one to follow.

Doris returned and handed me a white-rimmed Polaroid. Timmy Dushane was big enough to be imposing to most people, as tall as the Christmas tree in the photo, which was only about a foot and a half shorter than the ceiling, and fairly broad. His face was clean-shaven and still soft around the edges with youth—and tan, even in December; his expression somber, even on Christmas. I thanked Doris and tucked the photo into a crease in my notebook.

"What did Timmy do for fun?" I asked.

"He liked to tinker with cars, same as his daddy. He drove an old pickup day to day, but he rebuilt a 1968 Corvette when he was a teenager, and it's his pride and joy."

"Where is that car now?" I asked.

"In the shed out back, covered up, where it stays most of the time. Timmy only drives it after it rains. Says the dust ain't good for it. Willie says a car that's too prissy for dust is no good to anybody, but Timmy loves that old beast."

"What about friends? Who does Timmy spend time with besides Lucia?"

"He ain't spent much time with anyone but her in a year now. Before that, same bunch of boys he grew up with. There ain't that many options out here, we stick together. Three of them are married and daddies now." She gave me their names and addresses, and I jotted them down before I looked up.

"Do you mind if I have a look at his car?" I asked.

"Not at all. I'll get the keys."

She disappeared for a moment and came back with a black plastic key ring with four keys hanging off it. "Right back here."

I followed her across a wide stretch of dirt littered with dusty yucca and cacti to a barn with gaps between some of the weathered boards big enough to put a fist in. A thick orange extension cord snaked from the back of the house through the door of the barn.

She tugged a door open and waved me inside. "We don't have regular electric out here, just the shop light with the cord." She reached overhead and flipped a switch on the handle of the light, clipped to a board over the door.

"How long have you lived here?" I asked.

"Since I got married in 1979. Willie's folks opened this place in the spring of 1960. We moved into the manager's suite when we got married, and then into the house after Willie's daddy died the following year. Momma Dushane lived in the back bedroom until she died in 1984."

I only half listened as I lifted the tarp on the car parked directly ahead of the double doors and found a silver Corvette, the old-style hood ornament as shiny and perfect as the day it came off the assembly line.

"Wow," I breathed.

"Like I said, Timmy loves this car."

I peeled the tarp the rest of the way off. "It's a piece of art."

"You're into cars?" She cocked one eyebrow up.

"I had a friend who was. A long time ago."

She handed me the keys.

I glanced at the plastic and saw a partially rubbed-off logo of the motel and its address as I fit the round blue-tipped key into the door, wondering briefly why he would keep it locked out here, miles from the nearest neighbor. I guess they could never be sure what sort of guests would wander through.

The interior was just as pristine as the paint, red leather with white top stitching, every gauge behind crystal-clear glass rimmed with flawless chrome. I knelt next to the door and reached under the driver's seat, my fingers finding nothing but the track for sliding the seat and the floorboard.

Sliding behind the wheel, I lifted the top on the center console. It was tiny, barely big enough for a packet of tissues and some change. I picked through the coins, pennies and quarters mixed in with what seemed to be old pesos.

Three of the pesos had numbers on them: a five, a nine, and a three. I checked all the other coins but didn't find any others that were marked.

I put the keys down and laid the coins out carefully, snapping photos of both sides before I closed the console and turned my attention to the pouch on the front of the wide, flat dashboard that substituted for a glove compartment on this model.

The pocket held a user's manual—much smaller than the one for my truck, though paging through I saw directions for rewiring the electrical system and repairing a carburetor. Kind of made me wonder what there was about my pickup that required so much instruction.

A Polaroid photo of a pretty woman with golden-brown skin and thick black hair fell out of the middle of the book. I didn't have to read the faint chicken scratch on the bottom to know this was Timmy's girlfriend. I took a picture of the image, noting a tattoo on her right arm of a fairly standard red rose with a bunny directly below it, the whole business surrounded by stars, before I kept flipping through the little booklet.

On the next to last page, I found an address in Chupadero and a string of numbers that could've been a phone number, except it had a currency symbol in front of it. Even in pesos, that wasn't a small bit of money. I snapped a photo of that, too, laying the manual on the seat and checking the pockets on the dash again. A Chapstick, sunglasses, and in the very bottom of the large pouch, something cool and metal. I jerked my hand back and retrieved one of the tissues from the console, carefully pulling the pocketknife out and raising it to the windshield to examine it in the light.

I couldn't be sure without UV, but the staining on the edge of the blade and around the frame looked suspicious for blood. I put it on top of the dash and checked under the floorboard liners and the passenger seat, not even finding dust, before I stood, brushed off my knees, and went to the trunk. The air in the barn was thick, even in the utterly humidity-deprived broiler of a border-town August, the building like an overgrown Easy-Bake Oven, cooking everything inside by the light of the giant bulb in the sky. I used the door key to open the trunk and the flashlight on my phone to scan the interior, leaning in to inspect what looked like scratch marks on one side of the felt lining. They were long and thin, too thin to be fingernails, and I didn't see any other marks or staining.

I closed the trunk and stooped to pop the hood, glancing at Doris, who was on the other side of the shed. She leaned against what looked like a stable door and fanned her face with a small handheld garden spade.

"Almost done," I promised.

"Take your time, sugar. I'd rather you be thorough."

I reached under the hood and found the latch, raising it and looking down just as a low rattle started. Doris stepped forward. "Wait!" she shouted as the snake uncoiled and leapt at my face.

5

I screamed and dropped the hood, the heavy steel slamming down and cutting the rattler in half, his front end twitching enough on the ground to make me jump backward into Doris. She put her hands on my shoulders and stumbled backward herself.

"He's dead," she said with the confidence of someone who'd seen many a dead snake. "Damned things like anywhere they can hide. Sorry, I should've warned you."

I pulled in a deep breath, waiting for my heart rate to return to a healthy range. Dead people, I could handle. Live rattlesnakes were another story. "Not your fault, and everyone's okay," I said, sliding a foot back toward the car. "You don't think there's another one in there, do you?"

"They don't usually travel in packs," she said.

I gave the bloody snake remains a wide berth as I walked back around the car to pull the hood release again.

Shuddering, I slid my hand under the metal next to the back half of the dead snake and found the catch, managing to raise the hood slowly without getting snake guts on my hands.

I looked carefully around the tubes, belts, and battery. I unscrewed the wing nut holding the air filter compartment closed and lifted it, checking the underside of the lid and the filter.

"Can I ask what the heck you're looking for?" Doris peered over my shoulder, her breath unbearably hot.

She probably wasn't going to like the answer.

"Miss Doris, you said your son has a girlfriend who is permitted to illegally cross the border to visit him regularly, who has questionable associates in Mexico. And now your son is missing. I'm looking for anything that points to why that is." I used the gentlest tone I could muster in the sticky heat of the barn before turning back to the engine compartment. I found what I was looking for stuck to the back side of the engine block, hidden from view but easily accessible to anyone who knew what to reach for.

I pulled a homemade metal envelope out and showed her, watching her jaw fall open at the stack of cash I removed. I flipped through, estimating fifteen thousand or so.

"Who put that there?" Doris reached a hand toward the money, then took a step backward, shaking her head. "I know what you're thinking. You think Timmy was into smuggling or some such nonsense. He would never. We raised him to respect the law."

The whole bringing-his-girlfriend-into-the-country-illegally thing notwithstanding, apparently. I didn't think it would help anything for me to say that, though. What I knew was that in this part of the state, large amounts of cash and connections to shady characters meant a person was probably trafficking one of two things: dope or people.

"I'm not sure what I think right now, ma'am," I said carefully. "This is quite a bit of cash. Does Timmy have a bank account?"

"Of course he does," she snapped, clapping one hand over her mouth when she realized that didn't sound great for her son. "Maybe he was just going to the bank. He could have sold something."

She faltered such on the last two words that it didn't sound like she even believed them, but I muttered, "Sure," and smiled as I took photos of the money and the envelope over the open engine compartment, because I needed her to keep talking to me.

I handed her the money and told her it was better for her to keep it safe for him before I turned back to the car and, using the pronged end of a hammer from the workbench along the wall, flung the rest of the dead snake to the floor before I slammed the hood and replaced the cover.

I never thought I'd be so glad to step back into the August Texas sun, but the minutes in the little barn had plastered my shirt and jeans to me in some uncomfortable ways. Even the slightest bit of air moving around me was a welcome relief.

"You said Timmy didn't take his clothes or his computer?" I asked. "Do you mind if I look around his room?"

"I'm not sure I should agree to that." She twisted her mouth to one side and stared off at the mountains in the distance. "I want to find my son, but I don't want to bring him home just to watch him go off to jail."

"Do you have reason to suspect he's involved in something illegal?" I asked.

"I didn't thirty minutes ago," she said. "But I'm not stupid. I know what you're thinking. I don't want to think it, but that doesn't make it impossible."

There was no point or kindness in telling her I suspected Ratcliff's dead guy might be her boy. Once Jim determined something there, I'd broach that if I had to. But at least I had a place for him to start looking. I made a mental note to ask around about the local dentist and see if Timmy had X-rays on file. Assuming his head wasn't missing, they might come in handy.

Either way, I wanted to see if the computer held any leads on where the fifteen grand came from.

"I wish I could promise you that's not a possibility, but I don't know enough to say for sure," I said, curving my lips carefully into a practiced half-smile that said, *Trust me. Tell me your secrets. I will get you an answer.*

She held my gaze for a moment and sighed. "I respect your honesty. And I guess I'd rather see him alive in a prison visiting room than dead somewhere if that damned girl got him mixed up in something."

She waved for me to follow her and turned in the direction of the motel.

Doris stopped in the still-empty office and grabbed a ring of keys from a drawer before pointing to the first room outside.

"Timmy moved into the manager's apartment up here when he was nineteen," she said. "Someday this place will be his, so we didn't ever see much reason for him to move anyplace else."

My mind changed about what might've happened to her son with every third word out of her mouth. She was pragmatic and country in a way she shared with my Granny McClellan that made it hard to dislike her, but she was also clearly hiding something. I just couldn't figure out if the something was related to her son, her husband, herself, or maybe all three of them.

Maybe Timmy and Lucia had just shot a big old collective middle finger to everyone telling them what to do and disappeared. The most likely place to check that theory was with the border officer Timmy knew who'd been letting her cross, assuming I could figure out who it was.

Hell, maybe the cash in the 'Vette's engine was a bribe for the cop, and this whole sideshow wouldn't help me a bit in figuring out who was beheading and otherwise murdering folks down the road. But I had time to try to find out before Jim would be there.

The room was neat and way less musty than I expected, given the heat and the weeks that had passed since she said he'd disappeared. About twice as big as my standard Cherry Lane guest room, it had a queen-sized bed in one corner flanked by night tables, with a love seat and chairs facing a flat-screen TV mounted on the wall across from the bed and a teeny kitchenette with a half-size oven and two-burner cooktop, a microwave, a sink, and the smallest fridge/freezer combo I'd ever seen outside a dorm room on the opposite wall. A plain wood desk was on the other side of the refrigerator, stretching to the wall outside the bathroom door, and a black laptop sat closed and plugged in on top of it.

Pulling on latex gloves as I crossed the room, I paused at the closet and cracked the door, a row of shorts in denim and cargo styles and T-shirts hanging neatly over two pairs of boots and two pairs of sneakers.

"It's just like he left it," she said. "He even made the bed."

"Was that unusual?" I asked, flipping the computer open. A password prompt flashed up.

"About half and half. He usually made the bed if he thought anyone would be in here except him, not if he didn't."

I noted that and turned to ask if she knew what he might use for a password.

She didn't. I asked his birthdate, and she told me April 16.

I tried *Lucia0416*. Nope.

I opened a drawer under the center of the desk and rifled past a handful of paper clips and tiny plastic bags. In the back corner, I found a two-by-two-inch square of paper. It had several strings of random letters and numbers written on it. I tried two of them on the laptop before I got a warning screen that a fourth failed login attempt would erase the hard drive.

Timmy had some serious security on his computer for a roadside motel employee in the middle of nowhere.

I closed the computer and bent to unplug it. "Can I borrow this for a couple of days?" I asked.

"What for?" Doris asked.

"I'd like to see if our cyber security unit can get into it," I said. "The program he has protecting it is more than just an ordinary factory password, and I'm interested in why."

"Who will know what you find on there?" She twisted her fingers together. "I'll always see Timmy as a boy, but he's a grown man, and I don't want people to think poorly of him. Because of what he might look at on there."

"Miss Doris, I promise you I couldn't care less if your son is looking at porn on his laptop. No one I work with cares either, unless it's a kind of porn that violates the law. All I'm interested in is whether or not this machine holds a clue to why he disappeared or where he might've gone."

"Go on, then. Just don't tell me if you find...things on there."

"Yes, ma'am."

I noticed an iPhone on the bathroom counter and pointed. "Timmy's?" I asked.

"Everything is here but the truck."

"Did the local police put out an all-points on the pickup? And can I take the phone, too?" I took a photo of the paper with the jumble of numbers and letters.

"The local police didn't do shit but tell me he's grown and I can't use the law to stalk him," she said. "I'm his mother. Why don't they understand that?"

Another point for team flipping the bird, and an excuse to drop by the nearest sheriff's office. It was weird that he left his prize car and all that cash if he'd just taken off, but maybe he felt he didn't have any choice. Or maybe he planned to come back for those things and couldn't. Yet, anyway.

I flashed a smile at her and picked up the phone. "Let me see what I can do. Does your son have any tattoos or otherwise identifying marks?"

Doris pointed to her left arm. "He has a birthmark right above his wrist shaped like Texas. My husband always said he was the most Texan person we knew because he was branded with it by God."

I didn't even need to write that down. It wasn't the kind of thing I was likely to forget.

"You let me know if you think of anything else that might help. I'll be here for a couple of days."

She thanked me and locked the door to his room behind me.

I stashed his things in the closet in my own room, between two folded pairs of Wranglers, and pulled out my phone, scrolling through my contacts until I found a cell number for the Bexar County Medical Examiner. A tired voice interrupted the third ring.

"Bachman."

"Mr. Bachman, this is Faith McClellan with the Texas Rangers," I said. "We met a couple of years ago at—"

"You're Jim Prescott's soft spot," he said, metal on metal clinking in the background, probably from a tool hitting a tray. "But you're also the reason he still has his wife alive, to hear him tell it. So what can I do for you?"

From what I'd read in the newspaper, this guy was buried in dead bodies at the moment. I talked fast.

"Sir, I'm down at the southern border and wondering about five corpses our intelligence officer says were sent to your lab as crossing casualties between last September and now."

"You have questions about crossing deaths from eleven months ago?" The fatigue in his voice dripped out of the speaker before he laughed. "Are you serious? I have two refrigerator trucks in my parking lot housing bodies that have come in in the past six weeks. And they're full."

Of course he did.

"That's terrible," I said.

"It's a disaster is what it is," he said. "Between the ones farmed out from down there and the homegrown ones we're getting from the local gang-bangers, we flat can't keep up."

"Where would bodies sent up as crossing casualties have gone from your lab?" I asked.

"If the consulate couldn't identify them to send them back to their home country, they go to one of three area funeral homes for indigent cremation."

"And that's pretty immediate?" I asked.

"No reason to keep them on ice if no one knows who they are."

Which removing their heads would ensure, because he didn't have to say out loud that no one had time to look very hard with the number of bodies they got every week.

I thanked him for his time and went out to my truck.

I didn't have anything better to do than talk to the local sheriff right then anyway, and the sooner I found out what happened to Timmy, the sooner I could get back to Ratcliff's headless, unidentified murder victims, whether Timmy had anything to do with them or not.

6

Sheriff Connie Nava was half a foot shorter than me, with a personality big enough for ten people. Energetic ones.

"We don't stand on formality around here, Faith," she said, offering me a bottle of water from the fridge behind her desk. The entire station was one fifteen-by-twenty room with a small cell in one corner, separated from the officers' desks only by a thin plywood wall that had obviously been an afterthought. Nava didn't have an office: she used the desk furthest from the door, wore khaki shorts and a polo with the sheriff's office insignia embroidered over her heart, and had a metric ton of gorgeous, glossy black hair piled into a messy bun on top of her head that would make a shampoo model jealous. "It's too hot, and there're too few of us. Have a seat and tell me what you're looking for."

"Right this second, I'm interested in Timmy Wayne Dushane. His folks own the—"

"Oh, I'm familiar with Doris." Nava rolled her eyes. "Did she really call the Texas Rangers?"

"She did not." The words came out slowly as I watched her fold her arms over her chest and pinch her lips together. She didn't like the Dushane family, which I hadn't really expected. Typically in small towns, local business owners and law enforcement rely on one another in a thousand ways, and as such, they get along...well, better than this, anyway. "I'm staying there and was asking around. She mentioned that her son is missing."

"Did she also mention that her son is thirty-one years old and there was absolutely zero evidence of foul play? It's not a police matter if a grown-ass man gets in his truck and drives for the horizon."

"Thirty-one?" I pulled the photo Doris had handed me from my notebook and held it up. "I need to know what kind of moisturizer this guy is using if he's thirty-one. The way she talked about him, I'd put him at twenty, tops."

Nava took the Polaroid. "That's Timmy, sure. Ten or so years back, I'd guess?"

I returned the photo to my notebook. "I suppose I should've specified that I needed a recent photo."

"That may be the most recent one she's got." Nava sighed. "Doris thinks the sun rises and sets on Timmy, no matter how dark things around him get. I know why she's upset, but I can't violate his rights to help her."

"Of course." I perched on the edge of an old wooden desk. "I found some interesting things poking around their place this afternoon, though." I pulled out my phone and opened the photos of the cash and the marked pesos. "Any of this make any sense to you?"

"Why would Timmy have that much cash?" She tapped her finger on the edge of her desk.

"I'm wondering why he had this much cash and didn't take it with him if he left of his own accord."

"Yeah. That too." Nava bit her lip. "I really thought he took off." She muttered the words almost to herself.

"He may have," I said. "But I have a little extra time, and my curiosity is piqued. Do the numbers on these pesos make any sense to you?"

"I'm afraid not, but I will see what I can find out if you send me those images. Where did you say you found the envelope with the money?"

"Strapped to the engine block of Timmy's Corvette. His mother says he didn't drive it very often."

"That's a heck of a hiding place, though. Are the bills sequential?"

I shook my head.

"I'll check them against the bank's ATM records if you can get me some serial numbers."

I got her email address and sent her the photos. "The ones you can see here may be all we have to go on. Doris seems to be walking a line between wanting help finding her son and not wanting him to get into trouble if he was up to something he shouldn't have been."

"I've often wondered if they're not all up to something they shouldn't be," she said. "But I have no real evidence, just a gut feeling."

"Based on?"

"I've always wondered what else they do for money," she said. "Since I was a kid, it has seemed odd to me that they support their whole family with the motel. Upkeep has to cost them more every year, and we aren't exactly overrun with tourists around here."

"She told me they get mostly hikers," I said.

"But they only ever have, like, five or six rooms occupied at a time. At the most."

"Well, as a guest I can say the rooms are clean, but they are dated. It's not like they're doing big updates. If they own the property and their home, things might be tight most of the time, but I'm not getting alarm bells."

"I suppose." She pointed to my phone. "Then again, fifteen grand is a lot of money. And where it was hidden gives one pause. Which is why you're here."

"One reason, sure. Doris told me a story about some guys who made a big mess in the motel a few months back. Said she wouldn't let them come stay again and they've been camping in the area for a few days every few weeks. I'm also wondering if you know anything about them."

"Deputy Kirk said he saw a group of rednecks camping in pickups and SUVs back in the spring," she said. "They were just hanging out in the desert, no trouble."

"Doris told me a story about bloody bathtubs and sheets," I said.

She raised one eyebrow. "There hasn't been a murder around here in thirty-four years. I am quite sure I'd remember a call about a bloody motel room."

"Doris said there wasn't a body, so she didn't see a need to report anything. She thought one of them got hurt messing around with some stunt or something."

"Good of her to deputize herself," Nava said. "But what else is new?"

"What does that mean?" I asked.

"I'm thirty-one. I grew up in the valley, went to UT and got criminal justice and political science degrees, and came home and ran for sheriff when I was twenty-four. I won that first time by seventeen votes. I've been at it going on eight years, and not many people around here take me very seriously."

"They keep voting for you every few years," I said.

"They don't have much of a choice." She snorted. "After I chased old man Conklin into retirement that first election and then he died, I've never had an opponent to speak of."

"Do you have a lot of trouble with smugglers this close to the border?" I asked, keeping my voice light.

"Not as much as people probably think," she said. "There are easier places for them to cross a hundred miles or so down, and the part of Mexico across the river is just as poor as we are."

I noticed she didn't say none.

"What comes through here when you do see it?" I asked.

"The usual. Drugs, some prescription these days and some not. I've never had a bust big enough to draw the attention of the feds, though."

I noted that and finished my water before I stood, handing her a card. "Let me know if you think of or hear anything," I said. "I'll be around for a few days."

"Keep an eye on Doris," she said. "I wish I could point out exactly why, but my favorite professor in school said a cop has no more valuable tool than their gut, and there's something off about her. I suppose that's why I didn't take much notice when her son left—I was surprised he stayed as long as he had."

My gut hadn't really gotten that signal, but there was no point in arguing her feelings. And she lived here, I didn't—she might be onto something I had been too distracted to notice. But if someone was moving valuable contraband through this town, Archie's warning about cops on the take would certainly extend to the local law. Which was why

I didn't mention Timmy's girlfriend. I wasn't sure enough about Nava's motives or skill to spill everything, and I could always ask later if I needed to.

"I appreciate your time," I said from the front door.

"I have a lot of it, it's usually pretty quiet here. Come back by if you're so inclined."

I told her I would, staring a little too long as I tried to decide why my own gut was the kind of twisted up that meant there was something she wasn't telling me. Maybe a lot of somethings.

"Where can I grab a decent meal around here?" I asked.

"Mel's," she said. "Take a right out front and then the first left, about two miles down. You'll see it. Decent pancakes, best chili and tamales I've ever had outside my grandma's kitchen."

I waved as I stepped outside. In tiny, dusty towns like this one, gossip at the local greasy spoon was usually a treasure trove of information. Since Sheriff Nava hadn't been as helpful as I'd hoped, maybe someone there could tell me what no one was saying about Timmy Dushane—as long as I could get them to trust me.

Mel's Food and Fix It was right where Nava said I'd find it.

"Afternoon, officer," a woman who was probably my mother's age, but with evidence of a far rougher life etched into her face, said as she pulled a pen from behind her ear. The red plastic name tag pinned to her navy waitressing uniform gave her name as Edie. "Welcome to Mel's."

"I've never seen a restaurant with an auto shop attached to it," I said, glancing at the window wall that looked out into a five-bay garage where every lift was occupied by a vehicle in a different state of disassembly.

"It's a simple story: Mel's dad was the local mechanic for better than fifty years. He owned the land, and Mel is a good cook," she said. "The shop turns a good profit, and Mel's boys are all four mechanical whiz kids. One went off to the military and is a missile engineer, no kidding. Other three are out there." She pointed to the garage. "What brings you to our little corner of the world?"

"I'm in town to help a colleague with a case," I said. "Sheriff Nava said this is the best place in town to eat."

Her nose wrinkled at the mention of the sheriff, but she didn't say anything, and I couldn't ask why. Yet, anyway.

"We don't have a lot of competition, but we like to think that's not why most folks say that," she said.

The door nearest the garage opened, and an oil-stained young man in coveralls cupped his hands around his mouth. "Mr. O'Shea," he called. I turned my head, and an older man stood most of the way up from a vinyl barstool at the counter lining the longest wall in the restaurant, a slight hunch to his shoulders that looked permanent. He put two bills on the counter and shuffled toward the door.

"Definitely nicer than the waiting room at any auto shop I've ever been in," I said. "And the crossover business is probably good for the diner, too."

"It sure is," Edie said just as O'Shea drew back an unsteady fist and laid the mechanic out flat.

"Dammit, Rusty!" Edie screeched as a wiry man in a stained apron rounded the counter and grabbed the old man's arms, holding them at his sides rather than wrenching them behind his back.

"Highway robbery!" The old man's voice wasn't shaky or slow, booming through the suddenly silent room. "Thirty-five dollars for an air filter after you kept Bessie here for four days! I've never paid more than seven. If you're going to steal from people, you got to be prepared for the consequences, son."

I watched the exchange but kept my seat.

"He thinks it's 1967 most days," Edie muttered as the mechanic got to his feet, rubbing his jaw.

"You still got a decent right hook, Mr. O'Shea," the kid said.

"Rusty was the sheriff here for most of my childhood," Edie explained. "He's a good man. He's just confused and angry a lot of the time now."

There wasn't a trace of judgment in her tone, just resignation, matter-of-factness, and a tinge of sadness.

A large man in a Texas Rangers baseball jersey and an apron shuffled out of the back room, unruly salt-and-pepper hair poking out from under a triangular chef's hat.

"Our mistake, Rusty," he said in a calm, clear baritone, nodding slightly at the young mechanic. "Mark will get that invoice right for you in two shakes. You want a Coke while you wait?" He jerked a thumb at the cook holding the older man, who backed off slowly as Mark the mechanic scurried back to the garage and Mr. O'Shea went to the counter and took a red plastic tumbler full of soda from the man I assumed was Mel.

"I didn't mean to hurt your boy," O'Shea muttered.

"He's tough." Mel waved the apology off. "And like you said, he ought to know better."

"Gotta teach them not to gouge honest, hard-working folks, Mel," O'Shea agreed.

The rest of the room returned to their plates and conversations, and Edie turned back to me. "Never a dull day, anyway." She flashed a tight smile.

"Everyone was very kind to him." I sipped my ice water.

"We stick together around here," she said. "And people in these parts who ain't related by blood are related by marriage or by choice. Rusty gave this town the best years of his life. We take care of each other."

Mark returned with another invoice that Mel tore up, nodding for Mark to give O'Shea his keys and telling him to be careful.

"Buck's making his famous steak and potatoes tonight," Rusty told Mel cheerfully as he shuffled to the door.

"He's okay to drive?" I asked Edie, watching him climb into a vintage red pickup that would be right at home on the set of several dozen Hallmark Christmas movies.

"Perfectly fine. Just lives in the past," she said with a sad half-smile. "It started when Buck died a few years back. They were more in love than any two people I ever seen. I think Rusty's heart just couldn't bear it."

A woman at a nearby table called to Edie and asked for more ketchup, and Edie held up one finger and tapped her notebook. "Anyhow. What can I get you, sugar?"

The menu was traditional greasy spoon fare—burgers, sandwiches, deep-fried everything you could think of. "Vegetarian friendly" wasn't a menu category in places like this.

"Fries with a side of queso and a Dr Pepper, please?" I asked.

"Coming up." She scurried off to get the woman at the other table her ketchup, and I pulled out a notebook and wrote down the names of everyone I'd heard called by one. I wondered if O'Shea's condition might make him more likely to remember something that could be helpful to Ratcliff's case. In towns this small, crime—like motel management and professional car repair—tended to run in families.

———————

Stuffed full of decent fries and some of the best queso I'd ever eaten, I thanked Edie and took a giant to-go cup of icy Dr Pepper with me out of the diner, pausing in the nearest bay door to the garage. A mid-90s Chevy step-side pickup occupied the lift, and Mark the mechanic was under it, taking off the brake pads. I had swallowed a quarter of my soda before a shorter, younger version of Mel from the kitchen closed the hood of a red Mustang, wiped his hands on a red shop rag, and tipped his chin at me. "Something we can do for you, sweetheart?"

Mark turned, looking me up and down. "You ain't from around here."

"I'm not. What I am is wondering if you're Mark Jenkins."

"All day long," he said, reaching for a rag and stepping out from under the truck to toss the worn brake pad into a large yellow steel trash barrel.

"Doris Dushane tells me you're a good friend of Timmy's." I'd noticed his name in my notes from my chat with Doris as I ate.

I watched his face carefully but saw no sign of anything other than concern in his furrowed brow. "We been buddies since kindergarten." Mark tossed the grease-streaked rag into a heap of similar ones in the corner and stuffed his hands into the pockets of his coveralls, which had to be roasting him even with a dozen fans going in the shop. "I haven't seen him in a while, though. He's got hisself a Mexican girl he took up with. Spends a lot of time with her these days."

"When would you say was the last time you saw him?" I asked. "Not socially, just...at all. Has he been into the diner this summer? Come by looking for something for his 'Vette?"

Mark's brother walked closer. "You a cop?"

"Texas Rangers."

"Timmy in trouble?" He put his hands in his pockets, too, and Mark rocked up on the balls of his feet as his brother stopped next to him.

"I hope not," I said. "His mother is worried. I'm trying to help her out, just want to know if he's safe."

Mark nodded. "Hate for Mrs. D to be worried. She's been through enough in the past few years."

I watched his face as he spoke, nodding sympathetically like I knew what he was talking about and hoping he'd elaborate.

He scuffed one toe at the edge of the concrete, sending tiny pebbles of blacktop skittering.

"Timmy didn't say nothing to her?" he finally asked. His brother leaned forward and bumped his shoulder hard enough to knock him off-balance.

Smooth, dude. Like I wasn't standing there watching.

Mark didn't pay him any mind.

"She's always been good to us, you know?" he mused, talking so softly he might have been addressing himself.

"She seems like a nice lady." I kept my voice equally soft. "She just wants to know why her son took off without saying goodbye."

"Mark, we got to get back to work."

Mark ignored his brother, shaking his head before he looked up at me.

"That girl got him in with some real bad people," he said. "People who don't mind letting someone else take a fall for bad things they done."

"Mark!" Hand to God it was more of a bark than a word. Mark flinched and turned back toward the garage.

I took a step toward my truck, still listening to them.

"You can't be seen talking to a cop, 'specially not one that looks like her, who ain't from around here," burly brother Jenkins said, plenty loud enough to be overheard. "You're gonna end up right out there with Timmy if you ain't careful."

Right out there with Timmy...in the river?

I slid behind the wheel of my truck and cranked the AC, opening my Google Maps and typing in "dentist near me."

There was, of course, only one, just half a mile down the road.

I checked the clock—it was just after noon. Worth a shot.

I pulled up at the address, a white clapboard two-story home with what looked like a converted garage that housed Dr. Herb Strickland's office. Outstanding.

I tried the office first, noting the rust-patched pickup in the driveway. Locked and dark.

I crossed the gravel driveway, scaling the side steps to a wide, wrap-around porch with fans spotted along the ceiling at three-foot intervals. The doorbell was an old-school pull-style, which was somehow the most charmingly small-town thing I'd seen since I got there. I yanked on it and took a step back.

Steps came from inside, faint and far away at first, then louder. I saw the curtain on the transom window move and a blue eye peek out before the door opened.

"Can I help you?" The man who opened the door was a small mountain, probably six inches taller than my five-eleven and at least half as wide, huge hands cradling a ceramic Santa in a serape and sombrero.

I flashed a smile that had once dazzled pageant judges across America, pretending my face wasn't red, my clothes weren't sweaty, and my hair wasn't slicked to my head with oil and perspiration. Confidence alters perception more powerfully than most people think.

He smiled in return, fumbling with the knickknack and running one hand through his bushy white hair. It didn't tame it even a little bit.

"Dr. Strickland?" I asked.

"Last time I checked." His brow furrowed. "Do you have an emergency? Because the office is closed this week." His eyes landed on my badge. "But not for...the Texas Rangers? Really?"

"Faith McClellan." I stuck my left hand out so he could shake it with his free one.

"McClellan?"

"Yes, sir."

"What can an old country dentist do for you, young lady? If that smile is any indication, your teeth are just fine."

"They are. I'm actually here in search of some information—I'm looking for a local missing person, wondering if you have dental records we can use," I said.

"Somebody's missing?" He turned and put the Santa on a small table just inside the door with a few pieces of mail scattered across it and reached into his pocket, producing his key ring.

"Timmy Dushane," I said. "His mother asked me to help figure out where he is." I left out the part where there wasn't an official missing persons case open.

"Timmy..." He scratched his head with one hand and waved me down the steps ahead of him with the other. "I don't guess I've seen him in a while. But nobody said anything about him being missing. Doris is worried?"

"She is." I didn't offer any other details.

"I haven't seen him in a while," he repeated, stopping at the office door and unlocking it. "Where does the time go?"

"Any X-rays you might have will be very helpful," I said.

"Sure thing," he said, flipping lights on and pulling out the second drawer on a wide file cabinet.

"Here we are," he said, pulling out a thick folder and flipping back. "I started seeing Timmy when he was just a little guy. I've watched most of my patients grow up; now I'm treating their kids. Last X-rays I took were...two years ago. He had a cavity we filled." He pointed to a spot on the film. "I'll get you copies. It'll just take a minute."

"Thank you."

He disappeared through a door, and I looked around. The place was sparse but clean. Two folding chairs with a small table between them made up the waiting area. The tabletop held a photo book about the nearby state park in the center and a box of tissues toward the back. The walls were bare, a calming shade of blue, and an L-shaped desk sat in the middle of the floor with a crystal bowl of Trident gum on one corner and a silver-framed photo of a little boy on the other. The kid had red hair, brown eyes, and a missing tooth, freckles dusting his nose. He was cute.

"Here you go, officer," Strickland said, bustling back through the door and juggling the file folder and a stack of copies. "That should be what you need."

I flipped through the stack he handed me, finding the recent X-rays, as well as a dozen more sets that went all the way back to baby teeth.

"Thank you so much." I tapped them on the desk.

"I hope you don't really need those," Strickland said, his mouth turning down.

"Me too. But I appreciate you letting me interrupt your Sunday to get them."

"Let me know if I can help you in any other way," he said, opening the door for me and shutting off the light.

I waved as I started the truck, watching him stroll back around his porch and disappear inside. Jim would be happy I already had the dentals. Whatever they told us about Ratcliff's dead guy, I couldn't control. And I didn't have a great feeling about it after listening to Mark and his brother. But I'd learned a long time ago that not every case will turn out the way I want it to—my job was to follow the evidence to the truth.

7

The Cherry Lane's mid-century-not-so-modern rooms didn't come with Wi-Fi, so I opened my computer and used the hotspot on my phone to search for background on Rusty O'Shea and Consuela Nava, jotting notes as I read.

Rusty had first been elected sheriff in 1968, when he was thirty-one, after spending most of his twenties serving in Vietnam, where he'd earned a list of commendations as long as my leg, according to the Army database, including a Silver Star. He'd never married, had no children I could find a record of, and lived for the past sixty years in a ranch house he owned solely, according to the deed, off a dirt road about halfway between the Cherry Lane and the state park entrance.

I put two stars next to Buck's name in my notes and searched for Buck O'Shea and Terrell County. No results found. Just the word "Buck" got me more than five hundred hits about hunting season. I didn't have time to sift through that unless the former sheriff became more relevant to my case.

The internet had Nava's story pretty much as she told it: local girl, captain of the cheer squad in high school, she went away to the military —she hadn't specifically mentioned that part, but the computer said she was a member of the Texas National Guard for four years—and college before she came home to oust the sheriff who took over when Rusty retired in 1999 in an election that was decided by just seventeen votes. Her platform had been moving the county into the twenty-first century, smart policing, and a strong protection of Second Amendment rights. The former sheriff, Gary Conklin, had died of liver failure less than a year after leaving office, much of that time apparently spent writing letters to the local newspaper about how Nava cheated to win the election. I saved a few of those and searched county records for a marriage license with Conklin's name on it.

He'd married Edith Jane Lewis in 1996. A quick search of the local newspaper's online lifestyles archive told me she was a first cousin of Mel Jenkins, owner of the Food and Fix It. That explained why Edie didn't like Nava. I jotted the family tree down and went back to the DPS window, searching for Timmy Dushane.

The screen flashed with four records: his driver's license, which wouldn't be due for renewal for two years yet, two speeding tickets, and an arrest.

I clicked the arrest first.

Officer Ratcliff had booked him for drug trafficking. The weekend of July fourth, two months after his mother last saw him.

Ratcliff didn't answer his cell, so I left a message and flipped back through my notes. Jim would be there in about eighteen hours, and if Timmy Dushane wasn't Ratcliff's riverbed corpse, I'd be out of time to locate him. I was invested enough in his case by then to want to see it through, and the answer might give us a lead on the larger murder case—drug trafficking wasn't exactly an anomaly in this part of the state, but the town was small, which meant chances were good that most of the bad elements were intertwined.

Doris had said Timmy had a childhood friend in the border patrol, and Archie said his experience told him many of the agents weren't above taking bribes, the odds of which likely increased the less they were paid by the federal government. It looked like maybe Timmy accidentally crossed paths with Ratcliff in early July instead of the buddy his mom had mentioned. With the clock ticking toward Jim's arrival and Ratcliff not answering his phone, a visit with Timmy was my next play.

Arrests made by our border unit were processed through the federal detention center, and the cases went to federal court with a docket that was backed up for years. I could make the fifty-minute drive faster than I'd get a straight answer from anyone there over the phone. The idea that Doris had fretted over her son's whereabouts for months and that he hadn't contacted his parents, who he still lived with, raised a dozen questions in a blink. I grabbed my notebook and keys. The air conditioning in my truck worked better than the aging window unit in the room, anyway.

In the truck, I checked the gas gauge. The center was fifty miles down the road, and one thing lonely Texas highways teach quickly is that running out of gas is the dumbest mistake a person can make. I had nearly half a tank, but I stopped at the station three miles up from the Cherry Lane and topped off just in case.

Radio cranked to what Archie would call ear-bleeding levels, I sang along with Pat Green and Tanya Tucker and Janis Joplin as I let what I'd seen in what was turning into a very long day roll over in my head.

All I knew for sure about the bloated corpse in the river was that someone sunk it there—I'd guessed male, but wouldn't take even that as gospel until Jim confirmed it. Ratcliff said it was the latest in a string federal agents didn't want anything to do with, which told me something shady was going on with the local unit. That meant the question, beyond exactly what and who, was how far up the chain did it reach?

The more miles that sped by, the more convinced I was that Doris Dushane's wayward son might have at least some of the answers I needed.

"What brings the famous Faith McClellan to our humble little station?" The tone coming out of the Immigration and Customs Enforcement desk officer's face would have been right at home calling me a string of names inappropriate for polite conversation, his lips twisting into a near-snarl no matter how hard he tried to keep them pinched together when he wasn't talking.

I couldn't stop my eyebrows from going up. "Good afternoon to you, too," I checked his name tag, "Officer Wallace."

"Seldom a good evening to be had here for one reason or another." The look on his face said I was the problem with this one, but damned if I could figure out why. I had never laid eyes on the guy, and Ratcliff was my first brush with our border unit.

An entire childhood spent in corsets and heels competing for tiaras had taught me that I couldn't please everyone: a judge at the Miss Bluebonnet pageant when I was twelve had loathed me on sight, scoring me at half of what the other judges did in every category no matter how bright and skilled my smile or straight my posture.

Charity told me the next day that she'd overheard Ruth ranting at the Governor about his college girlfriend costing "us" a crown. Funny how I'd never seen Ruth squished and taped into a Miraclesuit, teetering around on three-inch heels with hair bigger than the Astrodome and fake lashes long enough for a bird to light on poking her in the face.

"Sweet girl, you can be your very best self on your best day, and some people just aren't going to like you," Charity had said, flipping her hair with the confidence of a young woman who was the loveliest and the smartest in most every room she entered. "You're a McClellan. Thick skin is in your DNA—you just have to find it. Do what I do: assume people who don't like you are bitter and jealous, and feel sorry for them instead of bad about yourself. Because you, baby sister, are going to change the world someday. And not by planning parties, no matter what Mother says."

She'd hugged me and grabbed her bag to take off for a class, leaving behind a cloud of Clinique's Happy perfume and a lesson that had stuck better than Ruth's swimsuit tape. Three decades later, I heard my sister in my head as I straightened my spine and glared right back into the swarthy red face of the officer at the desk. "I can make a phone call and have a Rangers captain reach out to your unit commander here if you really think that's necessary," I said. "Or you can just have someone put Timmy Dushane in an interrogation room." I paused two beats to watch for his reaction. His eyes narrowed, but the snarl faded into a slightly slack jaw.

"Either way, I'm going to get what I want out of the afternoon, so you go ahead and pick."

He muttered something that was probably better I couldn't make out and tapped keys on a computer so old it whirred and labored under a beige CRT monitor I would've only expected to see in a museum.

Looking around the front lobby of the rambling, warehouse-style building, every moldy ceiling tile and drywall crack joined the ancient, wheezing computer in highlighting federal funding priorities—which didn't include this place. I'd bet there were less sad and beaten-down federal dog kennels.

Picking up his phone, Wallace barked at someone to move detainee 4709 to conference room C and then come to the front.

Bingo. Bonus: Timmy wasn't dead. Downside: I was back to zero on Ratcliff's dead guy.

Wallace slammed the phone back down without a glance in my direction, guzzling a Red Bull and crushing the can with his meaty hand.

I walked to the corner just past the secured door, reading a small plaque on the wall. The building was dedicated in memory of Captain Herman Stillwater, a thirty-five-year veteran of the US Customs and Border Protection, in May of 1978—before there was such a thing as ICE. A quote attributed to Stillwater was etched into the brass: *"Never forget that this job is not about barriers or exclusion—it's about safety balanced with humanity and morality. Brave souls will never stop striving for a better life in the greatest nation on Earth. America at her best is not an elite private club, but a safe harbor for honest folks who want to work hard. Securing the border is about helping them navigate the system while keeping Americans safe."*

I read the words twice and then snapped a photo so I wouldn't forget to ask Archie if he knew this guy.

"Ma'am?" A low voice came from behind me, and I turned to find a uniformed officer with a smile much more inviting than Wallace's smirk.

"Beautiful words," I said, pointing to the plaque.

"More people here should read them every day," he said. "I'm Grady. I can show you to the conference room." He glanced over his shoulder at a scowling Wallace and shook his head slightly.

"I'm Faith," I said, ignoring Wallace. "Nice to meet you, Grady. Lead on."

He pulled the door open and waited for it to close behind us, taking a dozen steps down a hallway that had to be as long as a football field before he spoke again.

"Sorry about Wallace."

"It seemed I had personally offended him, though I've never met him."

"You're Chuck McClellan's daughter, right?"

"Am I wearing a sign on my back?" A wave of unease washed through me.

"Wallace...he..." Grady paused, throwing a glance at me before he focused on the concrete floor again. "I don't want to freak you out or nothing, ma'am, and I don't know the whole story here."

"In my line of work, it takes a bit to freak me out," I said.

He chuckled. "I suppose that's fair. Rumor has it Wallace worked for your old man years ago."

"Was he a Ranger?" I could hardly imagine that, and I hadn't mustered an inkling of recognition talking to the guy.

"No, ma'am, it wasn't anything official, if you know what I mean. Again, just a rumor. But whatever happened, he hates McClellan with the kind of fire that can eat a person up inside. The same kind of fire he loves Longhorns basketball with, as it happens. So you being who you are, and then busting Coach Richardson..."

"I'm not his favorite human. Check."

His gaze snuck sideways at me again as he unlocked a door at the end of the hall and a buzzer sounded. "Just so you know, it's nothing you did. Except show up here."

I followed him into a slightly brighter hallway with others snaking off of it every ten feet or so, filing that away. "Thanks for letting me know. What can you tell me about Timmy Dushane?"

"That he knows some bad folks," he said. "He got here in one piece, right after the fourth. By the end of that week, somebody had cut out his tongue and broken both his hands, though nobody seems to know how that could've happened."

It took a minute to process that for several reasons, not the least of which was Grady's casual tone. Did people here often end up mutilated with no apparent investigation?

I opened my mouth to ask why Timmy was still there if someone inside had hurt him that badly, the words stopping short when a door buzzed and then opened at the far end of the hallway, pandemonium leaking through for a full minute as a group of seven men in assorted uniforms filed through. I shuddered at the noises that had escaped the cellblock, drawing Grady's gaze.

"I've never heard a sound like that. Was that a person?" I asked, keeping my voice low.

"This place is like the eighth ring of hell," he muttered, standing up straighter as the group that had come from the containment area approached.

I adjusted my posture to match his. "Who is that?" I whispered. "And why are we standing here at attention?"

"We call them the enforcer posse," Grady whispered out of the corner of his mouth. "Derek Amin, Command Sergeant Major of the Texas Army National Guard, Jasper Aarons, Assistant Superintendent of the US Customs and Border Protection, their staff sergeants, and our warden. Here for a facility inspection. We get those on the regular these days on account of all the bad press."

But no one had thought to move Timmy Dushane to a safer facility after he was brutally attacked here? I raised my eyebrows but didn't ask that out loud.

"Unannounced inspections, I'm guessing?" I asked. "I mean, it's still Sunday, right?"

"Their visit was postponed from Friday because of an urgent something or other one of them had to handle," Grady whispered, saluting as the group closed in on us.

I fixed a smile in place as they paused in front of us, the sergeants fanning out behind them down both hallways, eyes scanning the area constantly. Damn. How dangerous was this place? My job often requires ducking inside a prison here and there, but I've never been in one where the people in charge seemed at once so wary and accepting of violence on the part of the population.

"Grady," the shortest and roundest of the men, at the center of the group and wearing a uniform like Grady's, only darker, said. "How are matters in D block?"

"Moving along, Warden," Grady said, his voice lower and with a harder edge. "No trouble this week."

"That's what I like to hear." The warden turned to the other men. "Grady here is one of our most conscientious and productive young guards. He's barely been here eighteen months, and already he's the day shift supervisor in D block. I wouldn't be surprised to see him in my office someday."

A tall, athletic man with dark curls and a small mustache and wearing beige fatigues with star-lined lapels smiled. He must be the National Guard guy. His face looked vaguely familiar, but I couldn't say why. I focused on his voice as he addressed Grady. "What brought you to work in the detention center?"

"I got a flyer in my mailbox about a job fair," Grady said. "I figured maybe I could make a difference in some of the stuff I've seen on the news. This place doesn't exactly have the most stellar reputation, sir."

Amin pursed his lips. "Some people would have us feeding these invaders steak twice a day," he said. "The warden here does the best he can with what he has, in my observation."

"Doesn't mean we can't use more guards who want the job for the right reasons. Sir." Grady held Amin's gaze without blinking.

"And just what would the wrong reasons be?" Amin's nostrils flared as he stepped forward. The warden cleared his throat and laid one hand on Grady's arm.

"He's a do-gooder at heart, but don't let that fool you, Amin," the warden said. "He runs a tight ship with the fewest injuries and the least whining in the south."

"Fewest injuries." Amin sniffed like the warden had just said Grady was drowning puppies on the state's dime. "Coddling criminals does no one any good in the long run."

Before Grady could keep the barb exchange going, I put my hand out and introduced myself. I only had so much time left before Jim arrived, and now that I knew Timmy Dushane was alive and locked up, I wanted to know if he knew anything that could help my murder case.

Amin's dark eyes turned to me, one thick brow rising as he looked me up and down in a way few people had since my last swimsuit competition. "What brings you to this godforsaken place, Ms. McClellan?"

"Just here to see a prisoner." I looked him straight in the eye, still unsure why I thought he looked familiar.

"What would the Rangers want with the kind of people who end up here?" Amin asked, the USCBP guy, Aarons, leaning into the conversation.

"Just checking every lead on my current case. I like to be thorough." I folded my hands behind my back and didn't say anything else.

"I've read about you, seen things on the TV, too," Aarons said, pointing with a thick finger. "You're the lady who always cracks the case."

"Indeed. I'm a fan of your work, as well." Amin's eyes had a sheen when he spoke that time. Something about the combination of the look and his voice was off-putting, but I kept the smile steady. This entire place had my skin crawling; he was just an accessory to misery.

"Thank you," I said, still holding his gaze.

He nodded slowly, his face spreading into a smile that stretched the mustache thin before he turned to the warden and Aarons. "Gentlemen, let's get on with it. I don't want to be late to dinner."

"Nice to meet y'all," I lied.

Amin saluted, his sergeant stepping forward to respond in kind and waving for him to walk ahead down a different hallway.

"Does that happen often?" I asked Grady as we watched them walk away.

"They do routine inspections every four weeks," Grady said. "I've never been sure what exactly it is they're looking for."

He pointed to a door just past the corner. "Dushane is waiting in there. I'm not sure how helpful this could be to you, given his injuries," he said. "Dude never said a word to anyone, as far as I know. Must have a secret somebody really wants kept."

Somebody who knew the penalty for assault was far less than the one for murder. He didn't have to say that part; it hung as thick in the air as the smell of mold and the feeling of despair. I've been in and out of most people's share of prisons, and this was the first that had sucked the joy entirely out of me with less than an hour inside. Maybe there wasn't that much joy to be had today, to be fair, but still. I shivered despite an ambient temperature roughly five degrees less than the surface of the sun.

What had I stumbled into? Something I'd probably be better off not knowing. But I was in it now—curiosity might have killed the cat, but it just drove me to work harder. Hopefully I wasn't quite out of lives yet.

Patting Grady's arm, I reached for the doorknob, swallowing a gasp as I swung it open.

Two of the man at the table would've fit easily into the shorts I'd seen in Timmy's closet. Both hands were engulfed in mitten-style casts, his sandy hair and beard both shaggy and dirty.

His head was bent, his eyes on the casts on his hands. If I squinted, I could imagine the hollow face in front of me filled out to resemble the one in Doris's Polaroid. But it took a good imagination to get there. I couldn't check for the birthmark because the casts covered half of each forearm, but I was pretty sure this was the guy.

What in the blue hell had happened to him? And why?

"I'm Faith," I said, shutting the door and pulling out the chair across from him. A small chalkboard with a scrap of white chalk attached to it lay on the table between us, and I almost laughed when I saw it. What the heck was he supposed to write with, his teeth? Someone made very sure he didn't have a way to communicate at all, at least for a while. Someone who knew that in a place like this, nobody would make much effort to chat him up.

Someone who didn't know an exceptionally stubborn Texas Ranger would stumble across his mother.

I sat down. Timmy didn't move.

"I'm here to help." I wasn't sure that was true, exactly, but I wasn't there to make things any worse, anyway.

Still not even a flicker of acknowledgment. If he hadn't been upright, I couldn't have sworn he was breathing.

"Timmy? I met your mother today."

That got him.

He raised his head slowly, tears brimming in hazel eyes sunken into a sallow face. I could see a ghost of the smiling man from the photo Doris had given me, but it was a faint one.

"She's worried about you." I kept my voice low, imitating the soothing tone Graham used with victims.

A tear spilled over and rolled into his matted beard, followed by another. He shook his head slowly, turning his hands over before raising one to pat his chest.

"You're worried about you, too?" I asked.

Timmy shook his head, then tipped it to one side and shrugged before he nodded.

"Maybe, but that's not what you meant."

He nodded.

"You're worried about your mom?"

He nodded, rolling one hand before he froze and glanced around the room, returning his hand to the table and his head to the bowed position.

"Your girlfriend?" I asked.

He didn't move, but the rigid set to his shoulders didn't match the defeated slump I'd seen when I first walked in. It wasn't that he didn't want to tell me. He was afraid to.

"Your mother mentioned that your friend was working for some dangerous people."

The shake of his head was so tiny, a half a blink would've obliterated it.

The men his mother worried about weren't who this emaciated, mutilated version of her son feared.

Grady had kept his eyes down and his voice low as he talked, too.

"Did someone who works here do this to you?" I whispered, hoping my voice was low enough to be garbled on the recording.

Timmy didn't so much as flinch, and I thought for a second he hadn't heard me, but then his foot slid slowly into the toe of my boot under the table. I took it as a yes. And read the fear on his face.

"You know, if you don't cooperate with law enforcement, we can't help you." I hardened my tone and leaned forward far enough on the table that my ponytail fell across my shoulder between my face and the camera on the wall, and my head was close enough to Timmy's for him to see me by rolling his eyes up. I flashed a smile to let him know I got it.

A low growl started in the back of his throat just before he launched himself out of the chair and across the table, knocking me and the chair to the floor.

8

Every molecule of air left my lungs when we hit the floor with Timmy's bony knees in my sternum, and I swung blindly as I fought to refill them.

Timmy grunted when my fist made contact with his jaw, but he didn't retreat. Grabbing my ponytail, he wrenched my head to one side and dove toward my face before I could get my hands up to block.

Alarms sounded, feet pounded in the distance. I shoved both arms against Timmy's bony chest, fighting for air as I felt his breath on my ear. He slid his knees to the floor on either side of my torso, pulling his head back just enough for me to see the tears welling in his eyes, his brow furrowed with urgency. I let my arms fall to my chest, sucking in a calming breath.

I wasn't being attacked.

Leaning close to my ear, Timmy Dushane was trying to tell me something. Without letting on that he was telling me something.

I kept flailing but stopped swinging hard as I caught a couple of gulps of air and tried to make out what he was saying.

The same four sounds repeated low and quick, over and over, less raspy and more frantic each time.

"Lay, eel, eel, ur."

The door slammed open, and Grady landed a boot to Timmy's ribs.

"What the hell's got into you, man?" Grady shouted, two officers behind him flanking the doorway with weapons drawn. Timmy landed on his right arm—and hand—with a short scream.

Grady turned to me, looking down with a furrowed brow. "He's never even so much as looked at anyone funny. Are you okay?"

Satisfied that Timmy was down, the other guards holstered their weapons and moved to help me off the floor. I waved them off with a weak smile, getting slowly to my hands and knees and leaning close to Timmy, who opened teary eyes and cut them sideways at me.

"Ew, do." His eyes went wide. "Ew. Ew. Do."

Grady pulled Timmy to his feet by his left arm, looking back and forth between the two of us before he picked up the chalkboard and shoved Timmy's shoulder in the direction of the door. "Back to bed, man. This just bought you a night in the hole. And you owe the lady an apology."

I followed them into the hallway and put one hand on Grady's arm. "Don't hurt him," I said. "Not on my account. I'm tough. He startled me more than anything."

"Don't pity him, ma'am. We can't have them attacking officers," the tall guy behind Grady said. "It's like dealing with animals around here half the time. If you don't establish a pecking order, they'll try anything."

I checked his name tag. "I appreciate the insight, Officer Bowden, but human beings are capable of far more complex thought and emotions than most animals, and this man has to be frustrated and scared half out of his mind. Imagine for a second the complete inability to communicate with anyone after a brutal assault. It looks like he hasn't been able to eat for weeks. Hell, I could get irritable enough to knock you on your ass over missing one dinner."

Grady snickered, covering his mouth with one hand.

Bowden's ears flushed red, and he opened his mouth to reply, then shut it without saying anything.

"Send him to solitary," I said. "I have no quibble with punishment. I just think he's been injured enough, and I'm fine."

This particular tightrope was tricky, because while I wanted to tell Grady to simply return Timmy to his cell and leave him be, if whoever had hurt him in the first place was paying even a little attention, word getting around that he'd jumped an officer and gotten away with it would raise a flag I didn't want to be responsible for raising.

Grady stopped at the hallway junction and spun Timmy to face me. I saw a tear fall when Grady yanked on his injured arm and couldn't stop myself from wincing.

"Maybe the lady is right, and you're just going a little crazy from all this." Grady waved a hand encompassing Timmy's injuries. "But you can't jump on an officer like that, you get me?"

Timmy nodded, keeping his eyes cast down.

"Are you sorry?" Grady asked.

Timmy nodded again.

"Are you going to do it again?"

Headshake.

Grady gestured to Bowden and the other officer. "Take him to the hole, but she's right—he's been roughed up enough already."

Bowden muttered something, and Grady stood up straighter. "What was that?"

"Nothing, sir." Bowden turned right while Grady pointed for me to turn left. "Let's go, Timmy."

Grady put a few paces between us and them before he murmured, "Some people aren't cut out for this job. He just likes an excuse to push people around."

"I appreciate you listening to me," I said. "That guy has been through a lot."

He paused with his hand on the door to the lobby. "What did he say to you?"

"Nothing," I said, trying not to let it rush out too quickly. "I mean, his ability to share anything is pretty much nonexistent, and I'm not psychic. I will let his mother know where he is, though. Any idea on a trial date?"

"Our courts are so clogged, it's usually more than a year," he said. "If they can afford a lawyer, it'll cut the time down. But the way I heard it, he was stopped with a toolbox full of pills and smack and a pickup bed full of guns. So I'm not sure a speedy trial helps him."

"It'd get him out of here," I said.

"And into the nearest federal facility." He shook his head. "A guy like Timmy won't last long in the federal pen."

"Do you know who he's working with?"

"I know the guy who picked him up was in the wrong place at the wrong time," he said. "He's one of yours, right? But at a post by himself a lot of the time?"

"Budget cuts," I said. "The state thinks the feds should pay for border security, so our manpower in the unit was cut by two-thirds last year."

"He should watch his back. And now that you've been here, you ought to watch yours, too."

I raised an eyebrow. "Awfully cryptic of you."

"I don't know who." He raised both hands. "If I did, I'd tell you. All I know is there are some bad apples around here, and Timmy got himself on their shit list and ended up mutilated and wasting away in a shitbox cell in the middle of nowhere. Whoever these people are, they don't mess around."

Goose bumps rippled so high it felt like my skin was crawling right up both arms as he spoke.

I'd spent the better part of a day looking for Timmy Dushane and had located him. Worse for wear, but alive. Box checked, mystery solved.

But I'd been so involved in looking for Timmy that I hadn't spoken to Ratcliff. Ratcliff, who'd arrested Timmy in the first place. Ratcliff, who found a mysterious and gross body in the riverbed and called me for help because he was convinced he was chasing a murderer.

Ratcliff—who wasn't answering his phone. He'd be easy pickings for anybody looking to keep his nose from poking further into this, working from his one-man outpost in the literal middle of nowhere.

I thanked Grady for his help and handed him a card before slamming the door into the lobby wall as I sprinted to my truck.

I rang Ratcliff's cell phone every three minutes for the entire hour it took me to speed back to the turn off the highway and got no answer.

By the time the gravel road dead-ended into sand about two hundred yards from the border operations trailer, where I could see his pickup parked outside, I had the accelerator on the floor, a dust storm flying in my wake.

Slamming the car into park hard enough to throw my ribs into the steering wheel, I flung my seat belt off and leapt out, running for the door. It wasn't locked—I didn't expect there were ever enough people around here to necessitate that.

There had been a fight.

Papers that had been stacked neatly a few hours before lay scattered over the floor, the desk, every chair—even under the refrigerator. The desk was askew, one edge popped out from the wall, and the ancient computer had been knocked to the floor.

"Dammit," I muttered. I checked the bathroom, which was undisturbed, before racing back out into the heat, my eyes landing on the small barn, my stomach twisting into a knot.

"Dodger?" I called, crossing the sand quickly and pushing the door open as my foot landed in a thick, sticky puddle. "No. Come on, y'all."

I didn't want to look. I grew up riding on my granddaddy's ranch and think more highly of animals than I do the vast majority of people. But the state pays me to look at shit I wish I didn't have to see every day. It's part of how I keep people safe.

A river of blood on a dirt floor could be from a horse or a man— without seeing the source, I didn't know what I was dealing with. All I knew was that in fifteen years working homicides, I'd never seen anyone walk away from losing that much blood.

I followed the trail to the center stall and pushed on the door. It opened about three inches before it stuck on something heavy on the floor behind it.

A faint whinny-whimper sounded behind the door.

Dammit.

"Dodger?" I couldn't budge the door and didn't want to hurt him. Spinning on one boot heel, I scanned the miniature barn for a ladder and found a four-step A-frame one folded at the end of a feed bench. I tucked it under one arm and barged into the first stall, a trickle of more blood coming under the dividing wall, separating around the hay on the floor and staining it bright red. "Hang on, sweet boy."

I scaled the ladder and found Ratcliff's horse lying on his side, a bullet wound just above the top of his left front leg. It was still oozing, but slowly. His ribs moved slightly with shallow breathing, his eye only half-open but rolling up to watch me as I put one hand and one foot on top of the stall divider and jumped over, landing in a crouch in the hay piled next to him.

"Hey, boy." I kept my voice low and soothing, unbuttoning my shirt and ripping one sleeve off to pack his wound as I dialed 911 from my phone. Hopefully stopping his bleeding wasn't that different than stopping a wounded person's.

"Terrell County sheriff, what's your emergency?"

"Faith McClellan, Texas DPS Rangers division. I was there this morning and spoke to Sheriff Nava. I'm at the Rangers border post and have a missing officer and a wounded service mount. Who's the best large animal vet in the county?"

"You don't suffer boredom, do you, Faith? This is Nava. You need Doc Porter. I'll get him out there, and I'm on my way now—is the area secure?"

"The only vehicles here are mine and Ratcliff's, and I haven't seen anyone else," I said, looking around and lowering my voice just in case. "The horse has been bleeding for a while, I think."

"Stay alert." I heard pounding feet as she ran for her car. "I'm on my way."

But she was better than forty miles away.

"Thanks," I said. "I'm going to call for backup from our guys, too."

"See you soon," she said, the engine roaring in the background as she hit the accelerator.

I ended the call and rested the phone on my knee, stroking Dodger's face as I closed my eyes and listened.

Nothing but his breathing—I didn't hear so much as the crack of a twig or shuffle of dirt under a foot. Nava was right to warn me to be vigilant, but my gut said whoever did this was long gone. My biggest worry right then was about Ratcliff, who probably hadn't left the premises of his own accord without his truck or his horse. What if he was bleeding somewhere in the scrub brush or the dry riverbed and I was in here hiding from no one and tending to Dodger?

I picked up the phone again and dialed Archie instead of the DPS switchboard, because he knew everyone and was owed favors by more than half of the law enforcement world, while I had exactly one contact in this area, who was currently MIA.

"You change your mind about coming home?" he asked when he picked up.

"Ratcliff is missing, and his horse has been shot." I kept my voice low. "I'm in the barn at the Rangers outpost, I haven't seen or heard anyone else, and the sheriff is on her way. But we could use some more manpower."

"I'm on it," he said, every trace of good humor gone from his tone. "Stay alert, and don't hunt for trouble on your own. I'll have thirty people to you in an hour."

"I'm good, Arch. Just get me enough guys to outgun whoever did this and set up a search grid for Ratcliff. They should consider him wounded."

"You got it."

I hung up and checked the horse's pulse. It was thready and too fast, but there.

"It's okay, boy," I said softly, brushing his mane back out of his face and checking his wound. My sleeve seemed to be stanching the blood flow.

I pulled my shirt back on and was fastening the last button when I heard an engine outside. A large one. I pulled my SIG from its holster and moved to the back left corner of the stall, where I'd be able to see anyone trying to use the ladder to get inside—hopefully before they saw me.

The barn door creaked when it swung in. "Hello? Officer McClellan?" A man's voice. He waited three beats and added, "Marty Porter here, I'm the local vet. Sheriff Nava said Dodger has been shot?" His feet came closer, following the blood same as I did, I figured.

"He's blocking the door," I said. "There's a ladder in the first stall."

"It's been a minute since last time these old knees were on a ladder," he said. "Let's see what I can do here."

I heard halting steps on the ladder's wide rungs before a head of wild salt-and-pepper hair poked over the top of the stall divider, followed by kind, bright green eyes behind wire-rimmed bifocals.

"I really am the vet," he said when he saw my sidearm in my hand.

I slid it back into the holster. Even if he wasn't, he was north of sixty and, judging by his full, red cheeks and the comment about his knees, not in great shape. I wasn't afraid of him.

"I believe you. Thank you for getting here so quickly."

"I'm afraid the problem is that I can't get down there with you." His fingers gripped the top of the wall. "My days of jumping over obstacles are so far in the past, I'd need photos to be sure they even really happened."

I glanced around. "Could you step down onto his water bucket if I turn it over?" I pointed to a steel washtub in the corner.

"I was never the basketball star my brother was growing up," he said with a shake of his head. "Even if I managed to clamber over this without breaking my neck, I'm looking at a drop of a few feet onto that thing."

"I'm not sure how much longer he has." I stroked the horse's silky nose, and he nuzzled my hand.

"Me, either, but we're going to do our damndest to make sure today isn't his day," Porter said. "That's a smart move, packing the wound with part of your shirt. Do you have any advanced medical training?"

"I can do wound care first aid, bleeding stop, and CPR. On people, anyway," I said.

"Better than nothing," he said, grunting as he hefted a large black leather satchel over the top of the wall. "Incoming!"

I stepped back, and the bag landed with a thud at my feet.

"I'll talk you through it," he said as my stomach turned to ice, flipping slowly when I realized this man thought I was going to operate on this horse.

I sucked in a deep breath and knelt between Dodger's chin and his wound. "Sorry I'm all you've got, boy, but I don't give up easily, at least."

9

By the time I heard sirens in the distance, I had found the bullet, removed stray bone fragments, and cauterized Dodger's damaged blood vessel as Doc Porter watched from eight feet overhead and on his iPhone screen so he could see the surgery field via FaceTime.

"You're to the easy part now," he said. "Just sew up the wound. The suture kit is in the silver case."

The sirens came steadily closer as I worked, more sweat dripping off every part of me. I clipped the last stitch as Nava ran into the barn.

"Doc, what the hell are you doing up on that ladder?" she said, huffing between words.

"Horse is blocking the door," he said. "Ranger Faith here might have saved his hide."

"McClellan?" she called.

"A little busy," I said as Dodger's eyes opened and rolled back to look at me. I stroked his face and murmured to him.

More sirens filed in outside, the backup Archie had called in for me, no doubt.

I heard officers talking to Nava and people discussing tools and taking the stall door off its hinges, but I stayed on my knees in the bloody hay with surgical tools strewn around me, petting the horse and talking to him.

"He likes you," Doc said, still perched on the ladder.

"I like him, too."

"You ever thought about being a vet?"

I laughed. "Math and science weren't my best subjects."

"I never understood why they make people take calculus to go to med school. You're not building a skyscraper. All you need to be able to figure is how many milligrams of meds per pound of patient will help without killing someone. From what I saw today, you'd make a damn fine one if you ever get tired of chasing killers."

"Thank you," I said.

A power drill whirred to life, and the door came down and was set aside in a couple of minutes. Doc Porter rounded the corner and knelt slowly, pressing a stethoscope to Dodger's side and listening for what felt like a long time.

"A damn fine vet." He stuck out his hand to shake mine, neither of us minding the blood. "I can't swear he's out of the woods, but he's a damn sight better than I'd have expected twenty minutes ago."

"Who will take care of him if we can't find Ratcliff, or if he's..." I let it trail off.

I had saved the horse. What if the minutes I spent in here had cost my colleague his life?

Doc Porter said he'd call for help and a trailer and have Dodger moved to his barn, where there was monitoring equipment, plenty of food, and air conditioning.

I gave the horse's sweet face a final pat and stood, scanning the crowd of peace officers in the barn for a familiar face, suddenly very aware of my bloody...everything...and my lopsided button down with the missing sleeve.

"McClellan?" A tall, barrel-chested guy in shorts and a Señor Frogs T-shirt flashed a Rangers badge and stepped to the front of the stall.

"That's me," I said.

"Morgan Dean," he said, putting a hand out and then pulling it halfway back when he saw the dried blood staining both of mine.

"Consider it shaken, and thanks for coming." I folded my hands behind my back. "I hope Archie didn't pull you away from anything too important."

I was pretty sure his shorts were actually swim trunks, and he smelled like sunscreen, which made me feel a little bad because we don't get an abundance of downtime, but at least he probably hadn't abandoned another case to speed out here.

"Fishing tournament." He winked. "My buddy just hauled in a nineteen-pound large-mouth bass. I wasn't going to win, anyway."

"Glad we didn't cost you a trophy."

"I don't know many people who wouldn't gladly skip out on just about anything if Archie Baxter needed a favor, ma'am. How can I help?"

"You can start by calling me Faith," I said. He was young, but not call-me-ma'am young. Maybe I needed a better eye cream. "We need a manhunt grid set up as wide as we can comfortably cast one with the manpower we have—Officer Drew Ratcliff went missing from this post sometime in the past four hours, his truck is still here, and his horse—"

"Is lucky you were here, from what I heard the doc say." Dean flashed a grin. "A few of the guys went to search the riverbed and the scrub brush out there, and we'll get a grid going." He turned his head and put two fingers in the corners of his mouth, the whistle drowning out every other sound for a split second. "Hammet!"

A stout man with a shock of orange-red hair and more than a smattering of freckles spun from Nava, who was detailing the terrain outside, to face Dean. "Sir?"

Dean took two steps toward him and reeled off instructions for setting up a manhunt grid, tapping his radio. "Let me know when you have people in position."

"Yes, sir." Hammet hustled out of the barn as I checked my watch. We had about four hours until sunset.

"My men are good at what they do," Dean said. "We'll find him if he's out there."

"What unit are you with?" I furrowed a brow, wondering if I should know his name.

"Recon," he said. "Just made lieutenant in June, so I won't let you down. I have things to prove."

I just bet he did. I peered closer at his face as best I could without being too obvious.

"I'm thirty-one," he said.

"Not as stealthy as I thought, I guess." I laughed.

"I'm just used to it." He pointed to a utility sink in the corner. "I'll tell you the story over a drink when we've found your guy, if you want. I'm sure you want to wash your hands. I'm going to go help."

He jogged out the door, his deck shoes flopping against his heels.

I went to the sink, spending the next few minutes wearing the nearly full bar of Lava soap down to a sliver and wishing I had something better to scrub under my nails with.

"You're going to start to wash your actual skin off, there," Nava said from next to my shoulder.

I picked at my bloodstained cuticles. "Probably."

She held out a light blue T-shirt. "It was in my gym bag, but it's clean if you want it."

I plucked at my ruined button-down and smiled, ducking into the vacant stall to change. "Thanks, Nava," I said, stuffing my once-white work shirt in a garbage barrel.

"No problem. You said you saw Ratcliff this morning?" she asked.

"Yep. I left him in the office about two hours before I came to see you."

"What were you talking to him about?" she asked. "I can't imagine a Ranger being interested in a bum like Timmy Dushane."

"He'd happened upon a corpse he wanted my help with," I said. Until I knew what was what, I wasn't telling anyone Ratcliff had been concerned about a string of murders—I had no idea if my handful of conversations around town had been enough to cause whatever had happened here, but since Nava was one of the people I'd spoken with, I didn't trust her.

"You think someone was murdered?" She sounded surprised. "And you didn't think that was more important that Timmy Dush—oh. You think someone murdered Timmy?"

No, but I didn't mind letting her chase that particular goose while I worked the case. "I'm not sure what I think," I said.

Her eyes went wide. "Oh, shit. I thought he left. Everybody around here thinks his mama is crazy. We didn't understand why he didn't leave years ago. Where did the body go? The JP is on vacation."

"I have a friend from Travis County coming out tomorrow to have a look at it. We didn't move...it." I said the last word slowly, a bad taste around it as I turned for the door, wondering if there was something about the body someone didn't want us to find—badly enough to assault a police officer and shoot a defenseless animal.

10

"Dammit." I pulled up short on the riverbank, resting my hands on my knees as I caught my breath. A mile on uneven sandy terrain in this heat was enough of a workout to make me glad I'd given up cigarettes more than a year ago.

"What on earth?" Nava was only a few steps behind me.

"Someone really doesn't want us to know who this was," I said between breaths, my eyes roving the churned-up mud of the riverbed and scattered pieces of what used to be a person. I walked along the bank, looking for tire tracks.

Fifty yards down, I turned to go back, shading my eyes with one hand and spotting the marks on the other side of the river.

I picked my way across carefully, not as worried about disturbing evidence Jim might need this far down.

Nava's footfalls squelched in the muck behind me. "Your legs are long," she said, and I turned to see her stretching to put her feet in my boot prints. "And while I understand your suspicion, it could just be idiots who didn't know what they were running over until they couldn't get away from it."

I shortened my stride slightly, slowing as I approached the tire tracks, which were wide but not terribly deep. Counting off the steps between them, I pointed. "This was a recreational vehicle of some sort. Probably a four-wheeler."

"There are easily a hundred of them in the county," Nava said. "And that's just the ones people bothered to register on my side of the river."

I circled the scene, taking photos of the tire tracks from several angles, and then turning and pointing the camera back up toward the mess in the middle of the riverbed. "Our people will set up a perimeter until the forensics teams can get here."

She could be right about the mess being an accident—I could see mudding in the empty riverbed being an interesting pastime in this part of the world, and it's not like your average civilian would think to be on the lookout for decomposing dead people.

But most average civilians would call the police if they ran over one.

I opened a text and sent Jim the photos of the scene. *The body I called you about has been shredded and scattered around the riverbed*, I typed.

My phone rang almost immediately.

"On purpose?" Jim said when I picked up.

"I don't know," I said, putting several paces between myself and the local sheriff. "It looks like a four-wheeler probably did the damage, though I just walked up on it because our guy that I was talking to down here this morning has disappeared. It could've been an accident, someone out mudding on their ATV. But the sheriff hasn't gotten a call reporting that anyone found the body."

"Back up to the part where we have a missing Texas Ranger?" Jim's voice was tight, and I heard a door close in the background.

"I don't know much yet. I called Archie, and he sent the recon unit, complete with their lieutenant. They're running the manhunt."

"Any signs of struggle or foul play?"

"The office was tossed good, and his horse had been shot." I didn't want Jim to get scared and refuse to come out, but I wouldn't lie to him.

"Somebody tore up the body you called me about, did God knows what to a highly trained officer of the state, and killed a horse?" Jim sighed. "This isn't even my jurisdiction."

"The horse isn't dead," I said. "I sort of operated on him. To remove the bullet. There was a vet there talking me through it. Kind of a long story, but he's on his way to rehab in peace at the vet's."

"I'd love to hear the story. I'm not so sure I want to come down there anymore, though."

"I understand that," I said. "And I can't say I blame you. I'm growing less interested in being here from a personal safety standpoint by the minute. But something is off out here, Jim. And not just a little off. It hasn't even taken me a whole day to see that, and I can't walk away and leave the people of this little dustbowl to fend for themselves if there's a murderer running amok." Especially not after showing my face and introducing myself all over town. Even when I can't help a situation, I try my level best not to harm it, and backing off now would be like waving a white flag at the local criminal elements. Not an option.

"I'm eighteen months from a fully vested state retirement," Jim said.

"What if I have the remains transported to you?" I asked. "I need your expertise, but I don't necessarily need you to be in the field here with this all torn up—there's not much for you to see about how the remains ended up here anymore. I can send photographs from this morning and this afternoon, and soil samples, too."

"I'd appreciate that," he said. "I'll find you every drop of information I can wring out of them."

"Perfect. Let me work out how to get this to you, and I'll let you know when they'll be there."

"You know what else I'd appreciate?"

"What's that?"

"Not having you end up on my table."

"We agree on that," I said.

"I'm serious, Faith. Eighteen more months."

"I have no plan to die anytime soon, Jim." I furrowed my brow at the edge of what sounded like desperation in his tone. "I can't walk away out here, but I understand completely why you'd rather stay clear of the scene. We'll get the bad guys. It's what we do. And I already have a few good leads."

"I'm sure you do. But it worries me that you're on your own out there—you have a tendency to run headfirst at trouble if it means you close the case. Some things are more important than the arrest, Faith. You can't help anyone ever again if you get yourself killed, and you just said you may well be chasing someone who's not afraid of your badge."

He wasn't wrong about any of that. And it probably wasn't pertinent to mention the border detention center's weird vibe or Timmy Dushane until I understood if any of that was connected to the rest of this. I knew how to handle myself, and right then that was what I needed Jim to focus on.

"Understood," I said. "Really. I get your point, and it's a good one. I'll be careful. And I'll try to keep these guys on the recon team in the loop. The lieutenant is young. He has something to prove and people to impress."

"I'll wait for your call about the remains."

"Thanks, Jim."

I hung up and walked back over to Nava, who stood in the same place I'd left her.

"We need a forensics team," I said. "I don't suppose there's a local one?"

"We have to call San Antonio or El Paso," she said. "Not that we have cause to do that very often. What do you need?"

"I need a collection of this site done and the remains transported to Travis County, and I need it now," I said. "The site can't be left unattended until the remains and any evidence are collected."

She reached for her phone. "I can help with some of that."

I thanked her and moved toward the skull resting in the mud, careful with where I placed my feet still, but not as concerned as I'd been earlier with the river bottom churned up—and any evidence likely obscured or destroyed. I squatted and leaned close, studying the destruction the tires had wrought and looking at the tracks around it.

It was detached from the remains, probably ten feet from the torso, the orbital sockets and teeth broken into several pieces, though some of them were held together by caked-on mud. I wasn't as good as Jim at studying remains—no one was—but I'd learned a lot from him over 124 murder cases.

Smashing the teeth was usually a ploy to keep a victim from being identified by dental records. Eye sockets were key to a facial reconstruction in cases where the remains were badly decomposed before discovery.

The pattern of the mud stuck to the skull told me someone ran over it forward and then backed up with the tires nearly in the same place before running forward over it again.

Which meant it probably wasn't a redneck out looking for some innocent ATV fun in the drying riverbed.

And while whoever did this had been trying to hide information, the effort itself gave a couple of things away: they thought this person had a US dental record I'd be able to access, and whoever this was, their identity was important to the case.

There was no other reason for someone to risk coming back to damage the scene.

Ratcliff's disappearance added a more disturbing layer: Jim was right, anyone who had something to do with that wasn't afraid of the Rangers, because if there's one thing that will drive a cop to the ends of the Earth to make an arrest, it's an attack on one of our own.

So the person I was hunting either wasn't afraid of going to prison, or they thought they were above the law.

Both were dangerous, but as I stood and turned back to Nava, my gut said I might well be dealing with the latter.

Which made me more than a little uneasy about what I had so eagerly charged into when Ratcliff called me for help.

11

"El Paso can have a forensics van with a team of three on the road in twenty minutes," Nava said as she slid her phone into her back pocket.

"Now far are they from here?"

"Four and a half hours or so," she said.

I checked my watch. It would be dark by the time they arrived, so we'd need lights. And power.

"I need every floodlight in the county. We are going to light this riverbed up like Permian High School's stadium on a Friday night," I said.

"I can manage that, too," she said. "And I have two deputies on their way to stand guard until the forensics team arrives."

I cast a look around at the mountains and hollows lining this part of the riverbed. "I'll wait with you until they get here."

"You don't have to do that," she said. "If my colleague were the one missing, I would want to help look."

"Our recon unit is the best in Texas at what they do," I said. "Manhunts are squarely in their purview. And I wouldn't feel right leaving you here alone when I'm not sure what we're facing. Or who might still be in the area."

"I appreciate that, but I'm not alone," she said, patting the sidearm on her hip. "And I may be a middle-of-nowhere sheriff, but I am a trained law enforcement professional. I can take care of myself."

I held her gaze, the uneasy feeling that she was trying to get rid of me zipping up my arms and leaving every hair standing on end.

"Of course you are." I flashed the smile Ruth had coached in front of her massive full-length mirror for hours when I was a kid. The one I always called my *Ruth-wants-that-crown* smile when I pasted it on for pageant judges. "But two good shots are better than one, especially out here in the open."

She narrowed her eyes for the barest moment. "Sure, as long as I'm not keeping you."

"Not at all."

She pulled her phone back out. "I'll get on those floodlights."

Relieved to avoid the unique hell of small talk for at least a little while, I found a rock wide enough for my backside poking up out of the mud and sat, scanning the hills around us for evidence of human activity. I couldn't see anything, but my vantage point was low. I texted Dean and asked him to send me an officer when he could spare one, dropping a pin so they'd know where to go, and made a mental note to ask his men to search the hollows and caves for signs that someone had been waiting up there for a chance to move or wreck the remains.

As Nava talked in low tones several yards away, I surveyed the river. Where could this guy have been dumped to end up here? And the more interesting—and pertinent—question: Why would whoever dumped his body care enough to come back and find it in the drought and destroy the identifying markers?

I pulled out a pad and pen. It wasn't a whiteboard, but it would have to do in this kind of pinch. I scrawled *where* across the top of a blank page.

Dean and his team would be better suited than I would to find a possible dump site, so I made a note to ask him about that. From the rivulets in the mud under my feet, the water flowed east toward the gulf. I turned to look west, wondering how far back the nearly dry, exposed part of the bed ran. The mud was devoid of even puddles in several places at least to the bend, which was probably a mile or so upstream. I jotted a note to find someone at Parks and Wildlife to search the section that ran through the state park for whatever the body had been weighted down by. With thousands of acres of protected—and therefore unpopulated, undisturbed, and perhaps most importantly, camera-free—land butting up to the border, if I were looking for a place to dump a body, this was a better location than many.

But once a body had been dumped, especially as efficiently as this one seemed to have been, it was usually forgotten. Which meant it was important to someone that nobody found this one.

Someone who had learned in the space of eighteen hours that Ratcliff had found it, and wasn't concerned with going up against a lone Texas Rangers border agent. But who either hadn't wanted to try or hadn't been convinced they had time to move the remains without being seen, because otherwise why not just take them instead of wrecking them?

The more notes I made, the faster I had to scribble to keep up with my thoughts.

New page: *Ratcliff* across the top.

He told me he'd happened upon the remains on a regular patrol yesterday evening. Who else had he told? Because someone had let word get back to whoever did this, assuming the damage I'd seen on the skull was evidence this was done on purpose. I try to avoid assumptions when I'm working a case, but this one seemed relatively sure—and wise, given the dangerous implications it carried and the fact that I was without my usual circle and unsure which of the locals were trustworthy.

Had Ratcliff come back out here and happened upon someone tampering with the remains after I left? I put a star by that, but then why would they have taken Dodger back to the barn and shot him? Or why would Ratcliff have come out here without his horse, especially in this heat?

I couldn't get those variables to balance. If Ratcliff had come out here without the horse, who in the world would go to the trouble—and risk of being spotted—to go to the Rangers outpost and shoot the horse? But if he'd had the horse with him, who would take Dodger back home?

And if he hadn't been here at all, what did someone think he knew that warranted an attack on a state police outpost in broad daylight? It was kind of in the middle of nowhere, granted, but still—someone could have shown up and sent their plan sideways easily. Hell, that someone could have been me if I'd left the detention facility a little earlier than I did.

I was so deep in thought I didn't hear Nava come up behind me. Her hand on my shoulder made me jump, sending the notebook into the mud.

"Sorry, I wasn't trying to startle you," she said. "My guys are on their way. They're picking up floodlights and going by the local garage. Mel Jenkins says he can show them how to hook the lights up to a car battery. He promises one battery will power them for days."

I picked up my notes and swiped mud off the back of one page with my index finger, wiping it on my jeans. "Perfect," I said, realizing as I stood how easily someone could have gotten the drop on Ratcliff out here, which made me wonder why he had ever been assigned to patrol this area alone. I hadn't given it much thought a few hours before, but now it seemed like something someone should have taken into consideration given the level of criminal activity in this part of the state.

Nava's phone buzzed, and she looked down. "El Paso forensics ETA nine thirty-five." She pointed to my notes. "You come up with any theories?"

I tucked the notebook into my hip pocket. "There are a lot of possibilities. I try not to lock myself into one mindset early in an investigation, because I've found it makes me miss clues I might have seen if I wasn't focused on a single track. Right now the only thing I know for sure is that the Rangers are a small organization to cover as much territory as we do, but we have the best of the best in Texas law enforcement in our ranks, and we will move every mountain out here if that's what it takes to find out what happened to one of our own."

Speeches were usually more Archie's thing, but he wasn't there, and I wanted to see how she'd react. I thought I remembered Ratcliff saying he'd notified other law enforcement of the body discovery yesterday, though I couldn't say for sure that meant she knew about it, since she'd seemed surprised when I spoke with her earlier. Between the Rangers, the US Border Patrol, Immigration and Customs Enforcement, the Parks and Wildlife park rangers, Nava, and whatever other federal agencies might have officers in the area, we were in the center of a jurisdictional hurricane here, and notifying other agencies could have meant anyone on that list.

"I would do the same if it were one of my men who'd gone missing," Nava said. "We're happy to assist the Rangers in any way we can."

Her voice was even and sincere, her facial expression open and concerned. It didn't quite fit what I expected based on my gut earlier, but my gut isn't always right and humans are complicated.

People I have trouble reading bug me as a general rule, though, and so far I wasn't sure what to make of her. At first glance, she seemed ambitious and smart, having landed the job she wanted as a young woman—but just behind that onion-skin-thin facade was a parade of facts that didn't match up. Low-paying, high-stress law enforcement jobs in the middle of nowhere aren't exactly in high demand, especially among locals who head for the city as soon as they're of legal age, the way Nava did. No one I'd spoken to, including Nava herself, had said anything about accomplishments since she took over the sheriff's office—and I know enough about politics to know young idealists usually come into office with a whole slew of things they want to change and do better. So if she didn't run for sheriff to change things, why did she run in the first place? And why was she still here almost eight years later?

"Thank you. I appreciate that, since I'm kind of a fish out of water here." Playing the clueless pageant queen usually works better to get men to talk to me, but I was going to be out here with her for a while yet, it seemed, so maybe I could use the time to pick apart what made the sheriff tick.

I gestured to the remains. "Is this a common occurrence here?"

"Dead bodies in the river?" She shook her head. "I know TV makes it seem like we find three a day, but in all my time as sheriff, I think there have been less than twenty. And three of them were children who got separated from their parents in the current."

"Jesus. I can't imagine things being so dire that people risk their lives and their children's lives to go to a better place."

Her head snapped in my direction, and I kept talking. "I'm not saying things there aren't that bad. Just that it's hard for me to imagine it."

"It was that bad when my grandparents came here in the sixties," she said quietly. "In many ways, it has gotten worse since." She paused. "You know, one of those three children was an American. A little white girl with blond hair like yours who was 'glamping' in a giant, overpriced RV with her parents. They were from Dallas, lived up the street from two NFL players, and were the very worst people I've ever spoken to in my life. Given my line of work, I'm sure you can appreciate the depth of that statement. At one point I had to leave the building and walk around the block to stop myself from hitting the woman." She glanced up at me. "I don't have much of a temper."

I felt my forehead wrinkle as I listened to her speak. "I remember that. The parents said someone took the child when they were hiking in the mountains, and she wandered off chasing a butterfly, right?"

"They said a *Mexican* took their child while they were on a hike. Specifically, because they knew that would scare people and create a panic." Nava stared at the mud, her tone flat and unemotional. Removed, even. "She drowned after she wandered out of the camper and into the river—it had been an unusually wet spring—because she woke up from her nap early and she was looking for her mother."

"The parents weren't there?"

"They were making a drug deal ten miles away. Painkillers, steroids, and diet pills they sold at their very expensive and exclusive health club."

"How was this not national news? That's the kind of stuff Lifetime makes movies out of."

"They had influential friends who kept the truth pretty quiet. Not totally quiet, but quiet enough. I knew twelve seconds after I sat down with those people that nobody had kidnapped their child, and I worked around the clock for weeks to prove it." Nava's flat tone turned bitter. "But money will buy most anything, including freedom, it seems. They plead out to six months served in a minimum security state facility and five years with ankle monitors."

"For neglect," I guessed. "You couldn't make the drug charges stick."

"That's because my witness wouldn't testify to what they were doing. I had traffic cameras that put their truck miles away at the time they initially claimed they were running through the desert chasing the person who snatched their kid. Once we found Lucy's body, the medical examiner in San Antonio was able to put her time of death that very afternoon. I found the traffic footage and brought in a couple of people who know the drug scene around here, and one of them ID'd them as people he'd dealt with for a couple of years. He'd seen them that afternoon, had the appointment alert in his phone for the same time they said they were hiking in the mountains with their daughter."

"But the deal you had to make with your informant to testify didn't include the drug charge, or he'd have been incriminating himself," I said. Because in the justice system, it never matters what we know. It matters what we can prove to a jury.

"Yep." She popped the *P* at the end hard. "The only bright side being that their fancy-pants Armani lawyer couldn't discredit my witness by giving the jury his criminal record without admitting why his clients were meeting with a drug dealer. But they left their toddler alone and let her die, and then tried to create a panic about a phantom kidnapper from south of the border to cover their own asses. And they got off. They're probably still just as rich and influential, and probably still selling pills, too."

"I'm sure you're probably right," I said. "But if it's any consolation, they'll slip again. In my experience, even if the justice system fails to adequately punish people, karma usually catches up to them eventually." I jotted a note to mention the parents' names to an old friend in the Dallas narcotics unit.

Sometimes karma needs a little help.

She sighed. "I hope so. Those people—they're my Moby Dick, you know? The one that got away."

"I know better than you can possibly imagine." I tucked my notebook back into my hip pocket.

She was quiet for a minute, her lower lip disappearing between her teeth.

"Oh, shit, your sister," she said. "I was a kid, but I remember that. My mother lit a candle for your family at church every day for a month. I'm sorry."

"That's very kind of your mother." I returned to my seat on the rock, scooting to make room for her to join me. I still didn't know what to make of her but was beginning to wonder if my first impression had been off.

"That's why you do the job, huh?" she asked, perching on the edge of the rock, careful not to touch me. It was too hot for that.

"I have saved more than a hundred families from the special ring of hell that comes with not knowing why someone you love was murdered. With not seeing whoever took them from you punished for what they did," I said. "Maybe someday I'll make Cold Case and find justice for Charity. But for now, sparing other folks is enough."

"That's cool." She lifted a foot out of the muck, a slurping sound issuing from the ground as she examined her boot. "I think these are done for."

I didn't miss the change of subject.

"Mine, too, probably. And I like these boots. So what about you? Why do you do the job?"

"Oh. I—"

"Sheriff?" A man's voice boomed over the brush lining the bank.

"Out here, Dawes!" She stood and walked toward the sound.

I followed, watching three brown-uniformed deputies stop for breath, setting halogen garage spotlights on various stands and a car battery down on the bank. A broad-shouldered truck of a Ranger followed, waving to me. I recognized him from the barn earlier; he had arrived with Dean's unit, wearing shorts and a T-shirt like the rest of them because it was their day off.

"Keep an eye on them." I shifted my eyes to Nava and her men and spoke softly. "And make sure no one touches the human remains in the riverbed. A forensics team is en route—let me know when they get here." I handed him a card and pointed out my cell number on the back.

"Yes, ma'am." He strode toward Nava's group and introduced himself, helping them set up the lights as I waved and turned back toward Ratcliff's office.

Maybe I was overthinking it, but the sheriff didn't seem to want to talk about herself much.

There could be a thousand reasons for that, and I didn't care about nine hundred and ninety-nine of them. I had a killer to catch. I could dig up more on Nava later if her story turned out to be important.

12

"The blood starts here outside the barn." Dean pointed to a pattern of oddly spaced drops. "And continues for at least half a mile east before it disappears into scrub brush. I have two guys still looking to pick up the trail."

I crouched, looking at the nearly black spatters marking the light-colored, packed dry ground in the rapidly fading sunlight.

I used two fingers to measure the spaces between the cluster of drops. There were three about two inches apart, and then another cluster about four feet away. I stood, walking toward the front of the office, scanning the ground. "There's nothing near the office or near his truck." It was a state-ment, not a question. I could see for myself the spatters began about five feet outside the door to the small barn.

So maybe Ratcliff was in the barn when the attack happened? I wondered if he might have tried to use Dodger to escape—getting them both shot in the process.

"There's a forensics team headed out here from the El Paso PD. I'd like samples of this dirt sent to the lab for analysis. I know they might not be able to get enough for anything conclusive, but it's worth a try since it's among very little evidence we have. I'll get Austin to send Ratcliff's blood type and medical files, and we'll try for a match."

Stepping into Ratcliff's office, I stood in front of the window unit air conditioner for a full two minutes. "I'm not sure I've ever looked more forward to a shower in my life," I muttered, mostly to myself.

Dean laughed behind me. "This part of the country will do that to a person in the summer. Nothing beats cleaning up at the end of a day like this one."

Turning to survey the mess in the office, I sighed. "I can't even tell if someone was really looking for something here, or just trying to make us think they were. I don't really know what was here, so I have no idea what's missing."

"I wish I could be more help," Dean said. "I'll say this: if this is for show, whoever did it is committed to their lie. They were very thorough."

"How much communication does your unit have with this post?" I asked, looking at the file tabs I could read without touching anything.

"We share reports on Tuesdays and Fridays. Ratcliff is a good guy. Quiet, keeps to himself. Seems to enjoy the solitude out here. He keeps good records, and he's made a few busts since I've been here. Those are fewer and farther between these days."

"Why is that? To hear the governor's press secretary tell it, the border is overrun with crime."

"I think you of all people know well how full of shit the average politician is." Dean smiled. "Not that we're hurting for more criminal activity—it's really more about the finesse required to make anything stick out here. International law is a different beast, deals are made in back rooms out at the detention center—we have to build airtight cases, lay traps. This job is at least as much about strategy as it is chasing bad guys. It's like a five-way chess match. And we have to be three moves ahead of everyone else."

Aside from the folder he'd sent with me, nothing was missing from Ratcliff's file stack. There were thirteen there now, and I'd counted fourteen that morning. But someone had gone through them in a hurry, the corners all jostled out of their earlier alignment. So had Ratcliff been interrupted in the process of sorting them, maybe heard a commotion—or the shot in the barn—and gone outside? Or was whoever did this looking for the folder I already had?

I went back outside, strode across the short distance to Ratcliff's pickup, and opened the door, pulling the hood release.

"What are the chances of finding two snakes in one day?" Again, I was talking to myself, and again, Dean answered me.

"Around here, better than even," he said, picking up a dried-out mesquite branch by the least-thorny end. He used it to bang on the top of the hot metal and waited. "You run across a rattler?"

"Under the hood of a car."

"Glad that didn't end badly."

When nothing moved—or rattled—around the truck, Dean waved for me to go ahead. "They make noise when they're spooked. It's a defense mechanism to scare off predators."

I reached gingerly under the edge of the hood and felt for the release, raising it slowly as he bent to peer underneath.

"All clear," he said.

Pushing the hood the rest of the way up, I pointed at the loose wires hanging ragged under a thick black hose. "Someone took his alternator."

Dean touched one finger to his chin, turning a slow circle and pointing to the edge of the road, where the dirt was just enough softer to be pock-marked with tire tracks. "But we have no way to track where an assailant came from or where they went, because there's been more traffic out here this afternoon than there's probably been all year."

"Where are the cameras, anyway?" I kicked the dirt with one muddy toe. "We have cameras everywhere, but not at an office staffed by one person?"

"Welcome to 1887. Ratcliff patrols on horseback. The office is a trailer, the horse practically lives in a lean-to," Dean said. "We just got broadband in this part of the valley last winter. You saw the fax machine in there, right? I have one too. That's how we share reports, because even with decent internet now, it's habit, and Ratcliff doesn't trust technology."

I covered my face with my hands, dragging them down it slowly and trying to swallow a frustrated scream.

"Sir!" We both turned west toward the shout to find Hammet waving an arm. "Wilkins picked up the blood trail through the brush with some work. It goes to the edge of the river."

Dean took off toward his subordinate at a loping jog, and I followed. "I could run a marathon next week with all the cardio I've done today," I said.

"Reminds me of football two-a-days in high school," he said, his voice not the slightest bit labored. "Our coach was such a prick. He made us run the length of the field until five guys threw up, every day for all of August."

"I've never understood why teenage boys put up with sadistic coaches," I huffed. "Why not just quit?"

"The football players got all the prettiest girls. Teenage boys have their priorities."

I snorted. "I always preferred baseball players, myself."

"I pitched in the state tournament my senior year."

"Of course you did." He was the poster model of the guy everything from sports to women to success had always come pretty easily for.

We stopped to catch our breath when we got to Hammet, then followed him to the edge of the riverbank. "Should we go across and see where it goes?" another officer, this one lanky with sandy hair and a long face, asked Dean.

Dean surveyed the opposite bank. "Stay in the riverbed unless I say otherwise." He looked at me and jerked his head toward the remains, thirty or so yards away and well guarded by the solid, stocky Ranger who'd relieved me earlier. He kept watch with military precision, Nava and her men watching other points from a decent distance away.

"Is that what Ratcliff called you out to help with?" Dean asked.

"It is. It's a dump—one arm is missing from where the body was weighted down, and the flesh on the other wrist and hand is stripped where the tie slipped off. Do you have a contact at Parks and Wildlife who can help us search upstream for the initial dump site?"

"Sure thing." He waved a hand in front of his face. "I'll never get used to that smell."

"Me either, and I've seen my share of dead bodies and all the rest of y'all's, too."

"What's that like? Working homicide day in and day out? Like, how are you not just the most depressed and paranoid person ever with what you see every day?"

I laughed. "I suppose some people would be. I don't dwell on the sad and scary aspects of what I do, which probably makes me a bit of a weirdo, but it enables me to be good at my job."

"What else is there to dwell on?"

"A long time ago, my partner told me that working homicide isn't about the victims. They're gone, nobody can help them or bring them back. It's about everyone else. My job is to bring closure to the people who loved the victims and see that the justice system keeps their killers from hurting anyone else. So that's what I choose to focus on when I walk up on a scene like this. I can't save him, but I can find the end of his story for the people who loved him, and maybe I catch the bad guy before someone else ends up in the river."

"You know what kind of bad guys dump bodies out here?"

"I know what kind the odds favor, anyway."

"Watch your back. And let me know if you need help. Beyond this, I mean."

The lanky deputy, who'd stopped about halfway between us and the corpse, turned back with his hands up. "It just stops. Right here."

Dean took a step forward. "That makes no sense. Where'd he go?"

I walked to the edge of the bank and knelt, staring at the largest spot I'd seen yet, dark and jagged, about as big around as my fist, before I pulled out my camera to photograph the faint tire tracks running to one side of it— just about as far to one side as Dodger's chest was wide, in fact.

We had followed the trail the wrong way. Ratcliff didn't run from the outpost with an injury. I turned into the brush and looked up, finding leaves just above my eyeline streaked with blood. The wonky spacing of the spatters we'd followed suddenly made perfect sense.

"It's not Ratcliff's blood. It's Dodger's. He was shot out here and went back to his stall."

13

"Does Archie Baxter still think the lab nerds hate him?" The El Paso lieutenant grinned up at me from a crouching pose, two sections of the damaged skull in his gloved hands, a shock of gray hair falling back from his eyes. He'd introduced himself as Dex Peterson and put his crew of three right to work, jumping in alongside them. In less than two hours they'd photographed, catalogued, and packed up most of the scene.

"Not all the time. And I happen to be a big fan of lab nerds. Especially ones who drive hours at the drop of a hat to help me out." I rubbed my arms, wondering how I could've possibly sweated my ass off all day only to be wishing I had a jacket. The desert got cold quick at night.

Peterson stood and settled the skull fragments into a nest of plastic packing in a large cooler. "I never make assumptions at a scene, but this is one of the more interesting ones I've seen. And I've been at this awhile. Started in the Austin PD many years ago and did a stint with the DPS, too."

"How'd you wind up in El Paso?"

"My son. His mother and I, we didn't work long term, and her family is there. It was better for him to grow up with such a large group of aunts and cousins. I settled into the department, got promoted to HDIC, and found my groove. My shrink says I'm a workaholic. I say my work is my life."

"Which is why you're out here at nearly midnight?"

"Nothing better to do."

"Well, no offense, but I'm glad."

"Me too." His brow furrowed as he gazed around, the garage lights giving the riverbed the glow of a working runway.

"If you were the type to make assumptions...," I prodded.

"Decomp tells me he's probably been under for six or seven weeks," he said. "And I'd have to look back over the river depth and condition reports from Parks and Wildlife, but that means he had to have washed down here and gotten stuck under that log pretty quickly after they dumped him."

"Which makes you wonder if whoever dumped him knew much about what they were doing."

"Indeed," he said.

"Could he have been submerged until very recently?" I asked. "Ratcliff said he'd been patrolling west of his outpost for the past two weeks."

"The river condition reports will tell me more about that."

"I noticed the missing arm and the stripped flesh on the right hand," I said, wondering if those details were more important than I'd realized.

"Both markers of being weighted down," he said carefully.

"Could they mean something besides that?" I asked, not wanting to put words in his mouth.

"No hands means no fingerprints." He pinched his lips together. "And given the specific damage to the skull..."

"I figured that was to make it hard to ID him," I said. "But I didn't think about the possibility that his arm and other skin were removed to the same end."

I turned to the cooler and peered in at the pieces of skull. "Who are you?"

"Your people are the best equipped to help you answer that," Peterson said. "The Rangers have the best forensic reconstruction team in the state."

"I've heard that, though I've never worked a case that needed to make use of it."

"This will make them work, but if anyone can help you, they can."

He turned to the rest of his team, busy counting and cataloguing evidence bags in large black plastic storage tubs.

"Do we have everything?" he asked.

"Yes, sir," a young woman with short dark hair and a serious, almost pinched look to her face said, closing the yellow lid with the large red "Evidence" sticker on the last tub.

"Where are we taking this?" Peterson asked me.

"I'll deliver it," I said, glancing around, unsure exactly why I didn't want to say where I was taking the remains even as I fixed a bright smile on Peterson and pointed to my truck, which I'd moved close to the river's bank just after sunset. He passed me a clipboard with a chain of evidence form on it, every bag and crate listed. I signed for the lot, then rolled the form up and slid it into my hip pocket, returning his clipboard.

Dean walked in front of the floodlight as I hefted a plastic crate, giving me something to focus on besides what I was carrying.

"Anything?" I asked.

"I wish I had better news. Assuming the blood trail we found does prove to be from the horse, Ratcliff is just gone. No discernible tire tracks, no blood, no prints that aren't his—or yours—in the office..."

"What about the hood and handles on his truck?" I asked.

He winced. "We got three partials that weren't enough for a hit, and several of yours."

"Dammit," I whispered under my breath. I knew better. "Sorry."

"I didn't get gloves either," he said. "I didn't think it was necessary."

"So we just have a missing officer." My biceps really wanted me to put the box down. I tried to adjust my grip, and Dean took it out of my hands like it weighed less than the average Louis Vuitton bag, tipping his head toward the truck and starting that way when I waved for him to proceed.

"Cops don't go missing for long," he said. "Every resource I can beg or borrow will be on this until we find him. I have four dogs coming tomorrow."

"I appreciate that. Keep me in the loop. I'll likely be back in a couple of days."

He loaded the box and walked around to open the door for me. "You need a guard for this stuff while you sleep?"

"I'm taking it where it needs to go now," I said. "It'll be hours yet before I can sleep after this day."

"Drive safely. I'll be in touch."

He shut the door and turned back to his unit, gathering them around as I started the engine. Peterson waved from the driver's seat of an El Paso forensics van as I drove slowly over the dirt toward the road. At the fork, I stopped and texted Archie and Jim.

On my way there with a dead guy in the back of my truck and a Ranger still missing after a six-hour grid search. They're bringing dogs in the morning.

I got two *be carefuls* in seconds.

Something is off out here, y'all, I typed. *Way off. I need a shower and a whiteboard and some more information.*

The conference room at HQ is closed, but we'll find you a board. Text me when you get home, your mother won't sleep until she knows you're safe.

I'm thirty-seven, Arch.

Doesn't matter. That was from Jim.

I sent a thumbs-up and pulled onto the road, thinking about Ratcliff— and how Timmy Dushane had vanished overnight a few months ago.

14

Every battle survived makes a warrior better at his craft.

The first target didn't go quietly—or cleanly.

A meeting under cover of darkness, a surprise attack, a series of unexpected complications. The executioner learned from every mistake.

His orders were clear: remove the threat. He watched hours of movies, men smaller than him on film beheading grown humans with ordinary weapons and single swings.

He arrived at the water early on a sticky late summer night, pulling a brand-new axe—the most expensive on the shelf, so therefore the best—out of the back of his car and stashing it behind a mesquite tree, congratulating himself on the simplicity of the moment. One little thing, and he was set.

He waited, the inky country darkness comforting, the water burbling along its well-worn path, the crickets chirping softly from the brush. Overhead, an impossible sea of stars so bright they didn't look real winked among wispy clouds.

He had always enjoyed being outside.

It made the things he didn't love about his life more bearable.

Headlights sliced through the darkness like a blade through butter, the truck rolling to a stop a few feet away, the mud on the tall tires fresh from the riverbed.

"The boss says you're getting greedy, my man." Everyone called him Javier, the man who swung down from the pickup's cab with a perfect Spanish accent. It wasn't his actual name, but it would do. "You're raising your prices every shipment," Javier continued. "He's losing patience. He can find other sources."

"Not with my selection or my resources." His voice was easy. Confident. Unruffled.

Showing weakness in battle was a fatal mistake, and he saw the butt of the M9 sticking out of Javier's jeans.

"With enough. I only came here to tell you to slow it down. Be thankful for all you have."

The executioner's eyes locked on the medal pinned to Javier's jacket. A patron saint of something, gaudy and gold with a filigree edge.

It was too warm even in the desert for a jacket tonight.

He reached behind the tree and grabbed the axe, swinging it deftly.

He hit the mark—but nothing else went as he'd planned.

Blood sprayed when the blade severed the carotid, but Javier didn't fall. Didn't die. He froze for a split second, his eyes wide, before he grabbed for the axe with both hands, fighting for the weapon as the executioner yanked the handle to remove it for another try.

The scuffle sent the blade deeper into the front of the target's neck. Just before the executioner retrieved his weapon, Javier's hands went to his throat, clawing around the blood pouring out as he fought for breath.

Interesting. He must've cut the airway.

Javier stumbled forward and flailed one arm at the executioner's face, striking his cheek hard enough to turn it, before he hit the ground.

Rolling him to his back, the executioner delivered another kick to his ribs. "I'm greedy? People who want the best need to pay the price."

A rustling in the brush drew his eyes to the side. A sleek, spotted cat crouched in a shrub, its yellow eyes shining in the night. A fellow predator. He rested the axe on the ground, wiped his hands on his pants, and gripped the smooth handle again.

It took four swings to collect his trophy that night. But it was the last time.

15

"A honeybee keeps the garden growing and gives us sweetener for my tea."
My granny's voice was muffled behind a beekeeper's hood. "He won't sting
you unless he absolutely has to, because he knows he'll die. A yellowjacket
is meaner than a snake and will sting anything he happens to light on." She
pointed to one that was, in fact, trying to sting a hollow log as she poured
thick beige powder into a hole in the ground next to the log. I backed up to
the barn door, but her voice followed me. "Two things can look the same,
but that don't always mean they are, sugar."

I flailed myself awake, swatting at the yellowjackets that swarmed out
around the log before they turned for the barn as a small, dark cloud.

Blinking, I could still feel the stings—there had been thirteen in total,
and I'd hobbled around with a swollen leg (my left one got the most stings
of any appendage with seven), baking soda poultices dotting my summer-
tanned skin like chicken pox for days while Granny argued with Ruth
about the absurdity of her demand that I not "ruin my face" at the farm if
they wanted me allowed back there.

Two things can look the same, but that don't always mean they are.

Timmy and Ratcliff, maybe?

Clearly, my subconscious had riddled something out. Maybe coffee
would help me catch up. Stretching, I walked to bathroom to brush my

teeth and sweep my still-shower-damp hair into a slightly unruly ponytail.

The coffeemaker was burbling when Jim rang my phone.

"Morning," I said around a yawn.

"Did you sleep at all?"

"Long enough for my brain to conjure up my granny to help with this case," I said.

"Um. What?"

I sipped my coffee before I even added the sugar.

"Never mind. Are you headed to the office?"

"I am. What's your ETA?"

"I'm in Waco," I said. "I realized when I hit the Austin city limit last night that I needed a garage to park the truck in given the cargo, and I wasn't waking my mother and Archie at three forty-five. So I came home. I'll be there in an hour and a half or so."

"Get a bigger coffee cup," he said. "And then bring a spare. You can only push yourself so hard, Faith."

"It's better when I'm busy."

"I'm more than a little concerned about what you're trying to stay busy with." He sounded more worried than I thought he should be.

"Nothing we haven't seen before, I'm sure." I changed the subject. "Hey, do you know anyone in the department that does the skull reconstructions at DPS?"

"That's a Rangers unit," he said. "Some high-tech toys and talented folks in there."

"Is that a yes?"

"I used to, but I haven't needed to call them in a long time. It's a good idea to try them at least if the skull is as damaged as you said, though."

"I'll come to you and then swing by headquarters while you work. I have a laptop to drop with cyber, too."

"You're not going to keep me company?"

"I've seen and smelled about all of this one I can take for one week. And I still have a missing officer down there. I'm hoping figuring out whose body is at least mostly in my truck will lead us to why someone didn't want us to know that."

"And then to what happened to the cop who found the body."

"Before he's dead, too. If he isn't already," I said.

"Is it weird that we finish each other's sentences?" Jim asked.

"It's a sign of intelligence and friendship." I added sugar to my coffee and stirred before taking another sip. It was good to be back on solid friend-zone ground with Jim. "Or so my psych textbooks said. See you in a bit."

Halfway to Austin, air conditioning blasting nearly as loud as the song blaring out of my truck's aging speakers, my phone buzzed in the cupholder. I didn't touch it—I'd seen the ways texting at seventy miles an hour can really ruin a person's face, and take lives, too. It fell silent. Whatever it was, it would wait.

Singing along with the radio, I let my thoughts wander to Timmy Dushane, rotting away in the bowels of the border detention center. Grady's parting warning danced around the edges of my brain, but if someone there wanted Timmy dead, he'd have been in the ground long before I saw him yesterday. Ratcliff's disappearance and the body he'd found just before he vanished took priority over a low-level smuggler with a controlling mother and a fabulous car.

I knew enough about my own brain to know the weird memory dream was trying to tell me something.

Look alike but are different. So which one was the yellowjacket, and which was the honeybee? Timmy had attacked me in the interview room. But he'd been trying to tell me something, I was sure.

I turned the radio down and concentrated on the memory of the sounds he'd growled at me, which had admittedly come through an adrenaline haze.

"Hey?" I muttered. "Heel? Wheel?"

I paused, pressing my tongue against the roof of my mouth and trying to say wheel with just my lips.

It was damned close.

Like the wheel on his antique 'Vette? Steering wheel or tire wheel?

I needed another look at the car, which shouldn't be that hard to arrange. Next word.

"Keel. Teal. Deal?" I tried the tongue trick. Maybe. What kind of a deal? Drug deal? Human trafficking? Something to do with Lucia?

I wasn't keen on the idea of calling Doris Dushane again just yet. Did she deserve to know where her son was? Maybe. He was a grown man, on one hand—who still lived at his parents' business, on the other. Certainly, Doris would have the time and determination to try to help Timmy. But could her attempt to get Timmy freed get one or both of them killed? I couldn't say no. Then again, I also couldn't say letting him stay in the detention center wouldn't end badly. The only evidence I had to work with there was that he'd been there for months and been maimed, but not killed. That meant someone wanted him alive. But without knowing why, I had no idea how long that would last.

One thing I was sure about in the whole mess: he had not asked for help or said anything about his mother. Whatever he was worried about, it wasn't going home.

I tapped one finger on the steering wheel, my thoughts veering in a direction I hadn't considered to this point: What if Timmy's mother wasn't looking for him because she wanted to make sure he was safe?

I had pegged her as a concerned mother, but for all I really knew, whatever landed Timmy in the detention center was a family affair. What if Doris wanted to make sure the blame all fell on him? A rattlesnake guarding the cash hidden under the car's hood, her reluctance to talk when I asked about some things but not others—those were easily explainable as either innocent enough or coincidence, but that didn't necessarily mean they were. And I had definitely seen stranger things.

Timmy might be better off sitting tight until I could check out the leads I had before I told Doris anything. The only problem was that I might not have time for that until after Labor Day, depending on what I could find out about the dead guy I was trying hard to pretend wasn't in several containers in the back of my truck.

The text was from Dean, who still had no leads. I sent him a thumbs-up, texted Jim that I was at the lab's loading dock door, pocketed my phone, and grabbed the chain of evidence form from the glove box. Jim stepped out a minute later to sign for custody of the remains and hurried back to his autopsy room, muttering about the heat making people extra volatile.

"Good to see you, too," I called after him.

"He's been so busy," Florence said in her trademark Janis Joplin rasp, taking the paperwork from me to separate Jim's file copies. She'd been his assistant for so many years, she knew what paperwork he needed better than he knew himself. "We've got two deaths of unknown circumstances from Austin PD, a suspected suicide from Travis County SO, and then your guy already piled up this morning, and that doesn't count his special case or the reports he has to sign off on from the weekend."

Special case? I didn't ask, because I knew her well enough to know it wouldn't do me any good. She guarded Jim like a Rottweiler guards a stash of T-bone steaks.

"How's he feeling?" I asked instead.

"He still doesn't seem to have as much energy as he used to." Her already wrinkled forehead wrinkled more with concern. "It takes him longer to do most things, he's more paranoid about the security at the front, and he almost never comes in early or stays late if the building is supposed to be empty. It really changed him. It's almost like his heart has gone out of this, you know? Jim has always been the most stubborn old cuss in this office because he cares what happened to the victims he sees."

"Nearly becoming one of them makes a person see things differently," I said. "Especially a person who didn't sign up for a job where people try to kill you on the regular."

"Speaking of people trying to kill y'all, how is that husband of yours?" Florence asked. "Jim was worried about his liver function for weeks after you got married. I think he actually tried to get a look at the surgical records while you were gone on your honeymoon."

"He's good." I flashed a smile. "The doctor said all his blood levels were back to normal at his last checkup."

She jerked her head toward the front of the truck. "He isn't with you today. Working a different case?"

"He's on special assignment right now." I managed to keep the smile as I tucked the paperwork back into the folder and wished her a good day. "Tell Jim to let me know when he's done with the skull."

She waved and climbed the steps to go back inside.

I started the truck and turned up the air, texting Archie to ask if he knew anyone in facial reconstruction.

He still hadn't answered by the time I got to headquarters, so I opened the door to the basement and jogged down the stairs, passing cold case limbo, with my eyes on the white linoleum.

I didn't look up until I opened the door to the cyber team's bunker. The back corner of the basement that once belonged to an in-house photo lab had been turned over to the computer guys twenty years ago, but the faint odor of chemicals still seeped out of the walls.

I peeked around the corner into Trey Morton's office, tapping on the doorframe when I found him hunched over his laptop. "Morning, Trey."

"McClellan?" He wrinkled his nose to push his glasses back up and stretched his back as he turned the chair, grinning when he spotted Timmy Dushane's laptop sticking out from under my arm. "You have something you can't crack?"

"*Can't* is a strong word. Don't have time to, don't have a lot of experience with—both are more accurate."

He clapped his hands, rubbing them together. "Let's have it, then."

I laughed as I handed it over. "It might be nothing. But he has some heavy security on this thing for a middle-of-nowhere motel employee, so I'd like to know why."

Trey waved one hand, dismissing me, as his brow furrowed when the screen lit up. "I'll call you when I have something."

"Thanks," I said as I turned back for the hallway, though I knew he was already so deep into the puzzle he didn't hear me.

Two drops in less than an hour. I followed signs to the forensic artists' office, knocking on the door when I found it.

"Come in." I opened the door, and a dark-haired guy in a lab coat who couldn't have been out of college more than a month looked up from a tub of blue putty and a gleaming white skull I wasn't even sure was real, it looked so perfect. "Good morning." He stood. "What can I do for you?"

"I'm Faith McClellan," I said, stepping and shutting the door. "I have a homicide with a possibly intentionally obscured victim ID, and I'm hoping you might be able to help me figure out who this guy is."

He flashed a smile and waved me toward a chair. "I'm happy to, though I usually need a skull to get started, and it doesn't seem you have any extras."

"It's at the medical lab with Jim Prescott at the moment, but as soon as he's completed the autopsy, I can get it for you. It's really not in great shape." I pulled up the images of it on my phone and turned the screen so he could see. "I think this damage was caused by four-wheel ATVs. So I'm hoping you're some kind of magician at figuring out what people would have looked like."

"No magic required, Miss McClellan," he said. "It's science."

His eyes fell on the rings on my left hand. "I'm sorry—Mrs. McClellan?"

"Mrs. Hardin, actually," I said. "Old habits die hard. I was Miss McClellan for a long time."

"Hardin, like Graham Hardin, the baseball player?"

"That's him," I said, running my right index finger over the cool platinum of my wedding band. "Though these days he's a commander in major crimes at the TCSO."

"The very first baseball game I ever went to, he was pitching for the Longhorns," he said. "I was five, and he threw a no-hitter. For years, I thought baseball was dreadfully boring, because no one got to hit the ball. It wasn't until my dad took me up to Arlington to see the Rangers play that I fell in love with the game—went to Baylor on a scholarship, in fact. When I figured out how special that first UT game my mom took me to was, I dug our ticket stubs out of my mom's memory box and looked up the pitcher's name. I was shocked he never played pro ball."

"He hurt his shoulder," I said.

"It happens earliest to the guys who can throw the hardest." He waved one hand. "Anyway—I hope you tell him the story and thank him for giving me a great childhood memory."

"Of a baseball game that was boring as hell to a kindergartener." I winked. "Will do." I wiggled the phone. "Hopefully this isn't boring."

He raised his eyebrows in a *May I?* gesture as he reached for my cell phone.

He flipped through the photos I had, turning the phone this way and that and pinching at the screen to zoom in a few times before he let out a low whistle.

"Where was this person found?" he asked.

"At the bottom of the Rio Grande," I said, leaving the minutiae out. "Does the water make a difference in the way the bones would be damaged?"

"Some," he said. "But mostly I'm thinking someone went to a bit of trouble to keep anyone from figuring out who this is."

"I know. My real question is, are they going to be able to keep you from getting to the bottom of that?"

"I can't say for sure. But I love a challenge, and I don't give up easily—I led my high school and college teams to more comeback wins than anyone who's ever played for either school."

"I do admire a good stubborn streak," I said. "It's a handy trait for good police work, Mr. ...?"

"Saunders." He handed me a card. "Noah Saunders. Call me when Prescott is done with your skull, and I'll arrange to have it sent over here. If I can't find out who your corpse is, no one can."

I pocketed the card and let myself out, hoping Noah Saunders's confidence was well earned.

16

Upstairs, I found Archie's desk vacant, the conference room door shut and guarded by a Travis County deputy, and an unusually empty and subdued bullpen for a Monday morning.

Archie had been up to his receding hairline in something no one else was allowed to know anything about for weeks now, with little sign of coming up for air soon. While the part of me that chased murderers was dying to know what was so important, the other part—the one that wanted to grow old and wear big hats and collect pets—thought I might be better off not knowing.

Wandering down a hallway, I checked brass nameplates on doors for Dean's boss, wanting to offer a commendation for the whole unit dropping their day off and working into the night.

Company Major Jack Livingston's door was closed, voices coming from the other side. I stood there for a second before deciding my comments would be better received if they didn't come in the form of an interruption. Before I made it back to the corner, the door opened.

Turning, I felt my jaw loosen when Captain Larry Jameson of the Travis County Sheriff's Office stepped into the hallway.

What was Graham's boss doing here?

"McClell—uh—Hardin?" His brows went up with his tone even as he took a reflexive-looking step back from me.

"Captain," I said. "It's been a while. How are you?"

I knew my even tone and flat expression were making him uncomfortable, so I kept them in place and stepped slightly to the side, blocking the hallway.

"Good. Good. Hard to believe it's August already." He feinted to the right, and I leaned on my left leg, sticking my hip out so he couldn't even turn and squeeze past me without making things very awkward. I had worked for this guy for a decade, Graham insisted we invite him to our wedding, and less than a month after we said "I do," when Graham was still recovering from being shot through the liver, Jameson had ordered my new husband out on an undercover operation that was stretching into a black hole, and I hadn't so much as been notified that Graham wasn't dead.

He owed me better than that. And the look on his face said he knew it.

"Is it? Funny, I was just thinking that the past three months have been the longest of my life. And when you grew up in Chuck McClellan's house, that's saying something."

"Listen, Faith..." Jameson's shoulders dropped with a sigh. "I know you must be concerned..."

"Concerned?" I kept my voice low, but my tone could've sliced glass. "I passed concerned just after Easter. I've left messages that have gone ignored. I haven't slept well in months. I'm barely hanging onto my sanity at this point. But it's nice to know all is well with you."

His mouth opened and then closed four times before words came out.

"We have...there are...you don't understand," he stammered.

"Explain it like it's my first day."

He stood up a little straighter. "Now look, dammit. I'm doing the best I can in a difficult situation. Security guidelines for this go way over my head. Way over yours, too."

"Security? Is there someone somewhere in this state who thinks I'd spill information that would put my husband in danger?" I was pretty proud of myself for speaking relatively normally. "I would appreciate being put in touch with this person."

Jameson flinched. "I'm just saying, this is a very delicate matter."

"And I'm just saying, I have gone to sleep every night for the past thirteen weeks only by convincing myself that if he was dead, somehow, I would know. Using my granny's old wives tales and romantic notions because it's the only way I can stop my mind from racing."

"Of course you would know." Jameson's voice softened. "If something had happened to him, you'd be my first call. He's a good cop, Faith, and if this goes the way we think it will, he's going to be a bona fide hero, too. I know it sucks, but hang in there. And try to keep your mind occupied."

He stepped close enough as he was talking to pat my shoulder awkwardly. "I have another meeting to get to." He turned sideways and slid past me, the static from the wall mussing his thick silver hair.

I stared after him until he turned the corner and disappeared, my heart full of the knowledge that Graham was okay and my anger still directed at Jameson over the assignment because I didn't want to be upset with Graham. I did know, in my soul, that he went because he wanted to—he could have told them to go to hell and had his pick of posts at other departments, including the DPS. Whatever he was doing, he thought it was important enough to leave, even though he knew the cover was so deep he wouldn't even be able to text me for as long as it took to finish the case. He'd told me as much as he packed a duffel two weeks after we got home from Aruba, our bedroom still full of boxes of his stuff we hadn't unpacked before the wedding. I'd since passed several evenings emptying the boxes, placing things around the house in a way that made it impossible to tell what was mine first and what came with Graham.

He was okay. They would tell me if that changed.

I was still frustrated with the whole damned thing, but that would get me through today.

I spun back to Livingston's office, rapping on the doorframe as I stuck my head in.

Empty.

I took a card from his desk holder—if I couldn't find him, I could email him. A letter might have more impact, anyway, and could be placed in Dean's file.

Antsy and looking for some direction, I wandered back to the bullpen and pulled out my phone and dialed Dean's cell number. He answered on the second ring. "Dean."

"Good morning. It's Faith McClellan," I said. "Checking for an update, and I also wanted to let you know I'm at HQ in Austin this morning, if there's anything I can do to help from here."

Dean sighed. "I wish I had better news to share, but we've had dogs out here for better than two hours, and we haven't turned up a single trail. Whatever happened to Ratcliff, he's gone, and he didn't leave the outpost on foot. We're in the process of shifting our focus to the highways and the border, but I feel like we're starting behind the eight ball here because of the location and timing of the disappearance."

"Which may well be part of what whoever orchestrated his disappearance was counting on," I muttered.

"You have any luck finding out who the dead guy in the river is?" he asked.

"People who are very good at that sort of thing are working on it," I said. "Nothing yet." I drummed my fingers on a vacant desk, flopping into the chair behind it. "Nobody needs me to be here today. They're going to ID the victim with or without me. Is Ratcliff's computer in evidence there?"

"We locked the office down with everything that was in there yesterday still untouched," he said.

"I'll be there in a few hours."

"Call me when you get to town."

I hung up, leaning back in the chair and staring at a blank whiteboard, Nava's story about the people who left their toddler in an RV and let her drown rattling around my head. If not for Nava's hard work on the case, they probably wouldn't have gotten the meager sentence they did—they knew people would assume the attack had come from outside, and they played it to their advantage.

Kind of like people assume a dead body in the Rio Grande is a nobody —a migrant who wasn't lucky enough to get across successfully. Ratcliff had taken the time to notice a few bodies that didn't fit that narrative, and now we couldn't find him.

Whatever was going on here, it all had something to do with Ratcliff asking about the bodies in the river everyone else was ignoring.

And I wasn't going to figure out why from an air-conditioned office in Austin.

————————

I'd had more than two hundred miles of open freeway to think about how the scattered dots I had found in the valley might connect, and I kept coming back to the bodies Ratcliff had found.

Everything from the vertebrae to the tendons had been sliced cleanly. No bruising or tearing of skin or muscle, no cracks or shatter marks on the bone that I could see in the photographs.

I dropped the photo onto a haphazard pile of a dozen or so others and tapped the touchpad on my laptop, making a note of the wounds and wishing I had remains from these cases for Jim to work his detail-oriented magic on.

It hadn't occurred to me yesterday that I wouldn't be able to talk to Ratcliff about the other bodies later, after I'd had a chance to look over the file he'd given me. I was thankful he'd kept such meticulous paper records: Ratcliff's file wasn't thick, but his notes were well organized and thorough for a guy who didn't work homicide by trade—and he kept exceptional notes on border activity in the area, too.

I'd found a folder labeled *Timmy Dushane* in Ratcliff's desk when I got back to the border outpost. Thirty-eight pages of notes on Timmy's border crossings going back four years were inside, along with a few photos. The activity—and volume of notes—had rapidly ballooned about a year ago, steadily increasing to a minimum of once a week between January and April, with the highest volume the week before Easter at three times back and forth. That week, Timmy had gone to Mexico twice in his truck and once in the Corvette. Those visits were also the only ones Ratcliff had recorded a vehicle for.

I noted the dates in my computer file and considered Timmy's definitely purposeful injuries. Could he be related somehow to whatever had gotten these other people killed?

How similar were the other remains to those Jim was hopefully examining even as I was plugging my laptop into the outlet under Ratcliff's desk and digging the files out of my bag?

Looking at the scene photos through the lens of victim identification—or really, obfuscation thereof—made them at once more fascinating and more frustrating.

"Five decapitations, two full dismemberments," I muttered. "Who is someone trying to hide the identity of these victims from?"

"Hide who from what?" Dean pulled the door shut behind him and stopped in front of the air conditioner, throwing a grin over his shoulder. "I talk to myself when I'm working, too. How was the drive?"

"I had a whole lot of empty miles to think." I flipped to the first fully dismembered body, which had gotten snagged on a rock back in January, dragging a dumbbell through the river bottom along the way. "Ratcliff was concerned about the volume of remains he's come across that were seriously damaged in the past year. I figured while I wait to see if the guys in Austin can ID the most recent one, I'd see if there were any similarities in the cases. It's more difficult to see detail in photos, but it looks like this first one was amateur hour compared to this most recent decapitation. I can see tearing and bruising on the muscle tissue in the shoulder where the arm was removed even after a substantial length of time underwater."

Dean took the folder when I held it out and scanned the report. "The trunk of the body was tied to a fifty-pound dumbbell with standard nylon cord." He ran one hand through his hair. "What kind of murderer would think that was sufficient to keep the body from moving? The gases produced during decomposition would float four times that."

"So either the person who did this was an idiot, or they didn't care if the body was found after a bit of time had passed."

"Cause of death?" He turned to the second page in the file. "Where the hell is the autopsy report?"

"Ratcliff said he had trouble getting anyone interested in these cases," I said. "I'm not sure if there wasn't an autopsy done, or if the paperwork didn't make it back here, or what. But given the situation with the body we found out there yesterday, I'd sure like to find out."

Dean was still reading Ratcliff's report. "No apparent wounds other than the missing appendages. So someone just cut him up while he was still alive?"

"Clumsily," I said. "Or at least in a hurry."

"Why sink him into the river, then?" Dean closed the folder and dropped into the chair on the other side of the desk, his eyes focused on the bulletin board on the opposite wall. "There are hundreds of square miles of nothing out here. You could bury a person and the only thing that might come across it would be a coyote."

"Water can cover some evidence if remains are left under it too long," I said.

"But a fifty-pound dumbbell wouldn't keep anything in place very long at all."

I tapped the photos. "Maybe it wasn't about keeping the remains still. Maybe they were supposed to move in the river and be found. At some point."

"To what end?"

"Sending a message to someone?" I mused. "Covering the place they were dropped in?"

He bobbed his head side to side. "I can follow sending a message. But then why not send the message directly? You're talking *Godfather*-style organized crime warnings—around here, those come from gangs and cartels. And they usually show up on the intended recipient's porch, or in their car, not in the river."

"What if this was a wide message? Or a sensitive one?"

He flipped through the other photos, making a face when he got to the one with the water moccasin swimming out of the hole where the victim's head used to be. "Jesus. Is that necessary?"

"It's memorable," I said. "Usually people who do things like this want at least some folks to know who's responsible. It's part of the reason for the theatrics."

"You said Ratcliff told you no one cared about these cases?" Dean touched one index finger to his chin. "But I don't remember seeing these in our reports." He gestured to the fax machine. "So who was he trying to get interested in them?"

"He mentioned the feds but didn't say which agency. Y'all have a few to choose from."

"You get the feeling he called another agency directly?" Dean asked.

"I guess I couldn't say for sure, but that was the way I heard it. Why?"

He tapped one finger on the edge of the desk. "That may mean he thought there was a rat at Joint Operations Intel."

"How would we go about finding out who that could be without asking him?"

Dean passed the folder from one hand to the other. "I have no idea. There are almost fifty full-time officers assigned to the team, from a dozen agencies. And information goes out to fifty-four border-area counties and a hundred and seventy-five law enforcement agencies."

"That's a small needle in a very large haystack."

Dean nodded, laying the folder on the desk. "Yeah. But just Ratcliff and me, we exchanged information every week. Why wouldn't he have mentioned dead people washing up out here by the half dozen?"

"How many guys in your unit?"

"Seven," he said. "And I would trust any of them with my child's life."

I stood and walked to the bulletin board, looking closer at the photos and reaching for one of a wide landscape my eyes had skipped over yesterday morning—before I knew the car in the center. It was nearly dark in the photo, and Timmy Dushane's Corvette was parked next to a pickup with a popup camper over the back and a tent pitched in the sand next to it. I held it an inch from the end of my nose and squinted, but I couldn't make out any people. I flipped the photo, looking for a date. The back was blank.

Two half sheets of copier paper tacked next to the snapshot had 3-D printing schematics for guns. Not as reliable as my SIG, sure, but everyone in F Company had fired the one Lt. Boone brought to a training last year. Three hours off the 3-D printer at the Waco Public Library, it would've killed anything just as dead as any other gun, provided it didn't jam.

Touching the printouts, I waved the snapshot at Dean. "How much time do your guys spend in this area?" I asked.

"Not a whole lot," he said. "We run special missions for DPS and the governor's office from an office just south of San Angelo. That's why it took us a bit to get out here when Baxter called yesterday."

"I see. And how do you know Archie?"

"Everyone who wears a Rangers badge knows Archie Baxter," Dean said. "The guy is a legend."

That was true. And half of them probably owed him a favor, too. I let the silence linger, plucking an index card with a local phone number and a set of what looked like map coordinates jotted on it from the board, not commenting on his nonanswer to my question.

I liked Morgan Dean—he was smart and capable and had certainly jumped right in to help when I needed it. But a little voice in the back of my head wondered why Ratcliff, who stayed in touch with Dean every week from this lonely post out here in the middle of nowhere, hadn't talked to him about the bodies.

I kept reminding myself that while I've always worked big cases better in groups, this guy wasn't Archie. He definitely wasn't Graham. He wasn't even Deputy Bolton. I didn't know him or how well I could trust him.

But I wasn't sure I could figure this out without him, either. So I had a tightrope to walk here. "Has Ratcliff said anything about ghost guns or arms deals in his weekly reports?" I asked.

He crossed the room to stand next to me, looking at the schematics. "No, but I know the ATF has guys running them down on the regular. It's like playing desert whack-a-mole, though, and frankly, the Rangers lack the manpower to join the game. Take out one ring, another pops up in its place."

I showed him the photo. "I know this Corvette. The guy who owns it went missing several months ago, according to his mother, who owns and operates the local motel. I saw him yesterday at the ICE detention center. He's missing his tongue, and his hands were so badly smashed in that attack they're basically useless." I watched Dean's face carefully as I spoke, my human lie detector on full alert.

He took the photo. "Someone cut out his tongue but didn't kill him? So someone with some clout thinks he's valuable."

"Marginally, at least. I thought the same thing."

"You said his mother owns a motel?"

"The Cherry Lane, out off Highway 90."

Dean tapped the edge of the photo on the desk before putting it on top of the pile of victim photos. "We see drug money move through motels a lot —it's an easy way to launder it."

"I found fifteen grand strapped to the engine block of his 'Vette in a heat-resistant envelope yesterday. Had to tangle with a rattlesnake to get to it."

"You had a room there?"

"Yeah. I'm about to again if I'm staying a few days."

"How many other guests?"

"None that I saw, though I wasn't there long."

"Is the place well kept?"

I raised one hand and wiggled it back and forth in a seesaw motion. "Kind of. It's clean, but everything is dated. Like, carbon-dated. And Doris, that's the mother, she mentioned that her son had a friend at the border patrol who let him cross back and forth to visit his girl in Mexico."

Dean grabbed his keys. "Let's go have a look around."

17

On the drive back to the motel, I filled Dean in on my conversation with Doris the day before.

He turned the radio off when I started talking and listened intently, nodding occasionally, until I sat back in the passenger seat of his white SUV and took a breath.

"Did you meet her husband?"

"No. She talked about him, but I didn't see him." I paused, an image of her kitchen sink, with a lone coffee cup and a single empty bowl in the basin, flashing through my head. "Or see any evidence of him. The sink had breakfast dishes for one waiting to be washed."

"You have a great eye for detail."

"You really think an old lady is laundering drug money through her family business?"

"I've seen weirder. Haven't you?"

"I have at that. And it would explain some of the guardedness I saw around talking about her son. She wants him found, but she was definitely holding something back when I spoke to her. I figure it has something to do with the fact that Ratcliff arrested Timmy for drug trafficking, but maybe it's more than that. What do we think happened to her husband?"

"I don't know enough to venture a guess. But it's weird to me that you said Ratcliff told you he was trying to get the feds to take note of his dead bodies, but he hadn't mentioned it to me," Dean said. "And the son, he's at the federal detention center. You saw him yourself?"

"He jumped out of his chair and knocked me to the floor," I said. "Yeah. I saw him."

"He what?" Dean tapped the brakes on the SUV and swore under his breath.

"What?" I asked. "He jumped on me, but—"

I didn't get the rest of the sentence out before he swerved to the shoulder and fumbled with his phone, finding the number he needed and putting it to his ear.

"Morgan Dean, Texas DPS Rangers Lieutenant, badge number 6047D9," he said. "I need to speak to Judge Estes about an emergency prisoner transfer order."

He tapped his fingers on the steering wheel as he waited for the call to be transferred, fixing a smile on his face and keeping every trace of stress out of his voice when the line was picked up.

"Good afternoon, Your Honor." Dean's voice was low and smooth, dripping an easy charm most people couldn't achieve with careful practice. "Keeping cool up there?"

He paused, and the volume on his phone wasn't high enough for me to hear the reply without leaning in way too close to be any kind of appropriate.

"I have a prisoner in questionable health at the Southern ICE facility whose life could be in danger if he remains there. I'd like an emergency order to move him to the Terrell County jail for the next few days until we can find a place for him at another federal facility, sir."

He nodded as the judge talked.

"Sir, I believe he's a material witness in a case that now involves a Texas Ranger we believe was taken by force from our southwest border outpost yesterday." He paused again. "The Rangers have been careful to keep this off the news media's radar as we search for the time being, sir. But it will certainly be easier for us to work with this particular potential witness if he's alive, sir, and if he's out of the environment of the detention center, which is high stress for him since he was attacked during his first days there."

Another pause. My fingers protested how tightly I was gripping the armrest on the passenger door.

"No, sir, I haven't spoken with him to offer him anything. But I believe he could be important to the possibility of our bringing Officer Ratcliff home safely." Dean turned his head and grinned, shooting me a thumbs-up. "Thank you, sir. I appreciate it. I will have someone there to pick that up and hand-carry it to the center in twenty minutes, sir."

He dropped his phone into the cupholder after he ended the call and pulled the vehicle back onto the empty highway. "I just hope twenty minutes is soon enough. If he attacked an officer, he wouldn't last long out there no matter who thinks he might be worth something. They have quite a few guards who are disillusioned cowboys with violent streaks, and attacking an authority figure—especially a female—is an excellent excuse to kill someone and get right away with it."

"I asked the guard I spoke with to make sure no one hurt him," I said, a tickle at the back of my neck rising with the worry that I hadn't done enough. "But they put him in solitary because I was afraid asking them not to punish him would tip off the wrong person that he'd been trying to talk to me. I think he was trying to tell me something, but he was afraid of who might see him talking to me if he just said it sitting at the table... Damn. I shouldn't have left him there. And then I found the horse and Ratcliff was gone, and Timmy slipped my mind almost entirely. I spent a whole day looking for him, and once I'd found him, my brain closed that case and moved to the bigger one."

But what if he was somehow connected to the bigger one? The town was awfully small.

"Don't worry yet." Dean slowed to turn into the motel lot. "Let's hope people are scared enough of the guard you spoke with to listen to him for at least a day."

I looked around the parking lot of the motel with a new lens, noting the utter lack of cars or bustle. "There's not even a vehicle that might belong to an employee," I said.

He parked in front of the office at the end of one horseshoe-shaped leg of the rambling building. The door was shut behind the screen, the air conditioner sticking out of the window rumbling and dripping condensation onto a rotten-looking spot on the wooden deck.

Dean turned the knob and pushed, stepping inside. A teenage girl with wide eyes behind thick glasses flinched as she looked up at him from a battered copy of *Fahrenheit 451*.

"Can I help you?" Her accent was much more New Jersey than South Texas. She sounded guarded just by nature, almost.

"I need a room," I said. "I'm not sure for how many days."

Her eyes jumped back and forth between us. "Sixty-five dollars a night, payable in advance. Towels for two?"

I opened my mouth to say no as Dean tapped my forearm and said, "Yes, thank you."

"Could we have room sixteen?" I asked.

She handed over towels and two keys, and I pulled the cash from my pocket for the first night and handed it to her. Her gaze lingered on my wedding ring as she took it, but she didn't say anything. Dean didn't wear one, though. What this young woman thought shouldn't have bothered me, but it did.

"Payment for tomorrow is due by noon if you're staying," she said, pushing a ledger across the desk for us to sign. She seemed careful to keep her hands on her side of the counter, like she didn't want to touch anyone by accident. "Otherwise Doris will clean out the room and keep whatever is still in it."

My eyebrows went up at that news. "Does that happen a lot?"

"More often than you'd think," she said, picking up her book. "I've seen her throw people out of bed in a dead sleep and lock the door while Jenny rounds up their stuff."

"Is Doris here today?" I asked. "I met her yesterday morning and have a couple of questions for her about a story she told me."

"She's out for the day." Her eyes shifted to the wall behind me, then the desk, then the cover of her beat-up old paperback. "That's why I'm here."

I glanced down at the book and tried to catch her eye. "Are you reading that for school?"

"Around here?" she snorted. "No. I just like to read. It lets me be...somewhere else. Bradbury was pretty smart for an old dude."

"I'm Faith."

She tipped her head to the side and stared at me for a good fifteen seconds before she spoke. "Ashton."

"You had to think about that?" Dean's voice was genial—gentle, even.

"I can't remember the last time anyone asked me my name. Or...introduced themselves to me."

"It's nice to meet you, Ashton. Do you know when Doris might be back?"

"I don't think until tomorrow."

"Do you know if Mr. Dushane will be around today?" Dean made the question sound casual.

Her brow furrowed. "I don't...I'm sorry, I'm not sure what you mean."

"She mentioned that she owns the motel with her husband yesterday," I said.

"I just wondered if he could maybe answer Faith's questions," Dean said. "She's the type to be bugged by things she's waiting to find out. You know."

"Sure, I get that," she said. "But I'm afraid I can't help you. As far as I know, Doris runs the place alone."

"Maybe she talks about a husband because she thinks it keeps her safer."

Ashton snorted. "Oh, she has no trouble there." Her fingers went to her lips, then she started picking at a small tear on one corner of the book cover.

I picked up the towels and the keys and tipped my head toward the door. "It was nice to meet you, Ashton."

"Sure. You too, Faith." She sounded sad.

We were in room 16 before either of us spoke again.

"Why would the old woman lie to me about her husband?" I said.

"To avoid questions." He flopped into a chair in the corner. "I can't figure out what kind of questions she's trying to skirt, though. Ghost guns, money laundering, missing people, dead people... This place is like the epicenter of border criminal activity, and I've never heard anyone make so much as a peep about it—I didn't even know it was here. What have you and Ratcliff stumbled over?"

It was a hell of a good question.

18

Google didn't have much on the Dushane family, and neither did the DPS database or the local criminal court records. By the time I finished searching everything and sat back in my chair, Dean came in with a pizza from the diner and two bottles of almost-cold soda. I took a slice from the cheese side and watched him wolf down a meat-laden one in four bites that he chased with half the bottle of Dr Pepper.

"No criminal records." He tapped his fingers on the edge of the pizza box. "I wonder how long this has been going on?"

"I wonder..." I turned back to the computer and typed into the search bar, looking for photos and news from the area in the 1960s, when Doris said her husband's parents had opened the motel. I knew the state parks had been a bigger draw for vacationing families back then than they were today.

I didn't find much, but the local paper did have a piece from 1964 on the Cherry Lane and how it had transformed the local landscape and boosted the county's economy. "This says that back in the sixties, this place pulled enough room taxes to the county in one summer to build a public library here—the first one they'd ever had." I opened another tab and typed more. "It's still there, too."

"People don't drive to state parks on vacation anymore, though," Dean said. "So maybe Doris and her son had to find another way to keep the place afloat?"

"That would definitely fit with some of the things I saw and heard." I took a bite of my pizza and chewed.

"I'll see if any of the federal guys I know have this place on their radar." Dean pulled out his phone. "Sometimes they really suck at sharing information."

I shook my head. "Don't ask them yet. I suck at sharing information on an active case, too."

"Even with other agencies?"

"I have trust issues."

"Those don't extend to your husband, I hope?" he asked. "He's Travis County, right?"

"He is the best man I have ever known," I said without hesitation. "He makes me want to be a better person and a better officer every day."

Dean smiled a soft smile that didn't show any teeth. "That's what my little girl does for me."

"How old?" I asked.

"She's four." He didn't need encouragement to whip his phone around with a photo of a little girl with summer sunbaked skin, wide, clear brown eyes, dirty-blond pigtails, and an adorably cheesy gritted-teeth smile.

"She's beautiful. What's her name?"

"Landry."

"Cowboys fan?"

"Her mother was." The sadness that etched his face was brief but unmistakable. Just being in the room with it made my heart twist at the idea of losing Graham.

"I'm so sorry," I said softly.

"Drunk driver, crossed the median. It's a sad and all-too-common story," he said. "Car seats work. Landry was four months old, strapped into her little bucket carrier in the back seat, and she didn't have so much as a scratch. I was at work."

"You couldn't have stopped that," I said.

"I know. I've been through the expensive therapy experience." He smiled. "I miss her, but I know she's proud of her baby girl, and I hope I'm doing half the job she would've of raising her."

"I'm sure she's proud of you both." And oddly, even though I'd known the guy for, like, thirty-six hours and change, that wasn't a platitude. There was something about him that even I really wanted to trust—and Lord knows I wasn't lying when I told him I have issues there.

"Sorry to drag everything down." He laughed and put his phone on the table.

"Not even a little," I said. "I appreciate you being here more than you could possibly know."

Here. In room 16 at the Cherry Lane.

I had requested this room because Doris said the crew she banned stayed in it, and then let myself get distracted by food and conversation. I knelt and peered under the bedskirt.

"What?" Dean's brow furrowed.

"Doris told me a story about having to kick out a group of guys last spring. She said they trashed a room and Timmy booted them and told them not to come back, and then later they were in the area again, camping in the desert."

"You think that's the photo Ratcliff had of the Corvette out at that campsite?"

"Very possibly. But right now what I'm thinking is about the comment Ashton made about Doris keeping stuff she found in the rooms. She said those guys trashed this one, but..." I turned a slow circle. "It looks just like the other one I stayed in here. Down to the undisturbed ancient wallpaper." I clicked on the flashlight on my phone and examined the paper, finding signs of sun fading on the wall opposite the window. "Except here, this paper is the same all the way around the room. The TV and bedding are the same as my other room. So is the carpet." I looked down at the patterned, tight-woven flooring, pointing to a path of clear traffic wear between the bed and the dresser that held the TV.

"You think she kicked them out because they had something she wanted?"

"I might. And I think I may know where we can find out what, with just a little luck."

"How sure are we that girl was telling the truth and the old lady isn't here?" Dean asked.

"I'm not sure why she'd lie, but with the week I've had, I'll give it fifty-fifty."

"We don't have a warrant, which means anything we find isn't admissible," Dean said as I pulled the door to the barn open, poking my head in and shining a light around.

"I'm not looking for a smoking gun. I'm looking for something that will tell us which path we need to follow from here," I said. "So I'm okay with that." Graham's distaste for breaking rules had me turning my head back toward Dean. "If you're not, you can wait here. Just holler if someone is coming."

He waggled his head from side to side. "Whatever is the fastest path to finding Ratcliff," he said, pulling the door wider and stepping inside. "Sometimes the end justifies the means."

"It does indeed." My personal philosophy is that criminals aren't following the law when they hide evidence and obfuscate facts, so if I have to bend it occasionally to discover something that will lead me to the truth about what happened to a victim, I can live with that. Admissible evidence rules are never far from any detective's mind, but I wasn't anywhere near the point in this case where something we found was likely to end up in a courtroom. That I could tell, anyway.

Dean let out a low whistle when I pulled the tarp off the car. "Damn, she's a beauty," he said.

"You know your muscle cars?" I kept my voice low more out of habit than a conscious fear of being discovered.

"My uncle owns an auto shop in San Antonio. I worked for him in the summers to pay for college."

I checked the driver's door, hoping Doris hadn't locked it yesterday after I left. No such luck. "Damn."

"Locked?" Dean asked.

"Of course."

"Why lock a covered car in a barn in the middle of nowhere?" he mused, picking his way around a graveyard of rusty gardening equipment to the tall workbench running the length of the far wall.

"I thought it was odd yesterday when she brought me out here, but I figured maybe her son was just paranoid."

"And then you found several thousand dollars hidden in the car, and you knew why," he said, plucking a small handsaw with a thin blade from a pegboard hook on the wall over the workbench.

"Still a little weird for Doris to lock it back. I handed her the cash yesterday before I left."

"Maybe it's a force of habit." Dean slid the saw blade between the window and the bottom seal, wiggling it around for a good minute and a half. The chrome lock button popped up like a Thanksgiving turkey timer. "Or maybe there's something else in here you didn't notice."

"Speaking of bending the law," I said, reaching for the door handle and nodding to the saw.

"I told you, I worked for my uncle. Popping locks on car doors went with the territory, and these old beauties weren't exactly built for security." He put the saw down on the hood. "You looking for something in particular?"

"I think Timmy was trying to tell me something at the detention center, but I had trouble understanding him because...well, because someone cut out his tongue. But I'm thinking one of the words was 'wheel.'"

"Which one?"

"I'll check steering if you want to take a look at the rolling ones. Just watch for scary local wildlife."

"Noted."

I slid into the driver's seat of the car as Dean's head disappeared below the bumper.

I felt under the steering wheel, brushing my fingers back and forth, but met only smooth leather and vinyl.

The wheel itself was open and thin, the adornments sparse. I tapped my fingers on the smooth, shiny red plastic. "What were you saying, Timmy?" I muttered.

"I don't see anything but some slightly worn brake shoes and an alignment issue in the front end," Dean called.

I scooted forward in the seat, running my hand under the edges. Nothing but dust so scant even Ruth would be impressed. Timmy took good care of this car.

So why was the front end out of alignment?

"Can you tell if something knocked that out of alignment?" I asked.

"Give me a second," Dean said, his voice echoing up through a very poorly insulated engine compartment into the passenger cabin.

I stepped out of the car and dropped to one knee next to the driver's seat, pulling out my phone and using the flashlight to examine the dash under the steering wheel.

Timmy had put some love into restoring this car. The leather was well oiled and smooth. So smooth I nearly missed the slit directly under the back center of the wheel.

"I'll be damned." I was a little too proud of my translation of what Timmy had said as I looked around for something I could slide under the leather. Standing, I grabbed the handsaw Dean used to open the door.

The blade didn't encounter any resistance slipping into the slot, but I stopped and nearly dropped it when I had it a quarter of the way in. Pulling it back, I held it in the flashlight's beam, sitting back on my heels and pulling both things close to my eyes.

"I think he hit something pretty hard," Dean said from above my head, opening a series of photos on his phone that showed repair work to the under- and back sides of the bumper. "Is that what you were looking for in here?"

"Two seconds." I set the saw carefully on the seat and reached one finger into the pocket under the steering wheel. Paper. I found the edge and slid my nail under it, pulling it free.

I smoothed the edges over the pristine floorboard, careful to touch in only a few places. "It's a map." I bit my lip.

"Of what?"

I picked it up by one corner and stood, laying it on the caramel-colored soft top of the car. "I think it's of...here."

I pointed to the saw. "I also think that's fabric and blood on that saw right there."

"Oh, shit," Dean said. "And I picked it up and got my prints all over it."

I waved one hand. "It belongs to the Dushane family. A first-year law student could convince a jury that their fingerprints being on their own tool makes perfect sense and doesn't prove anything."

"Thanks. For trying to make me feel better."

"I'm not. I'm telling the truth. I told you, I didn't come in here looking for a smoking gun. And that could be a thousand things, including Timmy's own blood if he's clumsy with tools. You see a plastic bag of any sort?"

Dean glanced around and disappeared as I studied the map. The river was in the right direction the way I had turned it, and the long lines could easily be the back of the motel, the other shapes the house and barn. An *X* was marked about a third of the way between the motel and the river—assuming I was reading it correctly.

Dean returned with a Piggly Wiggly plastic sack and handed it to me. "Best I can do."

"It'll work in a pinch." I used it to pick up the saw and then folded the bag around the blade. "You have an in at the nearest lab?"

"I have a good friend in Lampasas we can get it to. She can test it for whatever you like, though we'd need DNA to compare to since none of these people has a criminal record."

"I'll just have to figure out how to get some, then, won't I?" I closed the car door and laid the bag with the saw on the roof.

Picking up the map, I motioned for Dean to follow.

"What does that have marked?" he asked as I approached the door to the tiny barn's lone stall, which Doris had used her body to block from view the best she could the entire time we'd been out here yesterday. I just hadn't thought anything of it at the time.

"The spot on the map is outside," I said. "Riskier for being spotted, so I want to see what's in here before we go take a look out there."

I pointed to the combination lock hanging from the metal door fastener. "I've never met country people who like locks so much."

"Me either." Dean snagged a pair of bolt cutters from a metal garbage can full of shears and weeding tools. "And I have to admit a high level of curiosity about what else they're hiding."

19

Boxes—neat, unexpectedly dust-free towers of big plastic storage tubs teetered maybe a dozen stacks deep and half that many wide in the stall, which was roughly twice as big as I'd have thought before Dean opened the door.

"Christmas decorations? Cash? Dope? What's your money on?" I asked, pulling a chain overhead to bring the naked bulb hanging from the high ceiling to life. The light was a sickly yellow that washed out the black color of the center tubs to look like dark green.

"I don't think Santa is going to tell us where Ratcliff is. So I'm hoping for anything but decorations," he said, disappearing back out into the barn and returning with an A-frame ladder. "Pick a crate, any crate."

Absent anything resembling a label to work from, I pointed to the stack furthest from the door. All the tubs in it had red lids, while the others were about an even split between blue and yellow. "Try the top one back there."

He climbed to the third step on the ladder to reach the underside of the handle and tugged sideways, making the other nine under it sway such that I put hands on them to keep them from toppling over. "Maybe one more step."

"Definitely." He went up two more, to the last one before the top, and lifted the box by one handle to slide it free. "Kinda heavy."

I reached up to take it so he could come down the ladder, and my knees buckled slightly when he let it go. "Oof. If this is full of books, I'm going to feel like an idiot."

I squatted to lower the tub to the ground, wrinkling my brow when a *thunk* indicated something shifting inside it.

Dean rolled one arm in a *let's-get-on-with-it* gesture. "I'm going to die of dehydration from sweating if we don't get back into the AC soon."

I blew a rogue strand of hair off my sweaty face. "I sympathize. Here goes—big money, no whammy."

"Hey, my grandmother loved that show," Dean said.

"Mine too. My sister and I picked it up from her. We watched game shows on summer mornings while we waited for someone to come out to the pool with us. And my mother watched *The Price Is Right* while she worked out every day—probably still does. She's a master shopper, she'd win a fortune if she went on that one."

I unsnapped the lid and lifted it.

"Newspapers?" Dean's brow furrowed. "Who keeps this many newspapers?"

I pulled a copy of the *San Antonio Express News* from September 12, 2001, from the pile, a burning passenger plane buried in the side of a glass tower against an impossibly blue sky taking up the entire front page. Under it was a *Life* magazine from just after Princess Diana was killed.

Dean crouched at the other end, thumbing through. "November 1963— this one says it's from the twenty-second but has a headline about the assassination."

I paused at a copy of *Newsweek* in my own stack with JFK Junior's face on the cover, the headline about a plane crash off Martha's Vineyard. "Newspapers used to have morning and afternoon editions. I think by the sixties, most big cities had a morning paper and an afternoon paper. The ones that came out the evening of the twenty-second had the first coverage that day, but it was probably something they threw in last minute, stop-the-presses style."

"Wow." He pulled it free and held the yellowing pages gently, reading. "It's wild to think that not everyone had a computer and a camera in their pocket back then. Like these guys who wrote this didn't even know Abraham Zapruder was there filming yet."

"No one knew what was going on in the world until Walter Cronkite told them," I said. "That's what my granny used to say. I wonder what she'd think of reporters live tweeting things that will be history someday?"

He laid the paper gently on the ground and kept thumbing. "Wow. Vietnam, Eisenhower, Pearl Harbor... How old was this woman you talked with?"

"Probably not old enough to buy newspapers in 1941. I bet this was passed to her and she continued the collection. People say journalism is a rough draft of history." I pulled out a newspaper from August of 1977 with a headline about Elvis's death. "People are still making movies about him nearly fifty years later."

"Because he was the coolest guy who ever lived," Dean said. "My mom was a fan when she was a kid. She kept a record player in our house because she had all of Elvis's music on vinyl. I grew up on it—dude had some kind of range. And he was a nice guy, too. Super generous with everyone, from his staff to perfect strangers."

I stood, settling the papers back in the tote. "No argument here. I used to listen to my grandmother's records when I was a little girl. She loved his gospel albums, and man—his version of 'Peace in the Valley' still gives me goose bumps. But as cool as this is, it isn't what we're looking for."

He moved the box and retrieved another, and I laughed when I opened it to a life-size baby Jesus with a halo of gold under the head, turned sideways next to a wood manger and a plastic, blue-robed Mary. "Who had Christmas decorations?"

Dean picked up the statue of the baby and flipped it around, bobbing his hands up and down. "Hefty little dude."

"Probably weighted so it won't blow away," I said. "They look like yard decorations."

He put it back. "Maybe the red lids are personal stuff."

He turned to the next stack and retrieved a yellow-lidded box. I moved the ladder and got a green one from another pile. Groaning when I lifted it. "There are too many here to open one at a time," I said. "But I'm going to need a hand getting this one to the ground."

Dean hustled over to help, and we pulled the tops at the same time, yelping in unison.

"Bingo," Dean said. "Pills and wallets." He raised one end of the tub so I could see the jumble of amber prescription bottles mixed with wallets in every size and color. "The names on these bottles are all different. Who leaves their meds behind in a hotel?"

"Nobody. They're stealing. That's what Ashton meant when she said they kick people out and take their stuff if they don't pay on time for additional days." I reached for a thick, leather-bound accounting ledger. There had to be twenty of them in the green box, and there were a dozen boxes with green lids. I flipped the ledger open, my eyes nearly crossing at cramped rows of small, careful letters and numbers.

"This has last year's date." I tapped the top of the page. "I don't see a way this place could have turned this much business in the past decade."

Dean peered over my shoulder. "Those are codes," he said, pointing to the letters labeling the amounts.

"For what?"

"Something they don't want us to know." He put the book back with the others. "I have a forensic accountant friend at the DEA. He should be able to crack it." He smiled. "Nice work. I bet this will tell us what's been going on around here."

"I'm not sure it's going to lead us to Ratcliff, though," I said.

"It might point a direction, at any rate." Dean hefted the box and moved toward the door. "It's a good place to start."

I pointed to the box of wallets. "Any IDs?"

"Not one. Or anything else. All the cash is gone, too."

"What about the pills?"

"Plenty of those. If the labels are right, it's mostly painkillers, but we can have a lab verify. This would definitely be enough to indicate intent to distribute."

I picked up that box and turned left out of the doorway. "Let's see what Timmy thought was so important he marked it on a map hidden in his prized possession."

Leaving the storage crates and the plastic grocery bag containing the saw mostly hidden behind the low, spreading holly outside the back of the barn, I unfolded Timmy's map and tried to make it match up with the land. The river was maybe a half-mile away, barely visible at the horizon, so the spot marked on Timmy's map had to be a hundred paces or more from the back of the motel.

"We're just going to go out here and do this in the middle of the day?" Dean asked.

"It's not ideal," I acknowledged. "But after more consideration, I'm not sure we have less risk of being spotted at night, assuming Doris comes back or whatever hikers might be staying here return. Plus, I'm curious, and we have nothing more pressing to look at right now."

"True." Dean paused at the corner of the barn and looked around. There was nothing but flat land stretching to every horizon. "We can't dig up the whole desert." He waved a shovel and a pickax we'd found in the barn to emphasize the point.

"Let's see if anything marks the spot," I said. "Timmy didn't strike me as a brain trust. It may be nothing, but..."

"I'm with you."

We walked about a third of the way down the back of the motel before we turned toward the river. The expanse of flat-packed sand and dirt was spotted with brownish-green weeds here and there, but about halfway to the start of the riverbank, I spotted a splash of color.

"Flowers don't grow out here," Dean said when I pointed.

"Those look like flowers to me," I said.

Looking at the map, I walked to the flowers and looked at the back of the motel.

"Is that room sixteen?" I pointed to the small window in the bathroom, counting them to the corner. "I think it was eight or nine doors down from the corner."

"Maybe," Dean said. "One weird thing at a time."

I took the pickax and swung it at the ground next to the flowers. The shock of it meeting stone two inches in vibrated all the way to my shoulder.

I scraped the dirt away to make sure it was stone I'd hit and sighed. "Maybe just a coincidence."

Dean wandered a few steps away and knelt, sifting sand through his fingers before he stood and slid the shovel easily into the ground a few yards away. "Maybe not. This looks loose—at least relatively freshly turned."

I hurried over, helping move dirt with the broad end of the axe. We worked and sweated in silence for maybe ten minutes, making quick work of a fairly deep and wide hole.

"The lack of rain hasn't allowed this to recompact since it was last moved." Dean raised the shovel for another load. "But whatever was here, it seems somebody found it without Timmy's map. Or maybe Timmy moved it."

I glanced at the pile of dirt as big as the bed in my room that we needed to put back before we could go inside as Dean hoisted himself out of the hole.

I moved to follow, the toe of my boot catching on something about a foot from the river-side edge of the hole.

I raised my leg and stepped carefully around, bending to brush sand off a rock.

It wasn't a rock.

"Hey, Dean? You need to have a look at this."

"You found something?" He slung the shovel over his shoulder and walked back to the hole. "Cash? Guns? Dope?"

I brushed the sand away from a foot-shaped collection of small white metatarsals and lifted what looked like a tibia.

"Bones. And I'm pretty sure they're human."

20

"I have a friend at the university, an archeologist who specializes in bones," Jim said, his voice distracted. "We can certainly try to identify them, but I can't promise. Is there a full skeleton?"

"We seem to be missing two finger bones," I said. "But this is the strangest body recovery I've ever seen—they're completely clean. Almost too perfect to be real." I swiped a stray strand of hair out of my face and buried my nails in my scalp, trying not to get carried away until I knew for sure what this meant.

"I'd wager you have a better instinct for what's real and what's not than you'd think by now," Jim said. "But I know why you don't want to assume."

"Have you found anything useful?" I asked.

"Maybe. Your guy had a specialized implanted hearing aid. These are rare, and expensive."

"Do they by any chance have serial numbers?" I held my breath waiting for the answer.

"They do indeed, but this one got shattered by the vehicle that rolled over the skull yesterday. I'm not sure we're going to be able to make the number out, but we're going to try. I have to extract all the tiny little pieces from the remaining ear tissue first."

"And then put them back together?"

"Jesus, no," he laughed. "Even when my eyes might have been good enough to attempt such a thing, I have way too many bodies stacked up and too few personnel to even have anyone try. There's a computer program that can do it. It may not be able to get the type clear enough because it's teeny tiny, though. Just wanted you to know I might have a lead for you."

"I appreciate it, Jim," I said. "Anything else interesting?"

"He wasn't a stranger to violence," Jim said. "I've got five rib fractures with the kind of remodeling that comes with getting them kicked in. And the teeth are too far gone for a dental match, but he had some extensive crown work, pretty recently, and probably not in Mexico. I'll send you the details in a little while if you want to have someone reach out to dentists."

"I met the local guy yesterday. I can start there," I said. "I will call you when I figure out what we're doing with these bones."

"You're being careful, right?"

"Always."

I disconnected the call and turned back to Dean.

"We should get a team out here to take this place apart." He reached for his phone.

I put one hand up. "Not so fast."

He swept an arm around for emphasis, a pointing finger landing on the bones at my feet. "Why the hell not?"

"If we do that, we've tipped our hand. Everyone involved with whatever this is will know in five minutes that the jig is up. If we hang out, knowing what we know, this place is suddenly now the perfect base for getting to the bottom of whatever is happening out here, and it may be our best path to finding Ratcliff and getting him home safe."

My phone buzzed in my pocket, and I pulled it out to check the text. "Speaking of Ratcliff, his horse made it through the night." I tapped the screen and touched a smiley face and typed, *Thank you for the update.* "Doc Potter says he's slow, but he's up, and he ate some oats and apples this morning." I smiled as I tucked the phone away.

"So you don't want a team to search this place?"

"Not today. Once we're done with what we can learn here, absolutely."

He gestured to the plastic crates and the barn. "What now, then?"

I snapped three photos of the bones before I started picking them out of the sand. "We fill in the hole and get these to someone who can figure out who they belong to and how they got here."

Dean picked up the shovel and went to work.

Maybe the only good thing about finding possible human bits we needed to smuggle out of the middle of nowhere was Doris's barn: few buildings I'd ever been inside boasted such a collection of random objects. Including a canvas tool bag, a sheet of burlap that probably used to be a livestock feed bag, and a carrying case for a small chainsaw that Dean found in a corner near the workbench.

"I can't say this wasn't used to cut someone up," I muttered, shining my phone's flashlight at the chain on the saw and wrinkling my nose. "I bet a blood detection wand would light this place up with more purple splotches than the stands at a TCU game."

"As long as none of it belongs to Ratcliff."

"Are you guys friends?" I asked. This job has a way of forging bonds between the people who work it.

"Not spill-your-guts friends, but we get the occasional beer. He's a good man. And honestly, I have some selfish motive here: I don't want to think he got himself wrapped up in something he didn't think he could share with me and wound up dead. So I'm all in on bringing him home."

I slid my eyes sideways as I put the chainsaw back into its case and started wrapping bones in burlap strips Dean was cutting with a pocketknife. Once wrapped, I laid them carefully in the tool bag.

I wanted to know what else Ratcliff knew. And why he didn't share it with Dean.

We worked in silence until the burlap was gone and the tool bag was stuffed with bones.

Glancing around, I offered a thumbs-up. "Someone would have to be really paranoid to suspect anyone had been in here."

Dean pointed to the sliced combination lock dangling from the door. "Except for that."

"Doris's proclivity for imitating Fred Sanford to the rescue again," I said, holding up an identical-looking black lock—except this one was open. "It was under the tool bag in that drawer."

"It won't have the same combination."

"Hopefully she was telling the truth yesterday when she complained about her memory," I said. "She'll think she forgot. Or we can hope, anyway."

Dean stuck out his lower lip and bobbed his head from side to side.

"As last-minute plans go, it doesn't suck," he said. "I'd call this well done for a seat-of-our-pants operation."

"If only we could get away with jackets to cover this stuff until we get back to the room."

"That would stick out in this heat. But like you said, there's nobody here."

Still, we'd agreed carrying the giant plastic bins of accounting materials and drugs back to the room might be a bridge too far, so they were still out back where we could easily load them into a truck after the sun went down.

Dean pulled the chain to turn the light off, and I locked the stall door. We covered the car and laid the plastic bag with the smaller saw carefully on top of the bones.

He cracked the door to outside, where the air was somehow the exact same variety of hot and stale as the air inside. Craning his neck around it in every direction except up, he waved me over. "We're clear, I think."

We picked our way around the yard, moving due west from the barn to the back of the motel in a wide path around Doris's house in case she'd come home in the two hours and change that we'd been snooping.

Which made it that much more surprising when we rounded the end of the motel's shortest wing and walked straight into Ashton, the teenage desk clerk, who looked far more grown-up pointing a double-barrel shotgun at us than she had reading Ray Bradbury.

21

"Jesus." She loosened her grip on the gun but didn't aim it anyplace else. "What the heck are you two doing out here?"

"We, uh..." Dean paused for way too long, his eyes flicking from her to the gun to the horizon in a loop. I needed to make sure he didn't reach for his sidearm, or we might end up with the kind of trouble I really didn't want.

"We were looking for a change of scenery," I said. I didn't quite wink, but the tone implied it. Lord forgive me.

Her eyes went to the bag in my hand, her tone wry. "With power tools?"

"More toys than tools." I barely got the words out without laughing—or retching.

Dean sucked in a sharp breath behind me. *Don't speak, dude. I got it.*

Her eyes roamed over the sweaty clothes sticking to us with visible wet spots in several unfortunate places.

Eyes popping wide, Ashton pointed the gun at the sky as she covered her lips with her right hand. "Never mind. Everybody is into their own thing."

Dean opened his mouth, and I shot my hip bone into his leg and immediately cast my eyes at the dirt, giving my all to calling up my ability to flush on command on a pageant stage. "Sorry to scare you," I muttered, hoping I sounded sufficiently embarrassed and motioning for Dean to follow my lead.

"No worries. I've seen worse," Ashton said, shading her eyes from the sun's late-day glare as we walked past her with stolen evidence in broad daylight. Sometimes letting people assume what they will is the easiest path around trouble.

"You know she thought we were—" Dean waved his hand rather than finish his sentence.

"I also know she didn't ask any more details about what we're carrying, and she won't tell Doris anything we don't want her to know." I unlocked the door to room 16 and laid everything carefully on the desk before opening my overnight bag and emptying clothes to make room for what I hoped was crucial evidence. The hardest part was trying not to think about what kind of crucial evidence as I settled my clothes back around it, suddenly thankful for good dry cleaners. "I find that embarrassing topics are a great tool for wriggling out of conversations I don't want to have."

"I'll remember that." He resumed his chair in the corner, flicking on the lamp because it was still too hot out to open any curtains. "So why did the teenage desk clerk think she needed a shotgun to come see what was going on outside?"

"I was just wondering the same thing." I zipped my bag and set it gently in the bottom of the closet.

"Any idea how we might find out?"

"Maybe. Doris said the maid lives in room twenty-seven with her little boy."

"Got a name?" He stood.

"Jenny."

Dean opened the door and waved one arm. "After you."

I pointed to the next window down from room 27 and shooed Dean toward it. "A single woman living alone with her kid might be afraid to answer a knock from a random large dude she's never met."

"Fair." He stepped out of the way as I removed my badge and slid it into my back pocket. Like Archie said, this wasn't the kind of place where law enforcement equaled trustworthy. I rapped on the door.

I stepped back and waited. The curtains, drawn against the pounding sun and its unrelenting heat, fluttered so briefly a blink would've obscured it.

The chain slid across the back side of the door, and it opened an inch or so, a tiny woman with short blond hair peering up at me with a lone brown eye. "What?"

"Jenny?" I asked.

"Who's asking?"

"I'm Faith. I'm a klutz, and I spilled a Dr Pepper all over the bedspread in my room. I was hoping you could help me."

She stepped back and started to move the chain, then paused. "Why'd you come knock? How come you didn't go up and ask the girl at the front?"

Damn.

"She wasn't there," I blurted as the words popped into my head. "Doris told me the other day you lived on the property, and I saw the trike." I pointed to the red metal tricycle under the window, three streamers still clinging to the rust-speckled chrome handlebars.

She stared at me for a moment before she opened the door. "Laziest damn girl I've ever met," she muttered. "Good thing her auntie owns the place."

I kept my face flat, though that was interesting information to have.

Jenny pointed to the little towheaded boy curled around a well-worn stuffed blue puppy dog on the bed, his thumb in his mouth. He was asleep.

"I don't like to leave him, but I have an extra set of bedding in here in case he pees the bed," she said. "Potty training."

I looked around the room. It was almost exactly like mine, except the wallpaper was largely covered with taped-up crayon drawings of dogs, horses, and dragons.

She crossed to the closet and pulled out a giant plastic zipper bag with a bedspread, sheets, and pillowcases.

"You need the sheets, too, right?" she asked.

"How old is he?" I started talking before she finished.

"Three and a half." She raised her eyebrows, shaking the bag. "Sheets?"

"No, I whipped the covers back before it soaked through," I said.

"Oh." She smiled—just a slight one, but enough for me to tell she had a pretty smile. "So I can hang onto those in case. That's good."

She removed the sheets and handed me the bag.

"Thanks." I held it at my side with one hand and kept looking around. A blue metal toolbox sat on the floor next to a mini fridge, and I spotted socks and gloves hanging up to dry in the bathroom. "Have you worked here long?"

"Since just before he was born," she said. "Not many places will give you a home in exchange for working there."

I inched closer to the toolbox, looking around the room. "You've made a nice home here for him."

She snorted. "He needs a house with a backyard and a swing. He plays in a motel parking lot. And the folks we get through here aren't the kind of people a little boy needs to see sometimes."

She gave me another once-over. "What are you doing staying in a joint like this, anyhow? You got class."

I glanced down at my sweaty clothes and touched my mangled ponytail, laughing. "You're very kind. I'm here for work."

"It's in the way you carry yourself, your voice, seeping out of your pores. You can't learn that kind of class. So what is a lady who comes from money doing 'working,' sweaty and messed up, in an aging border motel?"

"What kind of people come through here who worry you?" I asked, furrowing my brow with just the right amount of concern.

"You didn't answer my question." Her expression went from guarded to wary.

"I'm passing through town, and there isn't exactly a broad range of lodging choices." I raised my free hand and smiled, hoping body language would help sell my story. She was jumpy, and flashing a badge might very well get me shown the door.

"This ain't the kind of town anybody passes through. We ain't on the way to anywhere." She put herself between me and the sleeping child on the bed. "If Carlos sent you, you can tell him I'm doing my goddamn best, and sending his guard dogs to fuck with me ain't going to get him what he wants any faster. The old broad don't know where Timmy went with his stuff, but somebody has to. I just gotta find Lucia. He couldn't do it in a month, what makes him think I can get to her in a week? He can go sit on his gross fucked-up middle finger and give me some time." She put both hands on her hips, not bothering to wipe at the droplets of spit that had started to fly as she spoke.

I listened to her whole spiel, the words more vehement and flying faster as she talked, wondering what to say next.

I went with the truth, pulling my badge from my pocket. "I don't know who Carlos is," I put the clean comforter down before I crossed to the door and opened it, motioning for Dean to hang in the doorway, "but if you'll fill us in, we can help you get him off your back and keep your boy safe."

22

"Cops are supposed to identify theirselves to you," Jenny said. "You can't use anything I told you."

Someone watched a lot of cop shows on the little antenna-topped TV. And had been doing something shady.

"I'm not here to arrest you, Jenny," I said. "Or to take your child. I think you might be in a situation you could use some help with. I want to help."

She held my gaze without blinking until my eyes were so dry it blurred my vision. "They'll kill me," she said when she finally closed hers. "He has nobody. I can't let them kill me."

"We won't let that happen," Dean said from the doorway.

She turned her head, blinking like she saw him for the first time.

"You can't stop it. They'll kill you, too."

I stared at her for five beats, the words ringing in my ears. I'd heard them a thousand times before, from people much scarier than a single mom in a bad situation in a sad little border-town motel, but they stuck out in a way they never had before.

Shaking my head, I reached a hand out toward her. "We are very good at what we do, Jenny. Who are you afraid of? Who's Carlos?"

She covered her face with both hands. "I was just doing what they said I had to. It's her fucking fault, you know. She dragged me into this."

"She who?"

"Doris." She sniffled, wiping her face. "She wanted me to follow Lucia. I got caught. Carlos made me work for him, watching Timmy. He said he'd kill my baby and make me watch before he killed me if I didn't do what he said."

"Jesus," Dean muttered.

"No one would blame you for trying to protect your child," I said.

"He's all I have. I thought I'd save up some extra cash and get us out of here, but I didn't realize who I was messing with. They don't let you go."

"Carlos?" I asked.

She nodded.

"But he's paying you?"

She pointed to a white wood panel on the wall near the bathroom door. "Doris pays me too. But it don't do me no good. If I leave, they'll find me."

"You said Carlos wanted you to watch Timmy," I said. "Did you do that?"

She pulled a drugstore spiral notebook with a bright yellow cover from the drawer in the night table. "I kept a log of every place he went, when he left here, when he came back."

"For how long?" I had to link my fingers behind my back to keep from snatching the notebook from her hands. She had to give it to me. I needed her to trust me.

"Since right after Christmas. That's when Doris and Lucia had that fight, and Doris sent me after her."

"Did she threaten you, too?" Dean asked.

"She offered me an extra hundred bucks a week to follow Lucia and take pictures of her with other guys." Jenny shrugged. "Who would turn that down?"

"And you met Carlos while you were doing this?"

"The second time Lucia left here without Timmy in the middle of the night, Carlos came out for a smoke, and he caught me waiting for Lucia to come back out of his place. It's not like I'm a detective or anything, and it's fucking dark out there at night."

My kingdom for a pen or a voice recorder. I was tired, and my brain seemed slower than normal at absorbing her words. But I didn't want to scare her, either.

"And all you did was pass Timmy's whereabouts to Carlos?" Dean asked.

"I swear," she said.

"How did you do that?" I asked.

"I wrote it down, and then I texted him." She pulled out an iPhone. "From this phone. Only this one. He gave it to me."

Now was the time.

"May I?" I put a hand out for the phone, and she passed it to me, along with the notebook.

I flipped to early May. Her handwriting resembled that of a fifth grader, but she had taken detailed notes.

"He left here on the ninth at 10:14 p.m. in the Corvette," I said.

"And he never came back." Tears spilled down Jenny's cheeks. "I didn't know they were going to hurt him, I swear."

He never came back, but the car did.

"Who?" I asked.

Jenny pointed at the phone, her whole torso shaking with sobs.

I unlocked the screen and opened the texts. Only one thread, last message at 10:21 p.m. on May 9th: *That bitch will learn what we think about stealing.*

I handed the phone to Dean and turned back to Jenny. "Do you remember where you went when you followed Lucia? Was it across the river?"

She shook her head. "She went to the park. The campground there. Carlos had an RV."

"When was this?" Dean asked.

"When does the book start?" she asked, pointing to the notebook. "It was the day before that."

Dean flipped to the front and then snapped it shut. "January sixteenth," he told me.

"Thank you, Jenny."

"For getting myself killed?" She slid down the side of the bed to the floor.

"We're really not going to let that happen," I said.

"He knows people everywhere," she said. "He knows way too much of what happens around here for one person."

"What does he do for money?" I asked.

"Drugs, girls, whatever." She waved a hand. "He knows shit about everyone, so everybody's afraid of him."

Dean held up the phone. "Who is he referring to in this last message?"

"Doris, I think. A lot of cash moves through this place, and you don't have to be a genius to figure it's not all on the up and up when the rooms are always mostly empty. Whatever she was doing for him, she must have been skimming. She's a cagey old broad, but I feel bad for her, you know? That would be a special kind of hell, to know I caused my child's death."

I put a hand out to help her off the floor. "Pack a bag for the both of you, and let's go," I said. "Nothing is going to happen to you or your son."

She pulled a worn canvas duffel out of the closet and started packing things, and Dean walked closer. "Are you sure about this? She's working for what sounds increasingly like a local crime lord—how can we be sure we can trust her?"

"We can't," I said, thinking about Timmy being led back to his cell. "But I'm not walking away from another potentially helpless person in a dangerous situation this week, and she trusted us when she didn't have to."

"Or she's setting us up," he said.

"I guess we'll see." I looked up at him. "Did your guys get Timmy out of the detention center?"

His brow furrowed as he pulled out his phone. "I don't know."

Mine buzzed in my pocket as Jenny finished emptying cash out of the space behind the panel.

A text from Jim: *Delivered the skull to your reconstruction whiz kid. I need to see you when you're back in town.* I sent back a quick thumbs-up.

Jenny bent over her son and shook him. "Come on, bud. We're going on an adventure."

"Like a quest?" he mumbled, digging at his eyes with both fists.

"Yep. Just like that."

"May I?" Dean asked, stepping forward and holding Jenny's gaze.

She stepped out of his way. He lifted the kid as easily as I would a pillow. The little boy looked at him for a few seconds before he wrapped arms and legs around Dean's torso and settled his head on Dean's shoulder.

We put them in his SUV and locked the doors as I waved for him to follow me back to room 16.

"Pull around and get those crates, and call your numbers nerd," I said. "Take Jenny and her boy to E Company HQ, and stay there. Try not to let anyone else know they're there. Archie knows everyone, I can have a US marshal here to put them in wit sec at least temporarily by morning."

"I'll run down what's going on with Timmy's transfer, too. Hammet is having some trouble getting to someone who will honor the warrant out there."

"Tell him to ask for Grady," I said. "And not to take no for an answer. If Timmy Dushane is involved in the larger crime ring here even peripherally, I might have put a target on him by going out there to see him—just because they didn't kill him after he was arrested doesn't mean they won't if they think we might get something out of him. Hammet is a Texas Ranger, for fuck's sake—tell him to use the clout to his advantage. Just don't give my name to the desk sergeant. It's a long story, but that won't help."

Dean glanced at his truck. "On it, don't worry. Where are you going?"

I shouldered my overnight bag. "I feel like I'm seeing more of my truck and the highway than anything else this week, but I'd like to take this to my friend in Austin myself. I'm hoping Jim has something for me on this mystery dead guy, and I want to see if there's any information in the file Ratcliff handed me that could help us. Can you drop me at the outpost so I can get my truck?"

"Of course. I thought you said Ratcliff told you no one was investigating those deaths?"

"No one he knew about," I said. "Maybe it's a long shot, but it never hurts to check every rock. Archie says eventually you always find the magic one that makes it all make sense."

I examined every variable I could remember about the case in the four-hour drive back north. Timmy, Doris, the ledgers, the bones, Ratcliff's bodies, Ratcliff's disappearance, Jenny the terrified hotel maid, Timmy's last outing, the crazy cowboys Doris had kicked out of the motel meeting up with Timmy, Lucia, and last but most considered: Carlos, the ghostly, menacing local small-time crime kingpin.

I told Siri to call Archie.

Voicemail.

"Hey, Arch, it's Faith. I need your contact at the ATF, because if you trust an ATF guy, he has to be a straight arrow. I also need a US marshal at E Company HQ for witness security as fast as one can get there. I know you're busy, but please call me when you get a minute."

I put the phone back into the cupholder.

Tomorrow, when Jenny was safe with the Marshals Service and I knew what Jim wanted, Dean and I would go out to the state park and pay Carlos a visit. For the first time in days, what I'd heard about him made some of this start to make sense as the miles passed—from the beginning, I'd figured Ratcliff's string of brutally murdered corpses was related to some sort of syndicated crime. Carlos could be the lynchpin that linked the bodies to the local drug trade—or maybe a larger smuggling operation, and to hear Jenny tell it, he even camped upriver from where the corpses were found. Timmy Dushane was in custody on drug-running charges, which could have been a setup orchestrated by Carlos for all I knew—especially since Timmy wasn't dead. That had puzzled me since I'd found Timmy, because he seemed too low-level from what we'd seen to be worth protecting. But that wasn't the case if his mother was laundering money for Carlos—or someone higher up than Carlos, even.

The more I thought about it, the more convinced I became that I needed to meet Carlos myself. And lock him up myself, too.

I turned the radio on, Reba's voice twanging on about the night the lights went out in Georgia. Jenny had the same twang in her voice, but Reba was from Oklahoma, not Texas.

He'll kill you, too. I still couldn't shake those words out of my head.

It took me nearly seventy more miles of songs to figure out why, and I nearly ran the truck off the road when I cracked it:

They, not *hey*. *Will*, not *wheel*. *Kill*, not *deal*.

Timmy Dushane had been trying to tell me something. But not about his mother or his car...about his girlfriend. And me.

"They will kill her. You too. You...you too."

Once the words clicked into place, they wouldn't budge. I could hear him saying them—and I knew in my bones this was right.

I grabbed my phone and told Siri to call Dean. "Get Timmy the hell out of the detention center, even if you have to take Jenny and the kid with you and carry him out yourself," I said when he picked up. "He was trying to give me a warning the other day, and I'm afraid I put his life in danger by showing up there looking for him."

Dean sighed.

"Faith, I'm so sorry. Hammet finally got through their asshole desk sergeant to your guy, Grady. Timmy's dead. They found him unresponsive in his cell this morning."

23

I didn't kill Timmy Dushane.

Logically, I knew that was true. But I felt terrible about his death just the same.

I pulled into my driveway after asking Dean to put his best tracker on finding Timmy's girlfriend, but I couldn't give him much to go on. "She's a prostitute, according to his mother, they call her Lucia, she has a tattoo of a red rose with stars and a bunny on her right arm, and that is everything I know," I said before texting him the photo I found in Timmy's car.

"We'll do our very best," Dean said. "You sound like you could do with some sleep."

"Not likely to come easy," I said. "But you're not wrong."

"Listen, I've got Jenny here waiting on the marshals," he said. "A guy out of the Austin office called about two hours ago, and they're sending someone. I will put someone on Lucia, and my forensic accountant has two grad students helping him go through those ledgers. Park rangers say the site Carlos uses has been empty for two weeks, but they'll call if they see anything unusual. We may have more questions than answers at the moment, but I have a feeling that is about to change, thanks to the hard work you're doing. Get some rest, and call me in the morning."

If the marshals were coming for Jenny, Archie got my message. But he didn't call me back. Which was weird.

I sighed. "Promise you'll call me if anything happens before sunup."

"Of course." He paused. "McClellan? We're going to find Ratcliff."

I smiled. "Thanks. I know you're right." And I did. I just hoped we'd find him alive—but I wasn't saying that to his friend. "And then we'll nail Carlos and whoever else is responsible for slinging dope and dumping bodies in the river."

"Good night, McClellan. Talk to you in the morning."

I put the phone on the table when I walked into the house and locked the door behind me, going to the kitchen to check the back door before I pulled a cold Dr Pepper from the fridge and Ratcliff's file on the bodies he'd found from my bag and settled on the sofa, turning on the TV for background noise. A decade of living alone and being comfortable in the silence had been entirely undone by a few months of having Graham's big, loud, easy-to-laugh self in my world.

The channel had a late-night *Friends* marathon running, and the group was playing touch football in the park on Thanksgiving.

I flipped the file open, looking for something I might have missed in my cursory glance two days before. Reading a homicide scene narrative written by someone who wasn't a homicide detective was frustrating as all hell. Ratcliff knew the bare-bones basics, but he had no idea what to measure or how to look for the kind of details that were often the difference between catching the bad guy and sending the case to join my sister in limbo.

"How deep was the water? The river hasn't been dry all year. What was the temperature that day? How were the remains oriented?" I muttered. Not that the pages answered me.

I got up to dig a magnifying glass out of a drawer at ten twenty, the TV catching my attention as I sat down. The hot actor guy and the dorky-but-funny one were hitting on the same woman, and when they asked her to choose, she picked dorky-but-funny. "Solid choice," I said, because looks fade much faster than intellect. Turning back to the file, I was only half listening as dorky-but-funny put his foot in his mouth and she left, telling them she didn't like either of them.

I ran the magnifier over the first photo in Ratcliff's file, taken last

September at the end of a not-quite-as-dry summer. The body was partially submerged, the level of decomposition high. No head to examine, but I spotted ink on the remaining flesh of one shoulder under a half-rotten blue T-shirt. It was hard to see, thin blue lines on gray, waterlogged skin, but they definitely formed a pattern. I studied the image, turning the photo every which way until I was pretty sure I was looking at the bottom half of an eagle with a sword in its talons and some letters I couldn't make out.

Which could be a Mexican symbol or an American one. Not terribly helpful.

I grabbed a pen and paper and sketched what I saw, writing "letters here" where I thought the type was supposed to go.

Next photo.

The same remains from a directly overhead angle. Through the muddy water, I could make out a torso and legs, though the angle and the water distorted the length. But with the right algorithm and a scale measurement of the femur, Jim might be able to use that image to estimate the victim's height.

Plopping the photo on the table, I sat back. I was kidding myself—and spinning my wheels, wasting time I could be sleeping. Height wasn't going to help me ID this guy, and neither was anything else I might see in these amateur photos. I know not every detective works homicide, but every Ranger has to take training in processing crime scenes because we often get calls for help from small departments all over the state.

Why were these victims documented so poorly? On a normal day, I'd say the officer was either incompetent or indifferent. But if Ratcliff didn't care who killed these people, why would he have called me?

I flipped to the photos of the November remains. Just as gross as Mr. September, and just as bland and useless, too. I dropped them on the table and laid the magnifier on top of them, pushing the button on the remote to silence the paleontologist guy, who was explaining something sciencey that none of his friends wanted to know. I was halfway to my feet, half wondering if there was something here I didn't want to know, when I saw it.

Reflected in the water surrounding the victim's chest, a police uniform shoulder patch.

I held the photo and the magnifier up to the lamp.

The "feds" Ratcliff called were US Customs and Border Patrol—possibly from the same circle as Timmy's buddy who was letting him back and forth across the border to do...whatever paid him fifteen grand in cash and got him hidden away and then killed in the past few months.

"I haven't had any coffee yet," I said, pushing my hair out of my face and shuffling to the kitchen. "Say that one more time: your accounting nerds stayed up all night and found what?"

"It's not just the motel," Dean said. "These ledgers show huge sums of money moving through three businesses: the Cherry Lane, the Food and Fix it, and the dentist's office."

"How much is huge?" I switched on the coffeemaker.

"More money than any of them would legitimately make in five years moves through there about every eight weeks."

I blinked, pouring sugar in a cup and sticking it under the spout. "That's not a small-time drug-dealing operation."

"There's nothing small-time about it, I've been assured," Dean said. "You and Ratcliff stepped into the middle of something these kinds of people would definitely see as worth killing for."

"I saw a couple of things in the file photos last night," I said. "There's not much to go on, but maybe a couple of bread crumbs. The victim from last September had a tattoo." I took my coffee to the living room and texted him a photo of the sketch I drew. "Looks like light blue ink, maybe a prison tat. There's writing I can't make out. I'm sending you a photo."

"Was it on his right shoulder, just over the shoulder blade?" he asked.

I checked the photo. "It was."

He was quiet for several beats.

"Dean? Why do you know that?"

"The writing says *custodire et ministrare*." Dean's voice sounded dull.

I sat down hard on the sofa. "To protect and serve. He was a cop."

"I'm no forensics expert, but my buddy Cody Rylan had that tattoo. He was DEA in this area for a couple of years. He got reassigned in February of last year."

"Reassigned where?" I asked as Dean said, "Who has his remains? The government should have DNA for a comparison."

"They went through Bexar County, but the ME there told me they have been cremated months ago. When he got them, they were listed as crossing casualties. Ratcliff said that he called 'the feds' and they weren't concerned," I said. "I couldn't figure out what he could've been talking about, but I caught a faint reflection in the water last night. A Customs and Border Patrol shoulder patch."

"It would make sense that he called them," he said.

"And given what the accountants found last night, it might make sense that they blew him off, too, depending on who he talked to."

I flipped through the photos. "You don't think they could all be law enforcement?" I swallowed hard.

"We don't have nearly enough to make that jump, but it's worth checking for missing officers from the units who work this area. God knows there are enough of them."

My phone buzzed with a text from Jim.

If you're still in town, come by when you get up. We need to talk.

"Can you quietly put feelers out about missing cops?" I asked Dean. "Use Ratcliff as your excuse, but don't mention the body or your other friend."

"Sure."

"The marshals have Jenny and her son?" I replied to Jim: *On my way in 10.*

"Since one thirty this morning."

"Good." I blew out a long breath. "I'm going to see the best medical examiner in the state and try to get a minute with Archie. He has friends everywhere; I don't see why border patrol would be exempt from that. Maybe if we can find out who blew off Ratcliff's concern, we'll have ourselves a real trail to follow."

24

I stopped so short when I stepped into Jim's office I probably would've fallen flat on my face if Archie hadn't stuck a hand out to steady me.

"Gentlemen." I stretched the word, my voice going up at the end almost like I was asking them something. Probably more polite than the *what the hell is going on* hovering on the back of my tongue. My hand closed around the strap on my shoulder bag.

"Come on in, McClellan," Jim said from the black leather chair behind his cluttered desk, the top invisible under teetering stacks of case files. His face had a pensive set: drawn-down brows and a worried jut to his jaw made my stomach turn a slow somersault. Jim was seldom worried about anything.

I turned my attention to Archie and a younger guy I didn't recognize to keep Jim's anxiety from rubbing off on me. Worry makes me miss details, and with lives in the balance, I couldn't afford to let even one pass without examination.

Archie shut the door behind me and slid the lock home before he took a seat on Jim's brown-and-orange plaid sofa next to yet another pile of folders and pointed me to the lone empty chair, opposite the new guy.

I lowered the bag to the floor at my feet, keeping one hand on the strap as I sat back in the chair and crossed my legs, waiting for someone to make introductions.

"Faith, this is Special Agent in Charge Kyle Miller from the ATF. Miller, Faith McClellan," Archie said.

"I didn't mean I needed you to call him down here." I swiveled my head slowly, looking at each of them in turn as I stuck out my hand and Miller leaned forward and shook it. I had just left that message a day ago.

"I was in town." Miller's voice was warm. "It's a pleasure to meet you. I'm familiar with your work."

"You were in town?"

"I run the field office in Richmond, Virginia, these days," Miller said. "But I'm here on a special assignment from Washington that exactly five people know the details of: Archie, myself, the director of field operations for the ATF, Senator Rooney, and the director of the CIA."

Jim's hand landed on his desk with a *thump*. "I don't need to be here for this." He stood.

Archie raised one hand. "On the contrary, Jim. We need your help."

Jim held Archie's gaze for nearly a full minute of flat, heavy silence before his eyes flicked to mine and he settled back into his chair. "Eighteen months," he muttered.

Miller raised a brow at Archie and me.

"He's retiring soon," I said.

"Ah." Miller steepled his long fingers under his chin, turning startlingly clear blue eyes on Jim. "I promise you and your personnel will be safe at all times, Mr. Prescott. If things go as I want them to, no one outside this room will ever know you're in this particular loop."

Jim nodded grudgingly as I leaned forward slightly in my seat, my heart rate picking up as I waited to see what Miller would say. Rooney was a three-term US senator originally from Abilene who sat so squarely in the moderate column on most hot-button issues, I was sure my sister would find his electoral success both a beacon of hope and a fascinating political science case study if she were alive. Hell, Charity might've run that guy's campaign for him. I don't trust politicians, but if I had to choose one who I could say was in it at least more for the greater good than his own ego, it'd be Rooney.

And right then I had a dead DEA agent, a missing Texas Ranger, and a witness who died in federal custody. That, even the CIA might be interested in.

But I hadn't told Archie any of that, which meant he was here because of something he heard from Jim. And if Jim called Archie about the body from the riverbed, they had an ID—and the ATF had an interest in the victim.

"Who is Ratcliff's dead guy?" I asked.

"Baxter tells me you're the best homicide detective in the state," Miller said. "I'd like to know what you've found so far before we get to that."

"Not much that makes any sense yet," I said. "We searched a suspected drug smuggler's former home and found some bones that sure look to be human." I pointed to the bag. "I brought them for Jim to examine."

"Buried?" Archie asked.

"In sand. No idea for how long." I cleared my throat. "The smuggler I mentioned has a girlfriend. Mexican national, prostitute, according to his mother, who also said she has ties to some bad elements on both sides of the border. He supposedly has a childhood friend who's a border agent and lets her cross back and forth. Possibly him, too. He drives a perfectly restored 1968 Corvette Stingray, and I found fifteen thousand in cash in a metal envelope strapped to the engine block. The last place he went before he somehow ended up maimed and then dead at the detention center was to meet a group of guys his mother suspects of unspecified illegal activity, and that was reported to a guy who sounds like the border town's answer to Don Corleone. They have money—a lot of money, according to forensic accounting—moving through three businesses in town. The numbers nerds say it's too much for a small-time operation, so we're trying to figure out how big this is and who's connected to what."

"You have a name for the wannabe Marlon Brando?" Miller pulled out a notebook and pen, his voice curious but unruffled.

"Jesus, you've been busy," Archie muttered.

"Carlos," I said. "No last name. Supposedly camps in an RV in the state park, but personnel there say he pulled up stakes a couple of weeks ago."

Miller's hand was a blur it moved across his paper so fast. "That's a lot to decipher."

"Welcome to my world," I said. "But I don't give up before finding the answer on a case." I tapped two fingers on my knee. "So I'll ask again—who is Ratcliff's dead guy from the river?"

Miller looked at Archie, who bobbed his head once.

"One of my field agents, who went dark about five weeks ago. The story is complicated, but he had been undercover on a weapons ring at the border for the better part of a year."

"You think they found out who he was?" I swallowed hard. That would explain why whoever dumped the guy didn't want him identified, but not why they didn't just plunk him in a shallow grave in Mexico instead of sinking him in the river.

"I have no idea," Miller said, rolling the pen between his fingers and letting out a frustrated sigh. "We haven't had any information from him in weeks."

"And we're sure it's the same guy?" I looked at Jim.

"All federal agents have DNA on file," he said. "We're running it now, so we'll know in a few hours for absolute certain, but that's who the implants were registered to. Archie called me before I had a chance to call you, and I mentioned it to him, and they showed up and now here we are."

"That would dovetail with the other thing I found, which is that the first victim in this chain might be a DEA agent one of our recon guys used to be friendly with." I pulled out the file and flipped to the photo. "If you look closely, you'll see a tattoo on his shoulder. Our guy says he was reassigned last February. Ratcliff found this in September."

Miller stared at the photo, muttering something I couldn't make out.

Jim put his hand out for the folder. "Where did the remains go?" he asked.

I shook my head as I passed it to him. "Bexar County as crossing casualties. Ratcliff said the feds told him they didn't have time to investigate dead immigrants in the river. I called Bachman, and he said they farmed them out to funeral homes who cremate them as indigents if they can't locate next of kin."

"What feds?" Miller asked, his tone a little sharp.

"According to one of the photos in there, Customs and Border Patrol was on at least one scene." I turned back to Jim. "Can you ID cremated remains?"

"Only in the luckiest cases," Jim said. "The heat even damages the DNA, so bone chips and teeth are often useless. And the extraction process is long and expensive."

"We are always short on time and money around here," I said.

"Indeed we are. Let me get some high-resolution scans of these photos, and I'll see if I can find anything helpful. In all my spare time."

I turned to Archie. "Why did you call Jim?"

"I was checking on you," he muttered. "I don't like you being out in the desert working without me or Graham."

"Graham is Lieutenant Commander Hardin?" Miller asked. Archie only nodded, but something in Miller's voice drew my eyes back to him. His icy blue gaze was edged with slight wrinkles. Sad wrinkles.

My heart stuttered and jumped into my throat.

"Archie." I reached for his hand.

"We don't know, Faith." He squeezed my fingers. "It's really important that you believe me when I say we don't know anything for sure right now."

I kept my eyes on Miller. "So tell me what you do know, and then tell me what you think."

Miller took a deep breath. "My office has been following a weapons trading ring for nearly three years that is suddenly bringing in mind-boggling sums of money. For a while, we thought their activity was localized in the mid-Atlantic, but we can't find a buyer who would pay the kind of money that's been moving through their accounts. My agent went undercover with an interjurisdictional unit down here, and we kept tabs on him through the Dallas office."

"And?" I knew what was coming, and my heart was going to pound right the hell through my ribs and onto Jim's threadbare brown carpet if someone didn't just say it.

"Graham's current assignment is to the same task force. He's inside the Zapata cartel. The feds had a guy who could position an officer in the room where bad things happen, and they sold Graham this idea that they could take down operations on both sides of the border." Archie's voice sounded like he was on the other end of a tunnel. I heard the rest of what he said, a few dozen placating words about how deep undercover my husband was working, and how that meant no one knew anything for sure. "All of their operations. Fentanyl that's killing kids, human trafficking, gunrunning, money laundering."

I knew exactly what kind of people they were talking about—and they were far more dangerous than anyone we'd ever dealt with. I also had a pretty good guess at what kind of bad things happened in rooms like that. Rooms my husband was currently in.

I swallowed hard. "I would know if he was dead," I whispered, remembering the increasingly heavy feeling in my heart in the days they spent searching for Charity. Days when I tried with everything in me to believe, but I knew in my bones she wasn't coming home.

I would know if Graham wasn't coming home.

"How?" I turned to Miller. "How did you get Graham embedded inside the cartel anywhere that would matter? Zapata can't be the kind of guy who picks up random strays to run his business, or he wouldn't have a business anymore."

"The task force has a guy who's been embedded for a long time. DEA, deep cover, limited contact. He's been inside for more than two years now, and Zapata quite literally trusts him with his life. They were able to use that to insert Graham as his cousin, Martin Peña, former Mexican military officer with special weapons training. Zapata is recruiting soldiers, because he's arming up for war."

Nothing anyone in that room said for the next twenty minutes fully registered or even mattered to me. Jim had a dead ATF agent in his cooler, and Dean thought one of the other bodies was a dead DEA agent, and my husband was another undercover cop in this mess. That was all I had the capacity to care about.

The Zapata cartel. What in the actual fuck could he have been thinking?

I couldn't wait to ask him, but I had to find him alive first. Which meant we had work to do. If dismantling a gun-smuggling ring and taking down a cartel was what it took to get Graham back safe and whole and breathing, so be it.

Taking a series of steadying breaths, I unzipped the bag and pulled out the bones, laying them on Jim's desk. The stricken look on his face as he met my gaze told me he would move heaven and earth to save Graham, just as I had once offered his wife a lifeline in her battle with cancer.

"Faith, he's a good cop," he began.

I raised one hand. "I know." I put the saw on Jim's desk before I stood. "Jim, that saw might be a weapon and needs to be checked accordingly. Archie, Agent Miller, we have an investigation to finish."

"Faith, if I thought for one second this assignment would be this dangerous, I wouldn't have let him take it," Archie said. "Jameson asked for my input about the task force, but I didn't know what they were into until Miller here showed up asking for my help with the gunrunning case, and by then Graham was already gone."

"If they convinced Graham they needed him, you couldn't have stopped him," I said through clenched teeth. It was true. Graham had worked a case last winter at a suburban high school, following the trail of a dealer who sold a teenager Fentanyl labeled as Dilaudid. That kid died, and three others in his neighborhood came damned close. Graham had dug deeper and deeper into locating the suppliers putting the fake pills on the street and made four solid arrests, which was probably how he wound up on the task force's radar. I sighed and put a hand on Archie's shoulder.

"You know that as well as I do." I shook my head. "I can't dwell on why he's there right now. I just want him back, whatever that takes. We have work to do."

25

Miller wadded up a gold Whataburger wrapper and shot it effortlessly into the wastebasket in the corner of the big conference room at Rangers HQ. "I miss Whataburger," he said. "The things you folks take for granted about living here..."

"They make the best milkshakes anywhere," I said, moving the straw to get the last drop out of the bottom of my cup.

"I might have to give Braum's the edge there." Miller flipped a page in the open case file as I shook my head, crossed to the whiteboard wall, and picked up a red marker. Milkshakes and burger nostalgia and building a whiteboard were what I needed to keep my head level and in the game. If I thought too much about Graham, I'd lose my ability to see anything except how much I wanted him in front of me. And getting him home safely wasn't even the only reason I couldn't afford to do that. Ratcliff's life was still very possibly in the balance here—or I was telling myself that, anyway.

"Too thick—it's not a milkshake if it needs a spoon." I kept my voice three tons lighter than it had any right to be. "I do love their peppermint ice cream, though."

Surveying the board, which had columns for the river corpse—nearly ID'd as ATF Agent Chad Godfrey—plus Timmy Dushane, Ratcliff, Doris Dushane, Sheriff Nava, Mel Jenkins, Herb Strickland, DDS, Morgan Dean, and Graham, I pulled the cap off the marker and added a column for each of the five other John Does Ratcliff had given me files on. I wrote in Cody Rylan's name with a question mark for September and just headlined the others with the month of discovery.

"You're going to run out of board." Archie ate the last two fries from his lunch and cleared the food trash from the table.

"Not as long as we're about out of suspects and dead people."

Miller raised one hand.

"We don't tend to ask permission to speak around here." I swallowed a laugh as I pointed to him.

"Sorry." He shook his head. "If I don't run an orderly bullpen, we might as well be on the floor of the New York Stock Exchange my guys are so loud. So—if that's victims and suspects, what's with the other LEOs up there?"

I pointed to the columns for Nava and Dean, making notes under each as I talked. "I can't put my finger on what makes me say I don't trust the sheriff, but my gut says something is weird there. All evidence points to some heavy criminal activity in the area, yet her jail was empty and she was idle when I went by there. Plus, Ratcliff didn't loop her into whatever he suspected with these dead bodies."

Archie leaned back in his chair. "That's what you don't like about the new recon kid—Dean. Right?"

"Dean told me he and Ratcliff exchanged old-fashioned faxes every week, updates on anything suspicious from either side."

"But the bodies weren't on there?" Miller made a note of his own. "Interesting."

"I told Dean you were in the area working a suspected body dump when I sent him out to the post to help you, and he sounded puzzled," Archie offered. "Truly puzzled."

I added that to the board, because Archie can spot a liar as well as I can.

"I like Dean. I don't get the same feeling about him that I do about the sheriff. But we have to look at everything objectively, from every angle."

"It's worth keeping one eye on what's going on with him," Archie said. "Though I think we have more likely geese to chase here."

"When was Godfrey assigned to the task force?" I asked.

"October seventeenth," Miller said. "We got regular updates from him until April, when they became sporadic. The last one arrived on May ninth."

"May ninth was the day Timmy Dushane disappeared," I said as I noted the date in both columns, drawing a line linking the numbers for good measure. I spun around, pacing the length of the board with my eyes on the carpet. There were four ground-in blobs of gum between the door and the far wall, and all had darkened to the same hazy brown patina as the rest of the carpet. Gross.

"But you said you saw Dushane at the border detention center?" Miller asked.

"I did, and he risked a beating from the guards to try to tell me something." I didn't want to think that decision had cost Timmy his life, but I did want to put maximum effort into making sure he hadn't taken the risk for nothing. "At first I thought he was trying to say something about a wheel, but I went back and searched his Corvette. Inside the dash under the steering wheel, we found the map with the location of the bones I left with Jim this morning. But then yesterday I thought I'd figured wrong and he was simply trying to warn me that someone would kill me. And a 'her' who could be really any number of women, from his mom to his girlfriend to an employee, and we have very little to go—" I stopped mid-sentence, spinning back to the chair at the far end of the table where I'd dumped my bag, digging until I came up with the little plastic evidence bag where I'd stashed the strange coins I found in Timmy's car the first time I searched it. "These were in the car's console. I thought they were coins, but they don't match any currency I could find on Google." I walked the bag down to Archie and Miller, who peered at the little silver disks from opposite sides.

"They do kind of look like pesos," Archie said. "But the kind you'd find in a museum."

"Could they be valuable?" I asked. "Part of someone's collection or something?"

Miller measured each one through the bag with a tiny tape he took from his pocket and jotted the numbers on his notepad. "Could be. My fiancée is actually really good with stuff like this—she's a prosecuting attorney in Richmond, but she spent time in Mexico and Central America when she was in college, studying archaeology before she decided to be a lawyer. Do you mind if I send her photos of these?"

"Archaeology to law?" I raised a brow. "That's quite a switch."

"She calls it Indiana Jones syndrome. She doesn't like snakes." He flashed a soft smile. "But she didn't want to teach, either. She says the law seemed like an honorable pursuit."

"Please ask for her input here." I made a go-ahead gesture with both arms. "I will take all the help we can get."

He pulled out his phone and snapped photos, then typed a long text.

"It's the middle of the day, she might be in court." He put the phone back into his pocket.

"When is the wedding?" I asked.

He blinked. "I'm sorry?"

"You said she's your fiancée."

"I did?" Miller's face went slack for a second before he put his hand to his chin.

Archie laughed. "You sure did."

Miller ran one hand through his close-cropped hair. "I better watch that before I actually manage to pop the question. I bought a ring months ago, but I haven't been able to come up with the perfect plan." He returned his attention to the whiteboard. "Anyway."

I put a hand on his arm, and he raised his blue eyes to mine.

"The moment will be perfect because you asked. Trust me."

He tapped his pen on the table and settled back in his chair. "How long have you and Hardin been married?"

I took a slow breath, turning back to the whiteboard and noting the silver disks. "Five months next Thursday."

"And he was your partner at the TCSO before you came to work for DPS?"

"Yep." I didn't want to talk about Graham. Keeping my mind on the case was helping me avoid panic. We had an officer in a dangerous deep cover situation, and we needed to get him back—that was all that could possibly matter, because I had to focus. He needed me to do my job, because not many people are as stubborn as I am. The bosses call it thorough, but really, it's rooted in the only good thing Chuck McClellan ever gave me: his nearly inhuman determination to achieve anything he set out to do. And he probably wouldn't have given it to me if he'd had a choice, narcissistic stingy prick that he is.

"And he hasn't contacted you at all? No strange messages, no emails from an address you don't know, no hang-up phone calls to your cell?"

"Graham has seldom met a rule he didn't like," I said. "He was a baseball player, college and then triple A, and he can still recite even the most obscure rules for the sport on command. He follows procedure. If they said no contact, he won't reach out to me or anyone else."

"I see."

Another deep breath. I scanned the board.

"I'd like to know what else has been going on in that area the past few months," Miller said.

I turned to Archie. "Do you know if HQ would have those reports Dean said he trades with Ratcliff on file?" I asked.

"When I worked down there many years ago, everything came here in hard copy once a month," he said. "I assume there's still some mechanism for that—it's standard procedure. They'd be in the records room—that's all sorted by company and then unit."

I led the way down the hall and around the corner to the maze of filing cabinets. "I'd like to see what he noted the week of May ninth in particular," I said, reading the labels on the drawers until I found the one I wanted.

"Me too," Miller said. "Godfrey was a good man."

I found the folder as my phone buzzed. An Austin number I didn't recognize topped the screen.

"McClellan." I pinched it between my ear and my shoulder, my hand on the file cabinet.

"Hi, this is Noah Saunders, from forensic art?"

"Oh, sure," I began. Before I could say that Jim had ID'd the body, he plunged on.

"I got a face ID match on the reconstruction you asked for. I'm no detective, but it's not a stretch to see why it was so damaged—the hit came up in the FBI's Most Wanted files."

I glanced at Miller and stepped away from him and Archie.

"And what was that?"

"According to this, your John Doe is Ferdinand Carlos Zapata, better known as Freddie Z, the youngest son of Emilio Zapata."

"The head of the largest drug cartel in Mexico," I finished for him, not missing that the middle name he gave matched the drug dealer Jenny feared.

"Yes, ma'am. I'm writing up the report now and will send it over to you when it's done, but I wanted to let you know right away."

"Thank you, Saunders."

I ended the call and slid the phone back into my pocket, my thoughts racing as I walked back to the filing cabinet.

"We're going to need that DNA match," I said, pulling the folder of May reports from D Company and flipping it open. "Our forensic artist says his facial reconstruction IDs the victim you say is your Agent Godfrey as Emilio Zapata's son, Ferdinand. He matched his facial reconstruction with the FBI's Most Wanted files."

Miller shut the door and leaned against it, letting his head fall back.

"The DNA will match," he said. "Because Chad Godfrey and Freddie Z are the same person."

Archie whirled in Miller's direction so fast he wrenched his bad knee and winced. "And this is something you didn't think we needed to know before?"

"I didn't know Faith had asked for a facial reconstruction, and my orders were to keep this information on a need-to-know basis. Orders aside, I didn't really think anyone needed to know that her husband is sitting in the middle of what's going to be the biggest cartel war in thirty years if Zapata gets wind that his son is dead before we get our people out of there. Both camps have enough weapons to arm a medium-sized nation."

I shook my head. "Not anymore. Mexico has tightened their gun laws considerably in recent years to stop that from happening." I furrowed my brow. "You're ATF. How come I know that and you don't?"

"Because it was only true for about six months," Miller said. "My smuggling case isn't about guns coming here from Mexico. It's about guns going to the cartels from here. Freddie knew the principal players in several cartels, and he was worried about his family. He was gathering intel that would help us take down the big fish—on both sides of the border. He reasoned that his father was better off in a prison where his name would buy him favor than dead, and he could save his mother and sisters."

"And now he's dead, and my husband is stuck behind enemy lines?" I could hear my voice climbing half an octave with every word, but I couldn't stop it. "Don't you people have some sort of an extraction team for situations like this?"

"Only in the movies," Miller said. "I'm assured that Hardin was briefed on the risks before he went in."

I paced. My skin felt three sizes too small, and I wasn't at all sure how much longer I could hold it together. I loved Graham with the fire of ten thousand suns. And I had never wanted to both hug someone and strangle them so badly at the same time.

But I could worry about how he could have taken such a risk later, when he was home.

What we needed was a plan for getting him back, and Miller's words had started a clock ticking—once Emilio Zapata found out his son was dead, no matter what Freddie had been up to, he would start a war. Not just with the Delgado cartel, but with the US government. And being the new guy would probably get Graham killed, no matter how convincing his cover.

26

"The guys that tore up the motel," I said, standing over the conference room table and tapping Ratcliff's report from May 12th. "They were camping in the desert on the night of May ninth. Timmy might have gone out there with them. There was a photo in Ratcliff's office of his Corvette pulled up at their campsite." I rifled through the reports, looking for other mentions of that crew. The May 9th entry was the first one, and they had been back in June, again in mid-July, and just last week.

"You said four young men in a pickup?" Archie asked, looking up from the folder with Dean's report digests, which was thicker. His unit was huge compared to Ratcliff's one-man throwback outpost, and they covered more ground, so the difference in incident volume was logical.

"You see something?" I dropped the folder in my hand and rounded the end of the long table to peer over his shoulder.

He pointed to the officer's narrative. "The recon team cited a group of four guys on May eleventh for poaching."

"Poaching?" Miller looked up from his laptop, where he'd been searching classified federal channels for anything that might help us get Graham out of Mexico; the only sounds from his corner for nearly an hour were keys clicking and the occasional frustrated sigh. "Is it still actually illegal to hunt anything here?"

"Lynx and ocelots, this says," I read. "The fur sells for a fortune, but the cats are endangered."

"And cute," Archie said. "Don't forget cute. People like to protect the cute animals."

Miller blinked and pushed the laptop back. "I'm sorry. I was only half listening to most of that. There was a group of hunters in the same area where Timmy Dushane, who we think was tangled up with some sort of unspecified bad element, and my agent Chad Godfrey—"

"AKA Freddie Z," I interjected. "I'm going to need the whole story on how that came to be at some point."

"Deal. But let's get your husband back and catch the bad guys first?"

I smiled softly at his unthinking prioritization of Graham's safety. I liked Agent Kyle Miller, with a vehemence I don't feel for many people right off the bat.

"Anyway—there was a group of men who aren't local in the area when both men disappeared?"

"That's what I've been told." I opened my own laptop, searching the recon unit's full reports for May 11th.

"So if these guys didn't have something to do with that, they might have seen something," Archie said.

"And God bless Morgan Dean and his unit, and the stupidity of one of those poachers." I turned the computer screen around. "Because someone swung at a cop and got arrested, and Dean's officers fingerprinted the lot of them and included scans of their IDs in the arrest report."

"Outstanding." Miller stood. "I have three federal agencies, including one most people don't even know exists, gathering any scrap of intel that might help Hardin."

"Thank you," I said, my eyes back on my screen. "Three of these addresses are in San Marcos, but one of them is here in Austin." I reread the street name and whistled. "A really sketchy part of Austin, but it's not far."

"I'll drive," Miller said, closing his computer and pulling out his keys.

As I walked out the door he held open into the noisy bullpen, he put a hand on my arm and spoke under his breath. "We won't lose him," he said. "You have my word."

And though I had only known him half a day and it made zero sense, I believed him.

"Oof," Miller said, rolling the car to a stop outside a building with more plywood and spray paint than actual brick holding the exterior together. "Do we think anyone actually lives here?"

"I don't know that I've seen worse, but I've probably seen just as bad. And there was a dead chicken in the hallway and a guy getting eaten by rats in a bathtub." I arched one eyebrow. "Who wants to go in first?"

"This isn't supposed to be the time when 'ladies first' applies, right?" Archie asked.

Miller looked a little pale as he put his sedan in park. "The rat guy was dead, right?"

I laughed. "Very. And this lady never minds being first. Come on, gentlemen."

We approached the front of the building in a fan formation, three sets of eyes scanning the area, searching every shadow, our stride a practiced sort of unconcerned. The car stuck out in this neighborhood, and our clothes probably did, too, but the worst thing a cop can do in a rough area is look even slightly concerned, never mind intimidated. Any passersby would have thought we frequented the place—it's a necessary safety function in places where the crime rate exceeds the graduation percentage at the local high school.

The door was behind a wrought iron screen with a brass knob, no locks or buzzers in sight.

I pulled the heavy screen back, flinching when it wobbled on its hinges but recovering quickly by reaching for the door.

Stale, rancid air heated my skin as the door opened and I realized the exterior was missing a crucial Texas element—I didn't see a single air conditioner. In heat this brutal, they aren't a luxury. People die without them every summer.

"Jesus. Maybe I hope nobody lives here." Miller raised one arm and crooked an elbow over his nose and mouth.

"No kidding," Archie said.

"We're looking for apartment three, which I bet is up those stairs." I waved in the direction of a narrow, graffiti-tagged set of steps that ascended into darkness, directly across from the door.

Halfway to the top, I noticed the window above me wasn't broken. It was boarded over, either to protect it from being broken or to keep the sun out.

"This guy's name isn't a riff on Dracula, right?" Miller must have noticed the same thing about the window.

"Faber," I said. "Julian Faber."

"Not here," a voice said from the darkness. A high-pitched giggle followed. "Gone, kaput, goodbye."

I jogged up the rest of the steps, a couple of them feeling dangerously squishy under my boots. Behind me, I heard two soft clicks as Archie and Miller unsnapped the safety straps on their holsters. "Watch the steps, a couple of them feel rotten," I said.

It was hotter in the hallway upstairs than it had been in the riverbed on Sunday, so I shouldn't have been surprised that the young woman just inside the door with the crooked, once-brass 3 on it was stark naked.

Three fans that were all probably older than she was hummed from different angles, every one pointed at her as she reclined against a dingy pillow, her bare ass resting on a faded blanket with a Texas Rangers baseball logo on it. Her glassy eyes said she was on something, but I didn't see evidence of what anywhere near her.

One window on the far wall was boarded up from the outside, though the glass was intact, just like the one in the hallway, but this one was open slightly. I wasn't sure that was helping the heat, and it definitely wasn't helping the smell: rotting food, sweat, and body odor combined for a retch-worthy stench that had me taking shallow breaths, unable to decide if it was worse when I breathed through my nose or my mouth.

The kind of giant cockroach my granny used to call a water bug scuttled out from under the edge of the blanket, and I stepped backward to avoid its path. Naked McJunkie, who was sitting on said blanket, didn't seem to notice.

I heard Archie and Miller in the hallway and stuck a hand out the door, holding up one finger. It was awkward enough for me to stand there, and I didn't need their help. Their footsteps stopped just shy of the door.

"Where did Julian go?" I asked.

Her head lolled to one side and back, like a damaged doll, her glassy eyes sliding my direction. "You're a cop," she said.

"I am."

"Is JJ in trouble?" She puckered her pale, cracked lips and giggled again. "I—"

"He ought be," she said before I could try to hedge that. "Rat bastard. You should check out the guns back there." She waved a limp hand in the direction of a short hallway. "How the hell can you call hunting a sport when you're literally fucking blowing the poor little things up? I asked him that." She touched her eye, where I couldn't tell if the bluish tinge around the socket was bruising or smeared makeup. "He smacked the shit out of me and said it's because he's smarter than the animals. Then he called me a bitch. You know, like a dog. An animal. He's not smarter than me on his best day." She tried to sit up, seeming to notice for the first time that she wasn't wearing anything.

"Holy shit," she said, covering herself the best she could with her hands. "You should've said something."

"I couldn't find the right words," I said, averting my eyes as she got unsteadily to her feet, one hand on the wall.

"'Chickadee, do you realize you're naked' would've been fine," she said, her eyes on the floor. I heard a snort followed by a cough from the hallway, and a couple of deep breaths later, she stumbled to a cardboard box in the corner and retrieved a T-shirt that swallowed her gaunt frame from shoulder to knee.

"There more cops out there?" She leaned against the wall in front of a blue-and-white oscillating fan and folded her arms across her chest.

"We tend to travel in groups," I said.

"Sure. I used to do that, too. Before JJ took off."

"Do you know where he went?" I asked.

"He said he was going hunting," she said. "Him and his boys went out to the desert to hunt these poor kitty-cat things. Been doing it all year." She waved a hand toward a countertop with a sink and a hot plate that probably passed for a kitchen around here. "That's why it stinks in here. They cleaned the damned things here, and he didn't take the trash out before he left again." She raised her arms, and I tried to avoid gasping. I could've closed my fingers around her bicep with overlap. "Like I could haul a hundred pounds outside even if I wanted to touch it. Which I don't."

That brought Miller around the doorframe.

"Do you mind if I take care of that for you, miss?"

Her eyes went wide as she looked up to meet his clear blue gaze, tugging on the T-shirt and smoothing her hair down. "I, uh...no, that would be nice, go ahead."

He smiled, and her cheeks flushed. "Thanks...?" He held the smile, waiting for her to offer her name.

I tried not to roll my eyes. Not like I haven't used my fairly wide arsenal of pageant smiles to butter up informants more times than I can count.

"Mikey," she said. "Short for MichaelAnn." She shuffled her feet. "My dad wanted a boy. Never let me forget it." A melancholy crept through the words that made me sadder for her than I'd been for anyone in a while.

"Nice to meet you, Mikey. I'm Kyle." He shot her one more grin before he went to the garbage can, using his arm to cover his nose and mouth again. Archie stepped inside and waved to Mikey before he hurried to help Miller with the animal remains in the open trash can. I stepped closer to her.

"I'm Faith," I said.

"That's a nice name." She plucked at the edge of the shirtsleeve with one hand.

"JJ was selling the fur from these cats, right?" I said. "Has he ever been gone this long on a hunting trip?"

"He just got back," she said. "Then he left again straight off, and he took a bunch of heavy artillery with him, too." She waved at the hallway again. "Like I said, I asked him how he was going to sell fur if he was blowing them up, and he smacked me. I didn't want to think about him hitting me, so I got wasted. I trusted him, but he's a rat bastard. They're all rat bastards."

Oh, boy.

"Can you show me the guns?" I asked.

The crinkling of the trash bag Miller was closing in the kitchen paused, and I put one hand behind my back where he could see it, turning my thumb up.

"Sure," Mikey said, stepping toward the short hallway and pointing to a door straight at the end. "Most of them are in there, but the bigger things are here." She turned and pulled open a set of louvered bifold doors that made up most of one wall in the hallway. "There used to be a washing machine in here, but JJ sold it. He said I can schlep clothes to the laundromat down the block and he needed the space for his business."

Pulling a chain overhead lit a bare bulb screwed into the ceiling of the little laundry closet, which was stacked front to back with large weapons. My eyes went wide as I counted a dozen .458 Winchester Model 70s, half that many two-bore rifles, a couple of what looked like .50-caliber rifles, and... "Are those..." My eyes stuck on the large, camo-green canister-style weapons in the corner. I counted eight of them.

"Surface-to-air rocket launchers?" Miller said from behind my shoulder. "They are, in fact."

"One shot from one of those can blow up a whole car," Mikey said, not appearing to mind Miller's presence in the least. "I've seen it."

Miller said he was looking for weapons traffickers—sure seemed like we'd found some. Which meant maybe we were on the right track to finding Ratcliff. And Graham.

Archie came back through the door and stopped short just outside the hallway when he got a look inside the closet Miller was efficiently inventorying under his breath. He didn't want to say too much with Mikey standing there, which I understood. Dealing with witnesses is tricky business, especially when they're involved with a suspect. Any little thing could shut her right up, so he focused on the guns, leaving the interview disguised as small talk to me.

I opened the door on the opposite wall, guessing correctly that it must lead to the bathroom. If you could call what I saw a bathroom—there was more rust and calcium buildup in that room than porcelain. Which gave me an idea.

Mikey here was an occupant of this residence. She was well within her rights to grant us permission to take it apart board by dingy board. She was also a sad young woman who'd been mistreated more often than not, from what she'd said. And we wouldn't have to worry about what we found or what it made her think if she wasn't there.

"Mikey, how would you like a swim in a nice clean pool, a bubble bath, and some clean clothes you don't have to schlep to the laundromat?" I asked. "Maybe a bed with air conditioning for the night?" I glanced at Archie over the top of her head, and he nodded and took a step backward. The Rangers have certain hotels that always make rooms available upon request for just this kind of situation. He just needed to find one that had everything I'd just promised her.

Mikey's whole face lit up, the skin stretching tight over her bones when she smiled. "That would be real nice," she said. "But you don't have to do that. Y'all can take whatever you need. I'm not sure what JJ and the boys are into, but I get the feeling it's something real bad. I don't think they're just hunting cats."

"Do you know what they are hunting?" I asked.

"He don't say much." She dragged her toe along a crack in the linoleum, making me unreasonably anxious that she was about to cut herself. "But when he forgets I'm listening or thinks I'm asleep, I hear stuff. He keeps me in this shithole apartment while he runs around with his buddies, because they can do what they want here, nobody's going to call the cops, and even if someone did, what cop is coming here?" She bit her lip. "Except you, I mean. What made you come here, anyway? Most cops don't even stop at stop signs driving through here."

"We're trying to save someone's life," I said. It was true, and the simplest way to put it.

Her eyes flew so wide her lashes touched her eyebrows. "JJ. I mean, you don't think he'd kill a person, do you?" Her voice had gone up a full octave by the end of the question.

"I have no idea." I honestly didn't. "All I can tell you so far is that we have a colleague who suspects JJ and his friends were into something illegal. Something more than poaching. I came here to find out how well he knows a man named Timmy Dushane, whose parents own a motel in Terrell County."

She wrinkled her forehead. "Did JJ and the boys get kicked out of there?"

I watched Miller count plastic cases of large-caliber ammunition out of the corner of my eye. "Yes, I understand that they did."

"He was real pissed at the people there," Mikey said, drawing my full attention back to her. "He said they stole something important from him."

"Like from his room?" I asked, thinking about all those plastic bins in the barn and Ashton's comment about Doris seizing property.

"I don't think so," Mikey said. "I got the idea it was like a business deal. You know, like on *Dynasty*?"

"When did that happen, do you remember?" I wanted a notebook more than I wanted my next breath, but I was afraid of spooking her silent if I took one out. My memory would have to do.

Archie reappeared. "The Sheraton at Four Points South," he said. "I'll send the key to your phone."

Mikey turned her head freakishly far around to look at him. "Me? I get to go to a hotel? With a pool?" Her earlier glassy eyes and slur were completely gone. Adrenaline is the best buzzkill there is.

"Do you want to pack anything?"

"How long can I stay?" Something in her voice tugged at my heart.

"Until tomorrow for sure, and then we'll see, depending on what we find," I said. "Is it okay with you if the guys continue to look around here and I come back after I get you settled?"

"Look away. Try under the floorboards in the bedroom closet, too. I swear he hides shit there."

Archie didn't have to be told twice. He pointed at the closed door and said, "Bedroom?" Then disappeared inside when she nodded.

She opened the bathroom door. "I'll be back before you can miss me," she said as she closed it behind her.

I turned back to Miller. "Anything helpful there?" I whispered.

"Oh, yeah." He was crouched on the floor, opening the ammunition boxes. "I could've looked for this guy for a year and not ended up here. Baxter was right about you."

"This was blind luck," I said. "I didn't come here because I thought this jackass was some kind of small-time arms dealer."

"Small?" Miller tapped one of the Winchester .458s and gestured to the rocket launchers.

"Okay, medium-time arms dealer," I said. "I was just looking for something on the motel owner's son." Something that might lead us to Graham. Or Ratcliff. Or both of them, in a perfect world.

"No, when he said you're his lucky charm," Miller said. "He said since the first day he met you, his life has been better because you're part of it. And that good things happen when you're around." He stood and opened his hands in the direction of the closet. "This is a very, very good thing for me."

"Seems like it's a good thing for whoever or whatever might not get killed with this stuff." I brushed one finger along the barrel of a two-bore. "You said your gunrunners are arming the cartels, right? Who the fuck needs anything close to this? It's not like people are hunting elephants in the Mexican desert."

"No, they're not." Miller pointed to the rocket launchers. "I think they're going to war. I just can't quite tell if it's with each other, their own government, or us. I think the answer to that may change by the week."

I opened my mouth to answer that, but before I could find words, both of the doors opened simultaneously.

"Miller, you're going to want—" Archie began.

"Is this okay?" Mikey asked.

Miller handed me his car keys as he moved past me to follow Archie. I turned to look at Mikey as they disappeared into the dark bedroom. She had smoothed her hair back into a neat ponytail and put on what looked like a pink bikini under a sarong she topped with a smaller T-shirt that came at least closer to fitting her. Everything was faded but in otherwise good shape.

"You look adorable," I said. "Ready to go?"

She held up a small bag. "I have a dress too. I don't want to forget anything."

"Are there any medications you take every day?"

"Not that I'm supposed to."

I gestured an "after you" and let her lead the way back to the street.

Pushing the button to unlock Miller's sedan, I was caught completely off guard when Mikey pulled a Ruger semiautomatic from the small satchel she carried and jammed the muzzle into my ribs.

27

Trophies belong to winners. The gold cup in the glass case. The buck's head mounted on the wall. The alligator skin, tanned and crafted into boots.

Survival and triumph live in the arena of the strongest. All hunters keep mementos of their victories.

The executioner built his own trophy case.

Even if he's the only person who's ever seen it.

Until tonight.

In a dark room, a glass freezer sits in a cool white spotlight. Five heads, eyes open, faces slack, stare out at nothing.

He sits in the white leather chair opposite the freezer and studies each face, contemplating his options.

His associates are getting greedy. Expanding operations.

Threatening his security.

He needs a more direct message.

A simple firearm will be a far more effective tool.

He runs his fingers over the cool metal of the M9 resting in the holster at his hip. Reliable, quick, and clean.

There is risk in this one. He matters more than any of the trophies in the case.

People will miss him.

People have to miss him before they find him.

Just as he needs to see the trophies before he dies. He needs to understand what he's a part of—what he's always been a part of.

The bell chimes.

The executioner stands. Opens the door. Shows the target into the cool, dark trophy room.

Shock twists an otherwise attractive face, his hands coming up to block the tableau even as he leans into it, peering through the glass.

"Surely they're not real," he says to no one in particular.

Wait.

Recognition dawns when his eyes reach the last trophy.

He coughs. Thinking about being sick, then thinking better of it. It takes a full thirty seconds for him to realize there could only be one reason he's here.

The bullet stops him before he can take even one step toward the door.

One shot. One little hole in the center of his forehead.

One full-size trophy crumpled on a black tarp.

Clean. Quiet.

The executioner rolls up the tarp and resumes his seat to wait.

All his training has taught him that messages like this one are best delivered while the rest of the world is sleeping.

28

"Give me those keys, and get in the car," Mikey growled in a voice I wouldn't have believed belonged to her just seconds before.

I let out a slow sigh, raising my hands. "You don't want to do this," I said as she unsnapped the holster strap under my arm and yanked my weapon out of it.

She laughed. "You think you know shit about what I want? Surviving is pretty much all I think about from day to day, but you're fixing to help me change that."

She jabbed me with her gun again. "Behave yourself, Faith. Like I said, cops don't even stop at lights around here. You'll bleed out on this sidewalk in broad daylight, and people will just step over you."

She was forgetting the two officers upstairs. Or was she?

My eyes went wide as I reached slowly for the door handle and scanned the street. Quiet.

She kept her gun on me as she rounded the car. I ducked quickly into the passenger seat, pulling my phone from my pocket as I sat and hitting the lock button on the door with my other hand.

Get out of there now, I texted Archie. *She's got a gun on me.*

Mikey yanked on the door handle and tapped the window with one gun as she fumbled with the other one and Miller's keys. I slid the phone back into my pocket.

"You stupid bitch," she snarled as she yanked the door open. "I could kill you."

"What?" I blinked, keeping my face blank.

"You think you're cute with the door? I have the fucking keys, stupid."

"I didn't do anything."

She waved her gun as she stuffed mine into the door pocket on the driver's side but didn't say anything else.

I stared calmly back. If she really wanted to shoot me, she'd have done it already. She seemed to think delivering me to someone would get her a reward of some sort. And if it meant I might get closer to figuring this shit out and getting my husband back, I was game to play along. Archie could track my phone, and the chances there wasn't a LoJack on Miller's government vehicle were pretty small.

I just needed them to hold at a distance until I figured out enough to know if this road would lead to Graham. Archie would know that—and Archie knew I could take care of myself, even if he usually worried anyway.

Mikey started the car and banged the gun on the steering wheel when her feet didn't reach the pedals. I flinched and threw my hands up. Maybe I should've qualified "she wouldn't shoot me" with "on purpose" when I decided to go with her. She wasn't the brightest bulb, though I had to give her points for a convincing performance upstairs. Right then she had me wondering how she came up with the idea to bait us so quickly. Like she said, cops didn't come to this neighborhood. It wasn't like she was waiting for us.

My head snapped up as she turned onto Riverside Drive.

Was she?

I liked Miller. But this week, I seemed to be surrounded by people I liked but wasn't sure I could trust. Had I seen him use his phone between headquarters and the stench-infused building where we found Mikey half-ass guarding her boyfriend's arsenal?

Not that I remembered. Then again, Mikey didn't know I'd used mine after she pulled a gun on me.

Focus, Faith. Breathe. In for five, hold for three, out for four. I counted through three cycles, my pulse slowing a bit with each. Whatever she was up to, I'd know soon enough.

Mikey picked up Highway 1 and drove straight out of town. The long stretch of flat road surrounded by flatter fields, corn withering in the summer heat in some, bright green and red combines clear-cutting hay for baling in others, would have been hypnotizing on any other day.

On this one, I was too busy making contingency plans for staying alive to notice much of anything but a golden-green blur.

No one had spoken since the car pulled away from the curb. Mikey had driven the entire way with her left hand, her right keeping the Ruger trained in my general direction. She hadn't realized that I was sitting there because I wanted to know where we were going, not because her twiggy little arm was pointing a weapon at me. That was probably better for me, though.

Ahead on the left, I spotted a cluster of metal buildings, maybe a hundred yards off the road. She slowed and turned into a long dirt drive, guiding the car through an open gate and stopping outside the largest building, which had both a garage bay door and a regular door facing the front.

"Let's go say hello." She swung the Ruger upward, and I opened my door to show compliance with her order mostly because I was curious, but partly so she wouldn't fire the damned thing on accident.

She knocked on the red metal door and stepped back, turning so whoever opened it would be sure to notice she was holding me at gunpoint.

The door swung inward to reveal a lanky young man with tousled hair caught back from his face by a blue bandana. He squinted into the sun, his eyes flicking up Mikey's left side and down her right, barely pausing at the gun or at what I hoped was an appropriately distressed look on my face.

"What do you want?" He hit the "you" hard, but with a tone that made it sound like he was referring more to something he stepped in than a person.

"You said there was a cop poking around, asking questions," Mikey barreled ahead excitedly, ignoring the slight or missing it altogether. "Here she is. She came by my place looking for you, and I tricked her into leaving alone."

The beaming smile on her face radiated so much pride, I almost felt bad for her.

The guy's face stretched from an expression of disdain to one of alarm as he shoved us both aside and stepped out, pulling the door shut behind him. "Are you out of your damn mind? Why would you bring a cop here? You didn't blindfold her or anything. Dammit, Mikey, do you have a brain at all?"

He raised a hand like he was going to hit her, and she ducked, her hands going to cover her face.

"I wouldn't do that, JJ." I guessed on the name, and admittedly didn't look my most threatening, but I kept my tone hard and authoritative, and he paused, turning an icy smile my way.

"Nobody asked you, darlin'. In case you haven't noticed, you're in no position to be calling any kind of shots."

Mikey let her arms down slowly, ducking her head the way Archie's dog tucks his tail when he's in trouble.

I was annoyed with her, sure, but in that moment, I couldn't feel much but pity for a young woman whose life had somehow landed in a place where she let this guy treat her like an abused animal and somehow kept trying to win his approval.

"That may be true right now, but you hit her and I'll make you regret it," I said. "That's a promise. And I keep my promises."

Mikey's eyes widened and landed on me, but she didn't speak.

JJ looked me up and down and cocked his head to one side before he shrugged. "Have it your way, killjoy. I don't have to hit her to keep her in line anymore."

Mikey looked puzzled, followed quickly by angry. Not that he noticed.

Grabbing my arm and putting his hand out for her gun, he drew us inside. A lone portable air conditioner worked overtime, rattling and whistling, to keep the temperature barely tolerable.

My eyes adjusted quickly to the dim light from a few high windows and some lamps scattered around the space. The walls were lined with wooden crates stamped with stenciled black letters identifying a dozen different kinds of weapons, some of them with manufacturers and some without. And those were just the ones I could see.

"Quite an inventory," I said. "Where'd you get them?"

"I'm not that stupid, sweetheart," he said. "None of your business."

"But you're selling them south of the border. Because the cartels can't get the weapons they want in-country anymore thanks to stricter laws there," I said.

"Very good. How'd you figure that out?"

"I have more to offer than just a pretty face," I said.

"She had all kinds of questions about your hunting trips," Mikey said. "I told you, she's the cop you were talking about."

"She's not. We've had that guy for days now." JJ waved a dismissive "shut up" hand at her, keeping his eyes on me. "So who are you?"

Ratcliff. I kept my face flat with a little effort. "I'm interested in who you're dealing with south of the border," I said.

JJ laughed, falling silent as he watched my face stay serious. "Why's that?"

I went with the most innocuous reason. "I'm looking for some information in a missing persons case in Terrell County. Timmy Dushane, his parents own a motel," I said.

"His mother owns the motel," JJ said. "The old man has been dead for almost a year. She just ain't telling anyone."

I blinked, remembering Dean's musing about that very thing.

"Why would she keep that a secret?"

"The government keeps sending social security checks if they don't know he croaked," JJ said. "To hear Timmy tell it, she put his bones in a hole in the backyard, and she sits out there and talks to him late at night sometimes. We saw her wandering around in a nightgown in the middle of the night back when we stayed there. She flipped her shit and threw us out. Wouldn't let us get our stuff, either. My favorite shirt was in that room."

"So you know Timmy?"

"He's buddies with Scott," JJ said. "Seemed like a decent dude, but a little Norman Bates around the edges with mommy dearest out there, you know?"

JJ paused, stuffed his hands in his pockets, and shook his head. "Why am I telling you any of this?"

"Because you don't care whether or not I find Timmy Dushane," I said. "He's not part of your operation."

"Or maybe because you're not making it out of this building breathing, so I figure the least I can do is answer your last questions." JJ folded his arms across his chest and leaned his weight on his back foot.

"Whatever you need to tell yourself." I pulled out my best Ice Queen Ruth McClellan voice and held his gaze.

He laughed again. "You got some guts, Barbie, I'll give you that. It'll be fun to get a look at them."

"But you have plenty of time for that. Indulge me—tell me about Scott."

"He's a border patrol guard. Knows the weak spots, especially with the river so low. Keeps his command busy with the streams of migrants coming north, makes it easy for us to pop south when we need to."

"For a price." I didn't bother to inflect a question on that.

"Sure. Gotta pay a man for his work."

I wondered for a beat if any of them realized how dangerous it was to get tangled up with two of the most volatile cartel leaders in modern history. Common knowledge had it that Zapata was convinced everyone from his wife to the cook was trying to kill him at any given moment. Though I supposed Miller's revelation about Freddie lent some credence to the idea that the old man wasn't so crazy after all.

The safety of JJ and his crew wasn't my problem, though. I wanted to ask him about Ratcliff so badly the back of my throat burned, but I had to time that right. Keep him talking. Get him comfortable. Let him be cocky and think he was running the show. I hadn't seen or heard another soul since we arrived, and the space was one big open room. If the fight was me against these two, I liked my odds, even with Mikey's Ruger tucked into the waistband of JJ's cutoff denim shorts.

"Do you know anything about Timmy's girlfriend?" I kept my tone casual, letting him think Mikey was wrong and I wasn't interested in him or what he was doing.

"I know Timmy thinks this Mexican whore, Lucia, is the love of his life. Follows her around like a puppy dog."

"You ever seen her anywhere else?"

JJ pointed his index finger at me. "You are something, you know? It's like talking to Sherlock Holmes, man. Yeah, she's one of Freddie Z's chicks. I think they were using Timmy's car to run dope across the border, on account of Timmy being friends with Scott."

"Scott doesn't let drugs come across the border? Do the Zapatas not pay well enough?"

JJ rolled his eyes. "For a smart chick, you got this mixed up. Sherlock would have it. Where's your Watson?"

Somewhere in Mexico, I thought. *That's what I'm trying to find out.* I couldn't say that, though.

I paused for a minute, letting everything he'd said roll around in my head. He watched me like I was on a stage, waiting for the next big reveal. It was unsettling.

"So you like to read, huh?" I asked, trying to distract him.

"No?" His brow furrowed. "You think I'd be here, doing this shit, if I liked to read? My sister, she was real good at school. She's an accountant up in Dallas. Nice boring life with a nice boring doctor husband and a really fucking nice house." His tone turned a little bitter toward the last, his eyes going to the floor. "I like the movies. Ironman is bad ass in everything."

I had to go all the way back to Coach Richardson smuggling painkillers out of Mexico to figure out what JJ was alluding to.

"The guards don't let the cartels make money on this side of the border if they can help it," I said slowly, the words tumbling out almost as the thought formed. "But you selling killing machines to the cartels is somehow justifiable. In terms of them looking the other way."

"Ding-ding-ding, tell her what she's won, Mikey!" JJ clapped.

Mikey looked up—at some point she'd taken a seat on the floor, and I hadn't noticed.

"What the fuck are you on about, JJ?" she asked.

His smile vanished as he stepped her way and drew one foot back.

"What does Timmy have to do with any of this, then?" I blurted, drawing his attention back to me. His foot went to the floor.

"Timmy? Not a goddamn thing. He's just a stooge who thinks that chick is going to marry his stupid redneck ass." JJ shook his head at me and delivered a swift kick to Mikey's side.

"I warned you, JJ." I spun and whipped one leg up, delivering a high, hard kick to his sternum.

He stumbled back, fumbling with his pants for the gun.

Mikey, tears streaming and one hand on her ribs, shot to her feet. I stuck an arm out to ward her off, but she didn't go for me, she hurled herself at JJ. "You rat bastard!" she screamed. "I have had just about enough of you hitting me!"

Good for her.

I watched for a split second as she grabbed his wrist with both hands. He pulled away from her and up on the gun at the same time.

The shot was deafening, echoing off the metal walls.

JJ screamed—a high, piercing shriek that might have been louder than the shot itself. Blood spurted. From behind his zipper.

Oh. My.

29

JJ and Mikey hit the floor hard enough for me to hear a crack that sounded an awful lot like a bone breaking. Mikey's turn to scream.

Oh, for Pete's sake.

"You shot me in the dick, you crazy bitch!" JJ howled when he could manage words. The dark stain on the front of his shorts reached the hem alarmingly quickly, blood running down his thighs and dripping onto the floor.

"You broke my arm, you rat bastard," she sobbed. "And I think my ribs, too. I'm turning your ass in this time, I mean it." She struggled to sit up and turned her blotchy face up to meet my gaze. "Officer, I want you to arrest him."

I blinked at her, trying not to laugh because she was flat-ass serious.

"I don't think he's a risk at the moment." I pulled my phone from my back pocket and dialed 911, reeling off my badge number and requesting medical assistance.

"Where are you?" the dispatcher asked. "The computer is having trouble triangulating your location."

Of course it was. "In a metal building in the middle of nowhere off FM 150. I saw a Gulf station a few miles back."

"It's going to be a little bit," she said. "I think I've got it on the satellite, but the nearest ambulance is twenty miles from you."

"Hurry. I think the bullet might have nicked an artery."

Dammit. I hung up and dropped to my knees next to JJ, whose eyes were trying to close.

"Don't you die on me, you prick, I'm not going to prison over you." Mikey leaned over him and brushed his hair back from his brow with her good hand as I unfastened my belt and pulled it free of the loops on my jeans, marveling at their choice of pet names for each other.

It's not often I run across people with a more dysfunctional relationship than my parents had.

I tried lifting his leg, and the blood flow increased. "Dammit." I poked Mikey. "Give me your shirt."

She took it off and handed it over, and I waved for her to come closer, feeling a little bad as she winced scooting toward me.

Taking hold of JJ's shorts on either side of the inseam, I pulled with everything I had and felt the thread give. Three hard yanks later, I had a better view of the entry wound. I couldn't say for sure about any other bits of him because I was very definitely not looking, but whatever else the bullet hit, it went into his thigh about an inch below his hip socket, at an angle. I stuffed a chunk of Mikey's shirt into the wound and leaned all my weight on it. He woke up enough to scream. I didn't bother to apologize, turning to Mikey and looking her up and down. I really could see every bone. I wasn't sure she was heavy enough to hold the pressure on the wound.

"Here." I nodded to the cloth. "Put your knee right square in the middle of this, and lean on it as hard as you can if you want him to live."

"I am not going to prison over his sorry ass." She gritted her teeth and did as I told her. I watched the cloth and didn't see an increase in the flow of blood.

"Just like that." I moved quickly to maneuver the belt under his leg and wrapped it along the edge of his pelvis, following the angle where his thigh met his hip bone and getting to my knees to yank up on it, fastening it as tight as I could.

I counted to thirty. "Ease up," I said.

Mikey rolled her knee off JJ's leg, whimpering as she moved.

I watched the cloth for a splash of red, seeing none. I lifted the edge gently, blowing out a long breath when I saw the blood had been reduced to a trickle.

"Now what?" Mikey asked. "Are you going to arrest him?"

"There will be time for that," I said. "He's going to the hospital for the immediate future. If he makes it through surgery, we'll see what's what."

"He's not a nice person," she said.

Neither was she, if her behavior today was any indication. But I didn't need to tell her that.

"I'm sorry you've had this experience," I told her as I touched Archie's name on my phone screen. "I hope your next relationship goes better."

"Faith, are you okay?" He sounded worried.

"I'm good, are you?" I asked. Since JJ was here bleeding on the floor, I figured the chances were pretty good that Mikey hadn't thought to send anyone after Archie and Miller.

"We're fine. You wouldn't believe the arsenal in this tiny little apartment," Archie said.

I looked around. "Oh, I bet I would. She brought me to a small warehouse in the middle of nowhere that is stacked with crates. I have a hunch you guys are on the tip of this iceberg there."

"But you're okay?"

"She was trying to use me to impress her abusive douche of a boyfriend," I said. "They scuffled over a gun he had stuffed down the front of his shorts, and...well, I'm waiting for an ambulance."

"Ouch."

"Her arm is broken, and he might bleed out, and all I really had to do was throw one decent spin kick."

Archie laughed. "Sounds like quite a day."

"Day's not over yet." I moved the phone out from my head, hearing sirens in the distance. "Let me get these two loaded into an ambulance, and I'll check in."

"Do not go off by yourself looking for the bad guys," Archie said.

"Roger."

"I mean it. Graham would say the same thing, and you know it."

"I know." I ended the call and stood as the sirens stopped outside. JJ stirred on the floor at the noise. Conscious was a good sign.

I opened the door and waved two paramedics inside, flashing my badge and collecting the Ruger that had done the damage to JJ as well as my own gun while they loaded him onto a gurney and discussed my makeshift tourniquet. I slid my SIG back into its holster and the Ruger into the back of my jeans, checking the safety before I put it there.

"It's holding. I say we leave it be," said the female paramedic, whose red hair was gathered into a high, no-nonsense ponytail, her face pretty even without a speck of makeup.

"He was bleeding a whole lot before I got that on him," I said. "If that helps you decide."

"I take it you don't want this belt back?" The guy grinned at me.

"He can keep it," I said, wrinkling my nose before I pointed to Mikey. "Pretty sure she sustained a couple of broken bones, too."

The woman locked her side of the gurney and waved her partner on before she crossed to Mikey and squatted in front of her. "Do you think you could stand with help?"

My eyes were on them as I tried to decide whether I would help Mikey or hurt her worse if I tried to lend a hand, so I didn't see the door open, I just heard the first shots fire.

By the time I turned around, the paramedic who'd grinned at me moments earlier was slumped over the gurney and sliding to the floor, his brains oozing out a cue-ball-sized hole in the left side of his head.

Mikey screamed, but not for long—the sound cut off when a bullet hit her square in the chest as the second wave fired from the doorway. The round exploded everything between her shoulder blades onto the crates and the concrete on its way out.

The redheaded medic didn't make a sound, she just dove behind a stack of crates. I scrambled behind a battered metal tool chest, the red kind with wheels like the one my granddaddy had from Sears when I was a little girl.

I only had a few seconds to process what I saw, but I was pretty sure we had a single shooter, firing some kind of hollow-point round from a semi-automatic rifle. And Archie wasn't coming, because I'd just told him I was fine.

Shit.

I flattened myself on the floor, hoping the angle was long enough that I could get a look at my adversary in the two-inch gap the wheels on the tool chest left between its bottom and the floor. I didn't dare try to look around the edge or over the top—a weapon like that could take off half my face or the entire top of my head with one good shot.

He hadn't come inside yet but was ducking in and out, using the double-walled metal door as cover.

The good news: he was in fact the only shooter I could see. And he wasn't wearing body armor, just a helmet. That gave me a chance.

The not-so-good news: his weapon was far superior to mine in terms of firepower and ability to inflict damage. And I counted three clips hanging from his belt. He had the clear advantage in sheer ability to overwhelm the situation before I could get a decent shot off.

I took three slow breaths, a thousand hours of training calming my nerves. Staying calm was the biggest thing I could do to improve my chances of walking out of this building alive.

And I did not intend to die in a shitty little metal box that served as base for some two-bit gunrunners.

The shooter didn't speak, just turned slowly, aiming his weapon in an arc as he went. His eyes fell on JJ, strapped to the gurney, and he stepped out from behind the door and crossed to it, raising the rifle high to pump a single, point-blank shot into the injured man's chest.

The bottom of the gurney exploded in a red river, chunks of JJ's chest falling to the floor with wet thuds.

I ignored it, because I had to.

The redheaded paramedic did not, a scream escaping before she managed to swallow it.

Fuck. I went from praying silently that the shooter hadn't had a chance to count bodies in the building in his haste to rain bullets over the interior to watching him turn toward the crates sheltering the medic.

He walked slowly, almost sadistically, every *thwack* of his boots on the concrete echoing off the walls around us—like he wanted her to be afraid before he shot her.

He was dangerously close to finding her before I could move, because I had to time it exactly right.

I scooted to the far right side of the tool chest, turning slowly and soundlessly onto my back before I sat up, tucking my feet under me and rising to a low crouch as he zeroed in on the six-foot-high pile of wooden crates.

Taking him down wouldn't save us, not for sure. I needed a kill shot. His head was covered, so I had to hit his jugular or his heart.

Moments like this are my least favorite thing about my job. Thank God they're pretty few and far between.

He stopped short of the crates, all his attention focused on them, putting out one hand and knocking the top crate to the floor. It broke open, a dozen guns similar to the one our intruder held clattering to the floor.

The medic—I had to hand it to her, other than the short, reflexive scream, she was handling herself better than some cops I'd worked with could—snatched one up by the muzzle, flipping it so fast it blurred, pointing it at her attacker.

It was really too bad it wasn't loaded.

The shooter saw that, his face dropping into mock horror before he laughed and raised his own rifle.

Go time.

I shoved with my legs and took one wide step to my right, aiming my SIG with both hands. He didn't notice. He was too busy waving the rifle in a small circle as the medic stood, jabbing her weapon forward and keeping her voice relatively calm. "I just want to leave," she said. "I don't even know these people. Step aside, and I'll go my way, and you can go yours."

Not bad, except it's hard to rationalize with the type of irrational personality it takes to hold human life in such low regard.

"I know something you don't know." He said it in a singsong voice, waving his own gun in rhythm with the words.

"What's that?" Her voice shook, but she kept her grip on the weapon, her eyes flicking to me.

"Duck!" I shouted as I lined up my shot and fired before he could start to turn.

She dove to her left. He stumbled forward one step and fell, crashing through the wall of crates and knocking two more to the floor.

The blood pouring into a pool on the concrete told me I'd hit my mark.

I swallowed hard and let a breath out, blocking the thought that he was dying on the floor because of me.

The medic was alive, and so was I—it was a good trade, and a justified use of my weapon.

That didn't make it much easier, but I'd take what I could get.

I crossed to the body and wrestled the gun—a standard military-issue M4—out from under him, sliding it across the floor a safe distance toward the empty half of the building. He was good and dead—bent unnaturally over the sharp corners of the fallen crates, glassy eyes staring at nothing, liters of blood around him. I checked his pulse anyway.

"He's dead," the medic said from behind me.

"I know. But it's always better to double-check." I stood.

She hugged the empty gun, her eyes glued to the shooter's body. "What the fuck just happened here?"

"Bad people do bad things," I said, reaching for the rifle. "That's the plain truth of it."

Her face crumpled and tears spilled down it, a deep, wrenching sob ripping from her chest as she let go of the rifle. I set it on the floor and patted her shoulder.

"You're still here." I never tell people at scenes that they're okay—of course they're not okay, they might not be for a long while. But she was still alive to try to get okay. I turned for the door and pushed it shut, throwing both locks. Just in case.

She pulled in a hitching breath and swiped at her face, her eyes following me and landing on her partner, lying twisted on the floor next to the gurney holding most of JJ's blown-out corpse.

"Brandon was supposed to get married in October."

"I'm so sorry." I felt every bit of the guilt of calling them here. Not that I had any way to know this would happen, but that didn't matter.

She turned to the dead guy and drew back one black-sneaker-encased foot, landing a kick to his middle so fierce more blood spurted out of him. I watched without comment.

"I hope you burn in hell." The redhead leaned forward and spit on the shooter.

Not that I didn't get it, but I did still want to go through his pockets.

"I need to search him," I said gently, putting out a hand.

"What did he mean, he knew something I didn't know?" She stepped backward.

"Your gun wasn't loaded. It just came out of the crate."

"Great." She shook her head. "I guess you can tell I'm not exactly the poster child for the NRA."

"You did an admirable job of keeping your head straight and keeping your cool right then," I said. "Seriously impressive. I know cops who get more rattled in life-and-death situations."

"I was plenty rattled." She sank to the floor like her legs had given out, crossing them in front of her and watching me squat to poke at the dead shooter's pockets.

"You hid it well and chose the smart thing in several split-second decisions," I said. "If you ever get tired of saving people in the ambulance, look me up."

"Where would I find you?" she asked.

I stuck two fingers into the shooter's front right pocket and came out with an iPhone, a wallet, and keys. "Jackpot," I said, flashing a smile at the medic as I stood and dumped his stuff on a table before offering her a hand. "Faith McClellan, Texas Rangers."

"Wow, we still have those?" She shook my hand but didn't get up. "I'm Melody. Melody Baskin."

"I'm sorry to meet you like this, Melody, but I meant what I said." I opened the wallet.

"Lucas David Lobban of San Marcos," I said, counting three hundred twenty-five dollars in cash and flipping a Costco card over. Same guy, same name as the driver's license. I tucked the wallet in my back pocket and tapped the phone screen. The "try Face ID again" box flashed up after half a second. I flipped the phone screen toward the floor and walked back to Lucas, crouching to put the phone in front of his face with its still open eyes, touching the button to try again when I thought I had it lined up reasonably well.

A photo of a rock formation flashed up, quickly obscured by a handful of apps.

I pulled out my own phone and took a photo of his home screen before I touched the password storage app and pointed the phone at his face one more time, searching for "apple" and finding what I wanted. "*This phone password 4*? Really, Lucas?" I shook my head as I copied it and opened the settings, resetting his lock screen code to my sister's birthday. The phone made me enter the password twice more to confirm the change.

Once I wasn't in danger of being locked out of the device again, I pocketed it in favor of my own phone, one stroke away from calling the local dispatcher back to ask for backup before I realized Lucas here showed up right on the heels of the ambulance I'd asked 911 to send us.

I tapped the side of my phone, turning to Melody. Maybe I was turning into a tin-foil-hat nut job, but I was a breathing tin-foil-hat nut job who still had a chance of getting her husband back.

"Where are we?" I asked.

She blinked. "How the hell should I know what this place is? You were here first."

"What county?" I asked, waving a hurry-up hand.

"Oh. Bexar, I think. This place is kind of in the middle of nowhere."

I opened my contacts, checking the clock. Somehow it felt like a thousand years since we'd left HQ, but it was only a little after nine p.m. Jim would still be awake.

I touched his cell number on my screen and surveyed the room, making sure I hadn't missed any hidey-holes.

"Faith? You okay?" Jim sounded worried when he answered.

"Still kicking," I said, not wanting to worry him too much. "I'm sorry it's kind of late, but I need a trustworthy contact in Bexar County who can come process a scene, and I don't want to call the local dispatcher right now."

"I'm not even going to ask why," he said. "I just want credit for my restraint because I'm as nosy as any decent cop."

"Credited and appreciated," I said. "You have a friend who can help, right?"

"Sure. Everyone loves me." He chuckled. "I'll call a guy and get you a team."

"Make sure your friend comes with them," I said. "And no local cops. I'll get my own people."

"You sure you're okay?"

"I am. Just not sure who to trust."

"I need a location."

"I'm going to send you a pin. Three victims, various gauge GSWs. No radio chatter—the last thing I need is the media screwing things up more here."

"On it." He paused. "Faith..."

"I'm watching my back. And my front, too," I said. "Thanks for caring, though."

"Eighteen months."

"Noted."

I touched the end button and looked around more before I turned my attention back to Melody, who was watching me with her lips slightly agape. "You think the local PD had something to do with this?"

"I have no idea," I said. "That's the God's honest truth. I think it's a little suspicious that Lucas here showed up right behind you and your partner earlier, but it could be a coincidence. I'm just not willing to risk anything I don't have to. Where are the keys to your vehicle?"

She pointed to her partner without looking at his body.

"I got it." I crossed the floor and searched his pockets, pulling his key ring free and walking it back to her. "I want you to drive straight from here to the hospital. Drop the bus off, find security, and get an escort to your car. Do not speak to anyone else, and don't tell security why you want the escort. Go straight home, park your car out of view of the street, and lock the doors and windows." It was overkill, I was sure, but I'd rather be too cautious than not cautious enough. I handed her a card. "My cell number is on there. Text me when you get home. An officer will call you tomorrow about taking a statement."

She sniffled, squaring her shoulders and jingling the keys. "Got it."

I led her in a wide arc around her partner's body and opened the door carefully, looking around before I let her out, then watched her get into the cab and start the ambulance.

Locking the door, I stared at Archie's name on my contacts list for a full minute before I went back to the list and chose another.

30

The thumping bass I had to hold my phone six inches from my ear to be able to stand told me Bolton was at a nightclub.

Damn.

"Mrs. Hardin?" His baritone was scratchy with effort, yelling over the music.

"Please tell me you aren't drinking," I shouted back, the noise echoing uncomfortably off the metal walls in the suddenly heavy silence around me.

"Not yet." The music muffled for a second, as did his voice as he muttered something to a companion. "Hang on, I'm going to my truck."

A few seconds later, the music vanished, replaced by road noise when he stepped outside. "What's up?"

I laughed, at first at the absurdity of calling Bolton out of nightclub, likely away from a date, to ask him to drive out to the middle of nowhere and babysit Jim's friend from Bexar County and his crew, as well as inventory this place. But then I couldn't stop. My shoulders shook. My vision blurred. After a couple of minutes, my sides ached. I couldn't turn it off.

I wondered for a split second if I was experiencing some sort of breakdown, more concerned when Bolton squeaked, "My God, are you crying?

Who died? Where do you need me to go?" In a voice that was two full octaves too high for him. Because his alarm just made me laugh harder.

I heard the engine in his truck rumble, and that sobered me enough to allow a couple of deep breaths. "So sorry. I'm okay. But I do need your help," I said between them.

"Anything." He still sounded worried, but not who-do-I-need-to-shoot worried.

"Go home and get your uniform, and come to the location I'm about to drop to your phone. I have a massive crime scene that needs to be inventoried and medical examiners coming in a little while to handle body removal. I need someone I trust here while they work, and I need to know what's here, but I have somewhere else to be."

"I get to run the scene? By myself?" He tried to sound professional, but I heard the excitement in his tone.

"Have you never done this before?"

"I'm up to the job, I swear," he blurted.

"I know you are," I said. "I was surprised to hear that because I know you can do this."

"Thank you. That means a lot to me, coming from you."

My, how far he'd come from the rookie former college defensive lineman who was positive a girl couldn't take him in hand-to-hand.

"You're welcome. Sending the location now. Text me when you get here, the door is locked."

"Yes, ma'am." He paused, and I started to hang up. "Mrs. Hardin?"

"Yes, deputy?"

"Is the commander okay? I'm not trying to...it's just that he's been out for a while now, and we all miss him, and nobody in the brass talks about him anymore. I've just been worried, is all."

"He's fine. Thank you for letting me know you've been worried." I swallowed hard, needing with every cell to believe I was telling Bolton the truth.

....

I walked a grid through the warehouse, peeking into crates and checking the floor for evidence of a cellar while avoiding blood puddles and bodies.

I didn't find a trapdoor. What I did find were a whole fucking lot of big, dangerous guns mixed in with more rocket launchers and a couple of military-style armed drones, even.

"These assholes are really into everything," I muttered, stopping at a workbench covered with an array of burner cell phones and papers, looking for anything that might give me a clue to what had happened to Ratcliff and wishing I hadn't tried to be so savvy about my line of questioning before JJ over there shot himself in the family jewels and then ended up with his chest blown onto the floor.

I moved a pile of specs on the drones, photographing the model numbers for reference. Under the books lay a stack of papers—a hand-drawn sketch of what looked like a desert road flanked by cacti and boulders, with a doodle of a skinny triangle in one corner. For a gunrunning, woman-beating douchebag, JJ had a little talent. I took a picture with my phone and set it aside, the next page a satellite map of Terrell County with three different locations marked.

I opened Google Maps and checked the Street View at each.

One of them was Ratcliff's outpost.

One was a small postwar ranch house.

And the other was in the state park, near the river about five miles along the riverbed from where Freddie Z was found. Carlos? I wanted a unit out there to check.

So. Could I trust Morgan Dean or not?

Only one way to find out.

I rang his phone. He sounded tired when he picked up, but not like I'd woken him.

"I hope to hell you're having better luck up there than I am here," he said.

"That good, huh?"

"We're into day two of a search and have found nothing. And when I say nothing, I mean not even a trail for the dogs to follow. It's like Ratcliff got beamed up by aliens."

"It was people, I assure you," I said. "I have a lead I'd like your help with —some addresses I'd like photos of. Don't approach, just send me photos."

"Sounds like there's a story in your day," he said.

"I'm looking at three corpses, waiting on a cleanup crew, and if I told you anything else about this evening, I bet you wouldn't believe me."

"Debriefing beers on me after the dust clears?"

"Make it a margarita and you've got yourself a drinking buddy," I said.

"Be careful out there."

"You, too."

"McClellan, if you knew what we're into here, you'd tell me. Right?"

Speaking of trust issues...

"I've told you everything I can," I said.

"That's not a straight answer."

"It's the only one I've got right now."

He stayed quiet so long I had to check to make sure I hadn't lost him. The line was still there, and I couldn't talk first. I pinched my lips together and waited. If I hadn't totally lost my people radar, he'd be okay with that after he chewed on it for a minute.

He cleared his throat. "Send me the addresses you want me to check out."

I thanked him and did just that, putting the phone on the table as it lit up with a text from Bolton: *Here. Did you call the army, too?*

I snatched the phone off the table, thumbs flying over the screen. *No. Why?*

There's a military transport vehicle out here. Back by the road. Government plates and everything.

I turned slowly to stare at Lucas Lobban, the license and Costco card flashing through my head as I pulled out his wallet slowly and checked it again. No military ID. My stomach did a slow flip as the new information registered and I tried to make it fit with everything else I knew so far—and around the holes I was still trying to fill.

I went back to the message screen and typed another text to Bolton: *Come straight to the largest building. Leave the truck for now, I'll check it out in a little bit.*

10-4, the reply buzzed a second later.

I crossed to the door to let him in just as the truck's engine cut off. I listened for his door to slam before I opened mine.

He jogged over and stepped inside, looking around before he shut the door behind him and locked it. He pulled in a sharp breath as he surveyed the warehouse, starting with a bloody, disheveled version of me and skipping through the carnage to the labels on the crates.

"What in the ever-loving hell is all this?"

I filled Bolton in the best I could, with strict orders to make a written inventory of the crates but to take no pictures and say nothing about what he saw, before Jim's friend Gary Montgomery arrived at the door with two forensic techs in tow and an unamused set to his mouth.

"Thirty years doing this shit and Prescott has me out here in the middle of the night, babysitting a hysterical female." He didn't even bother to murmur as he brushed past Bolton and me, pointing his techs to Lucas while he leaned over and flicked on a headlamp to study what was left of JJ and the dead medic.

Bolton's eyebrows shot to his close-cropped hairline while I tried to decide how—or if—I should reply to Montgomery. Assholes are an unfortunate fact of life no matter the profession, and I didn't care that he was pissed about being called out here after ten p.m. Inconvenient hours are part of the job—catching killers doesn't come with a standard eight-to-five workday. I did care that I wanted him there if Jim trusted him, which meant the barbed retort hovering on the tip of my tongue was best swallowed.

"I appreciate your help," I said instead, keeping my face vaguely friendly but my voice even and calm. "And your discretion."

"This was a high-powered hollow point fired at extremely close range." Montgomery spoke as if I hadn't, probing the edge of JJ's chest wound with one gloved finger.

"I know. I saw it happen," I said.

That got his attention. And Bolton's, too.

"I'm sorry?" Montgomery said, turning toward me.

"You what?" Bolton blurted close to my ear.

"I took the shooter down as soon as I had a clean shot," I said. "That's him over there on the floor—he announced his arrival with a hail of bullets that killed Mikey there," I pointed, "and the medic," I swung my arm toward Brandon, on the floor next to the gurney, "who had just arrived to help JJ there after he shot himself in the crotch."

My phone buzzed in my pocket, and I checked the text. "The second paramedic just made it home, thanks to her quick thinking—"

"And your marksmanship," the tech leaning over Lucas interjected. "I'd bet my house this bullet ripped straight through the aorta. This poor bastard didn't know what hit him."

I swallowed hard as Bolton laid a big, heavy hand on my shoulder. "I'm so glad you're okay. The commander would be lost without you."

"Commander?" Montgomery raised his eyebrows.

I knocked my foot into Bolton's before he could say anything else, waving off the question.

"Everything in this building is need to know only." I turned my head, meeting eyes with each of them and finishing back where I'd started, on Montgomery. "Don't tell your wife, your husband, your mother, your kid, or even your dog what you've seen or what you find. Bolton here is in charge and has my number if anything comes up."

Bolton followed me to the door and asked if he could call in help.

"Who do you trust the very most in your department?" I asked.

"Uh. Probably Lieutenant Commander Hardin, really."

I smiled. "That's nice. Can you handle this by yourself? As in, do you really need help, or do you want company?"

He considered that, looking around. "Probably company."

"I appreciate the honesty." I patted his shoulder. "Graham's life might depend on how few people find out what we're working on, so let's keep it to just us?"

He blinked. "Yes, ma'am."

I handed Bolton the Ruger Mikey had pulled on me a few hours that felt like several days ago. "This belonged to one of the gunrunners. See if there are any more like it in those crates." I wondered if maybe Lucas's shooting spree had something to do with JJ skimming merchandise. "You call me if you find anything interesting."

"Will do. Please let me know if there's anything else I can do."

I opened the door and stepped out into somehow more oppressive heat in the dark than there had been inside a metal building before the sun went down.

"Welcome to Texas summers, where the sun goes down, and the humidity goes up," I muttered as I pulled Miller's keys from my pocket, a smile touching my lips as I thought of how many times I'd heard my granny say that, shaking her head in the soft yellow glow of the porch lamp over her rocker as she shelled summer peas Charity and I had helped her pick in the garden.

I left my phone in my pocket as I started the car and made a lap of the building's exterior before I headed back toward the road.

Sure enough, an M35 military cargo truck sat just off the road.

"Surely not," I muttered as I parked the sedan and got out, pulling my SIG and approaching the truck slowly. Just in case.

I circled it twice, sidestepping with my weapon trained on the vehicle the entire time, before I was satisfied that Lucas had been the only occupant.

"What is it with this case and vehicle searches?" I asked aloud to the cactus growing wild a few feet away, its purple blooms open in the dark.

Heavy, camouflage-printed canvas shrouded the long truck bed. I raised the flashlight on my phone and peered inside, the long benches stretching over a floor full of metal boxes, each about the size of a standard suitcase. I wrestled the closest one to the edge of the tailgate and nearly yanked my shoulder out of its socket when the box slid off toward the ground.

"Holy shit, what is this guy hauling?"

I looked around carefully before I tucked my weapon into its holster and dropped into a squat, unlatching the top of the box and lifting the lid slowly.

Body armor. Military grade—this wasn't sporting goods store issue, it was the good stuff. Heavy as all hell, hot as at least the ninth ring, and packed neatly in the suitcase, which held two full sets, the helmets side by side on top.

But Lucas walked into the warehouse without any. Which meant he wasn't afraid of who he thought he was going to find in there. So he'd met JJ and his buddies and didn't consider them a threat, even in a possible group.

Lucas was confident in his skills and didn't expect to be challenged even enough to bother with the hot, heavy protection he'd driven here in this truck.

I picked up one helmet and flipped it over.

"Property of Texas National Guard," I read the stenciled letters inside.

The fact that the stencils matched the print on the crates of guns inside wasn't what made me drop the helmet, though.

I had it. Squatting in the dirt in front of a case of body armor behind a troop transport truck in the oppressive heat of the Texas near-desert, those stenciled letters were the last variable I needed.

Shoving the helmet back into the case and slamming it shut, I shot to my feet and hurried around the side of the truck, yanking the door open so fast the hinges squealed.

I found the hood release lever and pulled it, then rounded the front of the truck and hunted for the release button, turning my head and wrinkling my nose when I caught a whiff of burned plastic and...rotten egg? Release located, I raised the hood an inch and got a lungful of the foul smell, almost too preoccupied with coughing to notice the series of beeps coming from inside the engine.

But only almost.

Beepbeepbeepbeepbeepbeep...beepbeepbeepbeepbeep...beepbeepbeepbeep...

They were counting down, losing a beat each time.

"Shit!" I let go of the hood and ran, arms pumping, sweat beading and quickly dripping, pushing every muscle I had to the limit.

I dove behind the smallest metal shed as the truck exploded.

31

Ears ringing, I stood and peeked around the corner of the shed, recoiling from the heat even twenty yards away.

The paint on the rear driver's side of Miller's sedan bubbled and warped, smoke rising from the tires, the air thick with the acrid stench of burning plastic and rubber.

"Faith!"

I wasn't sure Bolton had ever used my first name, but I heard him bellow it and turned to see him running faster than I would've thought he could move up the lane toward me, his face reddening from exertion and proximity to the burning truck. He stopped next to me and rested his hands on his knees just as the heat got to be too much for the gas tank on Miller's car. Bolton jumped at the comparatively smaller explosion, and I dragged him behind the shed.

"I'm okay," I said, moving away from the hot metal of the little storage building and wondering for the first time if I should be concerned about what was inside it.

"I'm not sure I am." Bolton's eyes were fixed on his right leg.

"Oh, shit." I wasn't sure how I kept my tone relatively normal when I looked down and saw a chunk of Miller's car embedded in Bolton's shin, nor was I convinced I could keep it up.

I didn't see much blood, but I didn't want to touch anything near the wound for fear of changing that. I pulled my phone out and called Archie.

"Faith?"

I'd woken him up. I rattled off the highlights of my evening in an impressive two breaths.

"Jesus Christ." Archie's voice had no trace of sleep fog by the time I stopped talking. I heard a door open and close and water come on. "Get Bolton to a hospital, and let me know where to find you. I'll pick Miller up on my way out of town."

"Arch?" I paused. I couldn't remember ever having questioned his judgment.

"What?" His voice went up an octave.

"I just... Do you trust that guy? He's working with criminals, we don't really know him...I'm not trying to be difficult, but I have to know that whoever we're dealing with is going to help me get Graham home, not get him killed."

"I do," Archie said. "Miller is straight up and earnest, and he knows his stuff. And because of that, he'd be the first person to understand if you feel differently than I do."

"Can he help us?" I asked.

"I think so, yeah."

I blew out a long, controlled breath. "You better be right."

"That's easy. I'm never wrong."

"Not funny."

"It's a little funny."

"Next week it might be funny. Now, not as much."

"We'll get him back, Faith."

"We have to."

I ended the call and tapped the side of my phone, not wanting to call 911 for the same reason I had called Bolton instead of local law enforcement earlier.

Melody.

I clicked my messages and found her cell number, placing a call and gritting my teeth at the eleven o'clock hour. She picked up on the first ring, her voice strained but not sleepy. I don't suppose people who aren't used to being shot at sleep well after a day like the one she had, though.

"Melody, this is Faith McClellan from the Texas Rangers," I said. "I'm sorry to bother you so late, but I have an injured officer here, and I need your help."

"Huh?" She cleared her throat, pausing. "Why don't you call another ambulance?"

"You already know where I am, and I trust you," I said, a pleading note seeping into the words. "There was an explosion, and he has part of a car lodged in his tibia."

"Explosion? At that same place?" Her voice thickened. "I don't think I can come back there."

"We're near the road, and I just need you to help me get him to the closest care facility."

She huffed out a sigh, something that sounded like her fingernail tapping the back of her phone nine times.

"Fine. Twenty minutes."

"Thank you so much." I hung up and sat down next to Bolton. "Help is on the way."

"Ma'am?" He shifted his weight to his left hip.

"Yeah, Bolton?"

"Commander Hardin is one of the best people I have ever known, and I couldn't help but overhear your conversation a minute ago."

Damn.

"It's okay, Bolton," I said. "Graham will be fine, don't worry."

"I'm afraid he wasn't so sure about that," he said softly, his big eyes sad.

"What?" I grabbed his hand when he didn't elaborate. "What does that mean?"

"He came to my place before he left. I was outside shooting the shit with my neighbor, and Commander said he dropped by for a beer. Weird, because that had never happened before, but I thought maybe it meant, you know..." He ducked his head. "That he was starting to think of me as a friend. Then when we got inside, he told me he'd be out on a UC for a while, and that he needed me to look out for you. He said he was afraid what he was going into could get you hurt. I asked him, then, if it couldn't get him hurt, too, and he just said he knew what he was signing up for. He told me to keep you safe, even if he never came home."

I blinked hard and flashed a smile even though I wanted to scream.

Just a few weeks, he said.

Could be a career case, he said.

I won't be in any real danger, he said.

From what I'd learned today, two out of three of those were bald-faced lies. Graham had never lied to me.

And I had missed it. What the hell did that say about my human lie detector abilities?

That they didn't apply to my personal life—at least, they hadn't before. But how was I supposed to trust him again when I knew that he could look me straight in the face and lie so convincingly I didn't suspect a damned thing? How did women who don't talk to killers and thieves all day every day trust their husbands? My bullshit detector is more finely tuned than most people's, and I had completely missed this.

Until that moment, I'd always thought those stories about men who carry on affairs for years and then confess to their shocked wives were drag-ons-and-fairies-level fantasy. Who could really be so blind?

Me, it turned out.

"Are you okay?" Bolton asked.

I laughed. Not the scary, runaway maniacal laugh from earlier. A regular one at the absurdity of him asking if I was okay when he was literally sitting there with a burning chunk of car sticking out of his person.

"I'm okay. How you holding up?" I checked my watch, blinking at the insulting notion that only six minutes had passed and willing the hands to move faster.

"I'll live," Bolton said. "It's weird—it hurts, but not as bad as you'd think. My face hurt worse than this last time you punched me."

"You asked for that."

He smiled, but it was sad around the edges. "I suppose I did."

It made me wonder if this kid who had gone from obnoxious, ham-fisted know-it-all to Graham's favorite rookie knew more things I didn't know.

Right then, for the first time in my life, I couldn't bring myself to ask.

32

"I'm going to need another cup of coffee," Miller said, scrubbing a hand over eyes that were the kind of bloodshot that came from stress and lack of sleep. "That is a whole lot of information for this time of night."

We sat in black vinyl chairs in the surgical waiting area at the county hospital, where Melody said an injured first responder would get the best trauma care available in the area, waiting for the doctor to come tell us Bolton was okay. The ER doctors had sent him to surgery almost straight away after ultrasounds and scans showed that the chunk of twisted metal was embedded in his bone and dangerously close to a major artery. It had taken nearly the first hour of the surgery for me to give Archie and Miller the full details of my afternoon.

Archie flipped back through notes he'd been taking while I talked. "So this fellow who shot himself before the other guy showed up and really shot him...he said he knew where Ratcliff was?"

"He said he took care of the cop who was nosing around," I said. "I was working up to trying to finesse details out of him when they started scuffling over the gun, and things went south at record speed from there."

I pulled out my phone and opened my messages. "I did find some locations marked on a map, and I sent them to Dean to check out." I clicked the new message from him. "Let me see what he found."

I had five photos: three of a small house faced with dingy metal siding that probably used to be white—though the moonlit shot made it hard to tell exactly what color I was looking at—and two of an empty campsite at the state park.

I typed a reply before I flipped my phone around to show Miller and Archie.

Thank you. I'd like to know who owns the house and who has camped on that site in the past two months, if you can put someone on that.

I clicked send and moved to share the photos, surprised when the phone buzzed with a reply.

I'll get on that in the morning. Night, McClellan.

Good night.

I went back to the photos and handed the phone to Archie, my eyes on Miller.

His face showed the work he had put into this case: worry lines around his eyes even though he had to be at least a couple of years younger than Graham and me, dry skin, sunken, bloodshot eyes, eleven-o'clock shadow that was really probably a couple of days of beard scruff.

Archie trusted him. He'd known him for a while, too.

I had always trusted Archie. Quite literally with my life for a decent chunk of it. So I had to trust him with Graham's now. Or at least with this part of it.

"Do you have any contacts at ICE?" I asked. "Homeland Security oversees the unit that runs the detention center."

Miller looked up from the photos of the little house he was scrutinizing.

"I can find some if we need them."

"A prisoner was killed there yesterday after we delivered a request to move him."

"You mentioned this earlier, right? The guy you went to talk to from the motel who had been assaulted? I have someone checking into the center already, but I'll check for an update first thing."

The doors to the operating rooms opened, and a doctor in purple scrubs came out, pulling a mask down and smiling at us. "You're here for Deputy Bolton, right?"

"Is he going to be okay?" I asked.

"We were able to remove the object and clean out the bone fragments, and I think there's a good chance his bone will regenerate enough in the area to prevent the need for further surgeries. We'll know more about that in about four weeks."

"And his artery?"

"Not damaged. And because the metal and plastic were superheated by the explosion, all the minor vessels involved were cauterized as they were cut. All in all, I'd say the deputy was very lucky."

"Can we see him?" I asked.

"He's still asleep and likely will be until near sunrise," she said. "We're keeping him for a couple of days because he said he lives alone in a second-floor apartment—we'll give him some intensive physical therapy and train him up on the crutches to make sure we've minimized the chance of a mishap before we send him home. It's very important that he not put any weight on that leg. Can he work at a desk for a while?"

"We don't actually control that."

"I can make sure of it," Archie said with a kind smile. "Thank you so much for taking good care of the kid, Doc."

"I'm glad our outcome was good," she said. "Y'all be safe out there. No more makeshift shrapnel for a while."

We agreed and waved as she turned back for the surgical unit. No one spoke until we were climbing into Archie's truck.

"I'm picking up a rental at the airport when they open at five," Miller said. "If you two want to get breakfast and strategize, I can pick you both up on my way back in."

"That'd be great, thank you," I said.

"She's coming home with me," Archie said as he rolled to a stop in front of the Embassy Suites downtown. "We'll see you in a few hours."

"Sleep well, y'all." Miller shut the door and disappeared into the hotel.

"Don't argue," Archie said. "I can't make much of what the hell is happening here yet, but you're not going anywhere else alone until we're done with this one."

"I'm not arguing," I said. "But I do have something else to tell you."

"Still fighting the trust issues with Miller?"

I sighed. "I'm trying. I think I know where JJ and his buddies were getting at least some of the stuff they're selling. The truck that blew up tonight was a military transport. The shooter, Lucas Lobban, according to the ID I pulled off him, drove it there. Full of equipment and body armor marked property of the Texas National Guard."

Archie tapped the brake and turned to me at the red light. "You think they were running guns they got from the state."

"We both know someone else who did that once upon a time."

"But he was in a position to cover it up," Archie said.

I pointed. "Green." He started driving again.

"I know that," I said. "But maybe they have someone who is, too. I don't know if JJ and company were getting guns from Lobban or running guns opposite him, but we need to find his buddies tomorrow."

"If they're alive to be found," Archie said.

We drove several blocks in silence before he turned into his driveway and looked at me when he shut off the engine.

"I'd also like to know why Miller seemed to recognize the house in those photos Dean sent you."

"I noticed that, too. I kept waiting for him to say something."

"Maybe he forgot about it after we talked to the doctor. There's been a lot coming at us pretty fast."

"I'm trying to trust him because you do, and you said we need his help."

"I still believe both of those things, but let's see how tomorrow goes." He waved me into the house and handed me a protein bar from the pantry before he disappeared to find me an old shirt to sleep in and pointed me to the guest room. "The sheets are fresh, and there's a new toothbrush in the drawer in the bathroom."

I smiled. "Thanks, Arch."

"Go to sleep. Five thirty is going to come fast, and Graham needs you at your best."

"Yes, sir." I shut the door, going to brush my teeth and wondering what else Kyle Miller might not be saying.

33

"Faith. I have coffee ready."

Ruth's voice invaded a dream about twelve seconds after I closed my eyes. I opened them to find her perched on the edge of my bed.

"Hi, Mom." It had gotten much easier to call her that instead of Ruth in the past few months. "Thanks. For letting me stay."

"I understand it was more of an order. But thank you for not arguing with him. We both slept better with you here in the house." She sighed, plucking at the lace on her peach satin robe. "This probably isn't the time, but my therapist says I need to tell you that I'm sorry. For the way you grew up. And Archie said you were shot at and almost blown up yesterday, and I know better than any mother that tomorrow isn't a guarantee, and so..." She pulled in a hitching breath, appearing to stop the gush of words with sheer brute force of willpower. "I'm sorry."

She popped to her feet and started tidying the room, pointing to the mug on the night table. "Sugar, no cream. Right?"

I sat up and reached for it, taking a sip and flashing her a thumbs-up as she plucked a blanket from the arm of the rocker and folded it. "I've never understood how you're such a morning person."

"Makeup." She shook her head as she stowed the blanket in the closet. Um. "What?"

"I got up at four ten every day of my life because Chuck woke up at five, and I had to have my hair and makeup done before he woke up. You become a morning person or drive yourself slowly insane."

Holy shit. Her life had been so much sadder than I ever could've thought. I sipped more of the coffee and swung my legs off the bed. "I think I'm awake now. Mostly."

"I washed and ironed your clothes—they're hanging up in the bathroom. We'll be in the kitchen." She stepped into the hall and pulled the door shut.

I yanked my hair back into a ponytail and splashed cold water on my face, racing through getting dressed and wondering how I'd completely misread my own mother for so many years.

What was I misreading with this case?

I ticked through the facts as I stuffed my feet into my boots. Gunrunning. Drug cartels. JJ and his friends either acting as middlemen or rivals with Lucas Lobban, who somehow had the power to sell stolen state property under the radar. Timmy's assault and subsequent murder in the detention center and his friend Scott who kept letting these guys back and forth across the border. Ratcliff's suspicions and current status as a missing person. And somewhere in the middle of it all, my husband moving in this shadow world of drug runners and murderers. I had to get Graham back home safe.

For all the things I knew, there were too many that I still didn't. Today, I needed answers to some of those questions, and it looked more and more like getting them might entail a road trip south, probably with Archie and Miller in tow.

Maybe Miller didn't trust us any more than I trusted him. With a little more coffee and a few hours on the road, we might be able to rectify that—on both sides.

Miller drove while I pecked at my laptop keyboard in the back and complained about the shitty cell signal my hotspot was getting as we drove south through increasingly sparsely populated desert.

"Lucas David Lobban was born in Terrell in 1997, joined the Texas National Guard in 2015, no mention of his education. In 2019, he was dishonorably discharged for..." I clicked to go to the last page of his service record.

"For what? There's plenty of drama around this without pauses and bravado," Miller said.

"I'm not being dramatic, I'm waiting for the damned page to load," I said.

"Oh. Sorry."

"Theft. More than five hundred dollars," I said, clicking the charge when it loaded on my screen.

Nothing.

"Maybe he was stealing stuff from them and selling it even back then?" Archie mused.

"I'm sorry?" Miller asked.

"The stuff I found in the truck that blew up last night was still marked as property of the Texas National Guard," I said. "I think one of the purposes of that warehouse might have been removing that labeling before they took it to the border, just in case they got caught with it. But like everything else here, I know just enough to suspect I've got it figured out, but not nearly enough to really be sure."

I clicked another link that did nothing. "Weird. There are no details, and the link to the proceedings is ghosted." I went back to the main personnel page and looked for known associates. That wasn't there, either.

"All right, dammit," I muttered. "What are y'all hiding?"

"Y'all who?" Archie asked.

"Whoever erased most of this asshole's service file." I tapped keys as fast as the shit connection would allow, looking under the virtual hood of the Texas National Guard database for a back way into the site, where a little luck and a lot of know-how might turn up the deleted files.

"Given what you saw yesterday and what you're seeing now, we can assume Lobban is dirty," Miller said.

"Faith dislikes assuming anything, no matter how safe it looks," Archie said. "She's nothing if not thorough in her commitment to facts."

I tapped the edge of the keyboard as the computer labored with the thin signal.

There.

It loaded the database's core coding path. I scanned down the list, locating the deleted items folder, and clicked.

It loaded in less than two minutes with the terrible signal, which meant there wasn't a lot there.

Damn.

"We may not have time to track down every fact this time," I said, scrolling through a list of men Lobban had served with. "No shit?" I muttered, reading. Maybe there was just enough here.

"Something interesting?" Archie asked.

"Provided this name isn't more common than I think." I didn't take my eyes off the screen, opening another search window. "You ever notice how accustomed we've become to having information at the literal push of a button?" I asked. "A hundred years ago, agents had to wait for the postal service, or drive here, there, and yonder to look through dusty filing cabinets in musty rooms."

"On balance, technology has made our generation of criminals smarter and slipperier, too," Miller said. "Nobody at the ATF a hundred years ago was chasing ghost guns made on 3-D printers or military rifles that civilians can do so much damage with."

"Truth. I might prefer it their way." The TxDOT site finally loaded, and I typed the name into the search field.

Three hits. One guy in his seventies, one dead, and the one I was looking for: Gavin Daniel Kurczyk. Who served with Lobban in the National Guard in 2018 before being discharged after an injury, and who was also one of JJ's camping partners, according to Dean's arrest report.

"We need this guy picked up right now," I said after I filled Archie and Miller in.

"If he has any brains at all, he's hiding after what happened to his buddy yesterday," Miller said.

"Do you have anyone you trust who could go seek?" I asked.

He was quiet for a minute. "I'm kind of flattered you asked me that. I know you aren't sure about me, and I understand why. If DonnaJo were the one mixed up in all this, I wouldn't trust my own father, I don't think."

I reeled off Kurczyk's last known address, and Miller handed Archie his phone. "Text that to Mitchell Kelley. Give him the name, and tell him I need the guy's location ASAP. He's in the Dallas office, and he's the best we have at tracking people down. Two different judges on standby pretty much anytime for cell phone warrants, and we have plenty to justify it here. Just tell him to call me when he gets to that point."

"You think the guy went into hiding and took his phone?" I asked.

"You really think he didn't? People go everywhere with them, and you said yourself his pal JJ wasn't exactly running a think tank."

"I suppose that's true."

Archie poked at Miller's phone screen. "Okay, done," he said. "And someone named Nichelle messaged you, she has an urgent question."

Miller's brow furrowed as he put a hand out for the phone and said, "Siri, call Nichelle," into the speaker before he dropped it in the cupholder.

"Kyle, oh my God." The woman who answered sounded out of breath—or annoyed—and I couldn't tell which was more likely.

"Nicey, you're on speaker, and I'm not alone," he said. "Meet Archie Baxter and Faith McClellan of the Texas Rangers. Archie, Faith, Nichelle Clarke. She's a reporter in Richmond."

"And a friend," Nichelle chided.

"And a friend." Miller laughed. "Even when she's a pain in my ass."

"You have friends who are journalists?" I blurted it before I could stop myself. "How does that work? Um. No offense."

Nichelle laughed. "Nice to meet you, Faith. No offense taken. I work a little differently than a lot of my more overzealous and ambitious colleagues. And at least with Kyle, I have the benefit of knowing too many embarrassing things from his childhood for him to unfriend me."

"We dated. For years. A very long time ago."

"So are you from Texas, too, young lady?" Archie asked.

"Raised in Dallas, Mr. Baxter," she said. "It's very nice to sort of meet you, sir. I've read about your career relatively extensively, thanks to Kyle's raving about how flattered he was that you called him with a question about a case you were working last year."

"Thanks, Miller," Archie said as Miller shook his head and mouthed, *See? Pain in my ass*, in the rearview at me.

I swallowed a laugh. He wasn't a bad guy. I wasn't sure that meant I could trust him, exactly—what kind of cop has a close personal friend who's a reporter that he openly discusses investigations with? And drops everything to call on demand? Still—I truly liked this guy.

"You too, Faith," Nichelle said. "It's hard to work in the news business these days and not see your name all over some pretty big wire stories. I think you two must be single-handedly carrying the torch of the Texas Rangers' legend into the twenty-first century."

"Even when it burns us," I said, a little too melancholy for my own good.

"What's up, Nicey?" Miller asked quickly. I appreciated the redirect and let him know with a half-smile in the rearview. He nodded.

"This case you're supposedly not working on right now—there's a double switchback pattern to the origin of the gun shipments."

"A what?" Miller asked.

I poked Archie's elbow. We couldn't tell Bolton—who was in the hospital, thanks to me and this case—what was happening here, but Miller was telling a reporter? Archie nodded slowly, listening as Miller's journalist friend described the pattern.

"They're coming north from Texas in train cars, routing out in trucks from the rail yard here and the one in Baltimore, moving through local gun shows and online dealers before they go back south in rented trucks, all rented from the same company. And they end up with the same four guys, all of them with Texas addresses."

Miller mimed scribbling, and I pulled out a pen and pad.

"What's the name of the rental company?" Miller asked, keeping his voice low and even.

"G and L Interstate Rental." She paused. "You're not even going to ask me who owns it?"

"I know you looked. And I know you want to tell me."

"It's a subsidiary of a shell corp that's owned wholly by another shell corp that lists a sole proprietor of Luigi Edmionce."

"And who is that?" Miller asked.

"Joey says it's probably an alias for whoever is trying to muscle into the Cacciones' old territory here." Worry practically dripped out of Miller's phone into the cupholder.

"Does he know who that could be?"

"He won't tell me who it is. I'm not even sure he'll tell you, but I think it's more likely."

"I don't suppose me telling you to drop this is going to do any good?" Miller sounded tired. And worried. Who the hell was Joey, and what did this have to do with a mafia family Google had told me Miller took down last year, earning his post as youngest special agent in charge of a field office in ATF history?

"Not likely. There's a huge story here. I can feel it. What I don't understand is why you and Joey still pull this cloak-and-dagger shit on me after all this time. Haven't I proven that you can trust me? And also that I'm just going to find out whatever you're trying to hide anyway?"

The hair on my arm stood up, and it took all the restraint I could muster not to bark at her to stay out of an active investigation. Just like Skye Morrow—no regard for who might get hurt if she went blabbing about what we were working on before the public needed to know something was wrong.

Miller sighed. "Nicey, you don't understand—" he began.

"Because you won't talk to me," she interrupted. "I just shared some important information with you, and you know I'm not going to run anything until you've cracked the case and made the arrest. Everyone else is oblivious to this. I'm the only person following it. I can well afford to wait for the big headline and the whole story here, Kyle."

Miller drummed his fingers on the steering wheel, the muscles in his jaw flexing.

"You're not seriously considering telling her anything important?" I couldn't keep the words in.

"She's just going to go dig it all up on her own," Miller said through clenched teeth. "And she'll probably try to get herself killed in the process. With me out of town, she might succeed this time."

I didn't say what I was thinking, letting my head fall back against the seat.

"We have a very important corpse at the Travis County Medical Examiner's office," Miller said finally. "Taken in on Sunday. And there's a missing Texas Ranger, who is not the dead guy."

"And this is connected to the weapons ring?" Nichelle asked, computer keys clicking in the background.

"Off the record? I believe so."

Wow. I shook my head as Archie gave Miller some pretty serious side-eye.

Miller let go of the wheel briefly to raise both hands in mock surrender. To who, I couldn't tell.

"Did your digging figure out where the trucks go when they get back here?" Miller asked after a beat.

"It's not like I have access to LoJacks on them," she said. "The addresses in the billing logs are all the same four delivery sites over and over. But once they get there, the guns have become much harder to trace. Kind of like laundering money—the guns have a longer history in the system. I'm just not sure to what end. Maybe whoever the end buyer is won't take the time to read it all and will miss something? I'm still trying to figure that part out."

Miller's jaw muscles flexed again, but he didn't say anything about the origin or the destination we suspected for at least some of the weapons.

Four guys with Texas addresses. I'd bet my engagement ring when the guns came back here they were going to JJ and his crew, and then south to the border, riding along on "hunting trips."

I scribbled that down and tapped the pen on the notebook. Damn. It was easy to see once all the variables were there. For a reporter, Nichelle was smart. But so was Skye, and I wouldn't trust her as far as I could throw my truck, so I kept my mouth shut, watching Miller's eyes in the mirror.

"I know I'm likely talking to the wall here, but I need to say it anyway," Miller said. "Listen to Joey. He knows this type of people, and he knows well why you shouldn't mess around with them."

"My ability to get myself in trouble is about to be hampered by distance," she said. "We're headed your way. Tomorrow."

"You're coming to Texas?" Miller's brow furrowed. "Is your mom okay?"

"She's good for now. I'm taking Joey to meet her tomorrow. And I'm not sure which of us is more nervous."

Miller's forehead scrunched up more. "Has Joey not ever met your mom?"

"Not yet."

"It'll be fine," Miller said. "He's a good man, Nichelle, and for what it's worth, I think he's good for you. Lila will see that."

I couldn't bring myself to care about her personal anxieties, so I turned my attention back to my laptop, scanning Lucas's list of fellow National Guardsmen for any more names that rang a bell.

I found one on the second page and ran a few tangential searches while Miller finished his phone call.

"Thanks, Kyle," Nichelle said. "What would I do without you?"

She wouldn't have inside access to ATF intelligence, for one. That probably wasn't the answer she was looking for, though. I didn't say it out loud.

"Let's not find out," Miller said.

"Deal. Nice to meet you, Faith, Archie."

"Safe travels," Archie said. That seemed safe, so I echoed it.

Miller ended the call and shook his head. "I'm sure I can guess what you must be thinking."

"You mean, why in the world would you tip off a reporter about a case as sensitive as this one? I know you said you have a history with this woman, and I admit to a bias where the media is concerned, but I cannot get my head around that. Especially not when we have officers' lives hanging in the balance."

"Trying to get an ID on the people I mentioned will keep her busy for a day or two, especially with everything else she has going on," Miller said. "She gave us some valuable information, and she's good for her word—she won't so much as tease a story on social media before we have this sewn up. No matter how long that takes."

"You're sure about that?" I asked.

"I understand why you hate reporters," Miller said. "I would, too, in your shoes. But I trust Nichelle with my life. She's saved it a couple of times. She's far more interested in justice and truth than being first to break a big headline on the internet, though she manages to do both often enough to keep her paper in the black."

"Good for her," I said. "I have to admit, her idea about them running the guns around in a sort of laundering operation is intriguing, but I doubt Zapata cares where his weapons are coming from. What the longer trail probably does is make it even harder to trace their origins to the Texas National Guard."

"That makes perfect sense." Miller nodded.

"It does," I said. "Especially since this deleted material shows that Lucas Lobban served—and was even bunkmates with—Senator Rooney's son."

34

"But Rooney is one of the people who sent me here," Miller repeated for the fifth time in twenty minutes. "Why would he direct an investigation toward his own son?"

"I'm not saying he did," I said, tapping my phone to see if the signal had come back. No such luck. "On the contrary, I'm saying a United States senator would be in a good position to cover up his son selling property of the state if need be. And someone has gone to great lengths to hide Scott Rooney's association with this crowd."

"Which is just a sign that he's in the middle of whatever this is," Archie said.

"Not a fact, but an easy assumption," I said.

"I thought you said we needed to move to allowing assumptions." Archie turned his head and winked at me.

"That doesn't sound like something I would say."

"I believe I heard it as well," Miller chuckled, drumming his hands on the wheel. "I'm not a fan of assuming, as a general rule, but we may be running out of options given the speed at which people are dying. No one's phone has a signal yet?"

"We have to figure out what the motive is here before we go asking questions that might tip off the wrong people to what we've figured out," I cautioned.

"I know that," Miller said. "How are we going to do that without the internet?"

"Good point," I conceded. "Mine is out still."

"Ours too," Archie said. "Maybe that's a good thing."

Miller turned his head toward Archie. "Okay, I'll bite. How do you figure?"

"Eyes on the road," Archie said, though the road was flat, empty, and straight with heat waves shimmering off it as far as anyone could see in front of the car. "I realize I'm the only dinosaur here who remembers working a case before we had the internet to help us. One of the things that has been forgotten in the age of information flying around at the speed of light is that sometimes slowing down a beat is helpful."

"Being stuck in this car without cell service is pretty slow," I said.

"So let's use it. When so much comes flooding at us so fast, it's easy to miss things, at least until something else surfaces that points us to a clue we didn't notice before. Right now, let's look at what we already know about these people, because it's a fair amount, I guarantee. Miller, you have said several times that Rooney is responsible for you being on the case, which seems to make you doubt that his son could be involved. But what did he really tell you when he sent you down here? And does anyone in your chain of command owe this guy a favor—or want him to owe them one?"

"Not that I know of, but that's usually how those kinds of favors work. Public or even extensive private knowledge decreases their value in terms of what can be done or asked."

"That's true," I said. "And I've heard rumblings about Rooney being interested in higher office."

"There's not much higher office than the United States Senate," Archie said.

"There's one," I said. "I know a fair amount about what people with those sorts of ambitions will do to make that a reality. Spoiler alert: there's not much that doesn't make the list."

"You think this guy would throw his own son under the bus?"

"If push came to shove, sure he would. You don't think Chuck would've fed me slowly to a pack of wolves if it might have increased his polling numbers with some key demographic?"

"Chuck McClellan is a special kind of evil bastard," Archie said.

"Eh," I said. "Doesn't it almost take a special kind of evil—or ego, maybe—to seek the White House anymore? It's damned near impossible to get to that level of power and influence without having sold bits of your soul."

"Assuming you had one to begin with," Archie said.

"Could be a kind assumption in some cases," I agreed. "But the other thing I know about politicians is that avoiding a scandal in the first place is infinitely preferable to being a hard ass in the aftermath of it breaking."

"So you think maybe Rooney was trying to steer Miller in a different direction. Away from his kid."

I checked the bio Google had produced on Scott Rooney before my signal disappeared. "Publicly available information paints him as a golden boy who went to Brown to study business and play lacrosse. No mention of any military service."

"Are you sure it's the same guy?" Archie asked.

"Same date of birth, and the deleted service records list the senator's home address." I tapped the edge of the keyboard. "Someone who knows their way around computer coding removed all evidence of Lobban's connection to Scott Rooney from any publicly accessible page," I said. "I found the trashed code through a back door, but it took some work on my part. No reporter would go to those lengths, and most cops who would touch a case like this don't have the ability to."

"Nichelle has a guy who's good with computers," Miller said. "She's come up with stuff like that before. But she'd have to know where to look." He met my eyes in the rearview. "Which is to say, yes, I think you're right, erasing the connection from the obvious parts of the internet was probably good enough in ninety-nine percent of scenarios."

"And they did that before Lobban murdered two people and was killed yesterday, too." I wrote that down as I said it.

"How do you know that?" Archie asked.

"This kind of work takes days. It's not as easy as pressing delete, especially if you're not allowed above-board access to the servers." I stared at the beige-and-blue blur outside the window as the world zoomed by. "Miller, when Rooney asked you to come here, what exactly were you told? And why you?"

"I've been working this case for three years," Miller said. "I picked up rumblings about these guys when I was here and traced them to the mid-Atlantic. We took out one of their early sources of merchandise—with some help from Nichelle, actually—but y'all know as well as I do that crooks of this caliber don't give up."

"No, if they're not the ones in prison, they pivot," Archie said.

"Exactly. And then eighteen months ago, Mexico cracked down on weapons in a way no one has since Australia went house to house to buy them back after a mass shooting there twenty years ago. Among other things, it's very difficult to get a license to deal firearms south of the border these days."

"But the cartels weren't going to go without," Archie said.

"So they turned north, where guns are barely regulated and damned easy to come by here in the modern-day Wild West," I said.

"It's not like we just ignore massive shipments of weapons," Archie said.

"Sure, when we know they're there," I said. "But without Mikey, I wouldn't have known about any of the stuff we saw yesterday. Would y'all have known to look there? If Miller's reporter friend is right, they move them in plain trucks driven by people who get paid to avoid getting pulled over—all right out in broad daylight. Operating under the radar allows them to move literal truckloads of weapons at a time."

"Though honestly—if they were using many people to move them one at a time, that would work, too," Archie said. "I've gotten so used to people walking around with the damned things I barely notice anymore other than to note where I'd need to move to protect your mother and drop the shooter if some asshole starts spraying in the park or the grocery store."

"What a world, huh, y'all?" Miller sighed.

"Is it like this where you live?" I asked.

"Not quite yet, anyway," he said.

"So your case drew you back here because your dealers got a big new market with plenty of cash," I said, pulling the horse back onto the trail.

"We had just figured out that some of the guns we were tracking had crossed the border when I got the first call about working with the task force." Miller tapped the wheel, his brow scrunching in concentration.

"And how did you learn that?" Archie asked.

These were the kinds of small details he was so good at parsing, the ones other people with less experience often missed.

"Freddie mentioned to his CO that we should watch out for it, and I got a call. Then we got a tip from a border security agent," Miller said. "He was following a group of guys passing stuff back and forth across the border, and he had a Federale friend who came around asking him about American guns confiscated at the scene of a cartel shootout."

"So Zapata's son was already working with you at that time?" Archie asked.

"He was in another division working a fraud case from the inside out. His father's tequila distillery is one of a dozen or so legit businesses the old man owns. The bottles came through customs with one in each case marked for inspection, it passed, and then people died from drinking the others, but no one ever figured out why. The tox screens on every victim were clear for poisons and drugs."

"Doesn't that give the label a bad name?"

"That was the point. Someone was trying to undermine the distillery because it would cut off a lucrative and legitimate business for Zapata, giving the police in Mexico an easier road to taking him down. Freddie came to us and wanted to trade information on the other cartels to find out who was setting his father up."

"So someone had a plant inside Zapata's organization," I said.

"Freddie believed so with everything in him. He came to the US government for a lot of complicated reasons, I suspect, but I think the idea that someone was after his old man added some urgency to his decision. And we needed his help to stop people from dying. Eventually, he proved himself trustworthy enough that when he was moved to my command, it was as an undercover agent with an alias, and he was trying to help us catch the gunrunners before his father was killed."

"Why not go to the Federales in the first place? They have a whole unit dedicated to the cartels, right?"

"Freddie said it's so corrupt you could get drunk off the rotten apples in that unit," Miller said. "We've been very careful about the information we share with them because of that."

"Have you tested his theory?" Archie asked.

"How so?"

"Misdirection—filtering bad information through the ranks to see what happens."

"That could be a dangerous game, and what we're doing is working without taking the risk. So far."

"It is?" Maybe I shouldn't have said that out loud, but it was too late to take it back. "Forgive me for pointing this out, but you've been working this case for three years, and you don't even really know who you're trying to catch, from what I can tell."

"Do you know who you're looking for before you close in on the end of an investigation?" Miller asked.

"I've been on this for three days," I said.

"You're looking for a single murderer, I'm trying to take down organized crime on both sides of the border," he shot back.

"We are all on the same side, though," Archie said.

I pulled a deep breath through my nostrils. "We are. Sorry, Miller."

"I'm sorry, too. I get why you're on edge," he said. "But I really am here to help. I came here to get Archie's help but am happy to offer y'all the full power and bully pulpit of the United States government to get Hardin home safely."

"Thanks." I tapped my phone again and growled at the lack of service bars, closing my eyes. "In the vein of revisiting things we already know, I was called to the body recovery site in the first place because Freddie Z wasn't the first corpse Ratcliff found. He was looking for a common thread between these murder victims, and then he disappeared."

"Which probably means he was onto something," Archie said. "Killing or kidnapping an officer is an excellent way to distract police, which is helpful to...pretty much any criminal."

"True," I said. "The problem with that part of the investigation is that there was no medical examiner on the case, and then they cremated the remains, so aside from hazarding a guess based on half a tattoo and a possibly missing DEA agent who might just be really good at undercover...

we don't even know who they were. Which makes it damned difficult to find out why they died or who was behind it."

"And we're sure we really need to know that to solve the case we have in front of us?" Miller asked.

"I think it would help," I said. "I'm willing to work the case as if one of the other victims is DEA Agent Cody Rylan, based on the fact that we have identified the most recent body as an undercover ATF agent. But I think knowing who the others were and how they ended up in the river is an important piece of this." I swallowed hard. "If someone in the cartel is picking off undercover officers and serving them up as warnings, I need to know."

"Fair enough."

"Do you think Ratcliff will be the next one who washes up?" Archie asked. "What does your gut say?"

That I'd rather it be anyone than Graham, which was entirely logical yet made me feel like a horrible person.

"I'm not sure who took Ratcliff," I said. "It could be the cartel, I guess, but I think whatever happened to him is wrapped up in Miller's smuggling ring. JJ told Mikey they 'already had' the nosy cop when we first got to the warehouse yesterday, so I think whoever they've been getting their marching orders from is responsible for his disappearance."

"But he said 'had'? Not 'took care of' or something like it?" Miller asked.

"Exactly. Which is why I'm hoping one of the locations on that map I found is helpful with locating him."

"Fingers crossed," Archie said. "I'm wondering if there's some way we're not thinking of to pursue these other unidentified remains."

"Sure, if we had the manpower to cross-reference missing persons cases from both sides of the border with the scant file Ratcliff gave me." I sighed. "Unfortunately the current era of massively understaffed law enforcement agencies prevents such luxuries."

"I can get it," Miller said. "Once I can make a few calls."

"You have that many experts just sitting at the ready?" I asked. "What's that like?"

"The federal government is a big beast," Miller said. "We don't have that kind of idle manpower at the ATF, but I like to think outside the box. The military has all kinds of highly trained people who aren't particularly busy if we're not in the middle of a war. I have a few friends I can call."

Archie opened his mouth to say something but didn't get it out before my phone rang.

"Thank you, Jesus," I muttered as I picked it up and answered Dean's call. "Sorry, we've been driving through the land that cell towers forgot," I said. "How are things there this morning?"

"We went back this morning to check out the map's marked location in the state park, this time in the daylight," he said. "It's a campsite. And we found a family there down from Texarkana. Nice folks. Kids were playing with some unusual stuff they found in a cave near the site, about a hundred yards off the riverbank."

"Please don't tell me someone's children were playing with body parts."

"Not quite that unusual. They were building a fort, cutting the trees with a bone saw. And holding walls up with cinder blocks that had chains attached. Searching the cave, our guys found a stash of long, straight razor blades in a crevice. Like five feet long. Very likely bloody, but all brand new —almost like they were disposable."

"Or only good for a single use?" I shook my head. "You're thinking they might be responsible for the missing heads?"

"Not without a handle of some kind," Dean said. "But that's for your buddy Jim to tell us, isn't it?"

"I'll ask him." I sighed. "That indicates that the dumping ground for all the bodies was the same."

"Turns out the entry point to the river there is an easy grade, but once you're about halfway out, it's the deepest point for miles. We have a crew searching the water with a drone now."

"The ones Ratcliff found were all downstream."

"I'll let you know what we turn up."

"I'm on my way back down there with Archie and an ATF agent from Virginia," I said, thinking about Timmy Dushane's friend at border patrol and JJ's comment. "Can your guys round up the agents who have worked the border patrol in Terrell County in the past three months and have them at Ratcliff's outpost for questioning this afternoon?"

"All of them?"

"I hear they're horribly understaffed. Shouldn't be very many guys," I said. "I want to know who might have sold Ratcliff out to the cartel."

"To the what?"

"I have a lot to catch you up on, Dean," I said, trying to figure out what to tell him and what to hold back. "Send someone to round up the border agents, and meet us at the house that was marked on the map I sent you yesterday in an hour."

I disconnected the call and set the phone down, catching Miller's eye in the mirror. "Why did Archie think you recognized that house yesterday at the hospital?"

35

Miller sighed. "I should've known I wouldn't be able to keep anything from Archie Baxter," he said. "I know the place. It's a federal holding seized in a tax fraud case years ago and unsold because," he waved one arm, "this isn't exactly a hot real estate market. So the government has used it for various things: wit sec, halfway house, you know."

"Freddie Z?" I guessed.

"For a while, yeah," Miller said. "When he first came to the ATF, they kept him at a distance, physically and figuratively—it was vacant, and his assignment was to figure out if the tampering with his father's tequila was happening before or after it came across the border, so he had a local base when he wasn't staking out a shipment or talking to customs officers."

"A local base with plenty of built-in surveillance," Archie said.

"Naturally," Miller agreed. "But it helped him, because all anyone saw was that he really was committed to and invested in working for us. There was no dirt to be had on the guy, and believe me—we looked. He was one of the best agents I've ever worked with, because he knows how a criminal thinks. Like I said, it was Freddie who first figured out where all the trafficked weapons were going. He said he knew his father and his father's colleagues, and once guns got hard to find in Mexico, they would turn to the place they were easiest to get. Even before he came to our side, he saw a war coming—I think it might have been his biggest motivation to get out of there. He knew the life that was laid out for him, and he didn't want it."

"I can relate to that," I said.

"So Zapata needs weapons, and he figures he knows how to smuggle stuff out of Mexico," Archie said.

"And it turned out to be a lot easier to smuggle stuff in," Miller added.

"Especially if you could find a relatively stupid American who had a friend in the border unit and happened to be in love with a Mexican girl?" I mused. "This Carlos guy the Dushanes were laundering for could be part of Zapata's operation, right?"

"Sure seems like it," Miller said.

I wrote out an organizational chart, leaving question marks at the bottom under JJ's friends in case they were handing the guns off to someone else before they got to Zapata, and one at the top that was far more important to cracking the case. "I feel pretty good about this theory for how the middle of their operation worked on this side of the border," I said. "So what's your end game here, Miller?"

"End game? To find and arrest whoever is running this on our side of the border. I've led this investigation for three years, and the mastermind of this operation is damn well insulated. Knowing the mechanics and being able to ID the low-level guys is great and all, but in order to put a stop to this, we need the bigger, smarter fish. For the moment, though, knowing that your dead guy is our double agent means I want the bastard who killed him—and the one who ordered it, too."

"We'll get them," Archie said with more confidence than I felt. The massive resources of the federal government had been on this for literal years, and Miller was still over his head, best I could tell. How the hell were a couple of Texas Rangers supposed to do what the US government couldn't?

Right then, I couldn't bring myself to care too much. The victim that pulled me into this was a drug dealer turned cop whose family probably knew who killed him, if they hadn't done it themselves—my usual drive to fight for the victim had puttered out miles behind us on the lonely desert highway. All I wanted was to have my husband back.

If I had to help Miller catch his big fish to do that, so be it. But if I could get to Graham without it, Miller was on his own.

Miller's phone binged, and Archie picked it up.

"Agent Kelley says he has Gavin Kurczyk's phone number and is getting a warrant. Suspected involvement in smuggling and homicide okay?"

"Add imminent personal danger," Miller said. "It's true, and some judges who don't want to help us will grant a warrant to save a suspect's life."

Archie poked at the screen and then put the phone down. "Done. He says he'll call us when they have a location."

My own phone buzzed with a text from Jim: *If the same person killed all the people in these file photos, they improved their slicing technique over time.*

I noticed that, I typed back.

I also think the June victim's neck was broken before he was killed. At least from the photos. The bone shows fatal injury at the C-3 very close to the time of beheading. But the break should have been fatal.

I jotted that down.

Buzz. *He's also missing a fingertip on his left hand. The middle one. Hard to be certain with photo quality and decomposition, but this could be something he's had since birth.*

I flipped back to the notes I'd made after we talked to Jenny.

Was Carlos's "fucked-up middle finger" missing the end?

That might be helpful. Thanks for your time and your sharp eyes, Jim.

If the local drug lord had joined a DEA agent and a traitorous son in the river, maybe Zapata thought all three of them were working against him?

I picked up my laptop and reconnected it to the phone's hotspot, copying the full list of National Guardsmen in Lobban's company and noting his commanding officers all the way to the top of the chain.

Command Sergeant Major Derek Amin. I paused, the cursor hovering over his name.

Why did that look familiar? Something whispered around the edges of my brain, but I couldn't quite grab the thought.

No shot I would get a photo to load out here in this lifetime, so I wrote it down and put two stars next to it. Maybe my brain would get there before the signal strength did.

Going back to the search window, I started a hunt for everything the internet knew about Emilio Zapata and his son Ferdinand.

Miller unlocked the door to the stash house in Duncan and flipped on the light, a bare bulb screwed straight into the popcorn-finished, nicotine-yellow ceiling.

"Was Freddie still using this place when he was in the area?" I asked.

"He was," Miller said.

"So you had a cartel boss's kid working for the ATF? What does the DEA have to say about that?" Dean asked, walking the perimeter of the small living room and pausing by the window unit air conditioner in the corner. He laid one finger inside the vent and wiped it on the edge. "This has been off long enough for dust to collect here," he said, holding up his finger.

"The DEA has nothing to say about matters that are none of their concern," Miller said, walking over to take a photo of the dust line on the air conditioner with his phone. "The last time I spoke with Freddie was the weekend of July fourth. I looked through the security footage from the days leading up to it weeks ago, but there wasn't anything helpful."

"So before Ratcliff disappeared, you guys knew this ATF double agent was missing, and no one said anything to us when we launched a manhunt for Ratcliff in this area?" Dean's mouth twitched, annoyance clear in his tone.

"We brought McClellan in when it became clear that it was detrimental to both cases to avoid that," Miller said, his voice tight. "That's protocol."

"Drew Ratcliff is a good officer and a good man," Dean said, backing slowly away and holding Miller's gaze. "We better find him alive."

I stepped to the center of the room, pointing through the doorway at something that looked a lot like dried blood on the edge of the kitchen sink. "We need to work together if that's going to happen," I said, waving for them to follow as I crossed to the sink and pulled the chain on the overhead light.

Dark, brownish-red stains coated the white porcelain sink bowl on three sides, spilling down over the front apron to the cabinets. I knelt to check the droplets dotting the green-painted doors and staining the linoleum. "Jim said Freddie was shot," I said. "This isn't consistent with a gunshot wound."

"It might be consistent with someone having their throat cut, though," Miller said, leaning forward over the sink. "If I were standing here like this," he waved Dean over, "and you came up behind me and slit my throat..."

"It would run down over the edge of the sink," Archie said.

"It would also spray." My eyes roamed the higher walls and cabinets, catching a line of red-brown stains on the cream-and-floral curtains adorning the small window, along with streaks of clean cabinet about the width of my palm on either side of the sink. "I'll be damned."

"You think Zapata got a jump on his assailant? Or one of his assailants?" Archie asked.

I pulled my notes out and flipped through the pages. "Maybe. Or maybe Freddie Z was playing both sides of the fence, and he killed whoever died here but didn't have the opportunity to clean it up before someone came in and shot him," I said. "Ratcliff said the body that turned out to be Zapata was the sixth one in a year. Maybe he was the attacker in this one instead of the victim."

Miller pointed a finger at me. "I like that," he said. "Except I'd be more inclined to think he was under threat, either immediate physical jeopardy or threat of being dimed out. He never struck me as the type who would just murder someone if he had a choice."

"Assuming you're right, we have no idea whose blood this might be."

Miller pulled out his phone. "We have a forensics team in San Antonio."

Dean waved him off. "I have one at the lab in Lampasas." He pulled out his phone and made a call. "They'll be here in half an hour."

I touched one finger to my chin. "Does the local sheriff know that lab is there?" I asked.

Dean shrugged. "I would think she should, but I don't know."

"How well do you know her?" I asked.

"Not very. She tends to keep her department tight. They work traffic enforcement and run rescue calls and leave the heavy lifting to Ratcliff and me."

"She called a team from El Paso to the river to collect Freddie's remains," I said. "It took hours for them to get here. Hours she spent trying to ask me questions about the case before I walked away from her."

"Interesting," Miller said.

"She gave me her entire résumé the first time I met her, too," I said, pacing away from the sink. "I thought she was trying to impress me, or explain why she was working in this tiny little town, maybe..."

"But maybe she was trying to establish herself as an authority figure who had a connection with you?" Archie asked. "So you'd like her?"

"Watch it, Arch, people will think you've been studying psychology." I winked.

"I listen when you talk. Sometimes."

"I have one guy who's local to this area on my team," Dean said. "You met him the other day—tall, lanky dude. His name is Ben Langford. Let me see if he knows the sheriff."

He pulled out his phone and sent a text, and I closed my eyes, trying to call up the conversation I'd had with Nava. "She said she went to school somewhere away and then came back."

"I can run a background and credit check," Miller said. "See where she went and what she studied and if she carries heavy debt that could make her easy to compromise. What's her name?"

"Connie Nava," I said. "She told me she went to UT to study criminal justice and political science, but now I'm thinking objective verification wouldn't hurt."

He wrote it down. "I'll need a computer and a secure Wi-Fi connection."

"We have that at Ratcliff's office at the outpost," Dean said.

"We should look around here a little more," I said.

"Sure." Dean waved a "ladies first" in the direction of the hallway.

"I'm not sure that's chivalrous here," I said.

"It's a sign of respect," Dean said. "And, you know...self-preservation."

"Nice," Archie said, unsnapping the safety strap on his holster.

"Kidding, sir," Dean said. "Sorry if it didn't sound that way."

"Surely anyone who might have been here is long gone by now," Miller said.

I turned the knob on the bathroom door, the metal sending a shock up my arm that I couldn't swear was actual static.

Maybe I heard the flies. Or caught a hint of the smell.

Both flooded out of the tiny room in a nauseating cloud when I pushed on the door.

"If Freddie was in the river, who the hell is that?" Miller asked, his words muffled by his shirt collar, which he'd flipped up over his face.

"Good question," Archie said.

Taking shallow breaths through my own collar, I stepped closer to the corpse. "I hope the lab techs have a bug guy," I said, trying to ignore the fly larvae squirming in the rotting meat where the head used to be as I leaned in to peer at the tattoo on her arm. Her skin was partially liquefied, but I could see enough. The rose was probably fairly common, but the stars and the bunny matched the photo from Timmy's car.

"Odds are good this is Timmy Dushane's girlfriend. Lucia." I swallowed hard and checked her neck, pointing with the hand that wasn't holding my shirt over my face. "This isn't the same kind of wound the bodies in the river had, though." I glanced at Dean. "Her head was removed with a handsaw. See the marks?"

"Like the saw we found in Timmy's garage?" His eyes widened.

"You mean Doris's garage?" I replied.

I pointed to the door, waving them all back out and waving off stray flies once it was closed.

"This is the woman the motel lady said was a prostitute with some bad connections south of the border?"

"That's her. Based on what I know about the stages of decomposition, I'd say she's been there four to six weeks," I said. "And given the saw striations on the bone, I'd love for Jim to test the saw we swiped from the Dushanes' garage against her tissue. More than that, I'd really like to know what the hell she was doing here if this was the house Freddie Z used."

I pointed at the two remaining doors, which probably led to bedrooms.

"Miller, with me. Archie and Dean, take door number two. Anything that looks out of place, interesting, or messy comes with us."

I opened the bedroom door closest to me and screamed, yanking my SIG from its holster and aiming at the man in the corner, half-hidden behind the open closet door.

36

"Police!" I shouted in a remarkably steady voice, given the momentary loss of composure. Three other guns came up behind me, all trained on the guy in the corner.

He didn't move.

"Close the door gently, and put your hands where we can see them," I ordered calmly.

Not a blink, not a peep.

Archie took one hand off his gun to flip on the light. "I don't think he's programmed to comply."

A boxing dummy.

I laughed, holstering my weapon and bending at the waist. "I've shot a lot of things, from people to tires to even a toilet once—that was an accident. I can definitely say I've never drawn on a robot, though. Oops."

"I shot a tree once," Miller said. "I was a rookie at the Dallas PD, and you know, we don't have many trees. I was chasing a suspect on foot, he turned and I thought he was armed, and I fired before I had time to think about it. I didn't start off a great marksman, thank God. He wasn't our guy after all—I ran up on a drunk college kid carrying a walkie-talkie. He matched the description of our suspect, dressed similarly, same height roughly, dark hair. He panicked and took off when I hollered at him, and back then, I thought that surely meant he was guilty."

"It still makes me think there's a higher likelihood that someone is up to no good," I said. "But I don't fire unless I have no other choice."

"That drunk frat boy is the president of Rockwall Federal Credit Union now, a deacon in his church, and father of three. Someone was looking out for the both of us that day. I've never fired on anyone without being damned sure they were a threat to me or someone else in the moment since."

"But for the grace of God," Archie agreed, and Dean murmured, "Amen."

"I don't know a cop that doesn't have a horror story about a near miss. You got off easy, McClellan," Dean said. "This fancy punching bag almost doesn't count." He crossed the room and moved the door. "Holy shit."

We hurried the six steps that spanned the width of the room.

"Freddie's punching bag won the lottery," I said, my eyes on the four-foot stacks of hundreds between the closet door and the wall.

"Or Timmy's girl was here to set Freddie up," I said.

"How do you figure?" Miller asked.

"That's an awful lot of cash to be sitting there undisturbed for all this time. What kind of criminal comes in here and kills the girl a dozen steps that way, then just walks out and leaves this sitting here?"

"One who got interrupted?" Miller asked.

"One who didn't look in here?" Dean offered.

"One who wanted the girl dead, but also wanted it to look like Freddie Z might have killed her and like he was double-crossing the ATF," Archie said.

I turned and pointed at him. "Bingo."

"My friend Nichelle has a thing about puzzles." Miller put his feet up on Ratcliff's desk and took a bite of a grilled cheese sandwich from Mel's. "She used to keep a ladder in her kitchen, because she says when she's deep into a complicated section and having trouble finding pieces, taking the long view helps her see it differently. It's a philosophy I've applied to cases like this one with some success the past couple of years. We talked through the details on the way down here this morning, and we found some interesting new information at the stash house. Maybe zooming out is what we need."

"And how do we do that?" I looked up from my laptop, thankful to finally have a decent internet connection, popping a fry into my mouth and copying a paragraph on the Zapata cartel from an article in the DEA journal's March issue.

"What we have here is a huge network that spans not only multiple states but at least two countries," Miller said. "Maybe three if the intel we have on Chinese-made Fentanyl coming across our southern border ensnares Zapata. There are a lot of pieces to get mired in, but at the end of the day, the pieces can distract from the big picture. What we want is to get to the heart of the operation and shut it down. So what do we know that might point to someone who has the power to run something this large for years without getting caught?"

"That it almost has to be a dirty cop," Archie said, leaning back in his chair. "I did a stint in internal affairs back in the day—operations like this rely on the greed and corruptibility of people in positions of power."

I stood and went to the small whiteboard on the other side of the room, looking over Ratcliff's notes. "I don't see any names here that I recognize as law enforcement."

"Let's add some, then," Dean said, tossing me a marker from the pen cup on the desk. "You said you want to look into Nava. That right arm of hers, Deputy Dawes, has always given me a weird vibe. How long has he been here, I wonder? And then there're the border guards, too. My guys are bringing them in," he checked his watch, "twenty-five minutes."

Miller tapped on his keyboard. "Let's see what the federal government knows about Sheriff Nava."

He typed for a few seconds and leaned forward, putting his sandwich back into the white Styrofoam box.

"The shooter from the warehouse yesterday was National Guard?" he asked.

"He was. With Rooney's son."

"So was Nava. Served four years from 2010 to 2014, went to school in Austin on the state's dime. Her story about her education checks out. She graduated from UT in 2016, with two years of credit transferred from online community college."

I hurried back to my computer, searching her name in the state records. "She wasn't in their battalion, but she was on the same base at the same time," I said, reading the list of fellow officers. "Dean, your accountant friend said the ledgers showed money moving through three local businesses, and one of them was the garage-diner place, right? And it's owned by the Jenkins family?"

"That is all correct, yeah." He rounded the desk and looked over my shoulder.

"They have a son by the name of Jesse?"

"It's easy to find out." He pulled out his phone. "Yes. He's the youngest of the three brothers who currently run the garage, according to Facebook."

"He was in the same battalion as Nava. It seems crime could be a family affair for more than just the Dushanes."

Dean drummed his fingers on the table. "I know the older brother has a history of small-time drug deals and a hot head. One of my guys was off duty and in a bar out in Lampasas last year when he caught him selling in the john. He got a slap on the wrist, I thought because his parents called in a favor, but maybe there was more to it than that."

I tapped the marker on the desk, then jumped to my feet and paced the limited length of the small room.

"She does that when she's thinking," Archie said for the new guys' benefit.

"I've noticed," Dean said. "Care to share, McClellan?"

"It would be a hell of a smart way to get stuff back and forth across the border, using other people's cars that have been left for repair," I said. "I saw an older guy, I didn't think anything of it at the time. Over the weekend, he was at the garage-diner, and he got really pissed about his truck—said they'd had it for days and they were overcharging him for an air filter. Took a swing at the mechanic and made a big scene. The dad comped the air filter from behind the food counter, and they hustled the old guy out while one of the waitresses talked to me. She said he had dementia, played the whole thing down. Who keeps a vehicle for days to change the air filter?"

"So if the two largest local businesses and the sheriff's office are part of the network...," Miller said.

"Then the whole damned county is pretty much corrupt," I said. "Which is how Timmy ended up dead after I went looking for him."

"That wasn't your fault," Dean said.

"I know that. But I still want to catch the people responsible for it."

"Locating the local link between these folks and the border patrol is a good step in that direction," Miller said.

"Timmy's friend from school. His mother told me the guy let him and his girlfriend move back and forth across the border with no searches."

"And the girlfriend was dead with the tattoo in the shower at the stash house," Archie said.

Dean pulled out his phone at the mention. "Forensics is taking samples to see if the blood in the kitchen belonged to the girl and photographing the scene."

He tapped the screen again. "And my guys are fifteen minutes out. They have the entire unit that covers this area. Timmy's friend has to be in there somewhere."

Miller's phone buzzed. "Kelley has a steady location on JJ's buddy Gavin." He tapped his screen. "Oh, shit."

"What?" I tapped my foot, nervous energy thrumming in the air around me.

"He's..." He used two fingers to zoom in. "He's in a trailer. On the edge of the state park. Like maybe fifteen miles from here."

"Keep the tracker on, and have your guy ping you if he moves," Archie said. "Dean, can we send your unit to set up a perimeter and watch while we talk to these border guards?"

"On it, sir." Dean was already typing. "Miller, can I have that location?"

"Coming up."

I turned to Archie, keeping my voice low. "I can't stand sitting here. This whole operation is barreling toward a cliff, and the people in charge of something like this have to be well connected enough to know that. I want to go get Graham."

"We will. But we have to keep following this until we know where to look."

"What if nobody will tell us that?"

"We'll beat it out of them if we have to." His face said he was only half kidding, and I wanted to hug him for it. He squeezed my hand. "Nothing will happen to him, if it's the last thing I do."

Fear shot through me like lightning, the feeling so strong I actually flinched. "It won't be."

"I didn't mean it that way."

"You did a little." I squeezed his hand back. "Don't be a hero, Baxter. Leave that to the youngsters."

"Leave what to us?" Dean asked, moving toward the door. "They're almost here. How are we going to do this?"

"We need to split them up." I ignored his first question. "Get names, dates of service, commanding officers, and then grill them until they crack."

"This is the part I'm good at," Miller said.

"Happy to have you around today, then," I said, looking down at my laptop screen. I'd left off in the middle of the search about Nava. I clicked back to trace her chain of command and made a note. "Nava and all of the other guys we've tied to the Guard, including Lobban, had the same CO. Derek Amin. Why does that sound so damned familiar?"

Everyone mumbled noncommittal *I don't know*s as I opened a new window and typed the guy's name.

A photo filled the screen as I heard tires crunching the gravel outside.

"Oh, shit—I met this guy!" I pointed at the screen. "He was at the detention facility when I went to see Timmy." I clapped a hand over my mouth, searching my memory for whether we'd said who I was there to see as I stared at his title. Current Command Sergeant Major for the Texas National Guard.

"Don't think about that now. We'll get to it later. Right now, we need all focus on cracking fellow officers, some of whom might be corrupt," Dean said as a car door slammed outside. "I count six guys and four of us. There's not a lot of space here."

"I'll take the barn," I said. "Miller, you take the back room in here. Dean, you take this room. Archie...outside?"

"I'll take one of Dean's men along," Archie said.

"Put your other guy outside with the other two guards," I said to Dean. "I want their weapons before we do anything."

"Let's crack the case, y'all," Miller said.

37

"Have a seat." I pointed to a three-legged stool in the barn, positioning myself between it and the door.

"What the hell is going on here?" A stout border guard shuffled to the stool and glared at me before resting one foot on it instead of sitting down. "The Rangers pulled me out of bed and drove me to the middle of nowhere, then you take my gun, and now I need to consent to an interview in this shithole little excuse for a stable? I'm about to decide I want a lawyer."

"Do you need a lawyer, Brayden?" I arched one eyebrow and held his gaze, not blinking.

"You tell me."

"I wish I knew. It's actually one of the things I'd like to find out."

He kicked the stool over. "Aren't we all on the same damned side?"

I spread my hands. "We're supposed to be."

The calmer I seemed, the more agitated he got, which wasn't a good sign. As a general rule, people who act offended that they're being questioned are trying to cover fear because they're doing something they don't want anyone to know about. The question then becomes—is whatever they're trying to hide something I actually give a damn about?

"How long have you been with CBP, Brayden?"

"Almost six years," he said. "And my service record is spotless. Not so much as a dead Mexican. Ask anyone."

"I'll do that," I said. "Later. Right now I'd like to know why you're upset." I kept my volume low, tone even, face flat and unreadable.

He stared for a minute before dropping his head back to study the ceiling, thrusting his arms down his sides so hard it was a wonder he didn't flop them right out of socket. "You're telling me you wouldn't be annoyed if someone showed up at your home and hauled you in for questioning without so much as a thank you for your service? Do you know how hot it gets out here? The kind of horseshit we put up with, the sob stories we have to just fucking ignore? And nobody likes us—the migrants see us as their enemy, and the damned media can't shut up about everything we screw up, like any of them could do better with the skeleton-crew staffing level and absolutely shit budget we get from Washington." The words poured out of him on a wave of bile and frustration until he ran out of air and had to stop for a breath, his face red.

Huh. I tipped my head from side to side. "Thank you for your service," I said. That wasn't quite the direction I thought this would go, but I could work with it.

He bent and righted the stool. "You're welcome." He still didn't sit.

"How did you end up working in border patrol?" I asked.

"I grew up in South Texas. I wanted to be a cop from the time my grandpa gave me my first set of toy handcuffs, but I didn't make the obstacle course cut for DPS, and I lost my campaign for sheriff. I'm certainly not working for Connie Nava. So it was this or nothing."

I had five more questions teed up by the time he stopped talking.

"Did you go to school in this area?" I asked, studying his face and trying to place an age. I guessed enough younger than Timmy to know how he'd answer the next question before he'd answered that one.

"I did."

"Did you know Timmy Dushane? Parents own the Cherry Lane Motel."

"I mean, he was a lot older, I think he graduated when I was in like the sixth grade...but everyone knew of Timmy back then. He was a track star. Won state in the hundred meter. It was the first time our little school had ever won a medal at state."

Timmy? I tried to picture the guy I'd met as a superstar runner and couldn't quite get there. But I nodded like I knew exactly what this guy was talking about.

"So he was popular back then?"

"Sure. Damned shame how his life turned out. Chasing a Chicana whore back and forth across the border and living at his mother's motel. Everyone in town pities his sorry ass these days."

"He's dead," I said flatly.

"What?" The way Brayden's eyes bugged said he really didn't know that before I said it. "Did her pimp or her dealer get to him first?"

"He was killed two days ago in American custody at the ICE detention center."

Brayden sat heavily on the stool and put his head in his hands. "Jesus, Timmy," he muttered.

I stepped closer, lowering my voice. "Did you know Timmy well after high school? Say, better in recent years?"

He took a shuddering breath. "Kind of. He was Scotty's friend. From way back. We all knew that if his whore came across the river near the motel, we were supposed to ignore it."

I paused, thinking about the dust cover on the 'Vette and the weird tires, with the rear-facing door on Doris's shed.

"Did they drive his Corvette back and forth across the border when the river was low?" I asked.

"We were helping out a hometown hero, ma'am. It's not like we were letting rapists and murderers or dope across."

"I get it," I said. I even felt a little sorry for this guy. My gut said he had no idea what he'd been part of.

"Is Scotty here today with y'all?"

Brayden raised his head and pointed to the door. "He's outside with the old guy in the Stetson. I've always wondered why we don't get more respect, his daddy being a bigwig in DC and all. So much for all the complaining people do on the internet about nepotism."

I turned for the door and then turned back. "Scotty the border agent is Scott Rooney?" Formerly of the National Guard, but I didn't ask that part out loud. I grew up in a political family, and I saw the pattern better than most people probably would.

"Sure." Brayden looked puzzled. "That's bad?"

"It might be very good," I said. "Thanks for your cooperation today. You're free to go."

He offered a sad smile. "I hope you find whatever you're looking for," he said. "I need those Ranger guys to take me home. And I want my gun back."

I waved as I shoved the door open and ran toward the sound of Archie's voice on the riverbank. This whole damned thing was starting to make sense. And the senator's son was looking better and better for Miller's big fish.

38

Scott Rooney was the picture of unaffected, privileged charm in tailored khaki shorts and an artfully frayed-around-the-edges Rolling Stones T-shirt that probably cost more than he made in a week. Knowing who he was let me see things I'd brushed right past in my hurry to start questioning Brayden. To feel like I was doing something to move the case forward. Where Brayden had been afraid of getting in trouble, Scott exuded confidence that everything would work out okay for him in the end.

I'd bet he didn't know his dad was eyeing the White House and had sicced the ATF on him in the process.

"Hey," Archie said when he spotted me over Scott's shoulder. "Am I that much slower than everyone else?"

"I just had to come meet Senator Rooney's son," I said, putting my hands in my pockets as I joined them on the sand. "I didn't know you were among our guests today, but as it happens, I have a few questions for you."

Archie's eyebrows went up. "You're Rooney's son?"

Scott played it perfectly, with a slight smile and eyes dropped to his shoes. "Guilty." He looked up at me. "I'm sure you of all people understand why I don't lead with that when I meet people."

"Your father isn't in prison," I said.

Yet, anyway.

"Come on," Scott said. "You know as well as I do they've all done something that could get them locked up."

Was this fish bigger than Miller imagined? Because a corrupt sitting United States senator would be the Moby Dick of federal criminal pursuit.

"Why do you work a shit job at border patrol when you have an Ivy League education, Scott?" I asked. "The same reason you ended up in the Texas Army National Guard before college?"

His eyes went wide. "How do you know about that? The records are supposed to be sealed or expunged or something."

"There are ways to find anything that's ever been on the internet if you know where to look," I said. "But that makes me curious as to why you would want to keep your service record a secret. Especially in this political climate, having a son with a commendable service record is an asset to your father."

"I..." He stopped, shaking his head. His confidence was cracking. I just needed to keep chipping.

"I don't think our parents were ever friendly," I said. "Different parties make hostile bedfellows."

"They're all alike." He sneered.

"Mine was pretty controlling, with a very definite vision for my life that didn't include this job," I said. "How about yours?"

"He said he wanted me where he could make sure I kept a job. Called me lazy and ungrateful." His eyes went to the leather boat shoes on his feet again.

"Did you actually graduate from Brown?" I asked. "Google told me you went there."

Scott shook his head.

I pulled the baggie with the strange coins even Miller's archaeologist-turned-lawyer girlfriend hadn't really been able to help with.

"Recognize these?"

He leaned closer, peering at the bag.

"That's drug-dealer code," he said. "So the suppliers will recognize dealers approved by the cartel. Doesn't really mean much."

Damn. I stuck them back into my pocket and stepped back. "Tell me when you last saw Lucas Lobban."

His eyes came up to meet mine. "Luke? I haven't seen him in years. We knew each other in the Guard."

I made a sound that mimicked a buzzer. "Try again."

He raised both hands and looked me straight in the eye. "I swear."

"So you didn't get tipped off by your father or someone who works for him that I was in a warehouse in the middle of nowhere and send Lobban after me with an assault rifle loaded with hollow points yesterday?" I asked.

"Holy shit." His mouth fell open. "I did not." He paused. "You're standing here. Does that mean Luke is dead?"

"He is." I kept my cool, flat tone.

"Dammit, Dad," he muttered.

Archie raised one hand. "You're saying your father is the real villain here?"

Scott kept talking like he didn't hear the question. "I gave up my education, I worked under his guy at the Guard until I couldn't anymore, I've been down here trying to keep his shit from falling apart, listening to him when he says we're almost there." Scott sighed. "But we're never going to get there, are we?"

"To the White House?" I asked. "I know that ambition well. My father didn't deserve the honor, and it sounds like yours doesn't, either."

"I want a deal. I'll tell you everything I know, and I'll testify, but I'm not going to prison for that old bastard. He's had an iron grip on my entire life for too many years, and I'm done protecting him."

"Why would you protect him in the first place?" I asked.

"You didn't ever take advantage of being Chuck McClellan's daughter?" he asked. "I like the perks. Being the president's son was supposed to open doors for me. Allow me to finally have a life outside smuggling stolen guns and increasingly deadly dope."

"How do we know you know anything useful?" I asked.

He folded his arms across his chest. "I know everything, McClellan. I even know where your husband is."

I froze, my face falling before I could stop it.

A slow smile spread across his. "Looks like my intel is better than yours."

"Is he alive?" I asked, my heart hammering double time.

"He is. But the situation he's in is unstable. Zapata's right hand has evidence that Freddie Z was working with the ATF, and that has made them suspicious of the new guys. Your husband is new."

My heart stuttered between beats, and Archie put a hand on my elbow.

I took a deep breath, shaking it off.

"I want full immunity." Scott saw the weakness and pounced in for the kill. "I'll do everything I can to make sure Hardin is safe, and I'll hand you my father."

"Why would you do either of those things?"

"Because if we're not going to win it all, my father deserves to lose at his own game," he said. "You think I don't know I'm only here talking to you because he tipped off that ATF guy? He's trying to throw me under this bus he's been driving for years, and if I'm getting mowed down, he's coming with me." He took a breath. "And because I'm betting that you care as much about your husband as I do about my freedom."

Archie opened his mouth, looked at my face, and closed it again.

I stuck out my hand. "You know I can't promise you anything, but I will give the argument for it everything I have—so long as you hold up your end and you stay with us until I have Graham back safe."

Scott shook it. "Good enough. Can I go along when they serve my father with an arrest warrant?"

I thought about the look on Chuck's face when I snapped cuffs on his wrists.

"If you're telling me the truth, you sure can."

"His story checks out," Miller said. "His father was the congressman from this district before he was elected to the Senate sixteen years ago. Scott ran track with Timmy Dushane in high school, did two semesters at Brown before he withdrew and went into the Guard. I still can't find why he was discharged, but he was hired by CBP a month later, probably as a favor to his father."

"Because who doesn't want a United States senator to owe them one?" Archie asked.

"This one isn't going to like us if junior there is really telling the truth," I said.

Miller shook his head. "He's a hell of a good liar," he said. "I sat with him for thirty minutes and bought every word of how he wanted 'whatever might be happening' down here cleaned up."

"He counted on being able to plant enough evidence to frame his kid."

"And on no one believing the young man's side of the story," Archie said.

"Or maybe on us shooting before we asked any questions, even," I said.

"You sure your guys are good for keeping him under their thumb?" I asked Dean.

"He won't so much as take a leak alone."

"What now?" Archie asked the room. "He said Graham is in a shaky situation, but we can't exactly tackle the Zapata compound, just the four of us."

"See how many agents you can have on standby in the next twenty-four hours, and I'll do the same," Miller said.

Archie pulled out his phone, and I opened my laptop, an email flashing up from Morton in cybercrimes. I clicked the link and read the message twice before I opened the first attachment. "Morton cracked Timmy Dushane's laptop and found a whole folder full of encrypted spreadsheet files," I said, scanning some awfully big figures and whistling. "Holy shit. The Cherry Lane was moving seventy-five thousand a month, minimum."

"Dean's accountant friend told us that already, right?" Archie asked. "We should check those numbers against the ledgers you found and make sure they match."

"I bet they won't." I leaned closer to the screen. "Jenny was right about Doris—or someone—skimming money. In this second column, Timmy was keeping track of how much was coming off the top."

"Teeing his own mother up for the cartel?" Miller's eyes widened. "That's some cutthroat stuff, right there."

I opened the other file and found a calendar with dates marked from January to May, pulling out my phone to check the dates Ratcliff discovered bodies. If there was a pattern that matched, I didn't see it. I scrolled. "Every four weeks," I muttered. "What would Timmy be tracking every four weeks?"

"That Mikey girl said her boyfriend went hunting once a month," Miller offered.

I nodded, closing my eyes and hearing Grady's voice in my head. On the screen, I clicked back to the web browser, the photo of Command Sergeant Major Amin filling the screen again. "The head honcho at the Guard—he comes down every four weeks to inspect the detention facility," I said. "A lot of the stuff in JJ's possession, maybe all of it, was Texas National Guard property. Scott Rooney said he worked for his father's man at the Guard until he couldn't anymore. I bet he means this guy." I pointed. "Arch—something is bugging me here. I met him on Sunday, but I feel like my brain is reaching for something older. Do we know him?"

Archie crouched next to my chair on bad knees and peered at the screen. "The name rings a faint bell, but not loud enough for me to know why," he said.

I laid two fingers over the bottom half of the photo. "It's something in the eyes."

He leaned closer. "Oh, man."

"What?"

He stood slowly, leaning heavily on the arm of the chair. "He worked in the governor's office. During your father's second term."

I looked back at the photo and checked the bio dates. "He would have been about twenty-one."

"He was. He was a young guy who'd graduated UT early with some kind of international affairs degree, a prodigy. More than an intern, but less than the inner circle."

"You don't remember what he did?"

I stared harder at the eyes and could see them in the vestibule outside Chuck's office in the capitol. And in the hallway off the foyer at the mansion.

I grabbed the arm of the chair, closing my eyes. "He was at the house. It was late. I was a teenager, probably sneaking in..."

"A low-level go-getter with brains and ambition is the perfect missing piece for Chuck's case," Archie said. "No one would have suspected that guy of directing the guns one way or the money another. Not back then."

I searched for Amin's service record. "He joined the Guard as a captain the year before Chuck left office and was assigned to the requisition office six months later. He's spent twenty years working his way up through the ranks, and now he runs the whole damned thing. This right here is the center of your gunrunning operation. Care to go for two jumbo-sized fish today, Miller?"

"I'm going to need all hands on deck to reel them in," he said. "It's a smart scam—I bet no one in the legislature here bats an eyelash at someone ordering too many guns."

"So Amin sells the extras under the senator's political protection, and they split the profits: Rooney funds his campaigns, and Amin gets rich and has power," Archie said. "And they probably don't even think they're doing anything wrong, because the cartels are killing each other with their guns, and who's going to complain about that?"

I closed the computer. "I want a warrant for his arrest."

"Not yet," Miller said. "He's well insulated, and we don't want to tip our hand. Plus, if he's been into this since your father was the governor, he's not doing it without buying himself a few state judges. We'll take it to federal charges and courts. When we have the case sewn up."

"And when I have Graham back," I said.

"Of course."

Miller picked up his phone. "How do y'all feel about checking out this trailer where JJ's buddy Gavin is holed up while we wait for the cavalry and try to figure out a plan of attack? If Scott is right and Zapata's people know Freddie was working with us, they're probably responsible for putting him in the river, and they're likely covering tracks for any of the information he was able to get for us, too. It's time to go in. When we have the manpower."

"And when we're sure your people aren't leading us into another Waco," Archie muttered.

"No offense taken."

"There was a little intended."

"I like to think all of law enforcement learned from that." Miller's tone was polite but cool.

"Gentlemen," I said, putting a hand toward each of them. "We're on the same side this time. Nobody is going to do anything stupid." Not if I could help it, anyway.

"Let's go check out the trailer," Archie said, letting the door bang shut behind him on his way to the car.

39

"I've never seen a purple one before," Archie said, peering at the single-wide sitting alone in the middle of the desert outside the fencing for the state park. "It's certainly not inconspicuous."

"I only see one vehicle," I said.

"If you can call a half-rusted Gremlin a vehicle," Dean said. "Does that thing even start, or is it, like, Fred Flintstone powered?"

I snorted, shooting him a smile in appreciation of the levity.

Miller slowed the car about a hundred yards from the trailer as Dean's perimeter unit loaded up to leave. "I say we go in fast and loud. There are only three guys remaining in the group JJ was part of, and they might not all be here. But even if they are, we're not going to be outnumbered."

"It'll be dark in a couple of hours," I said.

"All the more reason to get in and out fast," Miller said, checking his phone. "I'll have a hundred agents here by morning. Let's do this, see if these jokers know anything useful, get some food and some sleep, and then go after Zapata. And Hardin."

"Sounds like a plan," I said.

Miller parked the car, the four of us drawing our weapons and fanning into a standard formation around the end of the trailer that had only one small, high window.

I followed Miller to the front door while Archie and Dean circled to the back.

Miller didn't knock. He just blew the thing off the hinges with one swift kick, moving inside and shouting, "Police!" in a voice so commanding I wouldn't have known it was him from our ordinary conversations.

I followed, turning a slow circle and taking in the scene. A glass bowl with three pills in the bottom sat in the middle of a scarred wooden coffee table. The small room had three bodies strewn across the carpet, but I didn't see any blood. In one corner of the couch, I recognized JJ's friend Gavin from his driver's license photo. He was wearing shorts and no shirt, hugging his knees to his chest and shaking from head to foot.

Archie and Dean stepped inside, bellowing, "Texas Rangers, if you have a weapon, drop it now!"

Miller and I kept our guns trained on Gavin while Archie checked the people on the slimy-looking brown carpet for signs of life. He stood after the third, shaking his head at me.

Dean flung the bedroom door wide, stepping inside and sweeping his sidearm from right to left before he muttered a string of swearwords and holstered his weapon.

"No, no, nononono."

I turned, my weapon moving, too.

"Go on. He's not going anywhere," Miller said, nodding to Gavin.

I ran into the bedroom and stopped short at the sight of blood and brain matter on the far wall as Dean hit his knees next to a wooden ladder-back chair that was tipped over on the floor, occupied by a dead man who was tied to it with bungee cords.

I didn't want to look. But Dean leaned forward to see how the cords were fastened, and I got a glimpse of the same blue plaid button-down I'd seen atop Dodger's saddle in the Sunday morning sun. The blood around the neat holes in the back of Ratcliff's skull had dried, his skin an unnatural shade of gray.

"Dammit!" I shouted, turning away from the scene and putting my foot through the flimsy wood of the door.

Archie hurried across the room, his eyes wide with alarm.

"What's going on, y'all?" Miller called.

"It's Ratcliff," Dean said, his voice thick. "Baxter, you got a knife? I can at least cut him loose."

Archie threw Dean a pocketknife, and I walked back to the living room as Dean made quick and careful work of cutting Ratcliff's body free of the chair.

⸻

"What the hell happened here?" Miller shook Gavin, raising a hand to smack the kid, who flinched and blinked, shaking his head.

"I don't know, man," he said, his voice high and whiny. "They all started, like, shaking and choking and shit. It was supposed to be Percs. Just a little pick-me-up. I heard a bunch of guys shouting outside and went to hide in the john. There were a few shots, and they took off."

He pointed to Ratcliff, whose body was next to the others on the floor now. "He was supposed to be taken to the drop tonight. I don't know who came for him or why. I swear to God."

"Did you not take any of these?" I watched the kid carefully, partly to see if he was lying and partly because it meant I wasn't looking at Ratcliff. Miller reached for the bowl with the pills in it, and I pulled on his arm with one hand. "Don't touch it. Some of that shit can get through your skin."

"I'm not," he said. "But thanks."

"Percs make me puke, man," Gavin said, shaking his head and pointing to his dead friends. "But I ain't never seen anyone do that."

"Where'd you get them?" I asked, keeping my voice even and calm. "Did they come from Zapata?"

"Sure, man," he said. "Just a bonus. You know, for good work."

"He's trying to clean up loose ends," Miller said.

"Tainted pills followed by a cleanup crew," I agreed. "Sure seems that way."

"I can't believe he killed his own son," Miller said. "Or told someone to."

"That has to be because he knows," I said.

"Knows what?" Gavin's eyes popped so wide he looked more cartoon than human.

I looked out the window. The sun was sinking impossibly fast. I didn't have time for this. I had no way to know if Zapata knew anything about Graham, and I was going to come right out of my skin if I didn't put my eyes on my husband before I slept.

I ripped my pocket I yanked so hard on my phone, pulling up photos from the day before. "JJ and Mikey were your friends, right, Gavin?" I asked, flipping the screen around. "This is how they looked after Zapata's guy got done with them yesterday." I didn't know for sure that Lobban was there at Zapata's order, but I didn't know he wasn't, and it worked—a wet spot spread across the mustard-gold sofa under Gavin as he stared at the photo and tried to breathe.

"I don't wanna die, man," he said when he could talk and before he broke into deep, harsh sobs.

I swiped to the woman in the stash house shower. "Do you know her? Recognize the tattoo?"

"Lucia?" he wailed, covering his eyes.

"Where can we find Zapata's crew?" I asked. "Anywhere outside the compound or north of the border?"

"There's a truck tonight," Gavin said. "Today is Tuesday, right?"

"It is."

"Yeah, tonight. A truck, their big shipment. Coming from the crew in Tulsa, straight through with no stops. Their new guys set it up. Amin was pissed. JJ heard them fighting."

New guys. Amin. I glanced at Archie. We had it pretty well figured out, it sounded like.

"Where, Gavin?"

He shook his head. "They didn't tell me."

I grabbed his bony shoulders and shook him so hard his teeth rattled. "Where, dammit?"

He cried harder but didn't talk.

"He doesn't know." Miller laid a hand on my shoulder. "You literally scared the piss out of the guy, McClellan. He doesn't know."

"Mikey wrote it down," Gavin said. "JJ called her his secretary."

I fumbled for my phone, scrolling to the photos of the pages I'd taken in the warehouse and finding the pencil sketch of the desert.

"Is this what you mean? She wrote it down here, with this map?" I asked, sticking the screen under his nose. "Do you know where this is?" Mikey's sketch was of a lonely road with some boulders and cacti and labeled only with a *CA* in one corner and a small triangle in the other.

Gavin sniffled. "It's usually off Highway 2," he said.

"Is 'CA' Ciudad Acuna?" Dean asked, peering over my shoulder.

Gavin nodded faster. "That's what they said, yeah."

I pointed at an asterisk off the side of the simple road sketch. "So we're near Highway 2," I said.

Dean nodded, pointing to the chicken scratch in the corner. "At eleven o'clock."

I peered at the sliver of an unfinished triangle. If it were a clock, it would say 11, straight up.

"Somewhere off Highway 2, outside Ciudad Acuna. Eleven o'clock," I repeated. "Sounds like we've got a date, gentlemen."

I hauled Gavin to his feet by one elbow. "He needs a cell. But not in Nava's jail. And we need a coroner out here."

"On it," Dean bit out, closing the door behind us as I nudged Gavin down the steps toward the car.

"Going to be a tight fit," I said.

Dean pointed at the Gremlin. "Does it run?" he asked Gavin.

"It's Sharla's," he said. "We rode here in it."

Dean ducked back inside and returned with keys, the Gremlin's engine turning over on the third try. "Y'all go back to the command trailer and see what kind of plan you have time to come up with. I'll get our lone survivor here settled in a cell and meet you later."

I slid into the back seat and let Archie and his bum knee have the front. No one talked as Miller drove. I spent the forty-minute ride to the Rangers outpost watching the sun sink, praying for Graham's life, and looking at how many miles of Highway 2 there were between here and Ciudad Acuna. We'd never find the meeting spot in time to set up an ambush—and an ambush was our only hope with only hours to prepare.

Miller let the car roll back toward the road, and I looked at my phone, coordinates for a pin I dropped on accident moving the map around in the upper-right corner. I let out a yelp and switched to my photos, finding the

Post-it note I'd noticed in Timmy Dushane's room. I typed the characters in with shaking fingers.

"What?" Archie and Miller both turned around.

"Timmy Dushane had a note with map coordinates in the back of a desk drawer," I said. "Guess which spot they mark?"

"Something off Highway 2 outside Ciudad Acuna?" Archie's long face lit with a smile.

"You win an extremely dangerous evening with your favorite step-daughter."

He winked. "No need for that 'step' nonsense, girl."

Miller met my gaze in the rearview. "We're going to Mexico?"

"We are going to Mexico."

40

The whore was the easiest kill, yet somehow the worst trophy. She was always watching him, even after he closed her eyes.

She'd been an accident, really, as much as he hated the term. He went to the federal stash house the pigs thought was a secret to hide cash—Freddie wasn't using it anymore, and their cameras were easy to locate and disable.

She'd let herself right in—his fault for not locking the door, even in the middle of nowhere.

She didn't see him at first, rooting through kitchen cabinets and calling out to Freddie.

Hunting more than one sort of fix.

He'd backed her up to the kitchen sink and sliced her throat with a kitchen knife, slumping her body over the sink while he went to the garage for a saw.

Far messier and more personal than his scythe. Probably why she was always staring at him, no matter where he sat or moved. He'd taken to staring back.

He wasn't afraid of a whore.

He was afraid of Emilio Zapata, though.

His entire situation had gone from bad to worse.

He'd expected his messages to motivate change, scare everyone into thinking they needed his protection while ridding himself of threats to his carefully insulated organization. Instead, his careful calling cards somehow landed at the feet of the only do-gooder cops left in a hundred-mile radius.

He'd sent someone to find out what the Lone Ranger out by the river knew, and they'd bungled the job almost comically, but some heavily laced pills would clean up that mess without getting his hands dirty.

The woman, though...she posed a problem.

People who mattered would care if she disappeared. Which meant he needed enough cash to disappear, too.

Faith McClellan had grown up to be a formidable adversary. A beauty queen, bringing down an international empire.

What an addition she would make to his trophy case.

41

"I don't know this crew from Tulsa very well," Scott Rooney said, leaning out the back window of an unmarked state sedan parked next to Miller's in the Mexican desert about a hundred yards from the road.

I wasn't sure if I wanted him talking to me or not, and would've cheerfully given my left arm for a set of binoculars, which we were somehow without between two government sedans and six officers.

"Do you know anything useful about this exchange?" I asked.

"I know Amin has been beside himself about making sure this goes down without a hitch. This is the first shipment they're routing through the new syndicate in Tulsa—part of the Dixie Mafia, if I understand things correctly. They were able to add three hundred units of body armor to what we were already running."

Miller's jaw did the flexing thing I'd noticed earlier, but he didn't say anything. I didn't comment on it, turning my full attention back to Scott.

"Where did the Dixie Mafia get three hundred units of body armor?" I asked.

"You put your old man in prison, and word of what he was up to spread quick." Scott laughed. "Crooks have no problem figuring out how to copy a successful scheme."

My stomach did a slow flip.

"How many are supposed to be here tonight?" Archie asked. It was his idea to have Dean's men meet us with Scott in custody, in case he could tell us something useful ahead of the drop.

I checked my watch for the thirty-ninth time since we'd passed through the Comstock CBP station.

Somehow we'd only been sitting there for twenty-seven minutes, and there were still thirty-five more until eleven o'clock.

"I'm going to lose my mind," I muttered.

"You're going to be just fine," Archie said, twisting so far in the seat that he winced.

"I'm glad one of us is sure of that." I'd never been so antsy. If I didn't move, I was going to spontaneously combust. But I couldn't get out of the car. We were kind of concealed by a combination of cactus, rocks, scrub brush, and thick, inky darkness. My pale skin and blond hair wouldn't exactly blend with the surroundings.

"I have it on decent authority that Zapata's new muscle is coming with his people," Scott said. "I'm pretty sure that's your husband. But no promises. It's not like any of these assholes are very trustworthy. I learned a long time ago not to count on or believe anything I haven't seen with my own eyes."

I swallowed hard and whispered a silent prayer. *Just bring him to me.* Graham and I were a good team—we could get out of anything, even this, if they would just bring him. And if he didn't fuck around and blow his cover when he saw me, a very real fear I hadn't considered until five minutes ago but one that had rapidly taken over the top spot on my long list of pressing anxieties.

"Archie, what if he freaks when he sees us and blows his cover?" I whispered.

"He wouldn't have been chosen for this assignment if anyone thought that was possible," Miller said.

"No one who sent him here expected me to end up in the middle of bumfuck Mexico waiting to ambush him," I said.

"We're not here to ambush him," Archie said. "We're here to observe, and to arrest anyone who commits a crime."

"Even though we're about as far outside our jurisdiction as a person can get?" I asked.

"We'll work a deal with the Federales," Archie said.

"I thought they were corrupt?" I pointed to Miller. "He said Freddie Z didn't trust them."

"Freddie Z was a criminal. It's only natural the cops he knew were corrupt—but not all of them are, and we have some inmates we can trade them," Archie explained. "Miller has been lining it up for weeks. That part will work out. It's this part we have to pull off right now that matters most. Just focus on the next hour or so."

I pulled in a deep breath, turning back to Scott.

"Who killed Freddie Z and the other officers?" I asked.

He shrugged. "It could be one of probably five people on either side. Whoever did it has covered their ass well and isn't bragging about it."

His borderline-arrogant tone gave me pause. Like Miller, I was sure the officers' deaths had been ordered by the cartel. But what Scott just said pointed to someone else entirely. Zapata would have called them out as cops and beheaded them in front of a crowd.

So what was I missing?

"Tell me how Connie Nava is involved in this."

"Nava? She's a pawn." He waved a dismissive hand. "She sticks to her traffic tickets and rescues people's pets, runs off coyotes, that kind of stuff. All they ask of her is that she turn a blind eye to the border activity, and they leave her grandmother alone."

"Her grandmother?"

"She's in-country. About an hour south of here. When we were in the Guard, Amin noticed how smart Connie was, and Zapata tracked the grandmother down in Piedras Negras. They sent Connie back to Duncan to run for sheriff after she finished school, and she's been there ever since. I feel a little sorry for her, to be honest. She's stuck. Which isn't cool, but at the same time, it's not really my problem, either. She's good for some information on who's dealing and who's buying every once in a while, but mostly she's just not a threat to us."

Watch check: that peeled off three whole minutes. I started tapping my foot, and Miller put the window up and turned up the radio. "He can't tell us anything else that's going to help. Head in the game, folks. It's almost time, things will move faster than you think possible, and we don't get extra lives or do-overs."

I patted the Kevlar vest we'd picked up at the CBP station and put a hand on my weapon, closing my eyes and taking deep, slow breaths. He was right. It had been a long time since I'd been part of a raid, and we only had one chance. Everything needed to go according to a very loose and hastily constructed plan.

And when did that ever happen?

42

A box truck with Oklahoma plates pulled up at ten fifty-six, and two men got out of the cab while seven more poured from the lift door on the back. All of the latter were heavily armed, while the smaller men who swung down out of the front had only desert-camo armored vests and automatic pistols—what kind, I couldn't tell from so far away.

Archie laid a hand on my arm. "You're shaking."

"I'm not trying to."

"We have to wait for everyone to get here and get into the deal," he said. "You know the drill."

"I know."

"McClellan, when we get out of the car, you watch for Hardin. If you see him and you can both get clear of any action without risk of life, do it. We can look out for ourselves."

"I..." I looked around the interior of the car, at Dean, Miller, and Archie. We'd become a team in the past several hours. "I don't want to leave y'all."

"We can take care of ourselves," Archie said.

"For sure." Dean smiled through two days' worth of scruff. "You get what you came for, and we will, too."

A sand-colored Jeep stopped behind the Oklahoma truck, visibly startling the crew surrounding it the way they raised their guns. We watched for a tense minute, but nobody fired. I peered at the guy who'd stepped out of the passenger side of the Jeep. Could be Derek Amin. Could be the tree Miller shot as a rookie if I squinted. We were too far away, and it was too dark for me to tell much of anything.

Miller held a hand out, palm down, like a high school quarterback in a state championship huddle. "For Ratcliff, on three?"

We piled our hands on, and Dean counted it off. "For Ratcliff," we said in unison, throwing our arms up.

Headlights appeared on the southern horizon.

We couldn't be more in the middle of nowhere. Our cell phones had lost signal back at the border, but Miller had borrowed a satellite phone that was in the front seat. He'd called for emergency backup from the ATF's Dallas office three hours ago. They'd promised to send any support they could muster and wished us luck. That was the last we'd heard from the ATF. Dean's entire unit was ready and waiting on the edge of Texas, looking for a signal before they breached foreign territory.

So there and then, we had only six officers—Archie, Miller, Dean, and myself in one car and Dean's lieutenants guarding Scott in the other. They were armed and would certainly help if things got out of hand, but the exchange wasn't their primary objective.

I didn't even care if Scott Rooney got away at that point. Where the hell was he going to go out here that he wouldn't die of either snakebite or dehydration? I understood why Miller wanted to take Rooney down, and objectively I knew how much that mattered and why. Personally, though, all I could think about was Graham.

"Vehicles approaching," Miller muttered, checking his weapon for the fifth time.

A jacked-up double dually pickup stopped first, followed by a smaller, shoddier box truck than the one that had come from the north.

I counted eleven men who got out between the two trucks, but damned if I could tell from out there if any of them was my husband.

A stocky guy walked forward with two large suitcases and handed them to the smaller guy from the bigger truck. So far nobody had guns trained on anyone else, but there were plenty of assault rifles milling around out there.

The smaller guy walked back and handed them off, pointing before the driver of the largest truck laid them on the hood and opened them, digging into the middle before he called something over his shoulder and closed them. Then he put them in the cab and waved one arm over his head in a circle.

The guys who'd poured out of the back of the biggest truck began hauling crates, some metal and some wood, out of the back of the truck. Each was stopped halfway to the other trucks and inspected. The stocky guy picked up a couple of the guns and spent several minutes poring over a case of body armor that resembled the one I'd seen at JJ's warehouse.

"That's Emilio Zapata," Miller murmured, nodding in the general direction of fifteen men.

"The stocky one with the gray hair?" I kept my voice low.

Miller nodded. "I wasn't sure he'd be here himself."

He stayed still, breathing slowly, his eyes on the action in the middle of the deserted road.

I watched the shadowy figures tote boxes back to the trucks, pounding my fist into my knee.

"Not yet," Miller murmured.

"Money in the suitcases, guns in the boxes," I said. "What else do you need to see?"

The Jeep's passenger rounded the corner of the box truck closest to us, calling something I couldn't quite make out to the stocky guy. "Did he say his invitation got lost?" I asked.

Archie nodded. "I think that's the National Guard guy who used to work for Chuck."

Zapata whirled. "Derek, go home," rang clear in the still night air. Amin advanced toward him, and Zapata's wheelman pulled a pistol.

The short guy from the Oklahoma truck backed away.

"Give it up, Amin," Zapata shouted. "*Traidor! Dónde estás, Freddie?*"

"He called Amin a traitor," I whispered.

"No, he called his son a traitor. The son he doesn't know is dead. That's what I wanted to know." Miller circled a finger in the air in a "go" sign. I leapt out of the car with more energy than I'd ever had in my life, falling in behind the guys as they crept across the sand under cover of darkness and lack of attention, because every eye in twenty miles was on the pistol that had materialized in Zapata's shaking hand.

"I don't know what you mean." Amin's voice was higher than I remembered, but clear and calm.

"If Emilio didn't order the hit on Freddie, I bet he's not responsible for any of the river bodies," Miller murmured.

I watched Amin's face as we crept closer. Zapata was upset. Amin was flat and unemotional.

"*Dónde está mi hijo?*" Zapata shrieked, shaking the pistol that was maybe a foot from Amin's chest.

"Zapata thinks Amin knows what happened to Freddie," Miller said.

"I think I agree with him," I muttered.

Miller turned his head so Archie and Dean could hear him. "If we can take them alive, great, but don't risk your own neck trying."

Dean nodded, all four of us moving steadily and silently across the sand. We were almost there, and no one had so much as noticed us yet.

"*Mijo!*" Zapata's voice was something between a scream and a wail as he fired the pistol.

And all hell broke loose.

Amin staggered backward, the bullet catching the top edge of his vest instead of splattering his brains all over the sand probably only thanks to Zapata's shaking hand.

Miller took off at a run and waved for us to follow, and I heard Hammet's and Langford's doors close behind us as they followed suit.

I sprinted, lungs burning, past Miller and Dean and straight for the back end of the trucks Zapata's crew had arrived in.

Bullets zipped between the factions, but no one could hear us coming over the gunfire, and they were so busy alternately trying to take cover and shoot the enemy that they didn't notice us.

Passing the front bumper, I caught the eye of a brawny man in a white tank top with a shaggy graying beard and a huge tattoo of a skull with fangs covering his massive forearm, blood dripping from the fangs onto the back of his hand. The inked art was big—big enough to see across a wide, dim space. The man narrowed his eyes and turned toward me as a bullet hit his chest and spun him completely around before he could fire or speak. He hit the ground hard enough to shake it, and I glanced over my shoulder in time to see Miller turn back toward Amin and the gunrunners, Archie on his heels.

Moving along the edge of the box truck, I heard arguing, in Spanish, from inside the back. The words were too fast and garbled for me to know what they were saying over the gunfire, but I knew the loudest voice with my whole heart.

Graham.

I slid to a stop near the back corner of the truck, my boots coasting over the sand so easily it might as well have been ice. I had to put a hand out to steady myself, stopping to listen closer.

Graham said something else. Another man shouted "*Estúpido!*" back at him and asked if he was just going to leave Zapata.

A third guy said Zapata was stupid and emotional and he didn't want to die over a vendetta when Freddie was a traitor.

Graham told them to shut up and fall in line. A crate lid squealed open, and five seconds later, Graham jumped to the ground with a Texas National Guard–issue M4 in his arms and rounded the corner of the truck.

I didn't have anywhere to go.

His eyes held mine, the look in them more stricken than the last time he'd been shot. He stumbled backward, nearly leveling a short, muscular guy carrying a similar rifle.

"*Policía! Policía!*" The second guy pointed, losing his grip on his rifle, when he spotted the CBP logo on my vest. "*Esta puta es policía!*" *This bitch is police.* He fumbled with the gun and tried to aim it but hit the back of Graham's arm.

"Martin? Martin! *Dispárale!*" *Shoot her.* He shoved Graham's shoulder and shouted again, drawing the attention of two other men. All of them eyed Graham with trepidation as he stood there with his gaze locked on mine and raised the gun. I saw his foot slide and knew he was about to turn on them. But there were too many, all heavily armed, and he didn't have a vest—they'd kill him. Even if we managed to limp away merely wounded, blowing his cover before Zapata was taken down would put a target on Graham that would cast a shadow over our lives for years.

I had half a second to make the most agonizing decision of my life.

I swallowed doubt and raised my sidearm. "Police! Drop your weapons!"

"*Jodete! Vete a la verga, cerdo.*" *Fuck you! Go to hell, pig,* the shorter man screamed, swinging his rifle and pulling the trigger. The metal side of the truck exploded behind my right ear, sending shards burning into my scalp and neck.

I fired back. My aim was better—one shot splashed half his brain across the sand.

When lives hang in the balance and everyone is running on an adrenaline high, critical decisions have to be made in fractions of seconds, and the hours I've invested in training pay off. I kept my breathing even and followed instinct, ignoring everything but the next threat: the tall skinny guy screamed and turned on me, spraying bullets from maybe twenty feet away as he shouted for Martin to fire.

He wouldn't. With chaos swirling around us, I knew in my bones that Graham would die before he made that choice.

So I made it for him.

I shot one foot out and kicked Graham's weapon out of his loose grip, turning my gun on him and watching the surprise register in his eyes before understanding dawned.

Be still, I thought.

Hand to God, I thought he nodded. Just the tiniest movement.

A bullet from the tall guy's rifle winged my left arm, sending a bloom of blood over my once-white shirt, and two more hit center mass. The Kevlar did its job, but the hits knocked the wind out of me.

I stayed upright and kept my arm steady, firing one shot into Graham's shoulder, a single tear that could be attributed to my own injuries escaping my lashes and rolling down my face.

Graham played it well, falling to the ground when the bullet hit him and giving me a clear shot at the skinny guy—I dropped him with two quick shots to the heart, but three more cartel soldiers ran in from the left, all shooting in the general direction of the truck. Retreating to the front bumper and hoping for cover, I kept firing but didn't hit much of anything I could see. The three newcomers watched the action around them for maybe five seconds before dropping their weapons and working together to grab Graham and the skinny guy, hauling them into the back of the box truck.

I puked in the sand.

I shot Graham. Myself. And they were taking him away from me bleeding.

I started back toward the rear of the truck, checking my ammunition. I might die if I went back there, but I also might die if they drove off into the desert with my husband bleeding from a wound I inflicted, good intentions be damned.

"Faith!" I turned when Miller screamed, my heart stopping when I saw him kneeling next to the pickup, Archie's blood pouring dark and thick into the sand.

"No!" I fired three rounds over his head, dropping three more guys. I didn't even know who they worked for, I just knew someone over there shot Archie and they were still waving guns.

"Damn," Dean said from behind my shoulder as I shoved a new magazine into my gun. "I'll take you for a partner in a gunfight any day. I got your six."

We moved in tandem, a slow circle facing away from one another as all the trucks roared to life, headlights blinding us and tires squealing.

In less than a minute, it was just Dean and me standing over Archie and Miller in the middle of a cool desert summer night, the lot of us surrounded by dead bodies.

"Where are Hammet and Langford?" I asked, looking around as Dean jogged away, calling for them.

"Oh, God," he said from the other side of the road. "Officers down!"

I looked at Miller.

"Baxter has a pulse," he said. "Go."

I found Dean standing over his men, both of whom were missing about half their head.

"Jesus Christ." He sniffled and dragged the back of one hand across his face.

"I'm so sorry." I knelt and closed the open eyes I could see, turning when I heard a woofing sound coming south fast.

"Thank God," Miller yelled as the ATF helicopter came into view. I turned on the light on my phone and pointed it up, waving my other arm.

"Come on, Dean." I tugged on his sleeve. "They'll help us get them home."

"Where's your husband?" He looked around.

"Zapata's men pulled him into the truck and took off," I said. "He was... he got shot."

His face fell as though I'd punched him. "That's... No. We were supposed to get him back. McClellan..." He shook his head, putting a hand to his chin and taking a deep breath.

I couldn't feel my chest, like everything from my collarbone to below my rib cage had been hollowed out.

What now?

"Jesus." Dean shook his head. "The joint operations intelligence group that Ratcliff didn't trust enough to ask about his stack of headless bodies— the Texas National Guard has more officers in it than anyone else. Amin... he's got to be giving Zapata the identities of the UCs in the cartel. And he probably knows them all."

43

"McClellan, I got this," Lieutenant Boone said, following me down a hallway at the Customs and Border Patrol station forty minutes later. "Go to the hospital and check on Baxter. Hell, you look like you could use some medical attention yourself—is your arm bleeding?"

"It's a scratch." I waved him off, counting doors until I got to the one Brayden had said would lead to Derek Amin. "I need to do this myself."

I had to know for sure which side of this mess had killed Zapata's son and the other agent—and how many dangerous people knew who Graham was. No one we could get on the satellite phone from the chopper had been able to tell me if information coming from Amin was the reason someone was picking off undercover agents in the Zapata cartel, but my gut said Dean could be right. As such, I didn't trust anyone else to talk to this guy— not even Boone.

I put one hand on the knob and turned my head, giving my boss a look that made him raise both hands and take a step backward. "Sure. I'll take the other guy, then. And maybe find an EMT to check your 'scratch' when you're done."

I was so focused on getting to Amin it didn't occur to me to ask the lieutenant what he was even doing there until after I'd opened the door.

"Miss McClellan." Amin spoke to the table in the center of the small office, his hands folded under it in his lap. "I'd say it's good to see you again, but I'm afraid I'd be lying to you."

"Funny how that works." I leaned forward to peer at the handcuffs fastened around his wrists. "I'm damn glad to see you sitting there with your shiny new accessories."

Dean's team had intercepted the Jeep as it crossed the river through the dry part of the bed near the spot where Ratcliff had found Freddie Z's body. Amin was in this room with me, and Boone was in with his driver—who had replaced Amin as head of requisitions for the Guard when Amin was promoted—which gave me a pretty good idea that Boone's guy was guilty of a few things, too.

"We'll see how long you can hold me," he said, still not looking up.

"Last time I checked, the penalty for a first-degree felony in Texas was life in prison," I said. "Conspiracy to commit capital murder should bring that with no problem, sir." I hit the last word hard.

That brought his eyes to mine. "What proof do you have of anything?" he hissed. "Ideas and supposition don't hold up in a court of law, no matter how clever you think you are."

"Confessions do." I pointed to the door, my voice even and unbothered. "You think your right-hand man in there won't sell you out to save his own ass?"

He sat back in the chair, his face spreading into a slow smile. "I'll wait for the proof. You'll never find any."

There was the crack I needed to get past his bravado: his own ego. He thought he'd insulated himself too well for us to make a charge stick. And from the lack of a real paper trail, I'd say he was right, but a head this big is almost always its own worst enemy. All I needed to do was keep him talking until I got him off guard. If I could trip him up, he'd do the rest for me. I held his gaze without blinking, everything I'd seen and heard in the past two days racing through my thoughts. Between Boone's finesse and my stubborn streak, we'd get what we needed. I just wasn't sure how long it would take. Or how long Graham had left before his cover was blown, if it wasn't already.

"What does your guy attach the razors to?" I asked, watching Amin's face carefully for a reaction.

He held it flat, shaking his head. "I'm not sure if I'm supposed to know what you mean, but I'm afraid you've lost me."

Dean's crew had sent everything they recovered from the cave in the state park to Jim by courier, but there was no way he'd had time to DNA test all twelve blades, and it was the middle of the night.

Amin didn't know that. But I was the worst liar in five states.

I tried anyway. "We have the DNA match for the blade that killed Cody Rylan in June," I said. "Best I can figure, they attach to some sort of scythe that takes off the victims' heads—which means whoever's swinging it is pretty strong. There was no shortage of muscle on Zapata's side of the firefight tonight, but I couldn't help noticing Zapata fired at you after he screamed about his son. Which makes me wonder if I've been suspicious of the wrong people all week." Wishful thinking, maybe—but it might scare him into reacting.

Amin didn't blink. "Who is Cody Rylan?"

I sucked in a slow breath, trying to hold my temper.

"I believe you know the answer to that, Mr. Amin."

"Commander, if you please. I earned the title."

"Earned? You were handed a job where you could perpetrate a fraud on the taxpayers of this state and the soldiers in your command." I paused to consider that. "But why?"

Amin shook his head, his lips curving up in a small smile as I tried to look at the situation from Chuck McClellan's point of view. The Governor didn't do favors. He furthered his own interests.

So why would Amin have been at the mansion so late at night in the waning days of Chuck's final term, the White House pulling further out of reach by the day?

"You were supposed to keep him in on the scheme." I shot to my feet so fast I flipped the chair over backward. "He gave you that job because he was going to continue running his weapons ring after he left office."

Amin shrugged. "I have no idea what you're talking about. I always thought your father was a good man and was honored by the trust he placed in me at such a young age."

I laughed. Loud—and for long enough to rattle Amin.

"I'm afraid I missed the joke," he said finally, his voice cracking.

"If you think Chuck McClellan won't throw your ass under a bus and back up to run over you as many times as it takes to save himself even a day in prison, you really had no idea who you were dealing with."

Amin blinked. "He'd be incriminating himself."

"We already have a solid case against him," I said. "And I'm liking the way the one against you is shaping up."

My phone buzzed, and I checked the text from Miller, my face spreading into a smile. "Judges who get woken in the dead of night because high-ranking state officials are implicated in smuggling and murder are pretty quick to sign search warrants. The ATF is taking your house apart as we speak."

The first flicker of fear crossed his face. "They have no cause. I want a lawyer."

"I'm afraid they're in short supply out here," I said.

"You have to get me an attorney," he said. "You'll have no case if you don't. I know my rights. You have to follow the rules, as your husband says." He smirked.

It took every bit of self-control I could muster not to kick his teeth in. He was right, on one hand—proving a conspiracy to traffic weapons and commit murder charge against a high-ranking state military official would take an airtight case.

On the other hand, I was damned tired of having to play by rules that didn't apply to the opposing team, and if bending this one might get my husband back home in one piece, I could live with that.

I leaned both hands on the table, putting my nose inches from his. "Any sense of duty I had to the law is on its way back to Zapata's compound with a bullet wound. I know someone is picking off undercover officers, and one way or another, I'm going to know who before we leave this room."

My phone buzzed again. I ignored it, holding Amin's gaze and keeping my breathing steady as I watched his quicken and his nostrils flare.

What was he afraid Miller's guys were going to find in his house?

My phone buzzed. I couldn't break eye contact right then.

"The ATF agents had taken Freddie as one of their own. And Cody Rylan has a cousin in the Dallas unit." I made that last bit up on the fly, but it sounded more convincing than any other lie I'd ever told as it passed my lips. "What are they going to find, Derek?"

He closed his eyes, his head falling back. "He's never coming home, you know."

My whole body went cold, every headless corpse photo in Ratcliff's piddly little file flashing through my head in a blink. Amin knew Graham was there. Amin knew something about the dead bodies, whether he ordered the hits or just supplied information.

"What have you done?" I asked. "Does Zapata know Graham is a police officer?"

Amin sat up straight, tipping his head to one side. "Who do you think told me?"

My phone buzzed for a fifth time, and I yanked it from my pocket, clicking a photo message from Miller.

A long room with dark walls, furnished only with a lone chair facing a console topped with glass cylinders containing masks. I watched the bubbles at the bottom that meant Miller was typing until the message popped up. *Mitch just sent me this shot of a hidden room behind a closet in his hallway. Dean says the head in the center is Cody Rylan. See the scythe in the corner? They're matching the blades to the ones Hammet found in that cave.*

I dropped the phone, my hand recoiling involuntarily.

"They found my trophy room." Amin's voice was cold as he studied my face.

"Oh my God." I didn't mean to say the words aloud, but I couldn't keep them in. I swallowed the *What kind of monster are you?* in favor of a more productive, "What do you mean Zapata told you who the officers were?"

"Zapata is old," Amin said. "He wants out."

I blinked. "Zapata is arming himself for a war," I said. "He's bringing in people with military experience, he's dealing with the Dixie Mafia to buy even more guns than you can supply. Those aren't the moves of a man who wants out."

"They are when escaping amid chaos is the only way out," Amin said. "It's not like either government would be willing to cut a deal with him. His only option is to set up a war—with who is immaterial, really—and to disappear once the battle begins."

I shook my head. "You're lying."

"I have no motive for lying if there are federal agents in my trophy room, Miss McClellan. The state will put me out of my misery soon enough. Emilio identified agents in his operation and passed the information to me because I had something significant to lose if they were able to connect me to the guns his men were using. I made sure the sensitive information stayed contained, but Freddie posed a problem. Alive, he was getting too close to being able to identify me. Dead, he would serve to make his father my enemy."

"So you changed your MO," I said. "You left his head intact and left him where he'd be found eventually. Because you thought Zapata would blame someone else." The words came faster the more convinced I became, Amin's head nodding.

"I didn't think he knew," he said.

"Until he shot at you tonight," I said.

He smiled. "Very clever girl."

"Who else knows about Graham?" I asked.

Amin shrugged.

"You said yourself you have nothing left to lose. Did Zapata really name him to you?" I slammed my hands down on the table, loud in the tiny room. "Talk, dammit!"

"Zapata suspects. Hardin was on a list of men to watch carefully tonight at the exchange. I have a former soldier working with the Dixie Mafia who keeps me in the loop. My presence tonight was simply supposed to show that they can't keep things from me."

"A finger in every pie, just like Chuck." I shook my head.

Amin bowed his head. "I'd like a lawyer now."

I turned for the hallway. "Probably be a few days. But I'm sure you'll be okay until they can find someone."

I slammed the door when I walked out and leaned against it.

We had cracked the case, and I even had a confession of sorts in there somewhere—Amin would be put to death for murdering Rylan, I had no doubt.

But I couldn't begin to care about anything besides the fact that Zapata was looking to create enough carnage to allow himself an exit window, and he suspected that Graham wasn't "Martin" after all.

Miller had his big fish, Archie was wounded, and Dean had lost two friends. But Graham was still behind enemy lines, and I had no idea if my shooting him earlier had helped his credibility or simply left him less able to defend himself if they turned on him.

For the first time in my career, I'd caught the bad guy, but I didn't give a single damn. And I didn't know what to do next.

44

"Hardin is a smart guy and a good cop." Boone parked a CBP sedan outside the hospital entrance and rounded the hood to open my door. "We'll get him back, McClellan."

I plodded through the door, following Boone to the OR waiting room on the third floor. He had to say that—not that Graham wasn't smart, but he was also surrounded and seriously outnumbered. And short of storming Zapata's compound with a wounded arm and a fervent prayer, I had no idea how to help him.

"No news yet," Miller said, rising to shake Boone's hand. Boone filled him in on what I'd managed to get from Amin as I plopped into a chair and stared at a sign on the wall about handwashing. I knew I needed to do something, but I'd never felt so unsure about what. The uncertainty was paralyzing—I didn't even want to talk to Miller, I was so shaken by Amin's story, but I had to know how Archie was doing, so I was there.

"Listen, McClellan, we wouldn't have made this bust tonight without Hardin." Miller dropped into the seat next to mine and handed me a Styrofoam cup full of coffee. "He pushed Zapata to be there himself, which meant Amin had to go, too."

"How do you know that?" I didn't look at him, my voice dull.

"I have another agent undercover inside the cartel."

I nearly dropped the coffee, my head snapping up to glare at Miller. "You what? And you didn't think I needed to know this before?"

"I didn't want to cloud your judgment," he said. "And before tonight, I wasn't sure how much to trust you." He at least ducked his head at the last.

"You weren't sure how much to trust me?" I stood, anger giving me strength I didn't know I could muster. "Me, whose husband is out there risking his life to try to save your case?"

"You haven't been married that long, and...well...you are Chuck McClellan's daughter. This whole setup was kind of your old man's brainchild."

"I also have a flawless service record spanning more than a decade, including the arrest of my dirtbag father." The words slid between clenched teeth on a sheet of ice.

"Like you shot your own husband tonight?" Miller asked, one eyebrow up.

I stepped toward him, not sure what I was actually going to do but really wanting to punch him.

"Everything okay in here?" Dean asked, rounding the corner from the men's room as Boone put a restraining hand on my good arm and muttered, "Miller can help you. Don't hurt him."

I froze. Miller, still in his chair, held my gaze.

"I'm sorry," he said. "I was wrong."

I stepped backward as Dean took the seat opposite Miller.

"Damn right you were."

I turned away from him and paced the length of the room. "What have they told y'all about Archie?"

"They took him to surgery as soon as we got here," Dean said.

I glanced at the clock, too many worries crowding into my head to allow me any semblance of cool.

"How long does it take to sew up a hole and get a man some blood? I dug a bullet out of a horse the other day in less than an hour and I've never stepped foot in a medical classroom."

"He was awake when they took him back," Miller said, pulling out his phone and reading something before he stood and stepped into my path. "You know that's a good sign."

"I'm not sure what I know right now."

Miller put his hands on my shoulders, his fingers sinking in when I tried to shake him off and walk past him.

"That text was from my UC. Graham is okay. It's a flesh wound, and everyone thinks he's one of them. We will get him back, but tonight, he's out of immediate danger."

I felt my shoulders deflate with the volume of the sigh that rushed out of my chest, my chin dropping to my collarbone.

"Who's 'we'?" I asked Miller's shoes. "You got your guy, didn't you?"

"I want the whole operation, and Amin was only a third of it," Miller said. "Rooney is peacefully sleeping in his townhouse in Georgetown, and you saw what Zapata's drugs did to those kids in the purple trailer."

"We're not DEA. Or FBI."

"I have a lot of friends." Miller put a finger under my chin. "Including you, I hope. I'm not leaving, Faith. We will get Graham home safe. You have my word."

"I've never been good at counting on other people," I said.

Dean walked up behind me, Boone moving in from the left. "You count on Archie, and you count on Graham," Dean said. "So for now, you can count on us. We've got your back, McClellan. We're in this together."

"All for one, something something," Miller said as Boone nodded.

I spun toward the sound when the door to the operating suite opened, the doctor pulling her mask down and flashing a smile. "Mr. Baxter is in recovery and out of the woods," she said. "His vitals are strong, and he's starting to stir. He's going to be sore for a few weeks, but he'll be just fine."

Miller grinned, Dean whooped, and Boone squeezed my hand. I closed my eyes and whispered, "Thank you."

Half of my world was right, then.

Now I had to get the other half back.

Sucking in a deep breath, I followed the doctor to Archie's bed, parked behind a yellow curtain in a dim, quiet recovery ward.

"Sorry, girl," he said, his voice thick with the anesthesia. "I'm good."

"So the doctor tells me."

"Graham?"

"I shot him, and they took him back to Zapata's." I couldn't even say it without choking.

Archie's eyes widened. "I'll want the full story later, but we'll get him back."

"That's what I told her," Miller said, stepping forward to shake Archie's uninjured hand. "Glad you're okay, sir."

"No small thanks to you, son," Archie said. "That was some damned fine shooting. A couple of times."

Boone clapped Miller on the shoulder. "The state of Texas owes you for saving this crusty old bear."

The guy. The tattoo. I raised one hand.

"Miller—I saw you take down the driver at the front of Zapata's truck when I ran by," I said. "Do you know if he got up, or where the Mexican authorities would take their bodies?"

Miller's eyebrows went up. "I can find out. Why?"

"That man, the one you shot as I passed him...he had a very specific tattoo on his arm."

"One you've seen before?" Dean leaned on the end of the bed.

I kept my eyes on Archie. "I didn't remember it until I saw it again tonight. I guess I've blocked out pretty much everything I could. But that tattoo was the last thing I saw before the closet door closed the night Charity disappeared. We never saw her alive again."

No Secrets Remain: Faith McClellan #7

A dangerous new threat forces Texas Ranger Faith McClellan to go rogue with an off-the-books investigation.

When a bone-chilling video message from North America's most notorious criminal reaches Texas Ranger Faith McClellan, she is gripped with fear for her family's safety. Realizing the urgency to protect her loved ones, she sets out to bring the sinister mastermind to justice. Despite opposition from her superiors and powerful federal officials, Faith silently launches a clandestine investigation.

Descending into the haunting depths of the shadowy criminal underworld, Faith's pursuit of the truth not only pushes her to the edge, but also unveils the eerie secrets concealed within the darkness, revealing the true extent of the danger that threatens her and those she cherishes.

ABOUT THE AUTHOR

LynDee Walker is the national bestselling author of two crime fiction series featuring strong heroines and "twisty, absorbing" mysteries. Her first Nichelle Clarke crime thriller, FRONT PAGE FATALITY, was nominated for the Agatha Award for best first novel and is an Amazon Charts Bestseller. In 2018, she introduced readers to Texas Ranger Faith McClellan in FEAR NO TRUTH. Reviews have praised her work as "well-crafted, compelling, and fast-paced," and "an edge-of-your-seat ride" with "a spider web of twists and turns that will keep you reading until the end."

Before she started writing fiction, LynDee was an award-winning journalist who covered everything from ribbon cuttings to high level police corruption, and worked closely with the various law enforcement agencies that she reported on. Her work has appeared in newspapers and magazines across the U.S.

Aside from books, LynDee loves her family, her readers, travel, and coffee. She lives in Richmond, Virginia, where she is working on her next novel when she's not juggling laundry and children's sports schedules.

Sign up for LynDee Walker's reader list at
severnriverbooks.com/authors/lyndee-walker
lyndee@severnriverbooks.com

Printed in the United States
by Baker & Taylor Publisher Services